CW01391642

In Russia the value of art treasures plundered by the Bolsheviks is immense – and their number virtually un-quantifiable. So who would know if some of them went missing . . . ?

But Konstantin Allington knows. A painting he last saw in Moscow over sixty years ago is now hanging in a London gallery and Allington approaches an English solicitor, Pip Spencer, to find out how it got there. At first, Pip is reluctant to take the case, even when Allington explains that the sale of Russian art treasures abroad is prohibited. Then he dies suddenly of a suspected heart attack – and Pip decides on a course of action that will lead to high-level intrigue and mortal jeopardy.

For someone in Moscow must move quickly to ensure that Pip can never get any closer to the truth. A beautiful young translator is despatched to London, and so begins an intricate game of cross and double-cross, with Pip caught in a spiral of ever-increasing danger. Set against the backdrop of the tumultuous events in Eastern Europe in 1989, *The Talinin Madonna* is a thrilling and original novel of suspense, love and mystery.

by the same author

THE ESTUARY PILGRIM

The Talinin Madonna

Douglas Skeggs

M

MACMILLAN
LONDON

First published 1991 by
MACMILLAN LONDON LIMITED
Cavaye Place, London SW10 9PG
and Basingstoke

Associated companies in Auckland, Delhi, Dublin, Gaborone, Hamburg,
Harare, Hong Kong, Johannesburg, Kuala Lumpur, Lagos, Manzini,
Melbourne, Mexico City, Nairobi, New York, Singapore and Tokyo

ISBN 0-333-55131-1

A CIP catalogue record for this book is available from the British Library

Typeset by Macmillan Production Limited

Printed and bound in Great Britain by Billing and Sons Limited,
Worcester

Prologue

Moscow 1986

The Rolls-Royce glided out through the suburbs of Moscow, its powerful 6.45 litre engine almost silent in the frozen air.

As it cleared the outskirts of the city and plunged into the open countryside, Vassily Krasin peered out into the darkness.

It was not yet dawn. The sky was clustered with stars but already there was a flatness, a slight opacity to the black that heralded the coming of day.

Krasin glanced down at the luminous hands of his gold Rolex watch. Timing was important. It was vital that they struck at exactly the right moment. It must be during the coldest hour, the indefinite lapse between night and day when the human body is at its most vulnerable, the metabolism slow, the mind demanding sleep and warmth.

It was bitter outside, ice particles blooming on the window pane. Even with the car heater on Krasin could feel the intensity of the Russian winter. He drew the collar of his coat around his throat and settled back in the soft leather seat.

'Have you brought some coffee?' he asked.

Chibatar nodded and taking one hand off the wheel he opened the glove compartment, took out a Thermos and handed it back to him.

It was piping hot, made from freshly roasted beans – no relation to the brown dust that Russian housewives accepted as coffee. Krasin looked at the back of his driver's cropped blond head with respect. Chibatar was a master at foraging, in many ways it was his greatest asset. He had contacts in the kitchens of embassies and foreign consulates from where he could lay hands on anything from asparagus to newly baked croissants.

'Where did you get this from?' he asked.

Chibatar took his left hand off the wheel and with a quick fluttering of the fingers he signalled that he had been given it by a friend.

Krasin gave a grunt of understanding. Stupid question really. The less he knew of these things the better. It saved him the task of having to ask what Chibatar gave in return.

Taking a flask from his pocket he added a tot of brandy to the coffee and sipped at it gratefully, thinking ahead to the coming interview, anticipating their arrival at the hotel, the words he would use to interrogate the Englishman.

By the time he returned Nina would be gone, he reflected – his mind drifting back to the previous night – washed and dressed and packed off to the State bank where she worked. It was just as well, he didn't like the company of a woman first thing in the morning. Skin that had glowed by candle-light looked grey in the dawn, eyes that had sparkled with pleasure appeared dull and grumpy. And Nina had become demanding of late. She wanted more than she was giving. It had been an amusing interlude, nothing more, and he guessed it was time to move on, look for something new.

Major Zakov was waiting for them at the hotel. As the Rolls drew in off the highway, its tyres crunching over new snow, he hurried out of the entrance lobby to meet them.

'Good morning, Colonel.'

Krasin stepped out of the car, nodding in return. The cold air gripped him, knocking the breath from his lungs so that he almost choked but he showed no sign of discomfort. Krasin never showed his feelings in front of his men. That way he remained aloof, an image of authority rather than a colleague.

'Have you spoken to him yet?' he asked.

Zakov shook his head. 'I was waiting for you, Colonel.'

The foyer of the hotel was deserted. The night-porter must have sensed their arrival, hidden himself out of sight. Zakov led the way up to the first floor.

'I've got his passport,' he said, handing Krasin the slim blue book with its gold embossed cover.

'And the key?'

'That too.' Zakov spoke with the slight gruffness of a man who is wishing he were back home in bed.

The passageway they had reached smelled of cabbage and stale cigarette smoke. A trolley littered with the remains of someone's dinner stood in their way. Impatiently Krasin pushed it aside. These damned waiters. It should have been tidied away hours ago. There was nothing Krasin detested more than Russian laziness, the slovenly attitudes, the lack of pride.

At the end of the passage two men slouched against the wall, hands thrust deep into pockets, faces wiped of expression as they waited.

6

'In case there's any resistance,' Zakov explained under his breath.

Resistance? Krasin smiled bleakly to himself. There was no chance of that. The Englishman was going to be so shit-scared it would be a miracle if he could move, let alone resist.

'Are you ready, Colonel?' Zakov had the key in the door. The two men had formed up on either side, legs braced, ready to move.

Krasin nodded. Get it over with, he told himself.

The key was turning in Zakov's hand.

Krasin watched him open the door a fraction, making no sound, and then stand back.

Raising his leg he kicked it with his foot.

This was the part Krasin found so distasteful. The moment of confrontation. It was sordid and brutal. But he knew it was necessary and it got results.

With a crash of woodwork the door burst inwards.

The two men on either side were surging forward into the darkened room, fanning out on either side, seizing control.

The lights came on.

The room was in disorder: a table with a bottle and glass, a suitcase opened, clothes spilling out on to the floor.

The Englishman had reacted immediately, springing up in alarm, eyes stretched wide, senses responding automatically.

In the same instant the glare of the lights struck him, the lethargy of sleep gripped him and he recoiled. Throwing his arms across his eyes he sank back on the bed, making slow caterpillar movements beneath the disordered eiderdown.

'How long have you been staying in this hotel?' Krasin inquired, flicking through the pages of the passport.

The Englishman was fumbling out of bed, groping with reality.

'What is this?' He looked ashen, surprise and fear draining the colour of his cheeks. 'What the fuck's going on . . . ?'

Krasin repeated the question.

Rubbing his hands over his face, the fingers furrowing through his hair, the Englishman looked stupidly around the tiny bedroom, at the two heavily built men who stood on either side of the door, at Zakov, silent and inscrutable, and finally back up at Krasin.

'What do you want?' he asked.

'Just answer the question.'

'I've done nothing wrong,' he complained mechanically. 'My passport's in order.'

'I'm not disputing that.'

The Englishman's eyes were growing accustomed to the light now. He blinked, screwing up his face, forcing it out of sleep, trying to bring his mind to bear on the question.

'Three days,' he said sulkily. 'I've been in Moscow for three days.'

'And before that?'

'Leningrad. Just for a couple of days.'

'And how long are you intending to remain in the country?' Krasin spoke with the courtesy of a tourist operator.

'Until tomorrow – I'm flying back to London tomorrow.' He grasped the hour of the morning. 'Or today, I suppose . . . what time is it?'

'Are you here on business or pleasure?'

'Business.'

A slight whine had crept into the Englishman's voice. Fear was settling down into resentment but Krasin wasn't concerned. He knew his man. This one wasn't going to start blabbering about his rights, demanding to see the British consul.

He asked him what business it was that brought him here to Russia. The Englishman gave a slight grimace.

'I'm an art dealer.'

'Has your trip been successful?'

'Moderately.' He didn't like having his abilities questioned. 'I've set up some useful contacts.'

'But not sold anything.'

'Not directly.' He admitted the failure.

Krasin was thumbing through his passport, checking the information with interest. 'I see you've been here several times in the past.'

'I make the occasional visit.'

'More than occasional,' Krasin corrected him with apparent admiration. 'You've been here regularly, two or three times a year for almost six years.'

'I'm trying to open a market in Russia,' he replied grumpily. 'It takes time.'

'I'm sure you're right. What is it exactly you deal in?'

'Paintings.'

'Where are they at present?'

'At the airport, ready to be put on the plane.'

Krasin looked around the bedroom, as though seeing it for the first time as he gave his orders.

'I need to see them before you leave. You will have them brought to my office.'

The Englishman was incredulous. 'But they're in store – all crated up.'

'That's no problem. You'll go to the airport with Major Zakov, have them taken out of store and brought to me.'

'I can't do that.' He sounded suddenly desperate. 'I'll miss my flight . . . my visa expires today.'

8

Poor bastard, Krasin thought to himself, he didn't stand a chance. Sitting there in his pyjamas, hair tousled, shivering with the cold, there was no way he could fight back. He would do as he was told and he knew it.

Krasin glanced down at his watch. 'I'll look forward to seeing you at nine. If that suits you?'

The Englishman had scrambled to his feet, was following him to the door.

'But I don't understand. I haven't sold anything here. I brought some paintings into this country a week ago and now I'm taking them away again.'

Krasin had paused in the doorway.

'I am aware of that,' he said lightly.

'What's wrong then?'

'There's nothing wrong – '

'Then why are you doing this to me?'

A slight smile curved Krasin's lips. 'I just want to make certain that the paintings you are taking away with you are the same ones as you brought in.'

There were forty-three canvases in all. They were wrapped in a protective covering of bubbled polythene and packed into six wooden crates.

From his desk, Krasin watched as the two men carried them into his office.

'Will you be requiring me to stay?' Zakov asked when the last one had been brought in and opened.

He shook his head. 'I'll ring if I need you.'

As the door closed, Krasin turned to the Englishman who sat slumped dejectedly in a chair. He had put on a sports jacket and grey trousers but his tie hung loose in his collar, his hair stood on end and he looked as though he was still in a state of shock.

'Where are they?' Krasin asked.

He glanced up, flitting his eyes around the room. Krasin read the gesture.

'There's no one listening.'

Jerking himself to his feet the Englishman went over to one of the crates and began to lift out the paintings.

'You might have warned me,' he said irritably.

'Possibly.'

'Bursting in like that. You nearly frightened me to death.'

'That was the idea.' Krasin wasn't used to apologising. 'If I'd given you any warning you wouldn't have reacted correctly. Zakov's

9

very quick to pick up on these things. I didn't want to arouse his suspicions.'

'Thanks very much.'

The Englishman had pulled five pictures from the crate and stripping off the protective wrapping he arranged them against the wall.

Krasin studied them thoughtfully for a few minutes.

'How much are they worth?'

'Together?' The Englishman made rapid calculations. 'About fifteen hundred.'

'Dollars?'

'Pounds.'

Going over to the bureau Krasin took out a thick roll of canvas, slipped off the band and unrolled it on the floor. There were five paintings in all, each one the same size and much the same subject as one of those the Englishman had brought from London.

Krasin compared the two sets of paintings thoughtfully for a few minutes before nodding his approval.

'Good,' he murmured, 'you've done well.'

The Englishman was taking tools from the crate.

'Left it until the last minute, didn't you?' he complained, crouching down by the paintings. 'I thought you'd forgotten.'

'I guessed you might.'

Strolling over to the window, Krasin looked down into Dzerzhinsky Square, noticing the queue that had formed outside the 'Children's World' toy shop. Was it Christmas time already? It seemed to come round quicker each year.

Behind him the Englishman was levering the nails from a stretcher. There were only a few holding the painting in place. When they were out, he lifted the canvas away from the stretcher, rolled it up and replaced it with one of those Krasin had given him.

'I assume I'm still going to catch my flight?' The Englishman was working on the next painting, laying the nails out on the floor as he removed them.

'I'll have a car drive you to the airport when you're finished. Zakov will make certain that the customs officials don't bother you.'

The Englishman had finished his work and straightened up. Five new paintings now stood in the gilt frames.

Krasin looked them over critically before asking, 'How much are they worth now?'

He shrugged. 'Two hundred – maybe two hundred and fifty thousand.'

The Russian's black eyes gleamed with pleasure.

'So, Tobias, it look as though you are going to have made a profitable trip after all.'

10

Chapter One

London
September 1989

Konstantin Allington looked much the same in death as he had in life: old, tired and cantankerous – a man who has reached the last chapter of his life and realised it isn't going to be a best-seller.

With a rattle of castors, the mortuary attendant pulled open the metal drawer, lifted the covering from the old man's face and folded it neatly around his bare shoulders.

It was like being buried in a filing cabinet, Pip Spencer thought to himself as he watched.

Detective Inspector Chatham came across to them. He'd extracted a cup of coffee from the machine in the passage and prodding it towards the corpse, he asked, 'Do you recognise him, sir?'

Pip Spencer nodded.

'Only we haven't been able to get a positive ID yet.'

'No, that's him all right.'

The old man was naked beneath the white cloth, his feet protruding from the bottom end. Tied to his big toe was a label. Why did they have to do that to the poor old sod, Pip wondered? It made him look as though he was going to reach the after-life by second class post.

'How did he die?'

'Heart attack.' Detective Inspector Chatham was dunking a ginger nut in his coffee. 'Knocked him over as he was walking up a flight of steps.'

'Where was this?'

'Holland Park tube station.'

'You're quite sure that's what killed him?'

Chatham nodded as he chewed on the sodden biscuit. He was a large comfortable man with shaggy eyebrows and weathered face and the slight corpulence that comes from regular hours in the pub.

'The heart attack wasn't fatal.' He qualified his earlier remark. 'But he fractured his skull falling down the stairs which comes to much the same thing.'

11

'Only in terms of life expectancy,' Pip observed privately as the body was rolled back out of sight.

'It would have been pretty quick.' Chatham felt a note of humanity appropriate to the situation.

'Did anyone see it happen?'

He shook his head slowly as though this needed extra concentration. 'He'd been dead some time when they found him.'

'So the cause of death is speculation.'

'Expert opinion, Mr Spencer.' Chatham was offended by the cynicism.

They left the mortuary and went out into the street. It was one of those bright, blustery days that come when summer has turned to autumn without anyone noticing the change. Pip breathed in the fresh air, glad to be outside again. As he was parting from Chatham he asked, 'Isn't there a lift on the platform of Holland Park?'

'I believe so.'

'It's strange that he didn't use it. An old man like that – over seventy, weak heart, in no hurry to get anywhere. You'd think he'd have waited for the lift.'

Chatham shrugged. 'They get impatient at that age. I can't see it matters why he used the stairs.'

He probably couldn't, Pip thought as he walked down the street, but it mattered a good deal to him. Because he distrusted coincidences. Like any other lawyer he knew that they occurred often enough but that didn't make them any easier to accept.

A vacant taxi was approaching but Pip ignored it. He wanted time to think, to put together the pieces in his mind. Somewhere near the concrete block of the Home Office he pushed open the door of a pub, a dismal place with etched glass windows and a cold buffet in an illuminated aquarium. Lights were chasing themselves around the fruit machines. On the tables little plastic signs reminded the devout that 'Le Beaujolais nouveau est arrivé' – possibly the least important news of the year.

He ordered a pint of lager and two rounds of cheese sandwiches. The girl behind the bar glanced at him as she took the money.

It was impossible to guess Pip's age but he appeared to be in his early thirties, a lean slightly intense-looking man with a wing of sandy brown hair falling across his brow. Not particularly good-looking, she told herself as she opened the till, but arresting just the same with deep blue eyes that smiled as he spoke.

The sandwiches arrived on a piece of exhausted lettuce. As he worked his way through them, Pip wondered why he had taken the time off to go over to Scotland Yard prying into the old man's death, raising questions that had been lying dormant.

Guilt probably, the feeling that he hadn't done his job too well.

Allington meant nothing to him personally. He had met the man only twice in his life. The first occasion he could scarcely remember; the second had been just over a week ago, the day he died.

Allington had barged his way into his office, flattening the secretary who tried to stop him against the door and launching straight into the attack.

'I've been waiting downstairs for over an hour,' he'd complained in a high, imperious voice.

'I'm sorry, Mr Spencer. I couldn't stop him.' Debbie had hovered in the background.

He'd told her it was all right.

'What's the matter with everyone in this place?' the old man had demanded, taking in the immaculately furnished office with one quick, disapproving glance. 'There's nothing here but a load of red tape and arse-lickers.'

It had not been the way Pip would have phrased it himself but not a bad description of one of the largest firms of solicitors in London just the same. He'd sat back and studied his new arrival with interest.

The old man had been dressed in a shabby black overcoat that appeared to weigh him down, scuffed shoes on his feet and a felt hat on the back of his head. His skin was brittle, the cheeks hollowed, giving him the dry, desiccated appearance of a dead insect.

'Do I know you?' he'd asked.

'Allington – Konstantin Allington. You did some work for me a few years back.'

'Ah yes.' There was a glimmer of recollection at the back of Pip's mind but he'd been in no mood to reminisce. 'So what can I do for you?'

Reaching into his overcoat pocket Allington had taken out a glossy catalogue and thumbed through the pages.

'Do you know the D'Este Gallery?' he'd asked.

'I can't say I do.'

He'd found the page he was looking for and slapped the catalogue down on the desk, prodding the photo with his forefinger.

'That painting is hanging in their window,' he said. 'Just hanging there bold as brass for anyone to see.'

'What of it?'

'I saw it in Moscow sixty years ago.'

Pip couldn't see that this was any reason to call out the national guard. 'It's probably been sold in the meantime.'

Baring his teeth the old man had given him a pitying look,

13

as though Pip had been kept wrapped in cotton wool all his life.

'The Russians never sell pictures, Mr Spencer. Don't you know that? They keep them in store, locked up tighter than a clergyman's daughter.'

'So how do you think it comes to be here in London?'

Allington had made a swift gesture of the hand, as though producing a rabbit from his hat and said, 'On the black market.'

'You mean it's stolen?'

'Stolen, smuggled out of the country. Call it what you like. The point is it shouldn't be flaunting itself around a London gallery.'

Two hours later he had been found dead, lying sprawled in the stairwell of a tube station.

Pip drained his glass and stared across the pub, trying to summon the intonation of the old man's voice, the exact words he had used.

Allington had been positive as he spoke, almost belligerent, ramming his chin out above the yellowed rim of his collar. Pip remembered thinking at the time that he was a disagreeable old sod and wondering who had the unenviable task of living with him. Looking into the old man's eyes he'd tried to detect tell-tale signs of fanaticism or senility but old age is a mask. There was nothing to be read in the pale blue irises and so he'd probed a little further.

'How did you come to see this painting?'

'I was brought up in Moscow.'

'You're Russian?'

'By birth – '

'If you'll forgive me saying so, Allington doesn't sound like a Russian name.'

'My father changed it when he came to England.' The old man wasn't going to be caught out so easily. 'He thought it might be hard to find work over here with a foreign-sounding name.'

'So why Allington?'

'Because that was the name of the ship we came across on – the SS *Allington Castle*. At the time it was the only English word my father knew.'

The explanation had sounded simple enough to be plausible but Pip couldn't see why the old man had brought the news to him.

'If you're right about this you should go to the police.'

Allington hadn't taken this well. At the mention of the police he'd screwed his face into an expression of disgust.

'The police?' He'd seemed to have trouble getting the word out of his mouth. 'What good would that do? They just write everything down and file it away. That's why you must go to them, Mr Spencer. You know how to make them listen. You know how to get them off their frigging backsides.'

'I'll need some evidence – '

Allington had been exasperated. 'I've given it to you. I saw that picture in Moscow sixty years ago. What more do you need?'

'Something more concrete,' Pip had replied slowly.

'You think I'm making this up?'

'I didn't say that.'

'Lost your edge, have you? The last time I saw you, you were doling out legal advice in a community centre in Finchley and glad to have the work. Too grand for that now, I suppose?'

'I can't start accusing art galleries of handling stolen paintings without some firm evidence, Mr Allington.'

'You want to talk about your fee, I suppose?'

'It would have to be discussed eventually' – there was no point in lying to him – 'but it's not the point at present.'

'Have you got the meter running, Mr Spencer? Do you know how many words you've said so far?'

Pip had begun to say that if he was given some sort of hard evidence he could act on it but he'd found himself talking to Allington's back.

Slamming out of the office he had gone downstairs where, Pip learned later from the commissionaire, he had celebrated the end of his visit by spitting into the umbrella stand.

Getting to his feet Pip left the pub and walked back across St James's Park where executives were exposing felt braces to the sunshine, secretaries eating their quota of high fibre and couples lying tangled together beneath the trees.

He wasn't proud of his conversation with Allington. He'd been off-hand, dismissive. He wondered whether the old man's gibe had been accurate. Would he have paid more attention to him if he had been dressed in a Savile Row suit? If there had been a thousand acres of farmland around his home?

Yes, dammit. Of course it would have made a difference. But that was the nature of his profession.

'Never forget we're running a business here,' his senior partner had reminded him on the day he started work at Evans-Greatheart. 'No moral crusades, no work on the side for friends. If you want to take up a cause, do it in your own time.'

The commissionaire greeted him as he came in through the revolving doors of the South Audley Street office.

'Lovely day, Mr Spencer.'

'Isn't it just,' he agreed. 'Not that we'll see much of it in here. Any post for me?'

'I had it sent up to your office.'

Pip took the lift to the second floor. As the doors opened

he found Max Fuller loitering in the door of his office, large and unshakeable, his sleeves rolled back from chubby wrists.

'I was looking for you,' he said amiably. 'I've got a table booked at Langan's in half an hour. Are you interested?'

'I've just had a sandwich.'

Max offered his condolences. 'Come along for the ride then.'

'Thanks. I was thinking of going rowing.'

'During lunch?'

'You should try it, Max. It would do you good.'

Max gave a chuckle, shooing the idea away with a flap of the hand as he turned back into his office. 'You've got to be joking. Lunchtime was designed for lunch, Pip – that's how it got the name. Anything else is a misuse of language. Besides, I don't think those little cockleshells were designed to take me.'

'Pity,' Pip chided him as he went into his office opposite. 'It might knock some of that paunch off your legal bearing.'

Debbie was waiting for the news of his meeting with the police.

'How did it go?'

'Nothing,' Pip told her, taking off his jacket and throwing himself down in his chair. 'They weren't interested.'

'But surely they're going to look into it?'

'It's not a police matter apparently. The old man died of a heart attack, the circumstances aren't suspicious and so there's no need to start an investigation.'

'Did you tell them about the painting he showed you?'

'Every word.'

'They must have thought it was quite a coincidence.' Debbie sounded indignant as she spooned instant coffee into a cup and poured water from the kettle.

'A coincidence and nothing more. They couldn't see there was any direct connection between the two.'

Debbie put the coffee cup on the desk. 'I can't believe it.'

'You can see their point.'

'But you'd think they'd look into it, if only as routine.'

Pip stared down into South Audley Street, thinking of an old man who had died suddenly and violently in the stairwell of the tube. Piece by piece he went back over their conversation, stripping it down to its component parts, testing his own responses. He was not sure what had done it. Maybe it was the belligerence, the high, carping voice that had convinced him that he was dealing with a crank. Now he was not so sure. The police might be satisfied by the circumstances of the old man's death but he was not. There were too many questions left unanswered, too many parts that didn't fit together.

He had come across a few frauds in his time and he knew how hard they could be to detect. Provided the method was simple enough they could slip by unnoticed for years. He'd seen it happen. Frauds were like those invisible planets on the other side of the galaxy that telescopes can't see. If it wasn't for the occasional flicker in the orbit of the other, visible planets, a tiny abnormality of behaviour, no one would know they were there at all. And that's what was nagging at his mind. Allington's death could be a coincidence as the police suggested. Equally it could be that momentary flicker in the system.

He turned from the window. 'Can you remember the name of that gallery he'd been to? It had a strange-sounding name.'

'The D'Este Gallery – '

'That's the one.' Pip was impressed. 'How did you remember that?'

Debbie smiled sweetly and sat down behind the typewriter, pleased to have caught him off guard.

'Isabella d'Este – she was a patron of the arts in the fifteenth century.'

'What a fund of information you are today.'

'I read History of Art at university. Didn't you know that?'

Pip didn't. Secretaries were rather like school friends – you worked with them half your life and knew nothing of any real value about them.

'Do you know where it is?' he asked.

'I can look it up in the telephone directory if you like.'

Chapter Two

The D'Este Gallery was in Grafton Street. It was small and prosperous with hessian walls and recessed lighting and the casual air of sophistication that comes from money made without physical effort.

As Pip came in the owner emerged from a back office, Gucci slippers hovering silently across thick pile carpet, his hand extended in greeting.

'Which painting do you have in mind?' he inquired.

'It was a picture of a beach with nude bathers.' Pip tried to describe the photo he had seen as he looked around the walls. 'I must admit I can't see it here.'

'Maybe it's been sold, Mr Spender.'

'Spencer – '

'We have a vigorous turnover.' The owner didn't conceal his satisfaction. He was an elegant figure dressed in an Italian suit of powder blue silk, a striped Turnbull & Asser shirt, gold cufflinks and matching suavity of personality.

'It was here last week,' Pip assured him. 'And it's printed in your catalogue.'

'What's your interest in this painting, may I ask?'

'I'm trying to trace it for a client of mine.'

'Client?' A slight chill had come into the owner's manner now that he appreciated Pip wasn't a prospective buyer.

'Konstantin Allington.'

'I can't say the name rings a bell.'

'He was here last week. White-haired, unshaven, probably wearing a black overcoat.'

'We get a great number of people in the gallery, Mr Spender. I can't be expected to remember them all.' Stray geriatrics didn't interest him. He glanced around the gallery, his manner suddenly abstract. 'And now if you'd excuse me I'm already late for an appointment.'

After he had gone, murmuring instructions to the receptionist in parting, Pip looked around the gallery. Framed oil paintings glowed on the walls, each one glossy as its photograph in the catalogue. Prices available on request.

Pip didn't know much about art. There never seemed to have been enough time for it, although his father had frequently encouraged him to buy pictures.

'Good investment,' he'd rumble, 'best there is. Movable capital, you see, nothing like it.' Not that he had ever taken his own advice. Pip's father hadn't owned a house until he retired from the army and when he died three years later the only movable capital that he had left behind was a few bottles of drinkable claret and a set of golf clubs. Not much to divide between four grown children. To make matters worse there had been several immovable debts to pay off. The house had been sold, along with his mother's few remaining pieces of jewellery, and it had been only through the intervention of an uncle that Pip was able to stay on at college. They'd been the poor relations, down on their luck. The disgrace had clung to them like a disease. And it had been this, as much as anything, that had given Pip the determination to succeed, to fight back, to reach the top. There never seemed to have been room for anything else.

A voice behind him broke through his thoughts.

'I saw the old man.'

It was the receptionist who had spoken. She was sitting behind a desk of inlaid marquetry in the corner of the gallery, her chin resting on well manicured hands.

Pip turned around.

'You did?'

She smiled at him lazily. 'I would have said something earlier but Julian doesn't like anyone butting in while he's talking.'

Getting to her feet she strolled across the floor. She was a haughty, long-jawed piece in a tight black skirt and high-heeled shoes with a silk scarf draped about her shoulders that hinted at a privileged background: buck's fizz and weekends in the country.

'He came in here about ten days ago,' she drawled. 'Julian didn't see him, he was out at one of his extended lunches.'

'There was one painting that interested him.'

'It's down here,' she said leading the way to a lower gallery in the basement.

The painting she showed him was of four water-sprites – looking much like undressed débutantes – who had tumbled out of the foaming sea and now lay sprawled on the beach, languid and abandoned, their well-shaved bodies white as sugared almonds.

'That's the one,' he said.

'It was in the window. The old man seemed fascinated by it. Just stood there staring at it.'

19

He could see why this piece of Victorian pornography had stuck in the old man's mind.

'Who's it by?'

'Albert Lecoque. He's a French painter of the mid-nineteenth century.' She had her sales talk ready. 'Rather underrated, we feel.'

'Is it valuable?'

'Quite – Julian is asking thirty-five thousand for it.'

Is he, by God. Pip looked at the picture with rather more respect. That worked out at around a thousand pounds a square inch – four and a half thousand per nipple in anatomical terms. Probably not the way to judge quality but impressive just the same.

She tossed the figure aside like a spent cocktail stick. 'It's nothing like the most valuable we have.'

'How long have you owned it?' Pip asked her.

'About a year now.' She shrugged and gave a little smile. 'We don't sell pictures as quickly as Julian likes to make out.'

'Do you know where it came from?' Pip was vaguely wondering what she'd be like in bed.

'I could check for you.'

The provenances of the paintings were stored on a computer. She tapped in commands with sharp-nailed fingers and scanned the screen.

'We bought it from Phillips.'

Pip was interested. 'And before that?'

'It belonged to a gallery up in Cork Street for a while. They bought it from a private collection.'

'Is there any mention of it ever having been in Russia?'

'Should there be?' she asked, the eyelashes dropping as she read through the information on the computer.

'I heard that it was in Moscow at the turn of the century.'

She shook her head. 'There's no mention of it here.'

Pip's intellect was untamed at the best of times. Educated at a windswept private school which had dispensed knowledge with a cane and a Latin lexicon, he had been protected from any appreciation of the arts but he had a remarkable intuition and as he walked down St James's Street he could feel the curiosity prickle in his stomach.

'Can I help you, sir?' The security guard held the door open for him.

'I need information on a painting.'

'Ask at the desk, sir.' He pointed across the green-carpeted floor. 'They'll be able to give it to you.'

Pip had been in Christie's only once before in his life. It had been on the occasion of a sale of bronze work about a year ago. His senior partner had taken it into his head to buy a statue for his wife's birthday and had invited Pip along to lend moral support and to take over the bidding should his nerve fail him at the vital moment.

The counter was staffed by three young men in tailored suits and a red-headed girl who was presently locked in conversation with a lady bearing an ivory figure.

'It must be old,' she was saying, 'my grandfather brought it back from the Far East and he's been dead for donkey's years.'

The girl looked unconvinced. Pip moved down the counter and catching the attention of one of her well-groomed colleagues he stated his business.

'I need to talk to an expert on Russian paintings.'

'You mean icons?' The young man's voice was uninterested, he looked Pip over with listless eyes.

'More recent than that. This concerns a painting that was in a Russian collection during the last century.'

'May I ask if you are intending to buy or sell?'

'Neither.' Pip didn't apologise. 'It's a legal matter, I need his professional advice on behalf of a client.'

The mention of the law had its effect, as it often did. The young man turned to the girl, interrupting the discussion as to the age of the ivory figure, and asked, 'Who does Russian art?'

'Try Bill Hargreaves.'

He picked up the phone, drumming his fingers on the counter. 'Is Bill there? No . . . it's someone to see him at reception.' The woman's voice could be heard still insisting that the ivory was valuable: 'But that's ridiculous, he would never have bought a copy – '

The young man put down the phone and turned to Pip. 'Mr Hargreaves will be down in a moment. If you'd like to wait in here.'

Gliding around the counter he showed Pip into a small interview room, closing the door behind him.

Pip took a seat by the window. Outside in the street two porters in long brown coats were lifting paintings from the opened boot of a Jaguar. He watched as they manoeuvred one up the steps and in through the porch. Easily movable capital, he observed to himself, just as his father had said. Thousands, possibly millions, of pounds contained in a stretch of canvas weighing no more than a few ounces.

The door opened at that moment to admit a man with thick spectacles and prematurely receding hair. There was a pleasant air of disorder about him. His tie was tugged to one side, the collar rucked up over a jacket that had been pulled on hastily as he left the informality of his office.

'Hargreaves . . . Bill Hargreaves.' He shook Pip by the hand and sat down, thrusting out his legs in front of him. 'You have a legal problem, I'm told.'

'In a way,' Pip smiled, making light of the matter. 'I'm trying to trace the whereabouts of a painting that was in Russia at the turn of the century.'

'Is it still there?'

'That's what I'm hoping to discover.'

'Tricky business.' Hargreaves commiserated with him over his square, television-screen glasses. 'It's not easy to track down pictures in Russia.'

'I can imagine . . .'

'I've tried it myself once or twice. The Russians tend to be cagey about their possessions.'

Pip didn't want to explain his predicament further than he needed but there was certain information that he wanted from Bill Hargreaves. He put this to him.

'Do you mind if I ask you a few questions?'

'By all means – fire away.'

'What became of privately owned paintings in Russian after the revolution?'

Hargreaves pressed his fingertips together, arching them painfully as he considered his reply. 'Those that hadn't been lost, burned, stolen or otherwise destroyed were nationalised.'

'You mean they were grabbed by the State?'

'In 1918.' Hargreaves put the situation more precisely. 'After someone tried to smuggle a Botticelli over the border, Lenin decreed that all art treasures in the country were the property of the Soviet Republic.'

'And where are they kept nowadays?'

'The majority of them are in the Hermitage in Leningrad or the Pushkin Museum in Moscow, although paintings by Russian artists tend to be put into the Tret'yakov Gallery.'

'And between them they hold the lot?'

'Not entirely.' Again Hargreaves's fingers strained backwards – an irritating habit in an otherwise likeable personality. 'The museums show the cream of the Russian collections but of course there are a great many lesser paintings that don't go on public view.'

'Why not?'

'There simply isn't enough wall space for them in the galleries.' He gave Pip the statistics. 'The Russian aristocracy had been collecting works of art since the time of Peter the Great; shipped them in by the yard. Collected together I imagine they have enough painted canvas to paper every room in Moscow.'

'So where are they held?'

Hargreaves wasn't sure of this. 'Presumably they're in some sort of reserve collection although I must admit I don't know where.'

'It must be enormous.'

Hargreaves nodded to himself; the thought of this wasted potential seemed to offend his professional pride.

'Have any of them been sold?' Pip put the question casually but Hargreaves jumped on it with enthusiasm.

'Oh yes. There have been one or two sales recently. The new spirit of Perestroika and all that. I don't like to sing the praises of the opposition, but Sotheby's have managed to open quite a market with the Russians.'

'Were any of their paintings sold before this?'

'Only for political reasons. In the late thirties Stalin sold off several Old Master paintings to boost the economy. Most of the profits went into defence – he preferred tanks to Titians.' The alliteration seemed to please Hargreaves. He grinned to himself and stroked the balding patch on his head.

'But presumably that was all at government level.' Pip wanted to be sure of his facts. 'There would have been nothing furtive in the sales, no one would try to disguise where they had come from?'

'Quite the opposite, it's proved to be quite a selling point.'

'And the years these pictures had spent in Soviet Russia would all be recorded in their provenance?'

'Absolutely.'

'So apart from those that were sold by the government, every painting that was in Russia at the time of the revolution is still there.'

'That's about the size of it.'

Pip asked the question that was uppermost in his mind. 'Is there any sort of black market operating out of Russia?'

There was a pause while Hargreaves leaned back and the fingers met and bowed to their fullest degree.

'I've never come across one.' He made his position clear, his eyes bright behind the thick shield of his spectacles. 'But there are rumours, as you'd expect.'

'Why do you say that?'

'A picture in Russia has no commercial value. It is merely the property of the State – or the people – however you like to see it. But in the West that same picture could be worth a fortune. Selling them into Europe on some sort of black market must be a tempting proposition to any enterprising Russian.'

Pip looked out to where the porters were still carrying pictures in through the front door of Christie's.

'So it would simply be a matter of smuggling them over the border?'

'Hardly simple, Mr Spencer.' Pip's naivety seemed to amuse him. 'If you did somehow manage to lift a picture out from under the Russians' noses without anyone noticing, it would still have to pass through customs and border guards. And then, when it finally reached the West, your problems would only be starting. A provenance for the picture would have to be manufactured and it would have to be watertight. Good enough to stand up to close scrutiny. No one in the trade is going to touch a hot picture out of Russia, not if they can help it. The risk would be too much.'

Pip pressed his point. 'But if it were done – '

'Then someone would make himself very rich.' Hargreaves finished the sentence for him and again he smiled. 'Oh yes, make no mistake, the potential is enormous. It's the logistics that are the problem.'

Pip considered Hargreaves's words as he walked up St James's Street. The weather had broken and a warm drizzle was falling from an opaque sky. Turning up his collar he caught a bus that took him up Park Lane. As soon as he reached Evans-Greatheart he went in search of Max Fuller.

Max's office was two down from his own. The door was open. Pip gave a knock to announce himself.

'Are you busy?'

Max looked up from *The Times* crossword puzzle, his round face crumpling into an expression of astonishment. 'Busy?' The word was new to him. 'Good heavens, no.'

'Could I have a word?'

'Of course, make yourself at home.' Max twisted around in his seat and opening a cupboard drew out a bottle of malt whisky. 'Care for a drink?'

'Not for me – but don't let that stop you.'

'It won't.' Max glanced down at his watch. 'The sun is over the yard-arm isn't it?'

'Provided your boat has capsized.'

He splashed whisky into a glass, took a pull at it and leaned back with a groan of contentment. Like so many men of sharp intelligence, Max Fuller preferred to hide the fact. The disguise he had chosen was that of indolence, affecting a perpetual laziness, arriving late in the morning, yawning in board meetings, so that only those who knew him well saw beneath the mask. Taking another mouthful of whisky he asked: 'What's on your mind then, Pip?'

'Didn't you have something to do with that arbitration case over Russian mineral rights up in the Antarctic?'

Max was not disposed to boast of the event. 'One of the less glorious moments of my career.'

'How did you handle the Russians?'

'With great care.'

'What I mean is, how did you get in touch with them when you needed to?'

Max gave the question rather more thought. 'We had contact addresses. Dozens of them. You've no idea what bureaucrats the Russians are, they bombarded us with paper work.' He studied Pip from behind the face of a middle-aged cherub. 'Why do you ask?'

'This is strictly off the record.' Pip felt obliged to give the caution but Max waved it aside.

'Don't worry, I'm not listening.'

'I have a vague idea, and it's only a guess at present, that someone is smuggling pictures out of Russia and selling them under the counter.'

'Good for them.' Max didn't hide his prejudices. 'What's your evidence?'

'I've got a Russian picture that doesn't admit it's ever been there.'

'Black market?'

'Looks like it.'

'So being a good boy scout you thought you'd sneak, did you? Break the bad news to Ivan.' Max had a way of making you feel as though you belonged to a lower life-form.

'Something like that.' Pip smiled in return. 'I thought it might be worth checking with them first. See what they have to say before making a fool of myself. What should I do – write to the Embassy?'

'God, no.' The very idea seemed to appal him. 'You'll have left London and retired to the country to grow vegetable marrows before they get around to giving you an answer.'

'Who then?'

'Take it right into the enemy camp.' Max evidently saw this as some sort of pre-emptive strike. 'Write to the ministry in Moscow. There's bound to be a ministry for the arts. The place is crawling with them – you can't fart in Russia without permission from a ministry.' Getting to his feet he browsed along the bookshelves, then drew out a thick paperback, tapping it on the cover. It was the *Blue Guide to Moscow and Leningrad*. He studied the index for a moment and then flicked forwards.

'Here we are.' He read from the page. ' "Further down the Ul Kuybysheva are the Ministry of Finance (no. 9) and the Ministry of Culture (no. 10)." ' He handed the opened book across to Pip.

'The Ministry of Culture – they're the ones for you.'

Chapter Three

Moscow

Dmitri Alexandrevich Podurets, head of the Department of Intelligence and Communication, was perspiring slightly in the afternoon sunlight which shone in through the single window of his office on the fourth floor of the ministry.

He'd taken a few vodkas at lunch. Not his usual policy but this had been an exception, a farewell party for one of the senior administrators. It was an honour to have been invited; to have refused a drink would have been an insult.

Taking out his handkerchief Podurets ran it around the rim of his collar. He was a short man with a round face, balding head and a body that failed to meet the requirements of any suit built in the Soviet Union. In the thirty years he had dedicated to the ministry he had worked his way slowly and methodically from a junior clerk's desk to his present office with its shelves of files and utilitarian furniture, its electric kettle with the withered flex.

Opening the lid of the box-file his secretary had put in front of him he began sorting through the contents. Podurets read everything that passed through his hands, articles, newspaper cuttings, letters that arrived with no name and more particularly foreign correspondence. It gave him a unique insight into the private life of the ministry, the rivalries, the petty jealousies that sprang up between departments. He made it his business to understand the power struggles, the shifts in the pecking order, often making notes – preserving the information, as he liked to put it – for his own use.

When he came to the letter from London he paused and read the translation a second time. Turning the smartly embossed notepaper he studied the picture pinned to the back. It was a vulgar painting of nude girls. His lips pursed in disapproval. Such things were not encouraged in the Soviet Union.

Dropping the pages on the desk he stood and leaned against the window frame. Across the tattered rooftops of Moscow the domes of the Kremlin glowed in the afternoon light. It was a view that never failed to please him and for a few minutes he gazed at it abstractedly before calling down the passage:

'Comrade Leskova, will you come in here please?'

He heard the scrape of a chair and then a girl appeared in the doorway.

'Comrade?'

'Come in, shut the door after you.'

Katya Leskova was a specialist in European languages. A tall, dark-haired Georgian who had only recently been transferred to the ministry from the State Institute of Technology in Tbilisi.

Crumpling himself into his chair, Podurets made small pouting movements with his lips as he collected his thoughts.

'How long have you been an interpreter, Comrade Leskova?' was the final product.

'Almost four years.'

'Would you consider yourself to be good at that job?'

'I think so . . .' The girl didn't like to commit herself until she'd discovered where the conversation was leading.

'So I imagine you read through what you translate before you return it here to me?'

'Naturally, Comrade Podurets.'

'Checking for all the fine details of grammar and spelling?'

'I try to make sure there are no mistakes.'

Podurets's hard eyes were on her. 'And do you then remember what it is you've written with such care?'

'Not for long.' She could see the trap now and her voice grew more wary. 'I hold the meaning of the words while I'm working but it goes shortly afterwards.'

Podurets pondered this reply, picking at his teeth with his thumbnail. His hands were plump and white, the two forefingers of his right hand stained yellow with nicotine like a meerschaum pipe. Picking up the letter he held it up to her.

'Do you recall this, for example, Comrade Leskova?'

She cocked her head to one side as she looked at the page. The spark of recognition in her eyes gave him the answer he was seeking.

'I see that you do.'

'You gave it to me to translate yesterday.'

'Indeed I did.' Podurets wasn't denying the fact. 'But do you happen to recall what is contained in it?'

'It was something about a painting in a London gallery. I didn't follow the details but I believe they were suggesting – '

'Accusing, Comrade Leskova.' Podurets tried to appear tolerant as he made the correction. 'They are accusing us of trafficking in artworks, of selling State treasures on the black market.'

The office was growing warm in the afternoon sunshine, the slitted eyes of Lenin smiled benignly down from the portrait on the wall. The girl listened to Podurets's words without understanding them.

'Black market? I hadn't realised . . .'

'Valuable paintings from this country are being sold in London galleries.'

'But I didn't see anything about that.'

'Oh yes, comrade.' Her innocence seemed to give Podurets some private satisfaction. He waved the letter to one side. 'At least that is what they would have us believe. Of course they have wrapped it up in pretty legal language. It's all very evasive, very non-committal. But the implication is there as clearly as if they had it printed on the front page of *The Times* newspaper.'

'I'd no idea, comrade . . .'

Podurets dropped the pages on to his blotter and sat back, composing his thoughts once more.

'Naturally this doesn't surprise me. Such unfounded accusations are to be expected from the West.' He comforted himself with the observation. As well as being director of the Department of Intelligence and Communication, Podurets was the party leader for their section, a card-carrying Communist, one of the faithful. He gave Katya an insight into the heavy responsibility this imposed on him.

'What concerns me at present is the long-term effect this might have on the ministry.'

'Effect? What effect can it have?'

He looked up at her as though she were simple. 'This matter has to be referred to Security, Comrade Leskova. Did you not know that?'

'But if the accusation is unfounded?'

'It makes no difference, it is still a question for Security. It is my duty to report it to them.' He spoke with the quiet complacency of one who knows his job. 'You see what trouble this letter of yours will cause, Comrade Leskova? You see what repercussions it will have? They might well make an issue of it, set up an inquiry. The black market is a sensitive subject in Moscow as I'm sure you are aware.'

The girl was looking aggrieved at being implicated in this business. It was not her fault that a firm of solicitors had written to the ministry. She wanted a way out.

'Could you not anticipate such an inquiry?' she asked.

Podurets wasn't listening. Running his hand across his head, he smoothed the limp strands of hair and voiced the fear at the centre of his indignation.

'The minister is not going to be pleased when he hears of this, not pleased at all.'

'But if you were to add your own assessment of the situation before passing it on . . .'

He looked up from the desk. 'What do you mean, girl?'

'They wouldn't bother to make inquiries if the answers to their questions had already been discovered.'

'Are you suggesting that this department should conduct an investigation?' Podurets tested the idea on himself.

'Ask an expert,' she replied. 'Find out whether it's feasible that paintings are leaving the country.'

He considered the possibility. A brief piece of research from one of his staff, signed by himself with a flourish of the pen. The subject closed before it could cause damage, nipped in the bud. Yes, it had its attractions. Such initiative wouldn't go unnoticed; it might even lead to promotion, another rung up the ladder.

Podurets hunched over his desk, white fingers drumming up a decision. 'And where would you go for such information?'

'The Tret'yakov Gallery?'

'The Pushkin would be more suitable in this situation.' His superior knowledge decided it for him. With a wave of his hand he said, 'Very well, get on to them. See what they have to say for themselves.'

Katya left the ministry by the side door and hurried up into Red Square, brushing the conversation with Podurets out of her mind.

After the stuffy atmosphere of the office the air was fresh and cool, the brief Russian summer drawing to a close, autumn already beginning to gild the trees in the Alexander Gardens.

A policeman was holding back the pedestrians on the corner of Kuybysheva Street, whistling shrilly at those who disobeyed. Katya waited on the kerb and looked across the square at the clustered domes of St Basil's.

The transfer to Moscow had come suddenly and unexpectedly. She had been given no time to prepare herself for the violent change in her life. After the sunlight, the spacious houses, the patrician elegance of Georgia, the move to the capital had been like entering another planet. It was not just the crowds and the queues, it was the mood of the place, the expressions on the faces, the sight, the sound, the sense of uncompromising grimness.

The policeman was beckoning her forwards with frantic gestures from his arm and more whistling. He looked pointedly at Katya's legs as she passed but she ignored him and dived into the subway alongside GUM department store.

The two Americans had said they'd meet her in the bar at four. It was already half past. With any luck they'd hang around for a while. They'd kept telling her there was nothing else to do in the city but drink.

The concrete shuddered as a train rumbled beneath her feet, smoke spurting up through the central gratings, separating the two columns of people who trudged through the half-light of the subway.

Tatyana was waiting for her at the far end.

'Where have you been?' she asked urgently, detaching herself from the wall where she'd been leaning.

'Podurets stopped me just as I was leaving. I couldn't get away from him.'

'That pig. What did he want?'

'He's fretting about some letter I translated. He wants me to go to the Pushkin Museum and sort it out.'

'Forget it,' she said. 'Let him do it for himself.'

Tatyana Vasnikova was twenty-six, two years older than Katya, several inches shorter, with a fierce vitality that filled the apartment they shared. She wore a flowing black dress that reached to her ankles, gold earrings and a string of golden coins round her head that jangled excitedly as they came up the subway steps on the corner of Gorky Street.

'Okay?' she asked.

Katya nodded. She had taken her purse from her bag and reaching under her coat she tucked it into her waistband well out of sight.

As they approached the Hotel Nationale she broke into a run, arriving at the entrance flushed and breathless.

The doorman held out his arm. 'You can't come in here, comrade.'

'Please, it's very important.' Katya smiled at him anxiously. 'I dropped my purse upstairs this morning. I must get it.'

'Not without a pass you won't.'

'I'm an interpreter. I was working here this morning. You saw me coming out with the minister, don't you remember?'

The doorman looked her over. Beneath her overcoat she was dressed in a crisp white shirt and blue skirt above polished black boots. A sleek, handsome girl, the sort who made you stop and wonder if things couldn't have turned out differently. He remembered her all right. Who wouldn't? But he wasn't giving in.

'You know the rules, comrade.'

'You've got to let her through,' Tatyana cut in angrily as she reached them. 'It's got all her ID cards. She'll be fried alive if you don't let her get it.'

'Please.' Katya's dark eyes were imploring him. 'It's so important.'

The doorman looked from one to the other and then dropping his arm he hustled her inside. 'Okay, make it snappy then.'

He must be new, Katya thought as she grabbed the temporary pass and ran upstairs. Falling for that old trick. He hadn't even asked to look in her handbag.

Five minutes later she returned, her heels tapping across the marble hallway.

'Did you find it then?' the doorman asked.

She waved the rediscovered purse, flashing him a dazzling smile as she went out into the street.

'Where was it then?'

'I dropped it in the ladies',' she called back over her shoulder.

The doorman leaned against the wall and watched her threading her way through the crowd, her dark hair splashing about her shoulders as she walked. He wondered what it was she had wanted so badly in the hotel. Certainly not her purse.

Tatyana was waiting for her around the corner in Gorky Street.

'Did you get anything?'

Grinning at her own ingenuity, Katya pulled three packets of cigarettes from under her coat – six hundred Marlboros wrapped in cellophane blocks.

Tatyana took them with a growl of interest. 'How much did they want for them?'

'Forty roubles.'

She whistled. 'You must have charmed them, Katska. They're worth a lot more than that.'

'They said it was enough.'

Katya was both pleased and shocked by her achievement. A year ago she would never have dreamed of abusing her job to get American cigarettes. But in Moscow you learned to adapt, to make the most of what you had. It was a simple question of survival.

And foreign cigarettes were wealth in Moscow. They could be used where money wasn't accepted. They opened doors, paid for the luxuries that had no fixed price.

'What are you going to do with them?' Tatyana asked, running her hands across the smooth cellophane, estimating their value in real terms.

'I hadn't thought. Perfume maybe?'

She shook her head, the gold coins fluttering. 'You can get more than that.'

'What then?'

'I don't know.' She handed them back to Katya. 'I'll ask around. See what's going.'

They parted hurriedly, Tatyana heading off towards the ministry,

Katya walking down the street past the old university building with its little garden.

When she returned to the office an hour later she found Podurets waiting for her.

'Where have you been?'

She went round behind her desk. 'I was down at the Pushkin, fixing a meeting like you said.'

'Why didn't you ring them?'

'I couldn't get through,' Katya replied airily. 'I thought it best to go down there in person.'

'And what have you arranged?'

'I'm seeing the curator at eleven tomorrow.' She sat down and smiled at him winningly. 'That is what you wanted, isn't it?'

Chapter Four

Pip walked down the platform of Holland Park tube.

Beside him the carriage doors rattled closed and the train lumbered forward into the tunnel, the lit compartments streaming past him, cold air rushing in behind, tugging at his clothes and hair.

He looked at the vaulted ceiling, at the posters and gleaming rails and thought of the time when these desolate tube stations had acted as air-raid shelters. He'd seen photographs of figures in sleeping bags huddled together in rows, heard talk of the spirit that had united them during those long hours. It was hard to imagine now. The few individuals on the platform that morning stood apart, remote from each other, paying no attention to Pip as he passed.

The way-out sign led up over the track into a passage of cream tiles above green. At the far end were two lifts. The doors of one stood open, bright lights and framed advertisements on the inner walls. A high-pitched siren was sounding, strident in the enclosed space, to warn passengers of its impending departure.

Pip paused in the passage and waited until the steel doors had closed and the lift rumbled away towards the surface. He watched the series of square lights on the control panel flickering upwards, registering its position in the shaft.

Walking back a few paces he began to climb the spiral stairway, flights of gritty steps interrupted by short landings. A thick ventilation duct snaked down the central core of the stairs; the walls were painted pale yellow, pitted and splattered with dirt.

Pip was not as fit as he would have liked but he'd been rowing regularly in the last two weeks and frequently went for a run in the morning before work. He was also forty years younger than Konstantin Allington but by the top of the stairway he found himself out of breath, the blood pulsing at wrist and temple.

'That's quite a slog,' he said to the ticket collector who stood at the barrier, his feet large in rubber-soled boots.

'You should have taken the lift, mate.' The advice was offered without enthusiasm as he took Pip's ticket. 'The stairs are only for emergencies.'

'Preventing or creating them?'

The question was received with an expression of blank incomprehension. 'What y'mean?'

'I hear that someone died down there a couple of weeks ago.'

'Oh him.' Understanding drifted into the ticket collector's mind and giving a slight backward jerk of the head he added: 'He was old.'

This apparently explained everything. Pip encouraged him to be more expansive. 'What happened exactly?'

'Heart attack.'

'Why do you think he came up the stairs?'

'God knows.'

Pip kept his tone casual. 'You'd think it would have been more sensible to wait for the next lift.'

The ticket collector paused, bringing his attention to bear on Pip for the first time. 'I don't know why he did, do I?' His voice was that of a reasonable man stretched to the limit of his endurance. 'The fellow was dead before I could ask him. Maybe you can tell me why he come up the stairs, you're the one that's just done it for yourself.'

'You're right,' Pip conceded the point. 'I just wondered whether the lifts were out of action that day.'

'There was nothing wrong with the lifts, mate. He come up the stairs because he felt like it.'

'Was anyone else there at the time?'

He shook his head. 'He'd been dead almost ten minutes before we found him – the doctor said so.' His eyes narrowed at the interrogation. 'What's it to you anyway?'

'Just curious.'

'You're not from head office?'

Pip assured him he was nothing so sinister and went out into the street. It was raining. Passing cars hissed on the wet road beneath a cloud of damp green foliage. He bought an early edition of the *Evening Standard* from a stall that had been pulled back into the shelter.

'Right to-do it was.' The newspaper-man, chubby in anorak and flat cap, picked up the story where the other had left off. 'They had the whole entrance to the station cordoned off. Ambulances, police cars, the works.' He peered up at the sky warming his hands on the memory. 'Plays hell with my rheumatics, this rain.'

'What time of the day did he die?'

'Around midday.'

'Was the station crowded?'

'No more than it is now, just a few people around. Didn't even

34

make the evening papers. It's a shame really – nothing like a bit of local news to boost sales.'

The power of the press, Pip reflected to himself as he headed up towards Notting Hill Gate. Burying his hands in his suit pockets he tried to picture the scene in the tube. Allington coming down the passage, arriving too late to catch the lift. Turning back impatiently, making his way up the emergency stairs. The effort would have made the old man's blood pulse, just as it had with him, but Allington hadn't paused to catch his breath. He had kept on going until his heart failed.

Pip stared into the window of a butcher's shop where rolled joints of beef, stacked chops, kebabs with red peppers and mushrooms skewered together lay in white plastic trays.

There was only one reason he could think of why the old man hadn't waited for the next lift, only one reason that he'd set off up the stairs, pushing himself beyond the limit of his endurance.

Someone had been following him.

Pip said as much to Max Fuller that evening. They were sitting in a wine bar after work. The rain had continued throughout the afternoon and now drummed against the window, distorting the image of the streetlights on the glass pane.

'I think the old fellow was frightened of being caught down there.' Pip visualised the deserted passage as he spoke, the draught sucking in the lift shaft. 'He thought somebody was after him and took the only other way out.'

'Have you told the police?'

'Not yet.'

'Why not?'

'Because I've got eff-all proof – just a sensation in the gut.'

'I know the feeling.' Max was solemn in their shared suffering. 'I get the same thing, only with me it comes after half a dozen oysters.'

'Do you think I'm being melodramatic?'

'Not necessarily.'

'I may have something more substantial to go on after I hear from that Russian ministry.'

'If you hear from them – the Russians only answer a letter if it suits them.' House claret and previous experience had made Max cynical on this point. He looked at Pip thoughtfully. 'I should leave it alone if I were you.'

'Why do you say that?'

'It sounds like bad business to me.'

'I need to know the answer.'

Max was not troubled by any such scruples. 'There are only a few rules to the legal profession,' he pointed out. 'Don't touch anything to do with politics or prostitution unless they're directly connected. Don't twist the law, don't fiddle your expenses and never on any account become emotionally involved with a case.'

'You think that's what I'm doing?'

'Leave it to the Russians. It's their problem. Let the blighters sort it out for themselves.'

Chapter Five

There were two armed guards on the door of the Lubyanka.
They stood with their legs parted, eyes shielded beneath the peaks
of their caps, ears protruding from shaven heads. Neither of them
looked at Podurets as he bustled up the steps.

He had put on his black overcoat and astrakhan hat and pinned
to his lapel was the Party badge to which he was entitled, the profile of Lenin surrounded by a garland of red enamel. It had started
to rain as he walked over from the ministry and the moisture now
gleamed on his shoulders and face, creating the impression that he
was sweating.

The duty sergeant checked his identity papers, barking directions
as he registered the name in the day-book.

Podurets knew the way. He'd been there a dozen times in the
past. It was an office on the second floor of the building. In the
high, granite-columned passage outside was a security desk. The
officer looked up from the phone as Podurets approached, cupping
his hand across the receiver.

'Yes?'

Podurets had come prepared. Setting his briefcase on the desk
he said, 'I have a document here that—'

The officer stabbed a finger across the uncarpeted passage.

'Wait over there.'

Podurets did as he was told, perching himself on a steel-framed
chair that had been designed for reasons other than comfort. The
window beside him looked down into an enclosed courtyard where
central-heating ducts dripped in the rain.

Podurets didn't mind waiting. He was vaguely aware that he
was never going to amount to much in the Party but he liked
to be of service to the authorities, hunting down small heresies in
the ministry, assessing the commitment of the girls in his charge,
filing reports on their conduct. It gave him a rôle, a private sense
of involvement.

A door opened further down the passage and a secretary emerged,
legs scissoring beneath a tight khaki skirt, buttons straining on her

37

blouse as she trotted past him. Podurets's eyes followed her down the passage. He preferred a girl with a bit of flesh on her, it was a sign of sensuality. The padded ones were best, he'd heard, the most compliant.

'Are you deaf or something?'

With a sudden jolt Podurets realised that the officer had asked him a question.

'I'm sorry?'

'What is it you want?'

'I have a document here that must be referred to your department,' Podurets replied. Opening his briefcase he drew out the letter from the London solicitor.

The officer scanned the sheet briefly and dropped it in the tray beside him.

'It'll be looked into.'

Podurets was not ready to be dismissed so quickly. 'I brought it over personally. It contains allegations that may require investigation by your department.'

The officer tilted back his head and stared at him. Beneath the high peaked hat he had a thin, fragile face with blue-veined skin and the kind of bony nose that grows raw and red in the winter. Getting to his feet he went back into the office.

Through the opened door Podurets could hear voices talking inside.

'We have the matter in hand,' the officer informed him as he returned.

Podurets walked downstairs. As he was crossing the hallway he was stopped by a call from the duty sergeant.

He turned, looked about himself.

'You mean me?'

The sergeant nodded. Putting down the phone that he held cradled in his neck he jerked his head towards the stairs.

'Back you go, comrade,' he said pleasantly. 'Colonel Krasin wants a word with you.'

Podurets felt a clutch of apprehension as he was taken back into the offices on the second floor. He had never met Colonel Krasin. He was just a name, a signature on ministry directives.

The lieutenant on the desk passed him over to a major, a short, powerfully built man with flat features. He was drinking coffee as Podurets came in.

'Are you the one with the letter?' he asked curtly.

Podurets nodded.

Crumpling the paper cup in his hand the major threw it into the basket and stood up. Without further explanation he led the way to the far end of the passage, knocked on a door and turned back to Podurets, looking him up and down critically.

'Take your hat off,' he ordered.

Dragging the astrakhan down the side of his head Podurets was ushered into the office.

It looked more like the drawing room of some private house. The walls were panelled in dark, polished wood, and a glass chandelier hung from the ceiling, the facets winking in the afternoon light. In the centre of the deep red Persian carpet was a desk the size of a billiard table.

Colonel Vassily Krasin was having lunch. In front of him was a plate of oysters on a square of damask table-cloth set with silver cutlery and a tall-stemmed glass. At his elbow a bottle of wine was crushed into an ice bucket.

As Podurets watched, he forked up the flesh of an oyster and put it into his mouth before lifting the shell to his lips and draining the liquid.

Standing behind his chair was a tall blond-haired man in a grey suit whom Podurets recognised as Chibatar, the Colonel's Ukrainian driver. His arms were folded, expression distant as though he were remembering something that happened years before. Podurets looked at him with interest. He was said to be a mute. Tortured whilst serving as an intelligence officer in the Afghanistan war if the rumours were to be believed.

Krasin touched his napkin to his lips.

'You are Dmitri Podurets.'

It sounded more like a statement than a question. Podurets wasn't sure whether to reply.

'That is correct, Colonel.'

'I see from your file that you are the head of the Department of Intelligence and Communication at the Ministry of Culture.'

Krasin looked up as he spoke. His eyes were hard and shrewd and quite extraordinarily black, the irises indistinguishable from the pupil.

With a small gesture of the fork in his hand Krasin added, 'What do you do in this department of yours exactly, Comrade Dmitri?'

Podurets had a number of answers to this question but none of them seemed appropriate at that moment and so he said, 'Translation work on the whole, Colonel.'

'I see.' Krasin was interested. 'And which languages do you speak personally?'

Podurets could feel the palms of his hands beginning to sweat.

'None, Colonel.'

'Your rôle is purely administrative, I take it?'

'I organise the work schedules.'

'It seems to be what we do best in this country.' Krasin made the observation with a hint of sadness. 'Italy produces great singers, France has its chefs while we appear to be nothing more than a nation of bureaucrats.'

He turned, gave a nod of his head. At once Chibatar stepped forward and removed the plate of oysters, putting a glass fingerbowl in its place. Krasin touched the surface of the water with his fingertips and dried them on the napkin. The action revived his interest in Podurets.

'A few minutes ago you delivered a letter to one of my officers. I can only assume therefore that you appreciate its content.'

Podurets wrung his hat in his hand, uncertain whether he was to be praised or reprimanded for this knowledge. Krasin was giving nothing away.

'Could I ask who else has seen this letter?'

'No one, Colonel.'

'It came directly to your department?'

'The delivery takes place first thing in the morning. No one else has time to see it.'

Flicking the napkin from his lap Krasin jumped to his feet and strolled over to the window.

'And what will be its destination once it leaves your department?' he inquired, his attention fastened on the crowded square beneath.

'It is normal to refer correspondence such as that to the minister's personal aide.' Podurets was on firmer ground now and spoke with a little confidence.

'You will leave it here,' Krasin corrected him. 'Major Zakov will give you a receipt for it.'

'Ah yes, I see . . .'

'You sound doubtful.'

'I will need to account for its transfer, Colonel.'

Krasin turned, looking at him with some curiosity. 'Why is that?'

'Its arrival in my department has been logged.'

'Then you will remove the reference from the files, Comrade Dmitri.' He nodded at the badge on Podurets's lapel as he spoke, reminding him of his loyalties. 'Do you understand me?'

'Completely, Colonel.'

'And should you receive any further communication from this source you will refer it to me directly.'

Krasin had turned back to the window. The door opened and Podurets realised the interview was over.

As he was leaving Krasin's voice held him.

'You say you speak no foreign language,' he said softly. 'Then who was it who translated this letter, comrade?'

Podurets had paused in the doorway, realising his mistake.

'One of the girls in my department.'

'Did she show any interest in the contents?'

With a sickening sensation, Podurets recalled the conversation he'd had with Katya Leskova.

'Yes, Colonel,' he said in a voice that had shrunk in the wash. 'I believe she has taken the matter up with the Pushkin Museum.'

Katya went over to the ticket kiosk.

'I have come to see Comrade Tokarev.' She gave the name of the member of the museum committee to whom she'd spoken the day before.

The women in the kiosk was counting through a book of tickets, licking her thumb between each one. She viewed Katya with suspicion.

'I have an appointment,' Katya added archly.

The woman closed the kiosk window for a moment and went next door.

'Wait here,' she instructed as she returned. 'He'll be down.'

Katya looked round at the cold, sparse hallway of the Pushkin Museum. A single flight of stone steps led up to the galleries like the approach to some ancient necropolis.

She wanted to put an end to this business as quickly as possible. Podurets had a way of exaggerating problems, building them up out of all proportion. Unless something was done quickly to squash the notion she could see herself being caught up in a long, time-wasting inquiry.

Tokarev appeared from a lower floor. He was a slight figure with sloping shoulders and round spectacles balanced on his nose. He was practically bald but what little hair he had remaining was brushed carefully over the crown of his head for maximum coverage. He listened to Katya's questions with an air of polite disapproval.

'What you say is quite impossible, young lady.'

'The ministry has received a report.'

'Then whoever sent it must be mistaken.' The subject held no interest for him.

'Are you sure of that?'

'You can take my word for it, no painting from the Soviet Union could leave the country unnoticed.' As he was speaking he led the way upstairs into the main gallery, a large sunwashed room of wedding-cake columns, and paused before a framed canvas.

41

'Do you recognise this picture, Comrade Leskova?'

'No, I'm afraid not.'

'Or this?' He moved further along the gallery wall flicking out his hand as though it was a duster. She shook her head again and felt Tokarev's disapproval deepening.

'I don't know very much about paintings,' she told him.

'But I thought you said you worked for the ministry.'

'As an interpreter.'

'I see.' The news served only to disappoint him. 'I would have thought they'd send someone with a little more appreciation of the subject.'

He turned back to the painting and perused it thoughtfully, his hands on his stomach, fingers pressed inwards as though holding in a paunch that he didn't possess.

'It's by Manet,' he told her eventually. 'Painted around 1874 at Argenteuil on the river Seine.'

The painting was of two people in a sailing boat. The man sat in the stern, sporting a straw boater and tight white vest and holding the tiller in his hand while his girlfriend leaned back, almost out of the canvas. She looked bored, Katya thought to herself, definitely wishing she was somewhere else.

'Although it appears to have escaped your own attention, this picture is particularly well known, as, I might say, are most of the paintings in this museum.' Tokarev's voice had assumed the high nasal pitch of the expert. 'Art books all over the world have carried reproductions of it and any picture dealer from any country would instantly recognise it. To steal such a major piece would be difficult, to sell it impossible.'

Katya listened respectfully, head bowed towards the picture, dark hair fanning out across her white shirt. She found the man's attitude patronising and didn't allow him to deflect her questions.

'But what of your reserve collection?' she asked. 'The picture that we were shown was not so famous.'

'The same rule applies.' Tokarev had moved away, less than amused at this cross-examination. It was not her place to interrogate a senior official and he gave his reply quickly and succinctly.

'All reserve collections in the Soviet Union are catalogued by artist, subject and dimension, but more importantly they are numbered. If one were missing, it would be noticed in exactly the same way as if one of your fingers was missing.' He allowed himself a small and wintry smile at this allusion. 'There would simply be one too few.'

'I see.'

'Do I make myself clear?'

'Yes, quite clear.' Katya wanted to ask him more but Tokarev had finished the interview. He swept the air with the thin blade of one hand, cutting short her questions.

'I don't know what your directive is in coming here, Comrade Leskova, but I suggest that you inform the ministry that if a painting were lost from this country it would be we who informed them, not the other way about. And as for reports from the West' – again the cold smile rebuked her – 'I recommend you ignore them in future.'

'I felt such an idiot. He kept showing me these pictures as though I should know them and I didn't recognise a single one.'

'That's their way.'

'After that he'd hardly talk to me.'

Tatyana wormed her way through the queue outside a butcher's shop. 'They like to behave that way, Katska, you don't want to worry about it. I think most of them only study art to make themselves sound important.'

'I just said I was an interpreter. The way he reacted you'd think I'd told him I was the ministry tart.'

'You'd get paid more if you were.'

On the corner of the Prospeckt Sapunova, beneath a tall building of crumbling canary yellow plaster, a woman was selling plums from a barrow. Tatyana stopped and darting out her hand she examined one critically. It was large and firm, the flesh glossy.

'How much?'

'Two roubles the kilo.'

She dropped it back as though it were red-hot. 'Who do you think I am, a tourist?'

The woman shrugged solid shoulders. She had a wide, placid face and small slitted eyes that looked as though they had been stabbed into the sockets with a knife.

'That's the price, take it or leave it.'

'I'll give you fifty copecks.'

'Eighty or I don't make a profit.'

'Okay.' Tatyana counted out the coins, took a bruised plum off the scales and changed it for another.

'Wasn't that a lot to pay?' Katya asked as they moved on.

Tatyana took a handful more out of her pocket. 'Not when you include these in the bargain.'

'Tasha!' She was horrified. 'You didn't steal those, did you?'

'Of course. The old cow ripped me off and I ripped her off in return. It's perfectly fair.'

A group of workmen were digging up paving stones in the Alexander Gardens. Resting on the shafts of their pick-axes they gave the girls a broadside of wolf-whistles as they passed. Tatyana turned and mouthed a four-letter word back at them and they howled with delight.

When Katya was first transferred to Moscow she had been allocated living quarters. The space came with the job – a gift of the State, as Podurets was fond of calling it. She'd had no say in where she lived or who she lived with.

The other two in the apartment had greeted her arrival quite differently. To Ludmilla, a pale Muscovite girl from the Records Department, it had been a matter of supreme indifference.

'I'm not going to be living here much longer, you see,' she had confided on one of the first evenings they were together.

'Why? Are you getting a transfer?'

'You could call it that.' She had smiled secretively, pouting small red lips. 'If a girl can't feather her own nest what can she do?'

'What she means,' Tatyana had explained some time later, 'is that she's a slut.'

The more volatile of the two, ever wary of having anything imposed on her against her will, Tatyana had been suspicious, almost hostile, when Katya first arrived, watching her from a distance. It wasn't until several weeks had passed that she'd finally dropped her guard, the hostility melting and turning inexplicably to friendship.

Looking around the park, Tatyana spotted an empty bench and hurried across to it.

'Have you still got those cigarettes?' she asked when they had sat down.

Katya nodded.

'I think I might have found a use for them.' Her eyes were bright in the shade of the trees. 'I have a friend in the fur trade, we might be able to do a deal with him.'

'What sort of deal?' Instinctively their heads had come closer together as they talked.

'I'm not sure, a coat maybe.'

Katya's expression was intent. A fur coat was the most treasured of possessions in Russia, something to be proud of. To exchange one for six hundred cigarettes was close to alchemy.

'You can do this, Tasha?'

'I think so, leave it with me for a bit.'

'It seems a lot for cigarettes.' She wasn't raising her hopes until she was sure.

'I'll have a talk with him.'

'But a fur coat's expensive.'

Tatyana grinned and rubbed her thumb across her forefingers. 'There may be something we can do for him in return.'

* * *

'What the hell does she think she's playing at?' Krasin asked putting down the phone.

His conversation with Tokarev had been short and to the point, a matter of listening rather than speaking.

'Did she give an explanation?' Zakov inquired.

'Just accused the museum of losing paintings from the reserve collections.'

'I bet they loved that,' he replied drily.

It was the motive that puzzled Krasin. He could see no reason for this girl to have taken the time off to go down to the museum, sticking her nose where it didn't belong.

'Bring me her file,' he ordered. 'Let's see who we're dealing with.'

When Zakov was out of earshot he turned to Chibatar who stood leaning against the wall.

'What's in it for her?' he asked.

Chibatar made no immediate response. He gazed at him with his pale grey eyes and then shrugged casually. He never seemed to show any sign of emotion but there was a serenity, a sense of fulfilment to the man that Krasin could never quite fathom.

'My guess is that she was put up to it by that little toad Podurets,' he said.

Chibatar nodded and indicated that it was more than likely.

'Thought he would be given a pat on the back for showing initiative and then shifted the blame on to her when things didn't look so rosy.'

They were interrupted by Zakov returning with a computer print-out in his hand.

'Nothing out of the ordinary,' he remarked, feeding through the densely printed lines. 'Katya Leskova – Georgian national, works at the Ministry of Culture as an interpreter, drafted to Moscow a year ago on one of the integration schemes.'

'No nationalist tendencies, I suppose?'

Zakov shook his head. 'Not that I can see. There is one interesting point. She shares an apartment with two other girls in the ministry. One of them is Tatyana Vasnikova.'

'Should I know her?'

'She's on the police records.' Zakov had a head for these details. 'She's been known to associate with dissidents, turns up at protest rallies – that sort of thing.'

Thoughtfully Krasin picked up his paper-knife and balanced it on the tips of his fingers. It was a German Fliegerkorps dagger, the type carried by trainee pilots. Krasin wasn't old enough to remember the war. The knife was a trophy of a different sort, confiscated during a police raid.

45

Zakov watched him turning the fine blade in his hands, the light licking down the tempered steel.

'Are you intending to do anything about this, Colonel?' he asked after a few minutes' silence had elapsed.

Krasin replaced the knife on his desk.

'Yes,' he replied lightly. 'I intend to go to the ballet.'

Chapter Six

It was a formal reception, part of the official function of the ministry, and the auditorium was filled with uniforms, jewellery and fur coats.

'Quite a turn-out,' Tatyana observed as they made their way downstairs in the first interval.

A growl of conversation drifted out of the opened doors of the dining hall. Medals and wine glasses winked in the chandelier light, high mirrors emphasised the space.

'Did you see the girl dancing the part of the nanny?' Tatyana had scandal on her mind as they came in. 'She had to stand in at the last moment when they found the other had got herself pregnant.'

'Where did you hear that?' It was Misha, a boy who worked in the Records Department, who asked.

'I saw a memo that was passed to the minister yesterday.'

Tatyana always seemed to be the first to know of such things, Katya reflected, looking round at the gilded ceiling and heavy velvet drapery; the powerful evocations of a previous era.

She had arrived late at the Bolshoi after being held up at a conference and had changed hurriedly in the ladies'. The dress she put on was of black silk. She'd bought it at the T'sum department store and then taken it to pieces on the apartment floor, cutting and restitching the seams to make it fit properly. It was simple and unpretentious but with her long hair and dark eyes she was looking sensational that evening and she knew it.

'They say it was one of the violinists who was responsible.' Tatyana was still discussing the unfortunate dancer.

'Well it wouldn't have been any of the male ballerinas, would it?' tittered Svetlana. 'You'd never find their fingerprints on a girl. Not their style.'

Across the floor Katya saw Podurets hovering close to the minister, ingratiating himself into the circle. He had left work earlier that afternoon to prepare himself for this occasion and now seemed in rare good spirits, smiling deferentially. Near him were one or two members of the ballet company, ghostly in their make-up, wearing flowing gowns over their stage costumes.

There was a cry of recognition from the crowd.

'Ah – there you all are!'

Katya turned to see Ludmilla approaching, her silver blonde hair piled up high for the evening, eyes painted. She was wearing a dress of some shiny golden material that looked both new and expensive. It was bunched at the waist into a large, propeller-like bow, giving her the appearance of a primitive flying-machine attempting to take off. Accompanying her was a frail-looking man, white-haired and timid, who was decaying unobtrusively into middle age. Ludmilla was in the mood to be disparaging.

'Such a bore, these ministry parties,' was her opening contribution as she joined them. 'Don't you agree? I can't think why we come.' She scanned the table beside her critically. 'And red caviare, there's only red caviare. When the Agricultural Ministry was here last month we had black.' She turned to her escort who was hovering in the background, attempting to infiltrate himself into the conversation. 'But that was Tchaikovsky, wasn't it, Mikhail?'

He nodded seriously, waggling his eyebrows, glad to be of service. Taking a roll of pickled sturgeon from a passing tray Ludmilla popped it between her red lips.

'I think you only get black caviare with Tchaikovsky.'

Katya couldn't see how the two could be connected but looked understanding. Ludmilla had been living in their apartment for over a year now but she still thought of her as a stranger, a passing acquaintance rather than a friend.

'Where are you lot sitting?' Ludmilla was relentless in her quest for supremacy that evening. 'I didn't see you during the performance.'

'We're up in the gallery.'

She seemed disenchanted by the information. 'I really think you should try to be down lower. There's so much you miss from that height – especially with Prokofiev.' At that moment she spotted someone she knew further along the table and moved on, fluttering her fingers at them in parting.

'Must dash – see you later.'

As they passed, with Mikhail still failing to speak, Katya and Tatyana exchanged significant glances.

'What's with the old man?' Katya asked Tatyana who accepted a glass of wine from one of the boys with a flash of white teeth.

'She says he's got blat.'

'He must have.'

Blat is a Russian word for which there is no direct translation.

It means influence, knowing the right people, having the right connections. Blat is the ability to get what you want from life, to twist the system to your advantage.

'I thought he was from the transport commission,' Katya said. 'How did he get invited?'

'Must know someone in the ministry.' As she was speaking Tatyana suddenly lowered her voice. 'Don't look now, here comes Podurets.'

Shouldering his way through the crush, glass in hand, Podurets was bearing down on them with an air of determined goodwill.

'Good evening, ladies.' His round face was scrubbed pink, hair parted centrally and slicked down smooth. He was wearing a black suit tightly buttoned over his white shirt and was perspiring slightly with the constraint of it. 'You are enjoying the performance, I trust?'

Katya told him they thought it very good and he nodded, apparently relieved that she should agree with him.

'Absolutely. I think the minister is to be congratulated on the occasion. Prokofiev is always the right choice.' He spoke quickly and awkwardly, fumbling his words as though reciting from a prepared speech. The reason for this became apparent when, stepping to one side, he indicated a man standing behind him.

'Comrade Leskova,' he began formally. 'May I present Colonel—'

Before he could complete the introduction the stranger had moved forward, taking Katya's hand in his.

'Vassily Krasin.' He gave the name quietly, dispelling the formality that Podurets had been attempting. 'I don't think we need to worry about rank in such surroundings.'

Podurets bobbed and hissed through his teeth at the implied reprimand. 'No. Quite . . . of course not.' His lips made rapid movements as he mouthed forward through his lines, searching for his place in the script.

'Comrade Krasin has expressed a desire to speak with you concerning the—'

Again Podurets's speech was interrupted by Vassily Krasin.

'I have been wanting so much to meet you, Comrade Leskova,' he said smoothly, taking over control of the conversation. 'You are an interpreter at the ministry, I believe?'

'That's right,' she said, allowing him to touch her hand to his lips, feeling his gaze flow down her arm into her body. The others had drawn back, she noticed, melting away from them like spring snow. Vassily Krasin gave a small gesture of helplessness.

'When I asked Comrade Podurets to introduce us I thought this would be the ideal place to meet, but now we are here' – he indicated the crush around them – 'I'm not so sure.'

'It is rather noisy.' Katya found herself agreeing automatically, encouraging him to continue. Her first impression of Vassily Krasin was one of intelligence, a quick, bright-eyed intelligence that was immediately attractive.

'The trouble with these ministry affairs,' he was saying, 'is that nobody dares to refuse the invitation in case it causes offence and so the place is always too crowded.'

'I hadn't thought of it that way.' Katya was aware of Podurets beside her as she was speaking, like a mother fussing over a gauche child, concerned that she should give the right answers, create the right impression.

'Maybe you could come back to my box for a few minutes.' Krasin was hesitant as he made the proposal. 'It's so much easier to talk there.'

'If you prefer,' she said but Podurets was quick to amend the reply.

'It would be an honour, Colonel.'

'I wouldn't go that far.' Krasin's eyes met hers for an instant with a flicker of humour, as though sharing a private joke with her. Taking the glass from her hand he placed it on the table, adding: 'If nothing else, at least I think we can improve on the wine.'

In the corridor outside, a general from the traffic police was talking with two women who had been stacked into satin evening gowns. His eyes followed Katya as she passed.

'The dark girl you were talking with back there,' Vassily Krasin said, dipping his head towards her. 'Who is she?'

'Tatyana Vasnikova – she's a friend of mine.'

'Ah yes.' The name seemed to be known to him.

'We share an apartment.'

'Remarkable-looking girl,' he observed. 'From her appearance I'd say she had gipsy blood in her. Would that be right?'

'I believe so.' Katya gave the answer cautiously as she walked down the curve of the passage, her heels silent on red carpet. She knew very little of Tatyana's past; it was a closed subject that they had never discussed.

'An extraordinary race.' Krasin filled the gap she had left in the conversation. 'Gipsies have no word for beauty. Did you know that? It seems curious at first until you realise that it obliges them to be more specific in their opinions. Instead of saying something is beautiful they will say it looks good enough to eat, or to touch or to kiss.'

'Do they have a word for ugly?'

'Several.' Krasin paused, his hand on the door to his box, his black eyes suddenly mischievous. 'And judging from some of the old women I've seen in Romania there's not one too many.'

He was laughing as he opened the door, ushering Katya into the box ahead of him. Inside there was a small group of people, silhouetted against the lights of the auditorium. They turned as Krasin came in, greeting him with the casual indifference of old acquaintances and returning to their conversations.

'First let me get you a drink,' Vassily Krasin said, going over to the table and lifting a bottle from the silver bucket with a rattle of ice. Finding it empty he drew out another.

Katya watched as he cradled the bottle in his hands to check the label. It was the first chance she'd had to study him at leisure. He must have been in his early forties. His features were firm, the dark hair cut short and brushed back from a high forehead. It was an artistic face, she decided, a face that implied strength and passion, but what intrigued her most at this first meeting was his clothing.

His pale grey pinstripe suit was impeccably cut, the trousers sharply creased, the jacket parting to reveal a double-breasted waistcoat beneath. The effect was severe, understated in its taste, but most becoming. It gave him the dignity and bearing of some of the city businessmen she'd seen in London.

But he was not a businessman, that much she knew. Very far from it. Vassily Krasin was attached to the Second Directorate, a colonel in the KGB. His job, as any typist or filing clerk in the ministry could tell you, was the internal security of art treasures in Russia.

With quick, expert fingers Krasin removed the wire cage from the bottle, twisted out the cork with a report of imploding gas and poured champagne into a glass, waiting until the bubbles had seethed upwards and fallen again before filling it to the brim.

'A beautiful creature, wouldn't you say?' A voice beside Katya took the thoughts from her mind. She turned to see a girl of much her own age leaning against the wall, half shrouded in shadow, appraising her with tawny eyes. She was dressed in a canary yellow dress that clung to her assiduously, exploring every curve of her body. Seeing that the point had been made, the girl smiled lazily at Katya and amended the remark.

'Beautiful, that is, for a peasant.'

There was spite in the observation, the cruel, bitter spite that is spawned in boredom. The girl considered Katya.

'Are you a friend of Vassily's?'

'No.' Katya gave her reply gravely. 'I work for the ministry.'

'Really?' Her eyebrows lifted, as though this one piece of information taught her all she needed to know. 'Some sort of secretary?'

'She's nothing of the sort,' Krasin told her, returning with the champagne and coming between them as he handed Katya a glass.

'Katya's an interpreter, my sweet. She can speak more languages than you've had lovers.'

The tawny blonde bared her teeth in a dazzling smile and turned away.

'Don't worry about her,' Krasin said as he led Katya towards the front of the box. 'She likes to play games with people. Her father is a member of the Politburo so maybe it's to be expected.'

He sat on the plush velvet parapet and looked down into the auditorium where cherubs were struggling with armfuls of gilded festoons. The seats of the stalls were nearly all empty now and the light from the deserted orchestra pit searched the sculpture of his features. For an instant it lent him an unnatural, satanic appearance.

Katya sipped at her champagne. It was dry to her taste, certainly not Russian in origin. Most of the good wines in Russia came from Georgia and she'd been taught to recognise them all from childhood. It must be French, she decided. They also made champagne.

'Do you enjoy the ballet?' she asked to bring his attention back to herself.

'Yes, very much.' Vassily Krasin gave his reply with a slight smile, as though she might find it hard to believe. 'But then I've been very spoiled.'

'Spoiled? In what way?'

'The first time I ever came here was in the days when Yekaterina Maksimova was still the prima ballerina.' He pointed up towards the upper gallery where Katya had been sitting during the first part of the performance. 'I can't have been more than seventeen and had no idea what to expect from such occasions. The only seat I could afford was up there in the gods but even from that distance her dancing was electrifying. When the curtain went down the whole audience was up on its feet and the stage was covered in red roses.'

Katya listened to him with interest. Vassily Krasin spoke easily, fluently but with a slight air of self-deprecation, as though keen to dispel any preconceived ideas she might have of him.

'They just rained down out of the darkness,' he was saying. 'It was an extraordinary sight.'

'And one that no other performance can live up to?'

'In a way. As I said, I've been badly spoiled.'

Katya drank some more champagne. 'At least you get a rather better view nowadays.'

'That's right, I do.' He nodded thoughtfully and then suddenly laughed, throwing back his head like a schoolboy remembering a good prank. 'And I have to admit I rather enjoy it here. These boxes are so close to the stage that you can see right into the wings and watch all the dancers as they are waiting to come on. It's really rather comical seeing their last-minute preparations.'

'Does that make it better?'

'Very much.' He jerked his head towards the Baroque splendour of the huge theatre. 'It helps to remind me that all this is no more than an illusion.' Without pausing to explain himself he changed the subject. 'Tell me, Katya. Do you know who I am?'

'I know who you work for, if that's what you mean.'

'Yes,' he said lightly, 'that's exactly what I mean. And does it worry you?'

'No, I don't think so.'

'Good.' He seemed relieved to hear this and relaxed once more. 'It's so much easier if we don't have to begin with explanations. The worst of being a policeman is having to apologise for it.'

Katya was intrigued by the remark. To her, policemen were irritable little men in grey uniforms who passed the day blowing whistles in the street. She couldn't reconcile the image with this sophisticated figure who sat drinking French champagne opposite her.

Vassily Krasin had turned away from the auditorium as he spoke and now placed his hands on his knees.

'I'd like to ask a favour of you.'

She smiled at the implied intimacy. 'What sort of favour?'

'I need some information. Recently a letter was brought to my attention. I believe it came originally from a firm of London solicitors, concerning an oil painting they had discovered.' He paused to let the words register. 'Do you know the one I'm referring to?'

'Yes, of course. I translated it a few days ago.'

'So I'm told.' He seemed glad that they were in agreement. 'I hear you took the Pushkin Museum to task over the affair.'

'I asked them for their opinion.'

'Wasn't that rather presumptuous of you, Katya?'

'I thought it would be a way of ending the matter.'

'It well might have been, but it was most unwise to take the law into your own hands, Katya. You must have realised that such behaviour wouldn't go unreported.'

'There was a complaint?'

'Naturally. The ministry received a call from one of the museum officials. He was most offended, claimed he'd been insulted by a rude and insubordinate member of their staff.'

Katya flushed slightly at the description, recalling how Tokarev's lips had pursed in disapproval as she talked to him. She'd had no idea the matter would go any further.

53

'I didn't mean to be rude. I was simply passing on the information in the letter.'

'I understand your motives entirely.' He leaned forward, his voice dropping in confidence. 'And in my opinion it's no crime to stick a pin into these bureaucrats occasionally, if only to check whether they are still alive or not. But matters of security must be handled by the authorities.'

'I just asked him whether it was possible for works of art to be sold out of Russia.' Katya's expression was petulant as she defended herself but he seemed interested by the question.

'And what was his reply?'

'He told me that such a thing was impossible.'

'I'm sure he did, but you've been in Moscow long enough to know that a denial means nothing in itself. No one here ever admits to anything. Drunkards will tell you they touch nothing but milk, mothers of large families will swear they are still virgins. It makes police work very tiring.'

The orchestra was returning, and over the murmuring of the audience came the brief, disconnected sounds of their instruments tuning up. Vassily Krasin glanced round at them and then back again. 'But he's right, of course. Nothing from the museums could disappear unnoticed. Unfortunately the situation is not as simple as that.'

'Is there some truth in it?'

He shook his head thoughtfully. 'Personally, I very much doubt it. But unfortunately the matter cannot be allowed to rest. There will have to be an investigation, if only as a formality.'

The lights dimmed in the auditorium, a hush was settling on the theatre. Krasin took her to the door of his box, touching her hand to his lips once again.

'In the meantime,' he said softly, 'I'd be glad if you kept this conversation to yourself. There's no need to repeat it around the ministry.'

'Not even to Dmitri Podurets?' Katya's voice was mocking as she stepped out into the lit passage. She'd intended the remark as a joke but Vassily Krasin replied in all seriousness.

'Particularly not with Comrade Podurets.'

'What did he want?'

'Nothing in particular.'

The curtain had gone up. It was the scene of Juliet's bedroom, a huge four-poster bed filled the stage and moonlight showed through the window, Prokofiev's music was smouldering in the orchestra pit but Tatyana wasn't paying attention to the performance.

'Are you in trouble, Katska?'

'Trouble?' She seemed surprised by the suggestion as she sat down, searching under the seat for her programme. 'No, of course not.'

'Podurets said that you were going to be reprimanded.'

'Why should I be?'

'For interfering in ministry business. He seemed very pleased about it.'

'It wasn't like that at all. He asked me some questions but he was perfectly friendly.' Katya was eager to describe her meeting with Krasin. 'And we drank champagne – French champagne, not the Soviet stuff.'

A man behind hushed them silent and they drew apart, turning their attention back to the ballet.

Juliet, dressed in a flowing white nightdress, was dancing alone on the stage, hesitant and delicate as a candle flame.

Tatyana watched her without interest. She felt an unaccountable fear at this meeting with Vassily Krasin. It hadn't been chance. He had left his box and come to the dining hall with the express intention of introducing himself to Katya. There had to be a motive, some reason. But what scared her more was Katya's complicity. She had gone back to his box without any hesitation, oblivious to the implication, returning flushed and exhilarated by the experience.

Tatyana studied her covertly out of the side of her eye. Katya was leaning forward in her seat, lips slightly parted, skin glowing in the stage lights. There was a blush of colour in her cheeks and she was watching the performance with a fervent concentration. Tatyana had never seen her looking more lovely than she was at that moment.

As if sensing her train of thought, Katya turned suddenly and said: 'He's only a policeman.'

'A policeman?' Tatyana sounded incredulous as she repeated the word. 'Is that what he calls himself?'

'Well what would you call him?'

She wasn't sure how she'd describe Vassily Krasin. He was one of the new breed of men in the Kremlin who seemed to have sprung from nowhere recently. Shrewd, capable men, matching ambition with personal charisma. Three years ago Vassily Krasin's name had been unknown in Moscow, now it was a commonplace. Such a meteoric success suggested influence, friends in high places – blat.

It was typical of him to be holding a party here tonight: where his predecessors had shunned publicity Krasin seemed openly to court it. Tatyana looked down at the cave-like apertures of the opera boxes where the nomenklatura parties, the new aristocracy, could be seen in the glare of the lights. Katya evidently found these élitist groups exciting. To her they were dangerous and frightening.

'I don't know who he is,' she replied honestly. 'But you should be careful of him, Katska.'

'Why's that?'

'There must be something he wants of you.'

'He just asked me a few questions, it's not as if he was particularly interested in the answers.' Katya had wanted her to share in the intrigue of this meeting with Krasin, and instead she was being grumpy and suspicious. 'You can be so paranoid at times, Tasha. You think everyone is part of some silly scheme.'

Again the voice behind hushed them silent and they turned away, each annoyed with the other for not understanding.

The stage had been changed to a street scene. Courtiers, soldiers and ladies in long dresses were filing in from the wings, the music had grown pompous with ceremony.

'Besides,' Katya hissed under her breath after a few moments, 'I don't know what you are getting so worked up about. It's not as though I'm going to be seeing him again.'

The following morning Podurets summoned her into his office.

'What day are you travelling to London?'

'Tuesday – '

'Until Friday afternoon, is that right?' Podurets prided himself on his grasp of detail. He took out a cigarette, pinched the paper filter between his fingers and set it in his lips.

Impatiently Katya watched him pat his cardigan pockets for his lighter, take it out and scratch the flint for a light. She was in a hurry to get down to lunch and brought him to the point.

'Was there something you wanted, Comrade Podurets?'

'As a matter of fact there is.' Podurets was not to be hustled. 'There has been an investigation into the picture that the London solicitor wrote to us about. I'm glad to say that his allegations are groundless, quite groundless. As I thought they would be. No paintings have been smuggled over the border, there has been no breach of security.'

'That's good – '

'You will say as much when you see him.'

Katya had turned to go but this last remark made her pause in the doorway.

'See him?' she repeated.

'Naturally he must be informed. You are in London this week, you speak his language. It would seem only logical that you should convey the message.'

56

He had Katya's full attention now. She came back into the room and stood above him.

'I already have a full schedule in London. It's all been arranged.'

'On the second day the delegation is lunching at the Russian Embassy. Your services will not be required.' Podurets was one jump ahead of her and smug with it. 'You can visit his office then, it is not far from the hotel where you are staying.'

'But what shall I say to him?'

'That will be explained to you. An appointment has been arranged with the curator of the Pushkin tomorrow morning.'

'Comrade Tokarev?'

'I believe that's his name. He will brief you fully before you leave.'

After their last encounter she wasn't looking forward to seeing Tokarev again. But as she hurried down to the canteen on the second floor Katya pushed the meeting firmly from her mind.

Tatyana was sitting at a table by the window with Alexsei Polyakov. A newspaper was spread between them, opened at the page of horoscopes.

'Does it say anything about travelling to strange and exotic places this week?' Katya asked as she slid her tray on to the table and sat down beside them.

'Nothing to do with travel.' Tatyana was working her way through the dense print. 'It says that with Mercury in your quadrant for the next two months your career is in the ascendancy.'

'Not if Podurets can help it.'

'Horoscopes are shit,' Alexsei told them disdainfully. Tatyana glanced up from the paper and jerked her head towards him.

'You know each other, don't you?'

Katya nodded.

'The stars are always saying that things are looking up,' Alexsei added. 'Everyone is going to be rich and happy, not today but tomorrow. They must be written by the Central Committee.'

Alexsei Polyakov worked as a cleaner in a factory during the daytime but he was better known as the manager of a jazz band, part of the cultural underground. He was often to be found hanging around the ministry.

'Where are you going this time?' he asked Katya.

'London.' She munched a tomato as she spoke, turning it in her fingertips. 'There's a delegation going over there to arrange a concert tour for an English orchestra next year.'

'Orchestras all sound the same. Why do we need an English one over here?' Alexsei was disparaging. 'It's just an excuse for a group of fat ministers to go on a trip to London and buy themselves Japanese video recorders.'

'I don't think they'll have much chance to do that.' Katya wasn't sure she liked Alexsei very much.

Dinara hove alongside with a loaded tray. 'Can I bung in with you lot?'

They made room for her around the table.

'While I'm over there I'm going to see that English lawyer who wrote to the ministry.' Katya addressed the remark to Tatyana.

'You are?' She looked up from the newspaper.

'Podurets told me just now.'

'You get all the interesting jobs. It's such a swizz.' Dinara talked like a schoolgirl in the hope of passing off her double chins as puppy-fat. 'I'm never even allowed to leave Moscow.'

'Are you seeing him alone?' Alexsei was suddenly interested. 'Without any sort of escort?'

'Seems like it.'

'Is that usual?'

'Katya's allowed to go wherever she wants.' Dinara was aggrieved. 'She's got the highest security rating in the department.'

Katya was looking at her watch. 'I've got to go now, I'm due at the institute in half an hour.'

'Wait for me,' Dinara bleated, rocking the table as she clambered to her feet. 'I'm coming too.'

After they had gone, Alexsei faced Tatyana across the table. He was a slight, sharp-featured man with a wisp of beard on his chin and the bright eyes of a night creature.

'She's ideal,' he said.

'I told you so.'

'Will she do it, do you think?'

'I'll have to ask her when she comes back from London.'

Alexsei didn't like the uncertainty. 'What if she refuses?'

'Then you'll have to find someone else.'

'Can't you twist her arm a little?'

'No.' Tatyana was emphatic. 'Katya's a friend. She will do it of her own free will or not at all.'

Chapter Seven

Katya had no clear image of English lawyers but she pictured them as shy, rather dusty figures hidden in the gloom of panelled offices.

Pip Spencer came as a surprise. For a start he was twenty years younger than she had expected and alarmingly self-assured.

She had found the address in South Audley Street without difficulty and given her name to the receptionist. A well-dressed secretary arrived, looking her over with a single appraising glance as she led her upstairs. Murmuring an introduction she ushered Katya into a large, thickly carpeted office.

'Miss Leskova to see you.'

The door closed silently. Pip Spencer stood and came over to her. He was impeccably dressed in a blue pinstripe suit with a gold chain stretched across the waistcoat. His hair was short and brushed back from a broad forehead, the expression in his deep blue eyes remote, professional, betraying no emotion.

'Have you been in London long?' he asked.

'Only since yesterday.'

He moved gracefully, she noticed as they shook hands. It brought a spark of recognition. Phillip Spencer reminded her of someone although at that moment she couldn't think who.

'Miss Leskova.' He tested the name on himself. 'I can't believe that's the proper way to address you, is it?'

'Probably not. My name's Katya.'

'That's much easier – mine's Pip.'

As he spoke he smiled, his eyes creasing into crow's-feet. The grave expression on his face was suddenly transformed. To her surprise she found herself warming to him and laughed at the strange-sounding name he had offered her.

'Aren't they the little stones in an apple?'

'They are,' he confided, 'but I don't think that's why they call me that. At least I hope it's not.' He offered her a chair. 'I always assume that it's short for Phillip.'

'Oh I see, a nickname.'

59

Her accent was irresistible, the vowel sounds drawn out into a growl in her throat.

'I had a call from your ministry,' he continued, taking his place behind the desk and meshing his fingers together. 'They told me you'd be coming in this morning but they didn't explain why.'

It was a question, she realised, phrased in the evasive language the English had perfected.

'You sent us a photograph of a painting hanging in a London gallery which you thought might have been recently smuggled out of Russia.' She began to recite the information that Tokarev had spent an afternoon giving her. 'Fortunately it's not true. One of our experts checked and found that we hold an identical painting in our reserves. It's probably a copy of the one you saw.'

'Really.' Pip's voice was non-committal.

'A great many of our paintings are copies of the originals. It was quite fashionable in the last century.'

'Did you see this copy yourself?' he asked.

Katya shook her head, flushing slightly at the question and he guessed that she was just a courier passing on information. He softened his approach slightly.

'Only I was wondering how you knew that your version was the copy rather than the one we have.'

'I'm not sure,' she faltered. 'I think art experts can tell these things.'

'There are probably some subtle differences in technique,' he agreed.

'Something like that.' She was grateful for the let-out and smiled in return, showing strong white teeth.

She was an enchanting-looking girl with her large, slightly slanted eyes and glossy brown hair. And somehow more poised, better groomed than he'd been prepared for. But then what had he expected – grubby overalls with spanners sticking out of the pockets?

'We were wondering how you knew it might have been in Russia,' she was saying. 'What prompted you to write to us?'

'A client of mine came to me with the picture.' He promoted Allington posthumously. 'He thought he had seen it in Moscow as a child.'

'Ah, that would explain it.'

'But evidently what he saw was the copy.'

'I think that is right.' The solution seemed to be acceptable to her. Uncrossing her legs with a rasp of stockings she was getting up to leave when Pip added. 'His death must have been a coincidence.'

She paused, turning round to him.

'Did you say death?'

'He had a heart attack shortly after speaking to me.'

Katya looked at him with dark, troubled eyes. 'I didn't know anything about this.'

'I didn't mention it in my letter. There was no reason why the two events had to be connected. He was old and probably suffering from a weak heart.'

She thought this over and then nodded, her brow clearing.

'Besides.' Pip didn't press the point. 'If the painting hanging here is a copy of yours, or the other way about, then the whole subject is academic.'

He accompanied her downstairs to the hallway.

'Now that you're here,' he said in parting, 'why don't you stay for lunch?'

'I'm afraid I don't have much English money.'

'I doubt whether you'd need any.'

Katya had hesitated at the invitation, inclined to accept. 'I'm expected back in a few minutes.'

'Another time maybe.'

'Yes,' she said seriously, 'I'd like that.'

Pip smiled, the same quiet smile that lit up his eyes. 'It's strange. I never expected to find myself regretting that I couldn't have lunch with a Russian.'

'Maybe that's because I'm not Russian,' she replied lightly, withdrawing her hand from his.

'No?'

'I'm Georgian.' There was a hint of pride in her voice.

'Is there a difference?' he asked.

'Do you think of yourself as an American?'

As she spoke Katya realised who it was Pip reminded her of. It was Vassily Krasin. They shared the same confidence, the same slightly conceited air of superiority. She looked up into Pip's clear blue eyes, feeling suddenly bold.

'But there is something you could do for me.'

'What is that?'

'You could buy me some magazines.'

When Pip returned to his office half an hour later he found Max waiting for him.

'Who on earth was that?' he asked.

'A Russian girl.'

'She can't be.' Max was not easily deceived. 'That one couldn't put the shot further than a few yards.'

'I'm not so sure,' Pip replied. 'I think she could be tougher than she looks.'

61

'What did she want?'

'She came to tell me that the picture Allington saw in Moscow was a copy of the one in the D'Este Gallery.'

'At least they've given an answer. Things must be changing over there.' Max nodded at the clock on the mantelpiece. 'Are you ready for a bite of lunch?'

'If you like.'

'There's one thing I'll say for Perestroika,' he added as he trundled himself downstairs. 'It's improved the appearance of their delivery service.'

Katya was pleased with the outcome of the meeting. She had told Pip Spencer of the copy, as she had been instructed, and discovered why he had written to the ministry.

There had been none of the problems that she had been told to anticipate. Tokarev had warned her that Pip might be secretive about revealing his sources but he had given her the information quite freely.

She stopped to look in the window of a jewellery shop. There was no mention of price, she noticed as she looked over the glittering display, but then Londoners didn't seem to worry about expense. Pip hadn't even asked the price of the magazines he had bought her. He had just collected them off the shelves, flicked out a credit card and scrawled his name on the receipt.

She crossed the street into Hyde Park. It was a still, damp day with a hint of woodsmoke in the air, leaves sticking like postage stamps to the path.

Sitting down on a park bench she unloaded the magazines she was carrying and began thumbing through the pages. Pip had grasped what she was looking for and given her the *Spectator*, *Time* magazine and the *New Statesman*: the political heavies, the stress on content rather than glossy appearance. Most of the articles were concerned with European affairs and of no interest to her but there were others covering recent developments in the Soviet Union.

A group of East Germans had walked over the Hungarian border into the West. No one had stopped them, the border guards had stood and watched. Others were waiting to leave the same way, camping in the grounds of the Embassy.

Katya had often wondered why she didn't defect while she had the chance. It would be so easy for her. But even as she asked herself the question she knew the answer. It was the families back home who suffered. If she were to defect, her parents would bear the brunt of the blame. Her father would lose his job, their home would be confiscated, everything they had worked for would be lost.

Besides, London was not her home. It belonged to young men like Pip Spencer with their credit cards, their secretaries and beautifully tailored suits.

It was unthinkable.

She glanced at her watch. It was after three. The time had slipped by without her noticing. Hurrying across to a litter bin she dropped the magazines inside. It was a waste. They'd be a valuable commodity back in Moscow but she'd never be allowed to take them into the country and so she threw them away and left the park by the nearest gate.

Chapter Eight

'Where in God's name were you?' Podurets screamed as she came into the office on her first morning back. 'The whole delegation was held up waiting for you.'

'I was delayed – '

'You were gone for four hours, Comrade Leskova. Four hours!' The veins on his forehead bulged. 'I've never heard of such irresponsible behaviour. I've had to apologise to the minister.'

'I didn't realise – '

'No, I'm sure you didn't. You didn't realise that you might have ruined the whole purpose of the visit, did you?'

'I was only a few minutes late.'

'I assume you have some explanation for your conduct?'

'The English solicitor kept me waiting for over an hour before he would see me.'

'But the meeting was arranged beforehand – '

'He was busy.' She had no hesitation in lying to Podurets. He wouldn't understand about the time she had spent in the park. It was easier to pretend that Pip Spencer had treated her rudely. That Podurets could accept.

'Why did you not lodge a complaint at the time?' he demanded.

'It didn't seem sensible.'

Podurets was on the point of contradicting her when the telephone rang on her desk. She picked it up.

'Are you ready, Katska?' It was Tatyana, excited and conspiratorial, calling from the floor below.

'I'll be with you in a minute.' She could feel Podurets's impatience as he stood waiting. 'You go ahead, I'll catch you up.'

'Do you know where it is?'

'I've got the address, I'll find it.'

'Was that a social call?' Podurets demanded as she put down the phone.

'No, an inquiry from the Finance Department.' Katya was moving away towards the door, trying to make her escape.

'I need a written report from you immediately.'

'Yes, I understand.'

'Your time must be fully accounted for.'

'I can't do it now,' she said as she retreated. 'I'm late for an appointment.'

Podurets's voice followed after her. 'Don't think the subject is closed, comrade, disciplinary charges will have to be considered.'

'Are you sure this is the right place?' Katya asked apprehensively, looking up the staircase.

'Quite sure. I've been here before.'

The landing they reached was small and uncarpeted, the bare boards amplifying their footsteps. Somewhere below a printing press was at work, the metallic chatter of its machinery reverberating through the building. The hard northern sun peered in through a grimy skylight above them and the air was heavy with damp and plaster dust.

'It's not the shop, just the cutting room,' Tatyana added, knocking on a locked door at the end of the landing. She seemed elated by the coming meeting and flashed a smile over her shoulder. 'But leave the talking to me. Don't try to bargain with him.'

Katya nodded. She understood the situation.

Tatyana's friend in the fur trade was a pale youth with black hair and soft, feminine skin. He couldn't have been more than twenty, his cheeks were smooth and there was only a faint shadow of a moustache on his upper lip. Tatyana introduced him as Yuri.

'Did you get my message?' he asked, drawing them inside and closing the door.

'I did. At least there was a note at the ministry which I guessed was from you.'

'I couldn't be here earlier, I was needed down at the shop for a fitting.'

The cutting room where they stood was in the eaves of the building. The ceiling was glass: cracked, repaired in numerous places and sloping downwards at an acute angle. Directly below was the work-table scattered with scraps of silk lining, tissue templates and heavy tailor's shears. Ranged along the walls on either side were makeshift racks hung with clothing.

'Where are the others then?' Tatyana asked, idly brushing her hand along a row of dresses.

'Out to lunch.' Yuri spoke in short bursts as though he had trained himself to overcome a stutter. 'I persuaded them to go together.'

'Really? They must have guessed you're seeing someone.'

'I gave the impression that a representative from the Writers'

Union was coming.' He saw her look round sharply and hurried on. 'But they are discreet about these things, no one will ask questions.'

'Still we must be quick,' Tatyana replied and then lightened the mood with a laugh. 'It wouldn't do to let them discover you're entertaining ladies in your spare time.'

Yuri didn't respond. 'Did you bring the cigarettes?'

Katya had been walking about the room, taking stock of her surroundings. The clothes she examined were of good quality, far better than anything you'd find in the stores, from which she guessed they were for the restricted shops.

Hearing Yuri's question she went over to him, pulling the cigarettes out of her bag. They were wrapped in brown paper; she tore it off and laid them down on the cutting table.

With long white fingers Yuri inspected the celluloid packets, checking that they were in good condition and Katya watched him with interest. She couldn't remember hearing Yuri's name mentioned before although that didn't entirely surprise her. Tatyana was often secretive about her friends.

'Good,' he murmured, setting the cigarettes down on the table and looking at Katya with his head cocked to one side. 'And now, if you'd take off your coat I'll see what can be done.'

Positioning Katya in front of a tall mirror, he began to take measurements with the cloth tape which he kept hung around his neck, running it swiftly from shoulder to elbow and then to the wrist, repeating the lengths under his breath to memorise them. His touch was shy, she noticed, his fingers just brushing over her body, scarcely making contact. When he came to the waist size he delegated the job: 'Could you put it round please – no, don't hold your breath in. That's right, and now the hips.'

The first coat he brought out was a silver fox. She didn't care much for the colour.

'Never mind that,' he said, lifting it off her shoulders. 'How about the size. Does it fit?'

'I'd prefer something longer.'

The fourth coat she tried on reached below her calf. It was dark brown, almost black, and embraced her with its weight and warmth. When she twirled her hips to one side the skirt of the coat lifted and spread, light rippling down its length as though over running water.

Tatyana looked at her in admiration. 'Do you like it?'

'It's wonderful,' she replied in a whisper, absorbed by the reflection that faced her in the mirror.

'You look like a princess, Katska.'

Yuri had returned with a matching fur hat. He set it in place and then, with his fingers resting on the point of her shoulders, he studied the effect in the mirror.

'Yes,' he said thoughtfully. 'That's the one. It's a good match for your complexion.'

Katya turned the collar up over her face, so that only her eyes showed dark and liquid from the cocoon of fur and then spun round on Tatyana. 'But I can't wear a coat like this.'

'Why ever not?'

'People will wonder where it came from.'

Tatyana shrugged the objection aside. 'They'll just think you've become the mistress of someone important.'

'Do you think so?' She wasn't sure she liked that.

'I'll let the hem down a few centimetres,' Yuri said, crouching beside her. 'You're taller than most of the women we get in here.' Taking back the coat he set it aside and laid it over a sewing machine.

Now that it was gone, Katya felt suddenly naked. She stood by the window, looking out over the roofs of the Kitay-Gorod towards the gleaming domes of the Kremlin. The radio in the corner was playing quietly to itself, Tatyana was talking earnestly to Yuri. Their voices were low so that she couldn't catch the drift of the conversation. After a few minutes Tatyana came across to her.

'Good, it's all arranged.' The golden earrings jangled in agreement. 'Yuri will make the alterations and have it ready for you next week.'

'It's so kind of you to do this for me,' Katya said. She felt grateful and turned to Yuri who now stood close to her. He was watching her with a strange, intent expression.

She sensed a catch.

'But there's something he would like in return,' Tatyana added and then seeing Katya hesitate she smiled in encouragement. 'You remember I said there might be a favour we could do for him.'

Yuri had dropped his spaniel eyes now and was looking away.

'What sort of favour?' Katya asked cautiously.

'He wants you to take something with you when you go to London next month.'

Katya looked at her in horror: 'I can't do that!'

'It'll be easy, Katska.'

'You don't understand,' she cried, 'it's not possible to take anything over the border.'

'This is just a few pieces of paper.'

'But I can't.'

'It wouldn't be difficult for you.'

She had no idea whether it would be difficult or not, Katya

reflected angrily. Tatyana had never been to the West, she had never experienced the restrictions. At customs control the baggage was checked methodically. Everything had to be accounted for, explained to the satisfaction of suspicious minds. There was no way she could smuggle anything through into another country. It had been tried often enough, usually with disastrous results. Hurriedly she tried to explain, the words coming out in a gabble. 'There's no chance, there are guards. It's impossible.'

'Not if you were clever – '

'This is hopeless!' Yuri's voice cut in accusingly. 'I knew she wouldn't be able to help.'

Tatyana hushed him silent but he carried on. 'You should have asked her first, I told you to ask her.'

'Be quiet, Yuri!'

He lapsed into silence and turned away. Taking Katya by the arm Tatyana drew her aside.

'Don't be cross, Katska,' she said when they were out of earshot. 'If you can't do it Yuri will understand. We're not trying to force you to do anything you don't want.'

'But why didn't you tell me before?' she asked bitterly. 'If you'd asked me earlier I could have told you there was no chance.'

Perching on the cutting table Tatyana took Katya's hands in hers, looking up at her. 'I thought it best to wait until you'd met him first.'

'They go through everything you have with you: handbag, pockets – everything.'

'I know, Katska. I didn't realise it would be so difficult for you.'

Katya felt trapped. 'You told me you'd already made the arrangements. I thought it was all fixed.'

'But you knew that cigarettes wouldn't be enough.' Tatyana sounded surprised. 'You said so yourself. The cigarettes are just to keep the other cutters happy.'

Katya glanced over to where Yuri now stood, hands in pockets, staring moodily out of the window. She didn't mean to be churlish. 'What are these pieces of paper that you have?'

'They're poems,' Tatyana replied evenly. 'Yuri's not allowed to publish here in Russia. The authorities have banned his work.'

'But why?'

She shrugged. 'Some of the things he says are not popular. That's why they must go to London. There's a publisher there who will print two editions of his poetry, one in English and another in Russian to be sent back here.'

'Samizdat?'

'It's important to him that he's read in his own country.'

'But can't you send these poems?'

She shook her head quickly at the suggestion. 'Anything going to a London publisher is likely to be opened at the depot. If he was caught he could be arrested.'

'And what of me?' Katya cried hotly. 'I could be arrested too, or have you forgotten that?'

'Of course I haven't.' Tatyana's reply came in a fierce whisper. 'But you don't have to be caught, that's the point. You're the one person who could get them through unnoticed. No one at the customs can read foreign languages. If you wrote them out with European lettering they'd be meaningless to the border guards. For all they know, they could be the address of the hotel you're staying in.'

Katya paused to consider. The fur coat still lay across the table, shining in the afternoon sunlight.

'And you always take notes with you.' Tatyana's voice was coaxing. 'I've seen them before.'

'How many are there?'

'About twenty-five in all. But they're short, they don't fill more than ten pages.'

'If the lines were joined together' – Katya was thinking out loud now – 'I suppose it wouldn't look like poetry . . .'

'It could be anything.'

'There are some speeches I've got to translate before going to London.' Katya could still feel the warmth of the coat, its weight about her shoulders. 'I could add the poems into the script, just little bits at a time . . .'

Tatyana's eyes were shining.

'And then take them out again when I arrive.'

'That's right.'

'They never check these things at the other end.'

'It'll be easy, Katska.'

Alexsei was waiting for them as they returned home that evening. He seemed pleased by the news.

'So, it's all arranged then.'

Katya didn't want to be hustled. 'I'll have to see – '

'You sound worried, Georgia.'

'It may be harder than we thought,' Tatyana cut in. 'She says the border control is very strict.'

'The guards won't give any trouble.' Alexsei was dismissive. 'They haven't the wits.'

Alexsei believed what he wanted to believe, Katya thought as they went inside. In that sense he was no different from Podurets.

It suited his conception of the world to think of the police as fools and so he'd convinced himself it was true.

'Where's Yuri?' Tatyana asked.

'He's coming on later.'

In the high-ceilinged entrance hall old Grigor was playing chess with a veteran of the Great Patriotic War. Tatyana leaned over the old man's shoulder as they passed, inspecting the arrangement of the pieces. Darting out her hand she moved the knight to one side.

'There, how's that?'

Grigor waved his arms in exasperation, as though brushing away a swarm of irritating flies, and mouthed curses through toothless gums as he did so but they had already gone. Clattering up the wooden stairs to the top floor, along the empty passage, past grimy windows where dust particles cruised in the shafts of evening sunlight.

'Have we got any sour cream?' Tatyana asked, checking through the basket she was carrying.

'We've got some of the normal stuff.'

'That's getting on, it must have turned by now.'

Katya nodded towards the opposite door, where a face watched them through the opened crack. 'If not we can always show it to Lubov, that would turn anything sour.'

They were laughing as they burst into the little apartment.

There was a silence. The room was still as though it had been locked for generations.

Standing in the centre of the floor was a neat figure – black hair and bright black eyes – dressed in a perfectly tailored suit.

It was Vassily Krasin.

Chapter Nine

Katya paused in the doorway, the smile dying on her lips as she recognised Krasin.

He stood with his legs crossed, one hand on his hip, the other in his trouser pocket. Against the shabby furniture, the meagre decoration, he looked svelte and thoroughbred.

The other two spilled into the room around her, their movements slowing, congealing into unease as they became aware of the presence of this well-dressed stranger.

There was a moment of complete silence, broken when Vassily Krasin smiled and said, 'I'm so sorry to butt in on you like this. I was passing by and thought I'd take the opportunity to call in.'

He looked directly at Katya as he spoke, his voice conversational as though there was no one else in the room.

'Your friend very kindly let me in.' He indicated Ludmilla who was curled in the armchair beside him wearing only her dressing gown, her hair tied up into a towel.

'She suggested I wait for you to return and has been entertaining me most charmingly in the mean time.'

Ludmilla pouted red lips at the praise. Katya's arrival had clearly interrupted the cosiness of this arrangement.

'I'm sorry,' Katya said mechanically and slipping out from between the other two she went over to Krasin. 'We've been down at the market.'

'So I see.' He picked out a mushroom from her basket, twisting it around in his fingers. His hands were strong, she noticed, sun-tanned and darkened with black hair but almost feminine in the delicacy of their touch. 'I called to ask whether you are free to have dinner with me?' He let the invitation hover as though it were inappropriate.

'We were going to eat here.'

Krasin dropped the mushroom back into the basket. 'Of course you will be, I should have guessed. Another time maybe.'

'No.' The words came before she realised. 'I can come.'

'I don't like to take you away from your friends.' Krasin was aware he was breaking up some sort of party. Katya looked across at Tatyana who now stood by the window and back at him again.

'It's all right. We didn't have anything arranged.'

He accepted the explanation with good grace and dropping his voice he added, 'In that case may I suggest you change.'

Katya flushed, suddenly conscious of the red handkerchief tying up her hair. Going into the bedroom she searched through her scant collection of dresses, pulling out the black silk. It was the same as she was wearing at the time of her last meeting with Vassily Krasin but that was too bad, it was the only good dress she had.

Tatyana came into the room as she was sitting at the dressing table, brushing out her hair. Without speaking she began to help, fastening the zip of the dress, pulling it up hard across her back. Katya could sense her anger.

'You think I should have refused him?' She wanted to get it out in the open.

'It's your decision.'

'He'd come all this way to ask me out. I could hardly say no to him.'

'Couldn't you? I thought you were going to be with us this evening.'

'What did you expect me to do?' She twisted around on the chair. 'Ask him to stay here for dinner with Alexsei? And Yuri turning up in a moment, his pockets stuffed with illegal poetry?'

'You could have sent him away, arranged another time if it is so important to you.'

'It's not so important – ouch!'

'What's the matter?'

'That hurt.'

'I'm sorry, I've broken the hook at the back.' Tatyana scrabbled in the sewing box below the table and took out a safety-pin.

'He'll see that,' Katya cried in frustration.

'No he won't, it'll be hidden under your hair.' She spoke with the safety-pin in her teeth. 'Besides, it'll remind you not to turn your back on him.'

Katya fixed two small pearl earrings, a present from her father when she'd left Georgia, dabbed on scent and reviewed the overall effect in the mirror. Her colour was high, the whites of her eyes bright against the darkness of her complexion. She felt the tickle of nerves in her stomach. Krasin's unexpected appearance had unsettled her and she fumbled with the cap of her lipstick.

'Good,' Vassily Krasin complimented her as she returned. 'Formal without being too severe. Are you ready to go?'

'Yes, I think so.' Katya turned at the door to say goodbye to the others but they were gathered around the kitchen table ignoring her.

* * *

72

'You keep strange company, if I might say so,' Krasin ventured as the Rolls drew away from the kerb.

'Why do you say that?'

'Wasn't that Alexsei Polyakov I saw back there in your apartment?'

'Probably.' Katya turned her dark eyes on him, regarding him gravely. 'I don't know him that well.'

'I'm glad. He's hardly the sort I'd expect to find a member of the ministry associating with.'

'We bumped into him in the street,' she replied with a shrug, looking straight ahead of her. 'I don't think he's a friend of anyone in particular.'

Krasin studied her out of the side of his eye. She was sitting well back in the seat, her long legs crossed, back straight as though she were riding a horse. A self-confident little minx, he told himself, apparently undisturbed by the opulence of the car with its sweet-smelling leather and veneered fittings. He would have expected her to be cowed by this visible symbol of wealth; most were, but her head was held high, emphasising the curve of her throat, and she was gazing casually out of the window as they sped up Kalinin Prospeckt.

She was a striking girl, there was no denying it. The high cheek-bones, the strong, slightly aquiline features gave her an imperious beauty. He'd thought as much when he first saw her at the Bolshoi and looking at her now he felt his interest quickening like a pulse beat.

'I hear your trip to London went off well.'

'Yes,' she replied politely. 'Everyone seemed pleased by the arrangements that were made.'

'I was referring to your meeting with the solicitor.'

'Oh, I see.' From the flash of her eyes he could see that she was taken by surprise. 'I hadn't realised you knew of that.'

'But of course I do.' Krasin spoke conversationally. 'Your visit to his office was my idea. I thought he should be the first to hear that we had resolved the problem of the stolen painting. Set his mind at rest. It's so easy to get the wrong end of the stick if you don't have the full information.'

The Rolls had turned into a side street, the purr of the engine falling as it slowed. Krasin made a window in the condensation with a gloved finger.

'But no doubt you explained the situation to him,' he added, looking out at the crowded street where women jostled around makeshift stalls.

'I told him that we had a copy of the picture he saw.'

'Good.' He turned back into the car. 'Why were you so late in returning to your hotel afterwards, Katya?'

She hesitated, assessing the privacy of the conversation. 'Do you want an answer or the truth?'

'Is there a difference?'

'Naturally. You said yourself that no one in this city tells the truth unless they have to.'

'Did I?' Krasin experienced a small shock as the girl threw the words back at him.

'I went for a walk in Hyde Park,' Katya said. 'I didn't notice the time, that's all. There was nothing strange about it.'

The car had drawn to a halt outside the Slavjanski Bazar. Chibatar was holding the door open.

'I can't blame you.' Krasin let the conversation settle on to a more general level as he stepped out on to the pavement. 'It's a beautiful park, especially at this time of the year. I often used to go for a run there in the mornings.'

There was a queue outside the restaurant but the doorman brushed them aside, flashing gold teeth in an obsequious smile.

'Have you been here before?' Krasin asked as they went upstairs.

'Once or twice.'

'In the course of your work?'

'That – and other times too.'

She wasn't going to concede him a point, he observed. It was strange, when he had first met her she seemed interested, accessible. He had sensed the invitation in her eyes, in her voice. But now Katya seemed colder, more impersonal as she stalked up the red-carpeted stairs ahead of him.

Maybe she was punishing him for arriving unannounced like that, for taking her away from her friends, or maybe she was simply responding to a ritual of courtship that was as old as history.

As he followed, Krasin cast his eyes up her legs to her waist, watching the way the black material of her dress rucked slightly with the sway of her hips.

The Slavjanski Bazar was crowded, noisy, boisterous. As they came in the head waiter led them to a private table on the gallery overlooking the floor.

'We can't be seen from here,' Krasin commented as he sat down.

'Is that an advantage?'

'The Russian aristocrats used to think so. They could bring their mistresses to these tables without being noticed.'

'Really?' Katya's tone was dry. 'And why do you come up here?'

'To protect your reputation.' He downed the little glass of iced vodka that had been set out ready before explaining himself. 'I'm not sure that your boss Podurets would approve if he heard you were dining with me.'

For a moment Katya's expression remained unchanged and then throwing back her head she laughed, a warm sound that came from deep within her, and with it the tension between them broke.

'I'm not joking,' he said, 'you'd be surprised how suspicious some minds can be.'

'Does that concern you?'

'Not really.'

'I thought not, Colonel.'

'I'd rather you called me Vassily – '

Katya's lashes dropped. 'If you prefer.'

'I do.' He flicked out the starched white napkin and dropped it to his lap. Waiters were humming around the table, laying out the little plates of hors d'oeuvres.

'I took the precaution of arranging dinner beforehand,' he explained.

'You must have been certain I was going to come out with you.'

'It was a risk I had to take. But like most risks it is all the better when it pays off.' He rattled the bottle from the ice bucket and filled their glasses. 'How long have you been here in Moscow?'

'Two years.'

'The move must have been quite a shock.'

'Not really. My mother's Russian. I have relations living in Moscow, that made it easier at first.'

'Really?'

Katya was the daughter of a Georgian architect, a prominent figure on the central planning committee of Tbilisi. He knew this already, although he could have guessed as much without reading her file. Katya's manners, her slim, small-breasted figure and more particularly the rather ill-advised boldness of her conversation told him that she came from a secure, affluent background. What she had in life she had been given. That was the difference between them.

'Aren't your parents worried that you might meet a nice Russian boy while you are living here and never go back?'

'Maybe, but they've no need to.' She sounded sure of herself. 'I've no intention of marrying just yet.'

'No?'

'All my friends had husbands and children before they were twenty. Most of them are already divorced.' She put a dab of black caviare on to her blinis. 'I think I'll wait for a few years.'

Krasin watched her eating, her shining hair spilled over bare shoulders. He imagined the lithe body hidden beneath the black silk dress and again he experienced the warm rush of desire. The sensation disturbed him. He could feel an intimacy developing with

75

this girl, an undercurrent of flirtation that he had not intended. It was something he was going to have to watch.

'That's why I accepted the job in Moscow,' she was saying. 'It's better than sitting at home bringing up children.'

'How do you find life with Comrade Podurets?'

'He's very efficient.' She glanced up at him appraisingly, testing the motive of the question but Krasin made it clear he was talking off the record.

'I imagine he's not always the easiest man to work with.'

'That's probably true,' she said lightly. 'But then I'm not in the office that often.'

'Of course, you travel a great deal.'

'I travel a little,' she corrected him mildly.

'Have you been anywhere apart from London?'

'Yes.' Her dark eyes were suddenly mischievous. 'But surely you know that already, Colonel.'

'How could I?'

'You've read my file at the ministry.'

Krasin was at a loss. 'What makes you so sure?'

'How else did you find my address?'

The answer was pert, provocative. Krasin touched the glass to his lips, tasting the wine, letting it scour across his tongue. He wasn't sure whether he wanted to continue indulging Katya in this flagrant insubordination or bring her to heel.

Either would be satisfying, he realised.

'I must admit it's one of the few perks of my profession and not one that I'm proud of.' His smile was quick, disarming. 'But how else was I going to find you after you left the other night?'

'You could have asked me.'

'That would have been forward.'

The waiter was pouring coffee, momentarily distracting his attention. Katya studied him through lowered lashes. He was very sure of himself, she thought, orchestrating the conversation, gently but insistently probing into her life, giving away nothing himself. She found him challenging and strangely exhilarating. The slight apprehension that had gripped her when they arrived had lifted to reveal bright possibilities beyond.

'How did you come to be taking morning runs in Hyde Park?' she asked as the waiter withdrew.

'I was Cultural Attaché in London for two years.'

She was impressed. 'That must have been very interesting.'

'It was.' There was a touch of regret in his voice. 'I must admit I rather miss it.'

'Can you not go back?'

'Not for the time being.' Raising his hand he made a quick gesture that took in their surroundings. 'My present commitments keep me here in Moscow.'

'Oh,' she said quickly, 'yes I understand.'

He ducked his head, suddenly confidential. 'Although if I can't discover how these paintings are leaving the country I will probably have to go over there.'

'I thought you'd solved that?' Katya was surprised.

'Why do you say that?'

'The copy you found – '

'There is no copy.'

She gave a shake of her head, trying to grasp what he was saying. 'But the meeting I had with the English solicitor. All those things I told him. I thought it was all cleared up.'

'A small deceit,' Krasin confessed. He sipped at his coffee, replacing the cup with exaggerated care. 'You see, the situation is rather delicate, Katya. I decided that it was too much of a risk to have outsiders involved.'

'You made me lie to him?' Katya felt cheated.

'Perhaps I should have told you earlier, but I thought it would only make your task harder.'

She looked at him with a mixture of horror and fascination. 'You mean paintings are being taken?'

'It would seem so.'

'But how?'

Krasin got to his feet, flicking an imaginary crumb from his suit. 'I'll show you.'

'I think the Russians are lying,' Pip said as he hailed a taxi in Curzon Street.

'What gives you that idea?'

'They have been too damned helpful.'

He gave directions to the driver and climbed into the cab, Max bundling in behind him. As they swept through the city, shop windows bright in the darkness, Pip described the worm of doubt that had been bothering him since he saw Katya Leskova.

'I suggested to the Russians that there might be some sort of fraud. It was only speculation. If I was wrong they could have just ignored the letter or written back telling me to get knotted. Instead they sent a very pretty ambassadress to my office, full of smiles and charming explanations.'

Max gave a grunt of agreement. 'Bit over the top.'

'I know things are loosening up over there but not to that degree. That was designer Glasnost.'

They had been entertaining a client, mixing business with pleasure in the time-honoured fashion and now Max was sitting slumped in the leather seat, well marinated in claret.

'What are you going to do about it?'

'I thought I might ask them to send me a photo of this copy they claim to own. They can't very well refuse.'

'If they're covering up you won't get a straight answer.'

'I might if I sent the letter to Katya Leskova personally.' Pip pictured the girl as he spoke, remembering the long shaft of hair, the rich husky accent. 'I may be wrong, but I don't think she knows any more about this than we do.'

The clock towers were striking ten o'clock as they came out into Red Square. The guards on duty at the Lenin mausoleum were changing, stamping back towards the guardroom with the slow, exaggerated step of clockwork automatons. Above them the castellated wall of the Kremlin stood out against the night sky, hard and sharp as a saw blade, and the huge red stars glowed on the towers.

'You're angry with me,' Krasin said.

'No.'

She wasn't angry. Curious and slightly bewildered certainly but not angry. All Katya wanted at that moment was an explanation, to understand what it was that had required such careful preparations.

In the light of the St Saviour Gate Krasin flicked out his pass from his inside pocket. The officer on duty glanced over it and handed it back, saluting smartly as Krasin went on inside.

The road led up past the Presidium of the Supreme Soviet, its yellow and white colonnaded façade ghostly in the glare of the floodlights.

'Where are you taking me?' Katya asked as she hurried along beside him, her heels clicking on the cobbled road.

'To see some pictures.'

'Pictures?' The vast statue of Lenin loomed up, almost lost in the shadow of the surrounding firs. 'What pictures?'

'Nothing of any great quality. But I think you'll find them interesting nonetheless.'

At the gates of the Great Kremlin Palace he told Katya to wait while he went into the guardhouse, returning moments later with a thickset officer in the uniform of a major.

Together they crossed the darkened expanse of the courtyard. A few lights were burning in the windows of the palace; apart from that the place seemed deserted. At the far side of the courtyard the major ducked into a doorway and stamped down a flight of stone steps.

'Not the most ceremonious of entrances,' Krasin told her as he followed, 'but this is the quickest way in. It saves going in through the palace which takes ages at this time of night.'

The major was unlocking a door at the foot of the stairs. They were below ground level now and the air was damp and clinging. Beneath her coat Katya could feel the goose-pimples rise on her arms and shivered quickly. Krasin caught the movement.

'Are you cold?'

She shook her head.

The door swung open on powerful hinges. The major stood back to let them through.

'Would you like me to wait, Colonel?'

Krasin told him not to worry. 'I'll drop the key back at the guardhouse on the way back.' He turned to Katya and held out his arm with a little bow.

'After you.'

Chapter Ten

The passageway they came into was high and vaulted. Functional bracket lamps cast pools of light on a stone floor and the air carried the dank, fungal smell of a cave.

Katya walked forward a few paces, her footsteps loud in the confined space, and looked around.

'Whatever is this place?'

'The central art repository of the Kremlin,' Krasin told her, flicking on more lights.

What she had taken to be packing cases she saw now were huge bare canvases stacked against the wall. Further down was a row of statues, some wrapped in cellophane, others uncovered.

There was a melancholy to the place, the desolation of a deserted theatre.

'I'd no idea there was anything like this down here.'

'Not many do.' He moved ahead of her now, one hand in his pocket. 'It's not exactly open to the public.'

The passageway intersected with another, wider and better lit. The walls were white-washed, cables snaking purposefully along the ceiling. Krasin led the way along it, passing several open doorways before finally selecting one at random.

'It's a reserve for the national collection,' he told her, clattering down three stone steps into a large vault. 'They were all put down here after the revolution for safe-keeping.'

High metal cabinets reached up to the ceiling. Grey frames bolted together, numbered and systematised, the pictures racked along them like books on a library shelf.

He walked down one aisle with Katya following behind, keeping close. Reaching up he drew a canvas down from the rack and showed it to her.

'What do you make of that?' Krasin inquired.

It was a crude, noisy little picture, a scene of a drunken party.

'Looks as if the neighbours will be complaining in a minute.'

He laughed. 'You sound as though you're speaking from experience.' Taking back the canvas he glanced over it, rubbing the hard

80

brown surface with his thumb. 'It's Dutch – a copy of a painting by Jan Steen.'

'How do you know it's a copy?'

'The paintwork's too meagre to be by him. There's no body to it, not enough development in the tones.'

'Shouldn't it have a frame?'

'It probably does, but frames are officially rated as furniture so they're kept elsewhere.'

'How very Russian,' Katya replied laconically.

'Isn't it.' He thrust the painting back in its place and drew out another. 'French Rococo.' He identified it without difficulty. 'One of a million pictures done in the style of Boucher.'

Katya looked at the scene of pink nudes splashing on the edge of a lake and found herself thinking of Ludmilla.

'Why do you smile?'

'I was thinking of something.'

'It's of no great value, just a piece of interior decoration. It was probably hung in the corridor of some private house in Moscow.'

'Is there any way of knowing who owned it?'

Krasin had moved further along, pulling down more pictures and looking them over with his keen, intelligent eyes.

'None,' he said over his shoulder, 'I don't think anyone was paying too much attention at the time they were acquired.' He enunciated this last word slowly, emphasising the irony of the image.

For the next fifteen minutes he went through the racks of paintings, picking out those that caught his interest to show to Katya. His knowledge was extraordinary. There wasn't a theme or style that he couldn't identify. When Katya commented on this he dismissed it.

'You think an understanding of the arts incompatible with my work?'

'No, but surprising.'

'Security is not just bully-boys in leather jackets,' he told her softly, as though confiding a secret. 'Have you never heard of Menzhinsky?'

'I don't think so.'

'The head of the Cheka during the twenties?' He seemed slightly amused by her ignorance. 'Now there was a man of true feeling for the arts. It's said that he used to write poetry on the back of death warrants during his interrogations.'

'He sounds like a monster.'

'But a good Communist.' Krasin's expression was veiled at that moment so that she couldn't tell if he was mocking her or not. 'He was never one for a uniform but he used to paint his fingernails red, just to keep his allegiances clear.'

'How extraordinary. I've never heard his name mentioned.'

'Well he's hardly set up as a rôle model. Of course to him art wasn't decoration. It was a symbol of power – as it so often is.'

Katya was about to reply to this when they were interrupted by the arrival of the janitor. He came quite silently. One minute they were alone, the next he was there beside them, grinning bravely.

'This is Georgy,' Krasin told her.

Katya's hand was on her breast. 'My God, he gave me a fright.'

'He looks after the place.'

'I saw the lights on – ' Georgy justified his sudden appearance – 'so I came to see who it was.'

'Quite right too.'

Georgy was at least seventy years old, a dwarf of a man with a head as bald as a boiled potato. Krasin flattered the old fellow's pride.

'There's absolutely nothing Georgy doesn't know about these vaults,' he told Katya. 'He's been working here for how long is it – forty years?'

Georgy dropped his eyes demurely. 'Forty-six, Colonel.'

'That's a long time,' Katya said admiringly.

'He was posted here in the war. Looked after the collection during the last months of fighting. And he's been here ever since.'

Georgy stood quite still as his credentials were given, feet straddled, hands clasped in front, his mouth spread into a shy, flat smile that split his face like the zip on a purse. At the mention of the war he lifted one finger for Katya's benefit and ran it over the patch of medals on his blue jacket.

'I was showing Comrade Leskova around,' Krasin explained, speaking slowly as though Georgy were slightly deaf. 'She's from the ministry.'

'Ah yes,' he nodded his understanding, 'from the ministry. We often have people from the ministry.'

It was only after the old man had gone, vanishing back into the passageway as quietly as he'd arrived, that Krasin returned to the business in hand.

'The trouble with this place is that there's too much stored here to keep track of it. The paintings alone fill fifteen chambers; the furniture and antiques a great deal more.' He spoke clearly, laying out the facts like cards on a table.

'Of course if nothing ever left here it would be easy to police. But unfortunately that is not the situation. There are offices that need furnishing, institutes, conference rooms, hotels, in fact every government-run organisation. Not to mention the apartments of high-ranking officials living in Moscow. There's an almost constant flow of traffic in and out of these vaults. And that's what bothers me.'

'But if something wasn't returned surely it would be noticed?'

Krasin nodded thoughtfully. 'But does anyone notice exactly what is returned?'

'I don't follow you.'

He strolled down the avenue of shelves, rippling his fingers against the spines of the canvases. On impulse he pulled one out.

'Take this picture for example. How do you think it is catalogued?' It was a view of green meadows, a distant church, cows lying in long grass beneath a laundry basket of white clouds.

'If you looked it up I dare say it would be described as "An English nineteenth-century landscape, measuring ninety centimetres by a hundred and twenty".' Krasin shrugged at the hopelessness of such wording. 'There must be a thousand pictures that could fit that description.'

'You mean it could be switched for another?'

'What could be simpler? This painting is taken out and another of the same size and description but less value is returned a few months later.' He thumped the canvas back into its place. 'No one would ever spot the difference.'

'But why should anyone bother? I thought you said there was nothing here of any great value.'

'Compared to the major works in the museums there's not. But still, some of the paintings down here are worth anything from ten to forty thousand American dollars.' He saw the look of wonder in her eyes and smiled. 'In the West, that is.'

'That's a lot of money.'

'Just one or two a year would amount to a fortune in time.'

'There must be someone who would notice though.' Katya could scarcely believe it could be done so easily. 'How about Georgy? He'd know what was going on.'

'He's a muzhik.' Krasin glanced over his shoulder as he used the Russian word for peasant. 'And practically illiterate. Anything that looks official impresses him. If an order comes on headed paper with plenty of rubber stamps on the bottom he'll obey it. I can't blame him but I can't rely on him either. What I need is someone intelligent down here, someone who understands the situation – someone like you, Katya.'

'Me?' She was taken aback.

'Of course.'

'But what could I do?'

'You could keep me informed.'

She'd thought he was joking, twisting the conversation into some sort of compliment, but she realised now that he was quite serious.

'You could tell me who comes and goes in these vaults, check over the paintings that have been returned in the last year, see if there's any discrepancy with their entry in the catalogue.' Krasin's voice rose slightly as he spoke. 'Apart from our friend Podurets you're the only other person in Moscow who knows of this.'

'But I have my job to do.'

'That's no problem. I can arrange to have you transferred here, on a temporary basis.'

The proposal had come so unexpectedly that she didn't know how to reply. Krasin gave a quick shake of his head, relieving her of the responsibility.

'That is, if you're prepared to help me, Katya. There's no way I can insist you do so.'

They went out into the night, walking back across the deserted courtyard of the palace. Chibatar was waiting for them in the road below the Borovitskaya Gate.

Krasin hardly spoke as they drove along the banks of the Moskva but stared out at the river deep in thought. When they reached her apartment he stood with her on the pavement for a few minutes.

'You'll think it over then?'

'Naturally – '

'There's no hurry. I can give you a few days to decide.' Taking her hand he touched it to his lips and then reaching forward he kissed her on both cheeks, his mouth just touching the corner of hers.

'Until next time then.'

'Good night, Vassily.'

In the act of climbing back into the car he turned to her. 'I want to catch him, Katya. If someone is taking paintings from those vaults I want to know who it is. I want that very badly.'

The door closed and the black shadow of the Rolls drew away into the night.

'How did it go?'

'All right.'

The bedroom was in darkness. Katya undressed quickly, pulling her nightgown over her head and fumbling her way into bed. Tatyana had been asleep when she came in but she'd awakened immediately and now lay watching her.

'Where did he take you?'

'The Slavjanski Bazar.'

'That's pretty crowded, isn't it?'

'And then up into the Kremlin.' Katya lifted herself on one elbow. 'Did you know there were paintings stored down there? Thousands of them.'

'I've heard it said. I've never seen them.'

'It's really spooky, Tasha. They're just stacked in there, rows and rows of them. No one even knows where they came from.'

With a flicker of movement Tatyana crossed the room to sit beside her. 'Why did he take you in there?'

'He wants me to do some work for him.'

'Work?' There was an edge in Tatyana's voice. 'What sort of work?'

Katya told her of the conversation they'd had in the vaults but Tatyana wasn't interested in the details, only in Katya's response.

'Did you agree to help him?'

'I don't know. It might be interesting – '

'You mustn't do it!' The words hissed out of the darkness.

'It's better than sitting twiddling my thumbs in endless conferences.'

'You'd be informing, Katska.'

'It's not like that.' Tatyana was overreacting. 'I'd just be telling him who came and went in the daytime.'

'That's the thin end of the wedge. Don't you see that? Once you start passing on information to those filth they won't let you stop – '

'Don't be so silly, Tasha.'

'Listen to me!'

Katya jerked up in bed. 'I am listening to you, for God's sake!'

'You mustn't do it.'

'But he only wants me to help him.'

'Why must it be you?' Tatyana was relentless. 'He has a thousand minions he could get to do the job for him. Why must you be the one?'

Katya didn't know. She didn't want to know. She had a sickening feeling that Tatyana was right. Vassily Krasin was not to be trusted. She hugged her knees and stared across the darkened room, wrestling with her own thoughts.

Tatyana interpreted the silence. 'You like him, don't you.'

'Yes . . . No – I don't know.'

She fell back on the pillow. How could she explain the confused emotions she felt for Vassily Krasin? He frightened her and fascinated her at the same time. She knew it would be wise to keep her distance but she was attracted to him, excited, more than she wanted to think about.

'He's dangerous.' Tatyana's voice was low.

'Yes . . . I know that.'

The window was open, a fine blade of air lifted the curtains. Outside a siren was wailing along the river bank.

Krasin had used her, pulled her strings to make her dance to his tune. But there was no harm in it was there? He had done it to protect her, to make it easier for her to approach the English lawyer.

In a small voice she asked, 'What shall I say to him, Tasha?'

'It doesn't matter.'

'He's going to call again after the weekend.' She wanted help.

'Just refuse him. Give him any excuse you like but finish it before it starts.'

Katya nodded, making up her mind, happier now she was certain. 'Yes, I will.'

'You must.'

Vassily Krasin went straight back home.

Switching on the Tiffany lamp on his study desk he poured himself a glass of brandy and downed it in one, feeling the spirit scorching into his stomach. For some minutes he stood quite still, thinking of the girl, going back over the conversations he'd had with her, carefully isolating points of interest and storing them in his mind.

Katya was clearly intelligent but quite unworldly. Well brought up and slightly pampered, with that radiance that comes to all women used to commanding male attention. But that was part of the attraction. The women he had known as a child had been hard and shrewish, brutalised by the conditions they lived in, by the world they worked in. Katya belonged to a different species, sophisticated and alluring, like some valuable possession.

She would do as he wanted. He was sure of that.

Clinking the stopper into the decanter he went out into the passage. Yekaterina's door was ajar, he noticed as he passed, the light still on. He nudged it open and looked inside.

She lay in bed on her side, one arm cast out and snoring heavily. He could tell from the inert slump of her body, the opened mouth, that she had been drinking.

Gingerly, his feet silent in the thick pile of the carpet, Krasin walked across to her. He rarely ventured into her bedroom. It was her domain, a private sanctuary of frills and pastel colours which she guarded jealously. The place was a mess, clothing dripping from chairs, shoes scattered about the floor, empty cigarette packets littering the dressing table.

She had fallen asleep whilst reading. The book was still wedged beneath her cheek. Reaching forwards he pulled it free.

It was samizdat, a translation of some American thriller. He recognised the crude print, the thick irregular pages immediately.

Silly bitch, a book like this could get you three weeks in jail – that is, provided you weren't married to a senior officer of the KGB.

He wondered where it came from. Maybe one of her admirers in the department had given it to her, one of the young bloods she liked to entertain in this powder-puff room when he wasn't around, rewarding them for their attention with boxes of chocolates and bottles of Scottish whisky and the damp clasp of her body.

Yekaterina stirred and rolled on to her back, the lamp bleaching the colour from her face, breasts slumping on either side of her chest like loaded panniers over a mule.

The sight disgusted him. But then he hadn't married her for her beauty. He'd married her for her family name; married her because her father was a general of the Red Army, a man both respected and feared, a man who had stood just four away from Brezhnev on those cold May Day parades.

Yekaterina's face had crumpled as she moved, as though she were suffocating. But now the breath sloughed out of her mouth and she steadied in her sleep once more.

Krasin dropped the novel on to the bed and left, wondering, not for the first time, how Yekaterina was going to take to being a widow.

Chapter Eleven

'Can I give you a lift, Comrade Dmitri?'

At the sound of his name Podurets started and then turning around he gave a little bow.

'Most kind of you, Colonel.'

'I was told I might find you here.'

It had not been difficult to track him down. Podurets was a creature of routine. On Monday evenings he dined with his married sister, on Wednesdays he played bridge and on Thursdays he visited a lady friend of his in her over-heated apartment near the Dinamo stadium.

On these days he wore his best suit and a clean white shirt and, oblivious to the tittering of the girls behind his back, he left the office promptly at four announcing that he had business in town.

Podurets thought of this placid and undemanding lady as his mistress and on occasion he honoured the word with a brief scuffle on the sofa. But most of the time he just sat drinking tea and talking, comforted by the chance to pour out his troubles.

That evening, as he was coming out of the apartment block where she lived, he had been astonished to see Krasin standing in the street. He had been sidling away up the pavement, hoping his presence there was a coincidence, when Krasin's invitation halted him.

'A friend,' he muttered, climbing into the Rolls beside Krasin. 'Friend of the family, that is . . . She's not been well recently.'

'And a most attractive one too, I'm told.' Krasin's manner was understanding, almost roguish, but it did nothing to calm his passenger.

'Yes, quite – most kind, Colonel.'

'I'm so glad to have the chance to talk to you,' he continued smoothly. 'I saw Katya Leskova yesterday, as I expect you already know.'

'Katya Leskova?'

'Didn't she tell you she was due to see me?'

'No, Colonel.'

'I'm surprised.' Krasin frowned quickly and then let it pass. Opening the walnut-veneered cabinet beside him he took out a bottle of lemon vodka.

'Can I offer you a drink?'

'Not for me . . . Oh yes, thank you.'

Podurets took the glass he was handed and waited while Krasin replaced the bottle and settled back in his seat.

'Are you satisfied with the work she does for you?'

'Katya Leskova is a capable interpreter . . .' Podurets left the sentence hanging as though this were only part of the equation. Krasin encouraged him to complete it.

'And apart from that?'

'I can't say she's a benefit to the department, Colonel.'

'Why not?'

Podurets licked red lips. 'Katya Leskova is insubordinate,' he said. 'She has no respect for authority.'

'Really?' Krasin stared away into space for a moment. 'Insubordinate. That's very interesting. It's exactly the word that Comrade Tokarev used that day he rang me from the Pushkin Museum. He described her as an impertinent and insubordinate girl.'

Podurets steadied his nerves with a shot of vodka.

'Do you know,' Krasin continued, 'I still can't understand why she confronted the Pushkin Museum in that way.'

'I couldn't say, Colonel.' Podurets was frightened by the drift of this conversation and when he was frightened he smelled.

Krasin opened the window a fraction.

'Whose idea was it?'

'I'm not sure, Colonel. It was some time ago.' He gave the problem his earnest consideration. 'It could have been hers.'

Krasin was sure he was right.

'I know you'd never have entertained such a preposterous notion,' he said, 'knowing how damaging it would be.'

'No, it was hers.' The memory was growing stronger. 'I remember it distinctly.'

'And you let her have her way. Now why was that?'

Podurets stared into his hands as though hoping that the answer to this question might be written on the bottom of his glass. But Krasin had nothing but admiration for his decision.

'I have to congratulate you on your foresight,' he said, opening the window a shade wider.

'Foresight, Colonel?'

'I imagine you suspected her motives?'

The wisdom of it returned to him now. Lifting his head he said: 'I did have my doubts.'

89

'I must confess I'd never have been so astute.'

They were passing a small park. Scraggy trees caged in with iron railings, photographs of the people's heroes displayed above the gate. Krasin leaned forward and ordered Chibatar to stop the car.

'So much easier to talk out here in the fresh air,' he observed as they walked together.

The evening had already anticipated the onset of winter. The air was cold, the sun sinking down through a molten sky. The figures who stood reading the newspapers around them were just shadows beneath the trees.

Krasin turned up the collar of his overcoat.

'There is something I think you should know,' he said, 'as it directly concerns your department. Last night Katya Leskova asked me whether she could have a temporary transfer to work in the reserve collection of the Kremlin.'

Honoured to be taken into his confidence in this way, Podurets frowned and repeated the request over to himself.

'Don't you find that curious?' Krasin asked.

'Extraordinary, Colonel.'

'I had no idea she would even know of such a place.'

'Nor I,' Podurets agreed. He made a contribution of his own. 'Did she say why she wanted to work there?'

'Not a word. But no doubt she has her reasons.'

For a few moments they stood together in silence, silhouetted against the blazing sky, before Podurets ventured a question.

'Could she be involved in smuggling paintings out of the country, do you think, Colonel?'

'It's a possibility we have to consider.'

Krasin was satisfied. The seeds were sown in Podurets's mind and already beginning to grow. He added a small threat for good measure.

'You do realise that you would be held responsible for any misdemeanour in your department?'

Podurets looked as though he wished he were living on some distant planet. Giving a slight smile Krasin changed the subject.

'Shall we go? It seems to be getting rather cold.'

They walked back towards the car.

'In the meantime, you will keep in close contact with me, Comrade Podurets. I want to know where she is going and who she talks to.'

'I understand, Colonel.'

'Nothing is too insignificant to be passed on. If anything should arise don't hesitate to ring.' He paused at the entrance to the park and pointed down the street.

'I believe you'll find the nearest metro in that direction.'

* * *

'Katya!'

The high-pitched voice belonged to Ludmilla. Bursting through the ministry doors, dragging on an overcoat, she scuttled up the street to where Katya stood waiting.

'Where are you going?' she asked breathlessly.

'Just shopping.'

Framed by her pale thistle-down hair, Ludmilla's face was pink with expectation.

'How did it go then?'

Katya moved on. 'How did what go?'

'The other night – with Vassily Krasin.' As if there could be anything else to discuss. 'I haven't seen you since to ask.'

Katya didn't want to talk about Krasin. She was seeing him later that evening and dreading the meeting but Ludmilla was not to be shaken off.

'Did he take you back to his house?'

'No, out to a restaurant.'

'They say it's amazing. One of the girls I work with had to go up there last month to deliver something. She said it was full of antiques and oil paintings with real silver cutlery on the table. And there was this enormous carved fireplace which she heard he'd had brought back from a palace in England. Just think of that.' Ludmilla's mind was a smoking ashtray of fag-ends. 'You should get him to take you there, Katya.'

'I'm not seeing him again.'

'You must! You'd be mad not to.' She was appalled by the waste and rubbed an imaginary coin with her thumb as though it were a currency she was describing. 'Now that one's got blat. I've heard that you'll find half the Politburo at his parties.'

Catching sight of a pensioner operating a set of public scales she darted across the street.

'I've been dieting,' she called to Katya as she climbed on to the wobbling platform, 'I want to see if it's taken effect yet.' The pensioner, in a white coat and beret, was flicking the weights along the scale, peering myopically at the calibrations.

'Damn,' Ludmilla said. 'I should have had a pee first, that always makes a difference.'

Katya watched as the silver arm began to steady.

'We should go out together one evening,' Ludmilla called from her perch. 'You and Vassily, me and my Misha.'

Katya couldn't think of anything she wanted less but agreed that they could think about it.

'It would be fun – '

She was interrupted by the pensioner's weedy voice reading out her weight. Leaping down from the scales she pulled off her coat and boots and told him to try again.

'But on second thought maybe that wouldn't be such a good idea,' she said, standing bare-footed on the enamel platform. 'Vassily's wife might not like it. I hear she's very possessive.'

Katya stood quite still, her face betraying nothing, and stared at the sparrows hopping about the pavement in search of scraps. Ludmilla had stepped down off the scales and helped herself to her clothes.

As they walked on the old man's voice followed them.

'Twenty copecks.'

'Your machine's wrong,' Ludmilla called back over her shoulder. 'I'm not paying you good money to hear lies.'

'Sod you, lady – it's twenty copecks whether you like it or not.'

'Whistle for it, grandad.'

'I'll have the police on you – '

'Pay him,' Katya ordered crossly.

Ludmilla took out a coin and tossed it down the street. She turned back to Katya, surprised by the sharpness of her voice.

'Didn't he tell you he was married, Katska?' Her smile was sweet and malicious. 'I'm sorry, I thought you would have known. I didn't mean to be the one to break the bad news.'

By the time Katya returned home that evening she was feeling tired and miserable. Going straight through to her bedroom she slammed the door and threw herself down on her bed.

After a few minutes Tatyana followed.

'What's the matter, kovshka?'

Katya didn't answer but lay facing the wall, hugging herself with her arms, the dark mantilla of her hair hiding her face.

'Did you speak to Vassily?'

She hesitated and then nodded. Tatyana sat on the bed beside her. Gently she probed deeper.

'Was he cross with you?'

'Not cross, just cold and detached.' Katya turned slightly, one arm across her forehead and looked up at Tatyana with troubled eyes. 'He said I was being selfish, thinking of myself and not the ministry.'

'What reason did you give him?'

'I told him I didn't want to be involved with something I didn't understand.'

'He can accept that, can't he? It's perfectly reasonable.'

'Oh sure, I've no doubt he can accept it. It just didn't please him very much.'

'He's not going to force you?'

Katya shook her head. 'I think he was surprised more than

anything else. He wasn't expecting me to refuse. I could tell.'

She looked pale and drawn. The meeting had clearly been a strain for her, much more than Tatyana had realised. Reaching out her hand she stroked the long brown hair.

'It's for the best,' she said soothingly.

Katya gave a brief nod.

'You wouldn't have wanted to do it.'

'I know.'

Katya lay quite still but she was like an animal in pain. Her back was arched and when Tatyana touched her she could feel the tension in the muscles, sense the struggle within.

'Did you know he was married, Tasha?' she asked suddenly, coiling up into a sitting position.

'Yes, I'd heard he was. I wasn't sure of it.'

Katya's face was close to hers now. She could feel the warmth of her breath as she spoke.

'He never mentioned her to me, never said anything at all.'

'Did you expect him to?'

She bit her lip and looked away. 'Probably not.'

'How did you find out?'

'From Ludmilla – she told me this morning.'

The little cow, Tatyana thought furiously. How could she do such a thing? She must have known how it would hurt. But no doubt that's exactly why she'd done it. To score a small victory over someone she considered a rival.

She put her arm around Katya's shoulders. 'Does it matter?'

'No – not really.'

Tatyana looked at her thoughtfully and then stood up.

'Take off your shirt,' she ordered going into the kitchen and returning with a bottle of oil.

Unfastening the strap of Katya's bra, she began to massage the oil into the smooth skin of her back. At once a rich, heady fragrance filled the room.

'What's that?' Katya asked.

'Lie still. It'll do you good.'

Tatyana's hands were strong and practised, the fingers following the flow of the muscles, seeking out the tension. Katya lay face down, holding her hair away from her neck.

'He asked me to go out with him tomorrow,' she said into the pillow.

The hands stopped.

'What did you say to him?'

Katya's voice was drowsy. 'I told him I was too busy.'

* * *

The following morning Krasin rang her at the ministry.

'I suppose there's no chance you've changed your mind, Katya?'

'I'm afraid not.'

The wind rattled the window beside her. It was one of those cold, bleak days that bring draughts and grumbles and the first snivelling colds into the office. At the next desk, Dinara was holding out chubby legs to the paraffin stove, clenching her toes into a ball for warmth.

Krasin sounded concerned. 'Have I offended you in some way, Katya? The other night I thought you wanted to help me.'

'It's not that.' She was speaking under her breath for privacy. 'I can't explain.'

'But I don't understand why you've changed your mind.'

Podurets had come to the door and was watching her with his inquisitive eyes. There was a wail from Dinara as she singed the bottom of her woollen stockings and clutched her foot in her hands.

'Is there no way I can persuade you?' Krasin asked.

'I've already given you my reasons. Please don't make me go over it all again.'

Krasin let the subject drop and changed tack. 'I'm going down to the country this weekend. Why don't you join me for a while?'

'I don't think that's a good idea.'

'You'd enjoy it, Katya.'

Out of the side of her eye she could see Podurets draw in closer, hovering within earshot.

'I can't talk now,' she told Krasin hurriedly. 'I'm late for a meeting. Ring me at home some time.' She put down the phone and went back to her work without looking up.

'Who was that?' Podurets was ferreting for information.

'Just someone I know.'

'I've warned you before about making social calls during working hours, Comrade Leskova.'

'It wasn't a social call.'

'Business?'

'You might call it that.'

'Then it should be referred to me.'

'It wasn't your business,' she replied archly, 'it was someone else's.' And taking her hat and coat from the overburdened hanger she stalked out of the office.

Getting up from his desk Krasin walked over to the window.

He couldn't understand why Katya was being so difficult. When he'd first met her she had been easy, compliant. Now suddenly she had become evasive. Maybe she didn't trust him, maybe she had some sixth sense. Or maybe it was that damned gipsy girl interfering.

Krasin stared down into the square, watching the sparks from the trolley buses as they jolted through the traffic, turning the possibilities over in his mind.

What he needed was a new angle, something to give him the edge on Katya Leskova.

On impulse he went next door, bursting into the office without knocking. Zakov jumped to his feet, hurriedly stubbing out his cigarette, but Krasin ignored his discomfort.

Throwing himself down in a chair he rapped commands into a computer. The screen lit, flooding with information. He typed in a name and Katya's file flashed up before him.

He had read it a hundred times before, he could practically recite it by now, but he went through it once again, concentrating on the entries evaluating her friends. After a few minutes he replaced it with Tatyana's file and then another.

Major Zakov watched him in silence. He recognised these moods of Krasin's and knew it was wise not to ask questions or attempt to offer assistance. Better to stand back and wait for orders.

Krasin's attention was locked on the computer. He fed in instructions, cross-referencing the names, summoning data from the vast store of its memory and as the screen cleared and filled an idea formed in his mind. He acted on it immediately.

'Call my chauffeur,' he ordered, getting to his feet. 'Have him bring the car to the door.'

Chibatar drove him over to the ministry, parking in the kerb some distance down the road, from where Krasin had a clear view of the main entrance.

He hadn't long to wait before he saw Katya emerge with Tatyana and two other girls. They were winding up scarves, chattering excitedly, their heads close together as they moved away up the street.

Krasin watched them without stirring.

A traffic policeman bustled up the pavement behind him, recognised the registration mark on the Rolls and passed by as though it were invisible.

Just as Krasin was beginning to think he had arrived too late, she appeared. He instructed Chibatar to move on ahead and jumping out on to the pavement he held open the door.

'Can I give you a lift?' he inquired.

Ludmilla stopped. For a moment she looked at him in surprise and then her face sweetened into a smile.

'That depends where you are going, Colonel Krasin.'

Chapter Twelve

The letter from England arrived two days later. The typed address had been crossed out and its cyrillic equivalent written alongside in red crayon. On the back was an embossed crest.

Podurets cut open the envelope and took out the printed page. It was in English. Leaning back in his chair he called down the passage:

'Comrade Leskova, will you come in here please.'

She appeared in the doorway looking fresh and chic in an embroidered skirt and broad black belt, her hair newly washed and shining in the winter sunshine.

Podurets had been on the point of giving her the letter but seeing her standing there, hands on hips, he changed his mind. What right had she to be in private correspondence with foreigners?

Katya was waiting, eyebrows raised.

'What are you working on at present?' he asked.

'The minutes of last night's conference.' It was an odd question. He had given her the job only an hour before.

'Ah yes . . . Well don't let me distract you.'

Later that day Podurets took the letter over to Dzerzhinsky Square. Krasin read it through thoughtfully.

'Has this been seen by any of your translators?' he inquired.

'None, Colonel.' Podurets stood before the desk, clutching his hat in both hands. 'It only arrived this morning. No one else touched it apart from myself.'

'So Comrade Leskova knows nothing of it?'

'When I saw who it was from I knew I should bring it to you, Colonel.'

'Yes, quite. You have done well.' Krasin acknowledged the plea for approval as he scanned the page. He picked on one line. 'What is this about magazines?'

'I don't know, Colonel – '

'It says here that he hopes she found the magazines helpful.'

Podurets squirmed under his scrutiny. 'Could he be referring to fashion magazines? I know they are very sought after by the girls travelling abroad.'

It was more than likely, Krasin thought to himself, but he encouraged Podurets to stretch his imagination.

'What are her political affiliations?'

'She has none to my knowledge, Colonel.' Podurets was surprised by the question. 'Politically she is an innocent.'

'But she shares an apartment with Tatyana Vasnikova who is anything but an innocent.'

Podurets was grappling with the problem. 'Could it be referring to some sort of subversive literature?'

'I would have thought so.'

Krasin dropped the letter to the desk and studied it, his hands clasped beneath his chin.

In the silence Podurets let his attention flicker around the magnificent office, taking in the carved panelling, the inlaid furniture, the silver inkstand on the desk. He was vaguely aware that such things shouldn't exist in the political ideology of the country but instinctively he knew they were right. These were the symbols of power, the outward manifestations of authority.

'Clearly Comrade Leskova failed to convince him of the truth.' Krasin glanced up from the letter. 'He now wants to see evidence of the copy we hold.'

'Can we not show it to him?'

Krasin's hard black eyes bored into him. 'I will have to consider the matter.'

'I trust I did right in bringing this to your attention, Colonel?' Podurets whined. It was not fair. He was carrying the blame for Katya Leskova's failure but Krasin had given him enough praise for one day.

'You will bring any similar correspondence directly to me.'

'Naturally, Colonel.'

'And continue to treat it with the utmost secrecy. It is imperative she knows nothing of this matter.'

When Podurets had left the office Krasin swore to himself. Hard, brutal words. But he uttered them softly and caressingly as though they were an endearment.

This English lawyer was becoming a nuisance. There was a tenacity to him that it was fashionable to admire. Krasin found it only irritating.

It reminded him of an incident that had taken place earlier that year. A factory worker had been shot during a dispute. When the police officer responsible was questioned he'd replied that the workman had come at him, refusing to stop when he was ordered. 'In the end I had to fire,' he had said. 'There was no alternative. I warned him over and over again but he just kept on coming.'

And that's exactly what this Englishman was now doing.

Krasin glanced at his watch. It was just after four in the evening. There was an hour's difference with British time. The solicitor's office would still be open.

Picking up the phone he dialled London, adding the number on the headed paper. The receptionist at Evans-Greatheart answered the call in a voice so clear it might have been in the same building.

'I'll see if he's available,' she chirped. 'If I can have your name?'

'Jablonsky.' Krasin gave the name of an officer he'd served under twenty years earlier.

A brief pause and Pip Spencer came on the line.

'Mr Jablonsky – how can I hep you?'

'Forgive me for ringing you like this,' Krasin was amiable. 'I am a colleague of Katya Leskova's.'

'Ah yes – '

Krasin detected the slightest flicker of hesitation in the solicitor's voice as he realised he was talking directly to Russia.

'I believe you two met recently.'

'That's right.'

'She has received your letter and passed it on to me in the hope that I might be able to help.' Krasin's English was fluent but rusty and he spoke slowly, enunciating the words carefully. 'There seems to have been some confusion, Mr Spencer. You have asked to see evidence of a painting that we hold.'

'That's right. I was told that you hold a copy of a painting that is hanging here in London.'

'I can find no sign of any such picture amongst the reserve collections.' Krasin sounded unhappy to be the bearer of bad news. 'I cannot think who suggested it might be there. Naturally Comrade Leskova is most distressed to have passed on false information.'

There was a pause while Pip digested this news.

'Are you trying to say that the painting presently hanging in London does belong to the Russian Government?'

Krasin looked down at the desk, running his eyes over the signature on the letter, marrying it with the voice, trying to evoke an image of the man to whom he was speaking.

'I think it is a possibility.'

'You're not sure?'

'Not without looking into it.' Krasin gave the conversation its direction. 'Unfortunately I am not in the position to carry out such an investigation.'

'No, I can see that – '

'You appreciate my problem, Mr Spencer?'

'You are hoping I'll do it for you?'

Krasin smiled to himself. It was a pleasure doing business with this man.

'It would be a great help to us if you could, Mr Spencer.'

'Why not the police? I would have thought this was a matter for them.'

'That is exactly what I thought myself, Mr Spencer.' Krasin sounded delighted that their thoughts should coincide. 'Although they would be forced to bring the subject to public attention and that, in the circumstances, could be a little . . .' he fought for the right word, 'embarrassing.'

'So what do you expect me to do?'

'If you could tell us a little more about the background to this painting you discovered, find out where it has been in the last few years, who owned it. Such information would be of the greatest assistance.'

'I see – '

Krasin could almost hear the solicitor thinking at the far end of the line. He sweetened the offer.

'Of course we will pay you for your time.'

The doubt lingered but it was melting now. 'I'm not sure that this is my concern.'

'Comrade Leskova would be most grateful.' Krasin altered his approach, putting it on a personal level. 'She is most upset by the misunderstanding she has caused you.'

'If I were to do it, how can I contact you with the results?'

Krasin's smile warmed his voice. 'I'll give you my private number.'

'If it's really just background information you want – '

'Nothing more.'

After Pip Spencer had rung off, Krasin stared across the room for some minutes, visualising the chain of events he had begun, estimating the outcome. Then, taking out his lighter he touched the flame to the corner of Pip's letter, turned it carefully in his hand until the paper had burned to a blackened wafer and dropped it in the ashtray.

'They want me to check up on that painting in the D'Este Gallery.'

'Are you going to do it?'

'I think I should. I can't very well ask them to play ball if I won't do so myself.'

Max sat slumped in his chair, hands folded across his waistcoat, looking like the effigy of a saint on his day off.

'I should watch them. Slippery blighters, the Russians.'

Pip was inclined to agree. 'But I can't see the harm in it. If that painting does belong to them I reckon they've got the right to know about it.'

'What was he like, this Russian?'

Pip recalled the slow, heavy accent, the carefully placed words. 'I imagine he's been over here in his time. He had quite a grasp of the language.'

'Did he say who he was?'

'A colleague of that girl who turned up the other day. She'd passed on my letter to him.'

'Do you trust him?'

'I've no reason not to, have I?'

Max put his hand in the semblance of a pistol and pointed it at him. 'Which would you prefer, a piece of advice or a drink?'

'Any chance of both?'

'Check up on this painting for him.' Max thumbed the cork from a bottle of Laphroaig, splashed a measure into two glasses and handed one across the desk. 'But keep a record of everything you do, starting with the conversation you've just had. Names, facts, the lot. I'll sign and date each page and hold it here in the safe. Any nonsense from Ivan and you can take it straight to the police.'

Pip nodded. It had to be sensible.

'And in the meantime, sting them for twice your normal fee.'

Krasin walked out of the Lubyanka, acknowledging the salute of the guards with a casual nod of his head.

The air was still and cold, the kind that catches at the back of your throat. The sun had sunk behind a veil of cloud and the city was buried in a faint, golden haze.

Thrusting his hands into his pockets he strolled down the Prospeckt Marksa, past the high, ornate façade of the Hotel Metropole. Braziers glowed in the pavement stalls, the smell of charcoal and roasting shaslik hung in the air.

Krasin looked at the figures huddled around them as he passed. It seemed an age since he had stood queuing for something to eat, scratching through his pockets for change, waiting to catch a little warmth from the red hot coals.

On the corner of Sverdlova Square, a student was selling carnations. Krasin looked them over, selected a dozen.

'How much do you want?' he asked.

The boy assessed him quickly, greedily. It was rare that anyone bought so many.

He said, 'Forty roubles.'

100

At least twice the going rate. Taking a card from his wallet Krasin scrawled the words, 'To Katya – in case you should change your mind.' Beneath it he added his private phone number.

'I want you to deliver this,' he said, tucking the card into the bouquet of flowers.

The boy's face was thin and pinched, the mouth a dark hole trailing breath in the cold air.

Sulkily he said, 'I don't deliver.'

'I've put the address on the other side,' Krasin informed him, drawing two notes from his wallet. They were American ten-dollar bills.

The boy hesitated as he saw them.

'I'll give you one of these now,' Krasin said pleasantly, as though reasoning with a wayward child. 'And if you can give me an accurate description of where you've been I'll give you the other when I come by tomorrow.'

The boy was eyeing the notes. It could be a trick. American dollars were wealth, real money. They were also illegal.

That's the way, Krasin told himself. Keep your guard up, sonny. Don't let them trap you. That's the only way to survive.

'What are you waiting for?' he asked.

With a snap of his head the boy took the ten-dollar note, stuffing it into his back pocket as he hurried away.

Krasin crossed the square. It was open, desolate, the distant bulk of the Bolshoi Theatre muffled in shadow. A performance must have just ended, figures were streaming out of the doors.

Nearby, Chibatar leaned against the bonnet of the Rolls. He had followed Krasin down the street, seen the deal he'd struck with the student but he showed no sign of interest as he held open the door of the car.

Krasin sat hunched in the seat as they drove across the city, his breath misting the window pane and stared out at the crowded streets. It was growing dark now and the lights in the shop windows silhouetted the passing figures.

He remembered the first time he had been over to the West, walking down the Graben in Vienna, looking in at the brilliantly lit interiors of the shops and cafés. It had been a cold winter's night, not unlike this one. A band had been playing in the street, snatches of waltz drifting to him on the frozen air. He'd felt an excitement all around him, a wonderful heady sense of pleasure. There were no queues, no ration books, none of the dreary resignation of State quotas. Here life was elegant and gracious.

That's when it had started, he supposed. As he'd stood out there in the cold night air, gazing at these fabulous people who brushed past him, he'd wanted to be part of it, to share in their sophisticated world.

At the time it had been a desire, a vague dream. The means hadn't come until later.

The Rolls slowed, drew in to the kerb before the Pushkin Museum. Krasin jerked his thoughts back to the present. He was so close now, so nearly there that he must be doubly careful. It was easy to slip at the last moment, to make some tiny mistake.

The museum was practically deserted. Thoughtfully Krasin walked through the galleries, hearing the crunch of his footsteps on the wooden boards.

In a passageway on the first floor he paused to study a small painting. The warden sitting next door noticed him there and wondered who he was. Not a tourist; there was something too determined, too proprietorial in the way he stood with his hands clasped behind his back, his chin resting on his chest. And the long black overcoat, the silk scarf were too formal for a tourist. He must be an official, one of the bastards from the government, someone to steer clear of. Averting his eyes, the warden retired back into the anonymity of his uniform.

After a few minutes Krasin moved on. In his mind he carried the details of the little painting, its size and subject, its precise position on the wall. Returning down the marble stairs he made his way to the gallery of antiquities.

Ludmilla was waiting for him.

'I thought I must have come to the wrong place,' she said petulantly as he came in.

Krasin turned and examined the marble body of an athlete. His late arrival had been intentional. He wanted her to be kept waiting.

Ludmilla was watching him.

'Why did we have to meet here?' she asked.

'It was convenient for me. I had some other business to attend to.'

'It's like a cemetery.'

Krasin turned and looked at her. She was dressed in a fur-trimmed overcoat, her hair fluffing out from beneath a woollen hat. There was something sly, acquisitive about this girl that he found distasteful. But he knew her, understood her motives and that made her easy to handle.

'You wanted to see me,' he said curtly. 'Why is that?'

'I've found what you wanted.'

A smile touched her lips as she spoke and Krasin guessed the little bitch intended to bargain with him.

'Go on,' he said.

'I've also discovered what I want in return.'

'I see.' He let the words freeze in the silence of the room. 'I've already told you I'm not making any deals.'

Ludmilla pouted her lips into a little wet raspberry. She was enjoying this confrontation.

'It won't cost you anything, Colonel.'

With a slight gesture of impatience Krasin walked out of the door but her voice held him.

'It's not fair – I've done as you asked, you must give me something for it.'

Krasin had turned.

'First you tell me what you have,' he said. 'Then I'll decide whether it's worth anything.'

Chapter Thirteen

Tatyana was arrested at four thirty-five in the morning; Katya saw the precise time on the report sheet later that day.

She had been asleep when they kicked in the door and the sudden crash of splintering wood as the lock gave way jerked her awake. She jack-knifed up in bed, hauling the blankets up with her in a sudden spasm of panic.

For a split second she thought she was dreaming. The room was in darkness and still cosy with night. Then the bedroom door burst open and the lights came on. Her eyes strained in the fierce glare of the bulb, sleep was dashed from her mind.

There were two of them. She saw them in an unfocused haze, large thickset men in black leather jackets who filled the entrance with their presence. They came through the door as one, blossoming out towards her.

Realisation came without understanding. Katya tried to scream but her body refused to respond and she felt herself cringing back, pulling the bedclothes up to her eyes and the only sound that came from her throat was a long-drawn-out gasp, more like a sigh than a cry of terror.

The two men scarcely noticed her huddled there in the corner. With quick, purposeful movements they went over to Tatyana and pulled her to her feet.

She hadn't reacted to the sound of their arrival. It was almost as though she was expecting them and she lay quite still, watching and waiting.

Taking her by the arms they lifted her bodily from the bed, her feet slapping to the ground as they took her next door.

Katya's fear hardened into indignation.

'Leave her alone!' She sprang to her knees, tousled hair falling over her eyes.

Neither of the two men appeared to have heard but the sound of her own voice gave Katya renewed determination.

'What do you want?' she demanded shrilly, leaping off the bed.

The blankets tangled around her ankles and she rolled on to the floor with a crash, her nightdress riding up over coltish legs. In any other situation it might have appeared comic. But then no one was looking. Cursing with frustration she kicked herself free and followed them next door.

Here another was searching methodically through the cupboards, not wasting time by breaking anything but feeling over the contents with the light, exploratory touch of a doctor examining a patient. He was dressed in a long overcoat and narrow-brimmed hat, the hair on his neck cut down to a shadow of stubble.

He glanced up briefly as Tatyana was brought in.

'Take her downstairs.'

In her white nightdress Tatyana looked small and defenceless. Her two captors held her high, so that her elbows were level with her head, bare feet scarcely touching the ground. She didn't try to struggle as they led her over to the broken door.

With her arms outstretched Katya dived between them, trying to prise Tatyana free. The officer took her by the scruff of the neck and pushed her firmly back into the bedroom.

'This doesn't concern you, comrade.'

He had been going through the kitchen drawers, removing every scrap of paper work and stacking it on the table.

'You can't just break in like this.'

'Don't try and stop them,' Tatyana called out, looking round over her shoulder as they pulled her out into the passage. 'It won't make any difference.'

Darting across the room Katya grasped one of the men by the arm, throwing her weight into his body.

He turned and hit her.

The palm of his hand came out in a quick jabbing blow that struck her on the forehead. It was hard and accurate. Katya was knocked backwards, her legs still running. The edge of the table caught her and she collapsed on the ground, banging her head against the wall.

Light splashed before her eyes, the room swam. She heard herself gasping for air. It was shock as much as pain. No one had ever hit her before. She had been put across her father's knee often enough as a child but never struck in the face like that. Shakily she picked herself up off the ground.

Tatyana had been taken away, only the officer remained.

'Go back to bed, comrade,' he ordered pleasantly, stacking the papers into his briefcase in the meantime. 'This does not concern you.'

'How can you say that?'

'Any interference on your part will be taken as an act of hostility.' He could have been reciting from the manual.

Katya rubbed the bruise on her head. In the harsh light of the overhead bulb the living room looked stark and unfriendly, an alien place rather than her home. The door stood open, the lock hanging loose. The wood of the frame was shattered into sharp needles.

'Look what you've done to our door,' Katya said, her mind grasping at irrelevant details.

'Report it to the janitor in the morning.' The feminine outrage drew a brief smile from the officer. He had small piggy eyes, she noticed, like a boxer who has taken too many punches to the face.

Going through into the bedroom he began working his way through the drawers. Katya watched him inspect her clothing, his fingers rippling between the layers of neatly folded shirts and jumpers, then moving up to the next drawer and searching through her underclothes. She felt a fresh rush of indignation.

'What do you want?' she demanded.

'It's just routine.'

'Then why has she been taken away?'

'She has not been charged, comrade.' He turned his attention to the bedside table. 'Simply detained.'

'You can't take those,' Katya cried as he took out a sheaf of notes and added them to those in his briefcase. 'That's part of my work. I'll need it tomorrow.'

His expression told her that he could do exactly as he liked. 'They'll be returned to you, comrade.'

'When?'

'After they have been examined.' He shut the clasps of the case and went out. Katya followed him down the passage.

'Where have you taken her?'

'You'll be told in due time.'

'I must know now.' Dimly she was aware of faces peering out at her from opened doors on either side. 'It's cold outside,' she said on impulse. 'I must take her some clothes.'

'They'll be provided.' The officer continued to speak with the steady tone of officialdom. 'You don't need to worry yourself.'

His footsteps were loud on the bare boards. The time-switch cut off and the lights went out with a soft plop. He put them on again with a bump of his fist. At once the elongated shadows of the wrought-iron banisters leapt back on the wall.

'But how will I know where to find her?' Katya scuttled after him, clinging to this last thread of contact.

'You may ask at your place of work tomorrow.'

'Why can't I know now?'

'Stay here, comrade.' He held out his hand to stop her. 'Don't try to follow, it's best not to be involved in these things.'

106

Katya watched him clatter on downstairs and heard the door to the street swing shut on its spring. She turned and began to walk upstairs.

Gradually she realised that she was not alone. Glancing up she saw her neighbours standing on the landing. They were still in their nightclothes and leaned over the banisters, gaping down at her with wary, suspicious expressions.

'What are you staring at?' she cried.

She turned around. There were more on the floor above, the grave faces watching her in silence.

'Have you nothing better to do than stand out here all night?' Katya screamed in sudden fury. 'Go back to bed!'

They made no movement. Walking on upstairs she brushed her way between them. At once they parted to let her through, drawing back from her as though she had the plague.

'I'm not sure whether he's come in yet.'

'Could you check please, it's very important.'

The secretary withdrew, leaving Katya waiting in the small hallway. A gas fire hissed in the corner, its flame bobbing in the draught. She drew her coat around her and looked at the utilitarian furniture, the dreary framed reproductions of official paintings.

She had been awake ever since Tatyana was arrested. For over an hour she had lain on her bed, trying to compose her thoughts, to plan some sort of strategy. But it was hopeless and eventually she had dressed and gone outside. Somewhere near the river she had met a group of street cleaners, large matronly women in rubber overalls who offered her a cup of sweet tea from a Thermos. Katya had explained how she came to be wandering the streets at this hour of the morning, grateful to have someone to talk to, and they had clucked and nodded their sympathy before moving on, leaving her to sit and watch the hard winter dawn come up over the Moskva.

The secretary returned. 'Comrade Rokotov will see you in a minute.' She spoke in the brisk, cheerful voice that people assume when they've first arrived in the morning. She looked Katya over with interest before adding: 'Don't you work upstairs?'

'That's right.'

'What's it like?'

Katya gave her the ghost of a smile. 'No different than it is here, I imagine.'

'But you get to meet all those interesting people.'

'We hardly meet them.'

'I tried to get posted up there but my typing wasn't good enough.' She didn't seem distraught by the loss. Poking her head back through the door she announced, 'Ah good, Comrade Rokotov will see you now.'

Katya went through into an office of varnished wood that gleamed in the morning light. From his portrait on the wall Lenin's face smiled down at her. Comrade Rokotov's didn't.

'You wish to see me,' he said. 'Why is that?'

'It is about Tatyana Vasnikova.'

Rokotov studied her with hooded eyes. He was a lean figure with dry skin and a large head, balding on top as though the cranium had burst through its covering of hair.

Picking up an elastic band Rokotov stretched it on his fingertips before asking, 'What do you want to know about her?'

Katya was not sure how much he already knew and replied cautiously.

'She hasn't come in to work this morning.'

Rokotov hitched his face into the semblance of a smile. 'That's because she was arrested last night, Comrade Leskova, as you very well know.'

'For what reason?'

'I believe it was for working against the interests of the State.'

'Working against the interests of the State?' Katya repeated the formula of words. 'What does that mean?'

'That I can't tell you.' His mouth hung open after he spoke as though he had trouble breathing.

'But you must have some idea.'

'I am head of the Finance Department, not a parole officer.'

The elastic band creaked and whined as Rokotov stretched it into new shapes. The mannerism infuriated her. She would have liked to smack his hand but instead she asked, 'Where has she been taken?'

'I have no idea.'

'Last night the officer in charge said I could discover where she was from her place of work.'

'Ah, well that would explain why I haven't been informed.' Rokotov found some gleam of satisfaction in the reply. 'Comrade Vasnikova doesn't work here.'

'What do you mean?' Katya spoke quickly. She was only just grasping the implication of what he had said. 'Tatyana has worked here for the last five years.'

'Until last night.'

Katya registered the details of Rokotov's face with extreme clarity at that moment. The open pores on his nose, the tiny split veins in his cheeks, the slight bulge of flesh over his collar. The elastic band stretched out wide and the taut sound as it rippled down his fingers broke the silence.

'She hasn't even been charged yet,' Katya said.

Rokotov offered her another of his smiles. 'Comrade Vasnikova's association with dissidents has been noted for some time. In the circumstances the ministry feels it cannot allow her to continue in her present position.'

'Just like that?' Katya could feel the tears beginning to sting her eyes. 'You'll sack her without a second thought? You haven't even spoken to her yet. It may be a mistake for all you know.'

'I hardly think that is the case.'

'You can't just wash your hands of it.'

'Take care of what you say, comrade,' Rokotov warned but Katya ignored him.

'You don't care, do you? You aren't worried where she has been taken or what will become of her. If she doesn't fit in with your scheme you just throw her aside and forget her.'

'That is enough.'

'What's the matter with you all? Don't you have feelings here?'

Rokotov snapped his hand shut. The elastic band flicked writhing in a knot on the table like a dark maggot and he aimed one finger at her.

'It is not for you to criticise the decisions of the ministry, young lady. If you value your own position here I suggest you guard your tongue.'

Katya left his office and stormed upstairs. She found Dinara chewing a toffee over her typewriter.

'Where have you been?' she asked through sticky teeth. 'Podurets has been looking for you all morning. He's in a real bait.'

'Too bad.'

'It's not too bad, Comrade Leskova.' Podurets stood in the door of his office, jacket off and cardigan tightly buttoned, the unbending expression of the self-righteous on his face. 'You were due in an hour ago.'

'I've been in the ministry since eight this morning,' Katya replied going round behind her desk without taking off her coat. 'I was down in the Finance Department.'

'On business?' Podurets utterd the sacred word.

'No, I was thinking of taking my holiday down there.' She picked up the phone. 'And this is business too, so you can listen if you want.'

'I hope for your sake that you are telling the truth.'

Holding the receiver in the crook of her neck Katya scratched in her handbag, drew out the little card and dialled the number it carried. The rapid tapping of the relays drummed in her ear and a receptionist came on the line.

'I wish to speak to Colonel Krasin.' Out of the side of her eye she could see Podurets taking in the name.

'Who's calling?'

'Katya Leskova – from the Ministry of Culture.'

'Just a moment please.' She put through the connection, a distant phone warbled and Krasin's voice came on the line.

'Katya.' He sounded surprised.

'I must see you.' With a swish of hair she turned away from Podurets, putting one finger into her ear to block out the sound of the office. 'It's urgent.'

'Certainly, why don't we have dinner one evening?'

'No, I must see you now – it can't wait.'

Krasin poured brandy into a glass and took it over to where she was sitting.

'Here, drink this.'

Katya hesitated before obeying. She looked exhausted. Her eyes were dark in her face, the thick mane of hair tangled across her shoulders. The spirit seemed to do her good. She gave a little cough at the initial shock of it and a flush of colour returned to her cheeks.

'Now let's start again from the beginning.' Krasin perched himself on the edge of his desk. 'When did this happen?'

'Early this morning. I don't know the exact time but it was still dark.'

'How many came?'

'Three of them.' She cradled the glass in her hands as though it were warm. 'They said that I could learn where Tatyana's being held if I went to the ministry in the morning. But they're not interested. They've sacked her.' She looked up at him wildly. 'That's not right, is it?'

He didn't reply to the question. Katya evidently believed in a god of fair play, a higher authority who could be appealed to for justice.

'Tasha's very good at her job,' she insisted.

'I'm sure.'

'And everyone likes her.'

And Rokotov was a sly old fox who wouldn't miss his chance to rid himself of a potential trouble-maker, Krasin thought to himself. He didn't want to hurt her with this observation however.

'Did they take anything away with them?' he inquired.

'Just papers.'

'Anything in particular?'

'No, everything – even my notes from work.' She wanted Krasin to appreciate the irrationality of it. 'They just went through the drawers and cupboards, stacking it all in a briefcase and then went away.'

Krasin pressed his point. 'Do you have any idea what it was they were looking for?'

A shadow passed across the girl's face. She could guess what they had been looking for, he could see it, but she wasn't telling.

'I think it was just routine.'

'Possibly.'

'I expect they always do that.' She sounded hopeful. 'Can you find out what's happened to her, Vassily?'

'I can try for you. No one can be held in jail for more than seventy-two hours without authorisation from the Moscow Procuracy. They may be able to tell me where she is.' Krasin stood up and walked her to the door. 'In the meantime I want you to go back home and wait for me to call. Chibatar will drive you.'

'I can't do that. I'm supposed to be at the ministry.'

'I'll talk to them.' His hand rested on her shoulder as he spoke. 'I'll tell them that your grandmother died unexpectedly, you've had to go to her funeral.'

For a moment she looked at him, uncomprehending, and then a smile flittered across her lips.

'That's better,' he said.

She spoke softly, urgently. 'I'm sure there's been some mistake, Vassily.'

'Let's hope so.' He kissed her goodbye. 'I'll make a few inquiries and call you when I have something.'

After she had gone Krasin walked down the short length of passage that led to his office. He pictured the arrest, the shock of it, the brutality, the dreadful feeling of helplessness.

He knew it only too well. His father had been arrested in the night. Even now he could remember the faces of the men who'd come for him, the smell of their bodies, the grunts of exertion as they'd dragged him from the single room they'd lived in.

Zakov was in his shirt-sleeves. He kicked his feet from the chair and stood up as Krasin came in.

'Did you learn anything from her, Colonel?'

'Only that she is scared out of her wits.'

Zakov rasped a hand across his chin. There was a cut on his cheek, Krasin noticed.

'What did you do to your face?'

He touched it, glanced at his fingertips to see if it was still bleeding and pulled a face.

111

'Women have sharp fingernails.'

'You should pick on someone your own size,' Krasin told him drily. He held out his hand.

'Let's see what you've got.'

Zakov took a box-file from the drawer, flicked open the lid and lifted out a thick pile of papers.

'I've sorted them roughly into subjects.'

Much of it was inconsequential: receipts, shopping lists, invitations. There were some letters held together by a clip.

He asked, 'Are those any use?'

'They're mostly from her parents, a couple from some boy in Tbilisi.' Zakov found no pleasure in rifling through other people's possessions. 'It sounds as if she broke something off when she moved here.'

Krasin nodded thoughtfully as he looked through the pages of scrawled handwriting.

'This is what you were looking for.' Zakov handed him a few sheets of pencilled notes.

Krasin glanced through them.

'I'll keep these.'

He went back to his office, pausing briefly in the doorway to say, 'She'll be coming back here later this morning. I suggest you make yourself scarce for the time being.'

It was half past twelve when she returned to Krasin's office in Dzerzhinsky Square. She had changed into a navy blue suit with broad white lapels, neatly tailored at the waist to make the most of her slender figure. Her hair was sleek and polished once more.

Krasin was astonished by the transformation. 'I can hardly believe it's the same person,' he said coming over to greet her. 'Did you manage to get some sleep?'

'Just an hour.'

'I'm so glad, you looked washed out this morning.'

She had taken a leisurely bath, glad to have it to herself for once, tidied the apartment and persuaded Grigor to leave the comfort of his basement stove to mend the lock on her door. Being busy had made her feel lighter, more optimistic. Only the quickness of her question now betrayed her anxiety.

'Have you found out anything?'

'Your friend has been detained at the militia jail in Ruzejnyi Street.' Krasin sat down behind his desk and crossed his legs, pinching the crease straight with his thumb and forefinger. 'There has been an application for extended arrest but it hasn't as yet been approved. That gives us a little time.'

'Can I see her?'

'I think that could be arranged. I've spoken with the officer conducting the case. He seems to be accommodating.'

'Will she be charged?'

'I can't tell you, to be honest. It's a police matter, although they'll have to leave the final decision to the Komsomol office.'

Katya stood by the window. It was one of those still grey days which deaden the sound of the city. Beneath her she could see cars and trolley buses fighting for position like some silent dance.

Krasin reached across his desk, drew a file towards him and flicked it open.

'In the meantime there is one problem.' He had the embarrassed manner of a man who can see both sides to an argument. 'During the search these were discovered in your apartment.'

He showed Katya the sheaf of handwritten pages. They were Yuri's poems, she recognised them immediately.

'Do you know what these are?'

She nodded. 'They were written by a friend of ours.'

'Yuri Stephanovich.' Krasin supplied the name. 'Apparently they were in amongst your notes, Katya. It seems you were transcribing them from cyrillic into European lettering.' He was not angry. If anything he was saddened by the discovery. 'I can only assume that you were intending to take these with you to England next month.'

In the street below two cars had collided. Katya watched the drivers jump out in the road to confront each other, arms waving frantically. The rear light of the front car was broken and tiny fragments of orange plastic were scattered over the road.

She said, 'I was taking them to a publisher in London.'

'You know that is illegal.'

'I was sorry for him.' She told him the truth. There was no reason not to. 'He had been banned from having his work printed in Russia. It didn't seem fair.'

'Ah yes, fairness.' Krasin studied her thoughtfully. 'That's important to you, isn't it?'

'Is it not to you, Vassily?'

He let it pass. 'You realise that this makes you an accessory?'

'No crime has been committed yet, has it?'

'Unfortunately that's not the way the militia will see it. Tatyana and her friends have been smuggling samizdat over the border for some time.'

The two cars had been pushed to the side of the street. Grey-uniformed policemen were taking down the registration numbers.

Katya had guessed Tatyana was involved in something of the sort but she wasn't interested in the past, only the immediate present.

'Can you get her out of jail, Vassily?'

'I don't see how I can. Unfortunately I have no authority in the situation.' Getting to his feet he came over to her. There was a strength to him that she found helpful, comforting at that moment.

'But those papers weren't hers. They were given to me. I was the one working on them, you said so yourself.'

'That makes no difference,' he said gently. 'The case is being handled by the militia. I could only intervene if you had been working under my orders.'

'Is that true?'

'We both keep to our own side of the fence.'

'But don't you see, Vassily?' She was suddenly radiant with confidence again. 'I could be working for you.'

Chapter Fourteen

As Katya was leaving the Lubyanka with Vassily Krasin, Pip Spencer pushed open the glass door of the Trenchard-Arnold Gallery.

There were only a few paintings exhibited on the walls, large abstracts with no frames. They were pale and impersonal, over-bearing in scale, savage in technique. The paint had been flicked and splattered on to the surface, dribbling and running down the canvas in oily rivulets. Graffiti had been scrawled into the wet colour, crude sentiments that seemed only to reflect a brutal and loveless world.

Pip could see no reason why anyone should want to own such things and as he looked at them he found himself thinking back to the spiral stairwell at Holland Park tube, to the dirty, pitted walls and the cold wind that came howling down after the departing trains.

Sitting behind the desk at the far end of the gallery was a young man in a double-breasted suit, legs crossed, one elegantly cut shoe dangling from his foot. He was tapping a gold pen against his teeth as he amused the secretary beside him with his conversation. Pip made his presence known.

'Are you the manager here?'

'At present.' His reply was dry, the question evidently an imper-tinence.

'I'm trying to trace the background of a painting.'

'Do you have it with you?'

'Only in reproduction.'

Pip showed him the photograph from the catalogue. At the sight of the marble white nudes and the cold sea breaking about them, the young man's eyebrows arched in disdain.

'And what has this to do with us?'

'You sold it.'

'I very much doubt that.' He managed to take the suggestion as some sort of insult to his good taste. 'It's hardly our cup of tea.'

'According to Phillips you sold this painting about three years ago.'

'Then it must be true.' The young man accepted the evidence with an air of weary resignation and offered the secretary a scrap of advice. 'One should never argue with an auction house – it's bad for business.'

'Unless they've made a mistake.'

'I don't follow you.'

Pip held the smile in his eyes. 'The provenance to this painting has been forged.'

There was a moment's silence in which the young man uncrossed his legs and sat back studying Pip with rather more attention. He understood exactly what he was implying. Pip pressed home his advantage.

'I was wondering if you could confirm whether you did own it at any time and if so who you bought it from.'

Again there was a pause while the other viewed him with a lazy hostility.

'You'd have to ask the director.'

'Director?'

'Adrian Trenchard, he handles the sales here – particularly when it comes to that sort of painting.'

'And is he here?'

'Not at present.' There was a slight tear in the young man's silky exterior now. 'He's attending an auction at Sotheby's.'

'When is he likely to be back?'

He gave a shrug as though the answer to this was obvious. 'Certainly not today, it's Friday, but he'll be in next week. If you leave your name and phone number I'll pass it on.'

'Unfortunately that's too late.' Pip recognised the polite brush-off when he saw it and took the offensive. 'But don't worry, I'll go up to Sotheby's and have a word with him there.' The idea seemed to appal the assistant; he looked at Pip aghast.

'You can't do that.'

'Whyever not?'

'He couldn't speak to you during an auction.' He was blustering now. 'It's a formal occasion. There's a protocol to be observed.'

Pip allowed his voice to carry the slightest hint of a threat as he turned to leave the gallery. 'I'm sure he'll find the time to speak to me – once he knows what it is I want.'

'Could you tell me where the auction is being held?'

'Which one would you be wanting, sir?'

The doorman stood in the arched entrance to Sotheby's dressed in a vivid green coat and top-hat that clashed with his pink face. His hands were clasped behind his back and he was rolling comfortably on the balls of his feet.

Pip paused to consider the question. It hadn't occurred to him that there might be more than one auction at any one time.

'How many are there?'

'Two on at present, sir. There's modern paintings and Japanese ceramics going down today.'

'Modern paintings, where would I find that?'

'Main gallery, sir. Up the stairs, straight ahead of you. You can't miss it.' He consulted his watch, calm and unhurried in his movements. 'It started over an hour ago, it'll be almost over by now.'

'I may be able to pick up a bargain at the end.' Pip made the remark lightly in passing but the doorman took it at face value.

'You might have done that, sir – if you'd come here fifty years ago.'

'I see' – Pip caught the irony in his voice – 'then I'm later than I thought.'

Upstairs the auction was in progress, the room hushed. Pip found a space at the back and sat down. There must have been over a hundred people in there, some filling the rows of chairs, others standing along the walls. He could feel their concentration around him like a field of static electricity.

'Four hundred and fifty thousand guineas.' The auctioneer's voice was low, almost lazy. The figure he quoted was of supreme indifference to him. His eyes skimmed the crowd, searching for the flicker of movement that registered a further bid. 'Do I have four hundred and fifty?'

The bid was offered. The auctioneer accepted it without emotion, smoothly increasing the going rate.

'Four hundred and sixty thousand guineas?' His attention moved back to the previous contender. 'It's against you, sir.'

Beneath the rostrum stood a porter, holding the painting on a green baize table. It was too far away for Pip to see clearly but it appeared to be a small cityscape, a white church and bony trees.

He turned to his neighbour, ignoring the protocol of the occasion and asked, 'What's that painting?'

'Lot number ninety-four.' The reply was hissed back in an undertone. 'The Utrillo of the Tour St Jacques.'

'The bid is four hundred and seventy-five thousand guineas,' the auctioneer informed the room.

Utrillos didn't come cheap, Pip reflected.

'Do I hear more?' The auctioneer's eyebrows were raised. There was a moment's silence, the last chance for a change of heart. And then the hammer fell, striking the rostrum with the sharp click of two billiard balls connecting.

'Sold to the Drayton Gallery.'

Pip watched as the painting was withdrawn and replaced by

117

another. There was something mesmerizing about the process: the quiet, unassuming voice of the auctioneer, the faint movement in the crowd that indicated a bid, the atmosphere of repressed excitement that only rippled to the surface after the hammer had come down.

Posted on either side of the room was a member of Sotheby's staff. Their job, he noticed, was to take the name of any buyer whom the auctioneer didn't recognise by sight.

Pip waited until there was a lull between lots before getting to his feet and approaching one of them.

'I'm looking for Adrian Trenchard. I believe he's here.'

The man's attention didn't stray from the auctioneer's desk. 'Over there. Far side of the room.' He had the audience visualised. 'Fair hair and glasses, reading his catalogue at present.'

Pip thanked him and slipped back into his seat. He moved to one side, adjusting his position until he had a clear view of Adrian Trenchard.

He was a lean man, touching fifty, dressed in a linen suit and bow tie. There was a brittle flamboyance to him, Pip observed. As the bidding continued he moved restlessly, tossing back his hair, toying with a pen, occasionally leaning forward to speak to the others around him.

The sale drew to a close. The auctioneer stepped down and the audience relaxed, talking freely amongst themselves, some of them getting to their feet and beginning to leave.

Adrian Trenchard stayed where he was.

Standing up Pip moved forward, taking the seat beside him. He introduced himself with a casual remark.

'Any luck today?'

Trenchard evaded the question. 'I wasn't bidding.'

'Just studying form?'

'One has to keep abreast of the market.' Adrian Trenchard didn't look up as he replied, his attention elsewhere. Pip dispensed with the pleasantries and pressed forward.

'I was hoping to find you here.'

'Really? And why was that?'

'About three years ago you sold a painting by Albert Lecoque.'

Trenchard continued to make annotations in his catalogue, an activity which demanded his full concentration. Pip prompted his memory.

'It was a painting of four nudes on a beach.'

Leaning back, Adrian Trenchard dropped his hands to his lap, directing his gaze on to Pip. Behind the spectacles, his eyes were of rinsed grey, red-rimmed as though he was suffering from hay fever.

'I'm sorry,' he said, 'do I know you?'

'Spencer – Phillip Spencer. I'm a solicitor.'

'Are you, Mr Spencer.' His head gave a slight quiver as he collected his thoughts. 'Yes, I sold a Lecoque, but I can't see why that is any business of yours.'

'I heard that it used to be in Russia.'

'Is that so?'

'It's not quite clear how it turned up here in England.'

Again the slight quiver of the head, the indignation of a man whose privacy has been violated. 'I can't see how that is any concern of mine.'

'I was wondering whether you could tell me where you bought it?'

'Really, Mr Spencer, you sound as though you are putting me on trial.' His voice was soft as he spoke, the eyes unblinking. Pip smiled pleasantly as he denied the allegation.

'Simply a process of elimination.'

'I see.' Trenchard gazed across the room, summoning the past to mind out of courtesy. 'As far as I recall I acquired the Lecoque from a private collection.'

'You remember it?'

'Vaguely.'

'Who was the owner?'

'I'm certain you know that already, Mr Spencer.' He was calling his bluff but Pip pursued the point.

'I'd rather you told me.'

'I bought the painting you refer to from an American collector.' Trenchard relieved himself of the burden of giving further, more mundane details. 'I imagine my secretary could give you his name and address should you wish to check.'

'It seems a strange thing for you to be buying.'

'Why do you say that?'

Pip nodded towards the rostrum from where the auction of modern art had recently been conducted.

'Victorian pornography – hardly your style, is it?'

The observation revealed Pip's ignorance of such matters and caused Adrian Trenchard some slight amusement.

'I have a living to make.' The disclosure was made in confidence and accompanied by another small tremble of his head. 'One has to earn a crust, like anyone else.'

Pip said, 'I see.'

There was nothing more to learn from this man. He would have to move on, check out the American collector.

Trenchard asked, 'Does that answer your questions, Mr Spencer?'

'For the time being,' Pip replied, getting to his feet. 'I won't take up any more of your time, Mr Trenchard. But I'd be glad of the name of that collector.'

Adrian Trenchard made no attempt to move. 'He won't be able to see you.'

'Why's that?'

Trenchard's smile carried a trace of triumph. 'Because he died three years ago.'

Chapter Fifteen

Tatyana was sitting cross-legged on the bed. She was still in her nightdress but over it she wore a loose robe made of some coarse material. A blanket was wrapped around her shoulders to keep out the chill of the cell.

Through the bars she looked like a caged bird.

'I'll need you to sign the release papers,' the warden announced, jangling a bunch of keys.

Katya nodded as she waited in the ill-lit corridor. There was a sour smell of unwashed bodies in the air. Pallid faces stared at her from the cells on either side, arms protruded through, clinging on to the bars as they watched her.

'Are you coming to get us all out, darling?' one of them called. The question was greeted with cackles of laughter that echoed around the bare space.

'Who's your fancy friend then?' another shouted to Tatyana.

'Keep it down!' The cigarette waggled in the warden's lips as she barked out the order. 'They never learn,' she grumbled to Katya as she turned the key in the lock. 'We get the same lot in here every bloody night, regular as clockwork.'

She clanked back the bolt and the cell door swung open.

Tatyana didn't move as Katya came in but grinned with pleasure, showing the two gold teeth at the back of her mouth. Katya sat down on the bed beside her and they hugged each other tightly.

'Are you all right?'

Tatyana nodded. 'Never better.'

'We've been so worried about you.'

Tatyana smiled faintly. The twelve hours she'd sat in isolation had given her time to think. 'They found Yuri's poems, I suppose?'

'Yes, they found them.'

Tatyana looked at her steadily. 'How did they know they were there?'

'It was just chance. I don't think they were looking for them particularly.'

'It wasn't chance.' She spoke softly but firmly. 'They knew they were there. That's why they came.'

Through the wall they could hear the voices of the other women shrieking at each other; one was banging on the bars with a metal mug. Tatyana jumped down off the bed. 'Come on, let's get out of this place. It stinks like an armpit.'

'I've brought you some clothes.' Katya pulled out the brown paper parcel that she had been carrying under her arm. At once the warden's voice interrupted them.

'You can change in the washroom later.' She stood in the entrance, legs straddled, uniform straining under the pressure of her enormous bosom. 'I want the sheet straightened, blankets folded on the end of the bed before you leave here.'

They signed the release papers and watched as they were rubber-stamped. The warden put on pink glasses as she filled in the forms.

'Did you have any personal possessions with you when you came?'

'None.'

'Then I'll need you to sign for that.' She pulled out a fresh set of papers and began writing importantly.

'Jesus, what a business,' Tatyana said as they came out into the street. She stretched out her arms and breathed in the city air. 'Have we got anything to eat back home? I'm starving.'

'Didn't they give you something?'

'Nothing edible.'

They caught the bus. It was almost empty and they sat together on the slatted wooden seat.

'How did you get me out?'

'It wasn't difficult.' Katya didn't want to explain the events of the day. 'They haven't pressed charges against you.'

'It must have taken blat,' she said suspiciously. 'No one is let out of jail just like that. I wasn't even questioned.'

'That's not important now.'

The bus drew to a halt, the doors hissing open to let in more passengers. Tatyana moved her legs to allow a woman to sit down opposite. Her voice was almost a whisper.

'Was it Vassily Krasin?'

Katya was searching through her handbag for a handkerchief. Tatyana wanted an answer.

'It was, wasn't it?'

'We'd never have got you out without him,' Katya replied quickly, twisting round on the hard seat. She wanted Tatyana to appreciate the debt she owed him. 'He's been wonderful, Tasha. If it wasn't for him you'd still be locked up in there. He found out where you'd been taken, arranged for you to be released – everything.'

Tatyana hissed under her breath. 'But why on earth did you go to him in the first place?'

'I had to. No one in the ministry would tell me what had happened to you. They didn't even seem interested.'

'Is that true?' The evening light gilded the dust on the window pane, framing Tatyana's black hair like a halo.

'Are you cross with me?' Katya asked.

'No . . . No, of course not,' she said gently. 'I'm sorry, Katska, I didn't mean to get you caught up in this.'

When they arrived back Katya inspected the fridge, took out eggs and a side of bacon wrapped in grease-proof paper. She warmed a pan on the stove and broke the eggs into it while Tatyana roamed about the apartment, looking at the new lock on the door, the neatly tidied bedroom.

'Would you like some bacon?' Katya asked through the opened door. 'It's good, I bought it in the market yesterday.'

Tatyana came and sat at the table.

'What have you agreed to do for Vassily in return?' she asked.

Katya concentrated on the bacon joint, paring off two thick slices and adding them to the pan where they clucked and wrinkled in the hot oil. Slipping the eggs on to a plate she arranged the bacon on either side and took it over to the table.

'What makes you think he wanted anything?' she said lightly.

'He didn't arrange this charade for nothing, kovshka.' Tatyana was eating hungrily, mopping up the egg with pieces of black bread. She glanced up from the plate. 'Are you going to work for him in the Kremlin?'

'There's nothing wrong with that, is there? I'll just be cataloguing a few paintings.'

'I thought so.'

Katya frowned at the implied reprimand. 'It's not like that, Tasha.'

'Isn't it?' She pushed the empty plate away from her and gave a quick lopsided smile. 'He's got you doing exactly what he wants, hasn't he?'

'It was my idea to work for him.'

'I'm sure he made you think it was your idea.' She leaned forward on the table. 'Men like Vassily Krasin are very good at manipulating, don't you realise that? He set you a problem with only one solution and then sat back and waited for you to find it.'

'He helped to get you out of jail.'

'Only because he had me put there in the first place.'

Katya shook her head, refusing to believe her. 'You're wrong, Tasha. You're just so wrong.'

'She seemed to be agitated.'

'That's hardly surprising in the circumstances.'

The angle-poise lamp on Podurets's desk cast sharp contrasts of light and shade on to Krasin's face, emphasising the lean, handsome features.

He detested this office, just as he detested this flabby, white-skinned bureaucrat who sat opposite him in his badly made suit. Christ, did he never wear anything else? No wonder he stank like a polecat. That mistress he kept tucked away up by the stadium must be long-suffering or short-sighted. Maybe both.

'I appreciate it's none of my business.' Podurets was trolling for more information. 'But would it be permissible to know what had upset her so badly?'

That was the other thing he detested. This fawning, sycophantic manner. Did the man have no pride?

Reaching in the upper pocket of his overcoat Krasin took out a silver flask and unscrewed the cap. 'Do you have a glass?'

Podurets scurried over to a cabinet, searched inside and returned with one. Krasin held it up to the light.

'It is not very clean, I'm afraid, Colonel.'

Krasin flicked out his handkerchief and wiped round the rim before filling it.

Realising that he wasn't going to be offered either a drink or an answer to his question, Podurets tried again.

'I couldn't help overhearing her trying to ring you, Colonel.'

Krasin filled the glass and took a mouthful. Good Scottish whisky, at least that wasn't affected by the surroundings.

'There was a raid on her apartment last night.' He spoke through the after-burn of the spirit. 'Her friend Tatyana Vasnikova was taken off to jail. And not a moment too soon in my opinion.'

Podurets made a murmuring sound that was presumably meant to show his agreement. Krasin drained the glass and rose to leave.

'In the meantime I have approved Katya Leskova's request for a transfer to work in the Kremlin vaults. It seems only sensible in the circumstances.'

'Absolutely, Colonel.' Podurets was struggling to see the sense of it as he held open the door.

'The transfer papers will be coming through shortly. You will handle them yourself.'

'Of course.'

'Maybe now we'll discover what it is she wants so badly.'

As he clumped down the linoleum-covered stairs of the ministry, his hands were dug into the pockets of his overcoat, features set in their accustomed impassive expression but under his breath he hummed to himself with pleasure.

It amused him to manipulate the evil-smelling bureaucrat. It wasn't difficult. Podurets already wanted to believe the worst of Katya Leskova. All he had to do was fan the resentment.

Outside it was cold, the still, sharp air snatching away his breath. Chibatar stood by the car stamping his feet as he waited. Seeing Krasin come out he stopped respectfully. His hands fluttered out a question but Krasin shook his head.

'I'll walk.'

He crossed the Moskvoretskiy Bridge. Above the lights of the city the sky was crusted with stars. Turning up his collar he made his way to a restaurant, one of the new co-operatives that had sprung up around Moscow of late. The service there was better than at the State-run establishments.

The manager greeted him at the door, snapping his fingers at the cloakroom attendant.

'Has my guest arrived?' Krasin inquired.

'About fifteen minutes ago.'

The manager led the way upstairs to a private room. Katya was sitting at the table. She stood as he came in and walked across to him, her eyes smiling in anticipation.

Krasin held out his hands towards her. 'You came.'

'Were you afraid I might not?'

'I wasn't sure – '

In the passage outside a waiter hurried towards them, a tray in his hand on which was balanced a bottle of champagne and two glasses frosted with ice. His orders were to serve it immediately at risk of losing his comfortable job at the restaurant. Giving a soft knock at the door he opened it with his back and went inside.

At the unexpected sight of the two occupants in each other's arms, he decided that he would risk the manager's wrath and putting down the tray he crept back into the passage.

Chapter Sixteen

The sound of the road cleaners woke Krasin.

He swung his legs out of bed and crossing the room still naked he looked down into the street. The lorry was crawling up the kerb with the laborious progress of a beetle, water fanning out from its rear end, the lamp on its cabin flicking orange light into the cold dawn.

Katya was still asleep behind him, her hair tumbled over the pillow. The blankets were pulled back exposing the smooth curve of her back and scattered about the floor were the clothes she'd been wearing the night before: the velvet dress, the black stockings and flimsy scraps of underwear. One high-heeled shoe was standing upright, the other lay on its side some distance away.

The disarray gave Krasin a unique shock of pleasure. To him it was the proof of supremacy, of female capitulation.

Going next door he moved the coffee table to one side. The apartment wasn't his own but one of several the department retained in Moscow to house important visitors.

Twenty minutes of strenuous exercises sharpened his senses and put a sheen of sweat on his body. He wrapped a towel around his waist and ran himself a bath.

He was fully dressed by the time Katya stirred, lifting herself up on her elbows and pushing the hair from her eyes.

'What time is it, Vassily?'

He went across to her. 'Just after seven.'

'I must get up.'

'There's no need, you can stay a while longer if you want.'

'I have to go back home and change.' Her voice was drowsy, eyes still seductive with the recollection of the night before. 'I can't go into work wearing an evening dress, everyone would guess what I've been doing.'

Krasin made tea, measuring the leaves into two tall glasses cradled in metal stands, adding a thick sediment of sugar.

'When am I going to see you again?' he asked as he carried them back into the bedroom. Katya gave him a lazy, contented smile over the rim of the glass as she sipped at her tea. She'd been worried he might not ask.

'When would you like?'

'I'm busy today.' He was adjusting his cufflinks, his voice more businesslike. 'Maybe later this week.'

He left, closing the door quietly behind him and went down to the hallway. Chibatar was leaning against the security desk, reading the morning edition of *Pravda*. He tucked it back into his overcoat pocket as Krasin arrived and greeted him with the usual pattering gesture of his hand.

It slightly disturbed Krasin that Chibatar couldn't speak. He was not one to tolerate any sort of familiarity from the men who served under him but he liked to understand their thoughts and motives. With Chibatar this was impossible. He was loyal, ingenious and completely dependable but remote. His silence made him inscrutable.

'Can you lay your hands on some French perfume?' Krasin asked as they drove through the morning traffic. Around him people were surging up the subways on their way to work.

Chibatar nodded and taking one hand off the wheel he signalled the two syllables of the word Chanel, then flashed five fingers to register the number.

Krasin nodded his approval. 'Have a bottle sent round to Comrade Leskova's apartment. Make it a large one.' The visual language that Chibatar had invented was not easy to read but it had the advantage that only a very few could understand it. 'And be on hand this morning,' he added as he arrived at Dzerzhinsky Square. 'I may need you.'

Krasin waited until ten o'clock before ringing General Alexandrei Chernov. It was always best to give the old man time to arrive, read the flimsies laid out on his desk and drink a glass of tea that he took spiked with the Southern Comfort whiskey that the American Embassy shipped over to him.

An assistant came on the line.

'The general's schedule is rather inconvenient this week, I'm afraid, Colonel. Is this a matter of urgency?'

'Naturally.' Krasin was not to be stalled. 'I would not have asked had it been otherwise.'

'The earliest I can make you an appointment is for next Thursday morning.'

'That will be too late.'

'I can ask the general if he can spare time earlier but I can't promise anything—' At that moment Chernov's voice cut in over the formal excuses of his assistant.

127

'Is that you, Vassily?'

Krasin wasn't surprised by this interruption. Chernov often listened to incoming calls on his desk intercom. He replied politely.

'I was hoping you could spare me an hour of your time in the next day or so, General.'

'Yes I can. We need to talk, Vassily.' Chernov had the high, piping voice that comes only with massive obesity. 'The Sandunov Baths. I'll be there at three this afternoon. We'll talk then, Vassily. We'll talk and we'll sweat.' He gave his girlish laugh as though the remark was a particularly good one.

'I shall look forward to it, General.'

'How did you hear about this girl, Vassily?'

'From the head of her department at the ministry.'

'Is he reliable?'

Krasin pictured Podurets as he'd last seen him, hat clutched in his hands, beads of sweat drilling themselves on his forehead.

'He's a Party member, General. He's been sending in detailed reports for the last twenty years. I see no reason to doubt his suspicions.'

General Chernov stared across the room and gave a grimace of disgust. 'I find this whole business embarrassing, Vassily.'

He was a mountain of a man. The magnificent physique that the Russian people had come to know so well in the years after the war through propaganda pictures in papers and newsreels had completely disintegrated. Over the years muscle had melted down to fat. The huge, bloated figure who now sat perspiring in the steam room of the Sandunov Baths bore no resemblance to the blond-haired boy of sixteen who had taken on the Panzers at Stalingrad – with the possible exception of the eyes. They were bright and watchful and set in his flat face like twin jewels.

Head of the Second Chief Directorate, the department for internal security in the KGB, a hard drinker, an incorrigible womaniser, Chernov was revered and feared in equal measure by his army of aides, advisers and assistants as well as by the departmental secretaries whom it pleased him to give a tuppenny upright against the wall of the office if they took his fancy.

He now vented his scorn. 'We have the finest border control of any country in the world. We keep accurate records of our people and yet this slip of a girl makes us all look like idiots.'

'I thought you should be kept informed, General.'

Chernov snapped his fingers at one of the steam-room attendants.

'Veniki,' he ordered stretching himself out on the wooden bench. 'Yes, Vassily. You have done well.'

Taking a bunch of birch twigs, the attendant began to beat Chernov systematically across the back, working down from the shoulders to the buttocks, stimulating the circulation, raising a rash of red weals across the white flesh.

'Good.' Chernov groaned with the pleasure it gave him. 'That's good.' The hot air was filled with the pleasant musk of the woods. He turned his attention back to the girl. 'She should be thinking of parties and dresses, counting the tea leaves to see how many children she will bear, not stealing paintings from the Kremlin.'

The skylights in the ceiling cast a sallow, greenish light on the misted baths. Ionic columns and ornamental tiles dripped with moisture.

Taking a plastic bucket Krasin threw water over the hot coals. At once a wall of scalding steam rose into the air. There were cries of 'Potepleye' – 'a little warmer' – from the other bathers who lay about the pool, their naked bodies just visible in the dense atmosphere.

Chernov had turned his head on the bench and watched as he returned to sit beside him.

'You keep yourself in good shape, Vassily.' It was an observation rather than a compliment. 'But then you've never starved, have you?'

'I spent most of my childhood trying not to.'

'As every man should.' Chernov brushed away the attendant and sat upright, his belly folding over his groin, obscuring the darkened area of his genitals. Krasin looked away in disgust and instinctively he found himself thinking of the wonderful, supple body he had slept with the night before.

'I hear she's pretty.' Chernov had somehow tracked his thoughts. 'Would that be a fair description, Vassily?'

'She's a very handsome girl.'

'And quite a tigress. Major Zakov tells me that she scratched him on the cheek when they arrested her friend.'

Krasin didn't want to discuss his relationship with Katya. 'She's Georgian,' he replied with a shrug. 'They tend to be hot-blooded.'

Chernov's hard blue eyes were on him. 'It's not always wise to be on intimate terms with these people.'

'I told myself the same, General. But this one responds better on a personal level. I've found she is more inclined to confide than to confess.'

'You may be right.' Chernov's shoulders suddenly shook and he gave his high, asthmatic laugh. 'More information is extracted in the bedroom than the torture chamber. Did you know that? It's human nature for you.'

129

Thrusting down on the bench with the palms of his hands he heaved himself to his feet and lumbered out of the room, steam billowing in his wake.

They performed the ritual of plunging into a pool of cold water, emerging with their skin raw and tingling, before moving through to the changing rooms. A plate of zakuski was brought to them with a bottle of vodka sheathed in ice.

Chernov filled the glasses, downed his in one and let out his breath in a rush.

'You realise she's going to defect?'

'I'm assuming that is so.'

'She's accumulated money.' Chernov drank more vodka. 'She'll be wanting to spend it. And that obviously can't be done while she's living here in Russia.'

Krasin stared at his glass which had clouded with condensation. 'She is travelling to London with a delegation from the Cultural Institute next month. She'll be under constant surveillance.'

Chernov nodded as he chewed at a roll of pickled herring with his mouth open. He thrust the plate towards Krasin but he shook his head.

'It's good for you,' Chernov told him. 'Replaces the lost salt, opens the pores of the skin, lets it breathe.'

And makes your breath stink worse than a trash can, Krasin added to himself.

Chernov shrugged at his refusal and picking up another roll of fish he crammed it in his mouth and ate eagerly.

'So you watch her. What then?'

'She is just a courier.' Krasin was beginning to dress. 'That much I'm sure of. It's her contacts in London that I want to discover.'

'Do you have any lead on them?'

'She's been in touch with an English solicitor. Last time she was over there she spent some time with him, returned to her hotel so late she disrupted the delegation schedule.'

Further down the bench two men were playing chess, the board perched on bare knees, their heads so close together they were practically touching. Chernov was studying him closely.

'I don't understand why she is doing this,' he said suddenly. 'Is it the money? Does she sell her heritage so she can buy herself a pair of American jeans? What is it she wants, Vassily?' His face remained open, vacant, as he asked these questions as though he was baffled. Krasin felt a stab of impatience at the affected stupidity.

'I imagine she wants freedom.' He supplied the answer quicker than he intended and felt Chernov stiffen.

'That's a dangerous attitude, Vassily.'

'But true – '

'It's human nature. There's nothing new in that.'

Krasin knotted his tie. He could feel the fine material of his shirt clinging to his back in the fetid atmosphere.

'To the people in the West, freedom is a state of mind.' He spoke factually, regaining control of himself. 'It is an escape from stress, an escape from the pressures of work. Here in Russia, freedom is living in another country. Freedom is just a short dash across a border, a jump over an electric fence. It's much closer.'

'A fantasy just the same.'

'That's what makes it so desirable.'

There was a dull ring as Chernov spat into the brass spittoon.

'I didn't know you were a philosopher, Vassily.' He stood up, a ludicrous sight in voluminous underpants, his vast belly balanced on two thin white legs. 'I knew you were ambitious. I knew you were stubborn. But I didn't know you were a philosopher.'

He spoke slowly, each word phrased carefully, and for a moment he stared at Krasin with small, cruel eyes. Then it passed and the mask of his smile was in place once more.

'But that's why it is good to come here.' He clasped Krasin by the shoulder. 'There are no uniforms in the baths, no ranks. It is true Soviet life, a place for men to meet and speak their minds.'

Chernov tugged on his trousers, pulled a shirt over his head and latched the braces into place.

'And we are lucky to have you,' he observed, 'you are the right man for this job. I've said that all along.'

'You have been most generous, General.'

Chernov was fumbling with his fly-buttons, doing them up with tiny pointed fingers. 'We must talk again,' he said, 'once this small matter is over. It is a long time since we discussed your future in the department, Vassily – far too long. I like to see good work rewarded.'

Silently the Rolls glided through the traffic. Krasin sat back in the leather seat staring out of the window. It was raining again; thick drops of water crawled across the glass pane, bifurcating and joining, blurring the image of the passing streets.

The meeting with Chernov had been unsatisfactory. He had said what he had come to say but he found it impossible to respect the old man. Chernov was one of the Old Guard, a war hero, a protégé of Stalin. He was still in touch with the ideals of the revolution. He thought of Russia as the Mother Country – a tough old matriarch who loved her children, looked after them and occasionally had to scold

131

them for their own good. To Krasin it was sentimental rubbish.

In Trubnaja Square a queue had formed outside a shop. He studied the resigned, patient faces as he drove past and then looked away. They were like cattle, these children of Mother Russia, standing out there in the rain in their shabby coats and rubber-soled shoes. Most of them wouldn't even know what they were queuing for. They joined on as quickly as possible, so as not to be last, and worried about what was for sale when they reached the other end.

Nothing ever changed, that was the bald reality of it. Russia was a nation of peasants ruled by an élite class. It always had been, it always would be. Anyone who thought otherwise was a dreamer.

The heating in the car was drying the atmosphere. He opened the window slightly to let in some fresh air and then slumped back in the seat, feeling the rain speckling against his face.

His father had been a dreamer. He'd believed in a Workers' State in which all men were equal. 'We'll work where we like and when we like,' he had told them proudly. 'And they'll pay us enough to eat meat-sausage every day of the week.'

Put like that it had seemed a great and beautiful idea.

As a child Krasin had been allowed to sit at the back of the impromptu meetings. They were never held in the same place twice. One time it would be in the basement of a shop, the next at the back of the works canteen, or in the boiler rooms below. The word was just passed about the shop floor.

Krasin could remember the low, excited voices, the urgent expressions on the men's faces, the acrid smell of tobacco smoke in the air, the hiss and splutter of the pressure lamps in the darkened rooms. But most of all he remembered the sense of illicit excitement that had run through the crowd like an electric current.

Krasin thought about his father occasionally but he felt no pain or guilt. He realised now that it was inevitable he should have been arrested. At the trial he had been found guilty of subversive acts against the State and given a life sentence of hard labour. Krasin didn't know where he was taken, or whether he was still alive for that matter, and he didn't particularly care.

That part of his life was dead.

The Rolls turned out of Neglinnaja Street into the broad expanse of Prospeckt Marksa, a policeman whistling them through the red lights. Chibatar glanced at Krasin in the rear mirror, noting how he sat deep in thought. He knew these moods of his. There were times when Krasin seemed to withdraw into himself as though in a trance.

He parked in front of the Hotel Metropole, jumped out and opened the rear door. Krasin stepped out, buttoned his overcoat and turned up the collar.

'Do you have it?'

Chibatar went round to the boot of the car and took out a large cardboard box tied with string.

Despite the shabby carpets, the security desks strewn with sheets of propaganda, the interior of the Metropole retained some of its pre-revolution splendour. Krasin went up to the second floor and brushed through the beaded screen of a small bar.

'You're late,' Ludmilla told him as he sat down opposite her. 'I've been waiting here almost an hour.'

Krasin ignored her. Nodding to the waiter behind the bar he asked her what she was drinking.

'I've been on lemonade.' Her gaze was fixed on the cardboard box. 'But I'll have a brandy now.'

'Will you,' he replied drily turning to the waiter. 'Make that two.'

Ludmilla said: 'You've brought it then.'

'I said I would.' He pushed the box towards her. With eager fingers she pulled aside the string and removed the lid.

The fur coat lay in a bed of tissue, dark and gleaming. She ran her hand across its rippling surface and the sensation drew a smile to her lips.

'It's what you wanted.'

'Does Yuri know you've given it to me?'

It was a stupid question. 'As far as he's concerned it has been confiscated.'

'That's good.' Ludmilla was talking automatically, still fascinated by the coat she had earned.

'I would suggest you take care of where you wear it.' There was sarcasm in Krasin's voice. 'It might raise some ugly questions if your friends were to see you with it.'

'I'll keep it at the ministry.'

The waiter flicked two mats on to the table and set the glasses of brandy on them. Krasin waited until he had gone before asking: 'Have you seen anything of Yuri since Tatyana was arrested?'

'He came round late last night with Alexsei.'

'What did they talk about?'

Ludmilla twisted her face into an expresion of consideration. 'Yuri thinks he's going to be arrested.'

'He flatters himself – '

'He's very frightened. He told Tatyana that she should have hidden his poetry more carefully. Alexsei agreed. They argued about it for a long time.'

The waiter brushed past them carrying a tray loaded with glasses of lager. The television behind the bar was ploughing its way through a wartime soap that had been running longer than the war itself.

133

Krasin took a shot of brandy, letting it scorch across his tongue. It was good, he thought to himself, there was nothing like fear to set friends at each other's throats.

'They know that Katya is going to be working for you,' Ludmilla told him. 'Alexsei was furious, told her she was a lackey.'

'How did she take that?'

'Not too well. She slammed out of the room.'

Krasin took two American dollars from his pocket, which he estimated to be enough to cover the price of the drinks, scattered them across the table and stood up to go. Ludmilla watched him.

'Is that it then?'

Krasin paused. 'What more do you want?'

She gave her slow, bruised smile. 'Katya didn't come in last night.'

'So what?'

'Maybe there are things I could do for you too.' There was a hiss from the coffee percolator on the bar. Ludmilla was playing her one trump card. 'I'm better in bed than her.'

Krasin took the back of her hand in his. 'You've already been rewarded for your part in this.'

Ludmilla tried to remove her hand but he held it tight.

'You're hurting me – '

'The information you passed me served its purpose. The State has shown its gratitude. But make no mistake, you're a squealer.' His voice was soft. 'What you've done to your friends is despicable.'

Ludmilla's red lips puckered into another sad smile. 'You put these things so clearly, Vassily.'

He relaxed his grip and snapped his fingers. 'Where is it?'

'Where is what?'

'The security pass. I gave you one to get in here.'

She took it from her handbag and handed it to him. 'No one else is allowed to win, are they?' she said bitterly.

Chapter Seventeen

'The bastard tried to kill me,' Pip said. 'As certainly as if he had sent me a letter bomb through the post.'

He was shocked by the implication of what he was saying, shocked by the simplicity of the attempt on his life and the ease with which the intruder had broken into his flat. But in particular he was shocked by how narrowly he'd escaped.

'Do you realise that if I'd switched on the lights the place would have gone up like a fireworks display?'

Pip took a sip of red wine and placed the glass back on the table between the ashtray and the ketchup bottle. Sitting here in the pub with Max, the air full of office gossip and cigarette smoke, the distant explosions of the space invaders machine butting into their conversation, the events of the night before seemed grotesque and improbable.

He had been in no hurry when he arrived back home. For once he'd had the evening to himself. There were a few papers in his briefcase that he wanted to go over and a re-run of *The Maltese Falcon* after the nine o'clock news. He was reckoning to put in an hour's work and then get a curry from the take-away in Queensway.

The lights were out in the corridor and he'd taken the lift up to his flat. Unlocking the door he was groping for the switch when there'd been a crash from the floor below and a wail of despair. It was one of his neighbours. She was standing in the entrance to her flat, keys in hand, trying to support a loaded paper bag on one knee while groceries spilled out on to the floor.

'Are you all right?' he'd called out. Another rock-fall of perishables had given him the answer. Going downstairs he'd helped retrieve spaghetti, tins of tomatoes and a box of tissues. 'I couldn't get my key into the lock in the dark,' she'd explained. They'd agreed that they must say something to the caretaker in the morning. The lights were always fusing. She had been grateful for his help. 'Thank you so much, that's very kind. No, I've got it now.'

Feeling his way back to the door of the flat, Pip had reached down to pick up his briefcase. It had been then that he smelled gas. For a moment he'd frozen, uncertain of the source, alarm bells going off in his head. Carefully he prodded the door open wider and at once the sweet, sickly stench of gas rolled out into the passage.

Clamping a handkerchief over his face he'd darted inside, barking his shins on the coffee table as he crossed the living room. In the kitchen he'd found one tap of the cooker open, quietly hissing gas into the confined space. He twisted it off, angry with himself, his lungs beginning to tug for air.

Throwing open the little kitchen window he hurried back next door to open some more, get a bit of draught through the place. As he was crossing the floor there had been a crunch beneath his feet. He'd reached down, picked up a small, sharp object.

The night air was breathing into the room now. The last traces of the gas dissolving. Pip had switched on the side light and examined his discovery. It was a piece of glass, opaque and slightly curved. For a moment he couldn't identify it. Then he'd glanced up at the ceiling.

The light bulb had been broken. The exposed filament was protruding from the socket, the shattered remains lying beneath.

Pip stared across the pub, reliving the moment, the sudden shock of realisation.

'It had been turned into a detonator,' he told Max. 'One spark from that thing would have blasted the place to bits.'

Max was rebuilding his fortifications on steak and kidney pudding. 'Are you sure?'

'You bet. I tried it later.'

Pip had waited until there was no danger from the gas and flicked the switch. The filament had given a sudden brilliant flash and burnt out.

'The beauty of it is that it would have left no trace. If forensic found the glass they would have reckoned the bulb shattered in the blast.'

It was so simple, so professional and that's what frightened Pip.

He had cleared out of the flat, spent the rest of the night in a hotel off Oxford Street, a sterilised, cosmopolitan place with lift doors that tinged as they opened like a microwave oven and a foyer full of rubber plants, soft lights and tourists asking about day-trips to Stratford. Feeling faintly ridiculous, he'd signed in under a false name, changed his room an hour later and left it to come into work at six that morning.

Max was chewing thoughtfully. 'You think that Russian who telephoned you is responsible?'

'Well it wasn't the lady from meals-on-wheels.' Pip pictured the burnt-out filament, the tiny wires twisted like singed hairs. 'It was a set-up, Max. He knew exactly what would happen once I started asking questions around London.'

'Did he give you a name?'

'Called himself Jablonsky. I doubt if it's true.'

Max gave a nod of agreement and washed it down with a mouthful of Guinness.

'He must have given you some sort of contact address?'

'A phone number. I tried ringing it this morning. It's been disconnected.'

'I could get it checked out if you like,' Max offered. 'I've someone in the American Embassy who owes me a favour.'

'Could you? That would be useful.'

An artificial log fire was burning in the grate, the one-armed bandit nearby winking and tweeting to itself as it calculated how to avoid shelling out money.

Max held up his fork, giving the piece of steak a few seconds' reprieve. 'What did the police make of it?'

'They said they will make inquiries. Which I imagine is their way of telling me that it's not something they want to touch.'

'Have you any idea of who set this bomb up?'

'I could hazard a guess.'

Later that afternoon, he put a call through to Christie's.

'I'd like to speak to Bill Hargreaves,' he told the switchboard. 'I believe he works in the picture department.'

'Just a moment, please.'

'You won't remember me,' he said as Hargreaves came on the line. 'My name's Spencer – Pip Spencer.'

The name drew a blank. 'What can I do for you, Mr Spencer?'

'I was talking to you some weeks back about Russian paintings – '

'Oh yes,' Hargreaves's voice suddenly animated with the recollection, 'I'm with you now. You were the lawyer with the enigmatic questions about the Russian reserve collections.'

'That's the one. I wonder if you could spare me half an hour of your time? I need the answers to a few more questions.'

'Sure, how about later this week?'

'As a matter of fact I'm in rather a hurry. You're not free this afternoon, are you?'

He found Hargreaves cataloguing a forthcoming sale.

With his jacket off, hands thrust into trouser pockets until his braces strained and surrounded by stacks of dusty canvases, he

137

seemed quite at home in the huge picture warehouse of Christie's and more relaxed than he'd been before.

'Good to see you again, Mr Spencer,' he said, greeting Pip with a grin and a handshake. 'Sorry about the mess.'

'Glad you can give me the time.'

'How can I help you?'

'I need information on a dealer called Trenchard.'

Light winked on the square lenses of Hargreaves's spectacles. 'What sort of information?'

'Anything you have.'

'He runs a gallery up in Cork Street.'

Pip's nod indicated that he already knew this much.

'And another in New York. Specialises in Contemporary art, new trends in the market. It's all very slick, very polished; he gets himself a lot of media attention.'

'He's successful, I take it?'

'I think you could say that.'

'Do you know him well?'

Hargreaves shrugged. 'I see him around the place. He's a sociable animal, likes to be seen at opening nights and such. What's the interest?'

'I need to speak to him.'

'His gallery is walking distance from here.'

'On neutral territory, that is – '

'You mean somewhere like here?'

Before Pip could answer, he changed the subject, pointing to a small canvas covered in brilliant smears of paint that stood propped against the wall.

'Look at that,' he said in disgust. 'It happens every time.'

'What does?'

'Last month we sold a Van Gogh for a record price – you probably saw it on the news. Since then a tidal wave of undiscovered masterpieces by him have come in through the front door.'

Hargreaves picked up the offending painting and sniffed it critically. 'I don't think the paint's even dry on this one.' He dumped it back in place. 'God knows who lets these things in.'

'What shall I do with it?' asked the assistant who hovered nearby.

'Drop-kick it out of the back door in the general direction of the owner.'

He turned back to Pip, his voice lightening. 'Is this important?'

'I think so.'

'I'm giving a lunch party on Friday,' he said, coming to a decision. 'I'll ask Trenchard along if you like. Are you free that day?'

'I've got an appointment but I can change it.'

Hargreaves nodded. There was a slight smile on his face as he waited for an explanation. 'Are you going to tell me the reason, or is it another of your mysteries?'

'No mystery. Trenchard has been handling stolen pictures.'

Hargreaves's gaze didn't waver. 'From Russia?'

'You got it.'

He said, 'Holy shit.'

'Do you want to change your mind about lunch?'

'I don't think so.' Hargreaves was still watching him with interest. 'Who knows, it might even breathe a little life into the conversation.'

It was growing dark as Pip pushed through the swing doors of his hotel. A coach tour had arrived and their luggage cluttered the foyer. A pair of porters in cerise jackets with gold trimmings were circling about, fussing it into order.

'I'll be leaving first thing in the morning,' Pip told the girl at the desk.

He'd paid in advance and she flashed a smile of acknowledgement as she tapped the information into her computer.

Going to his room Pip packed the few belongings he'd brought with him, zipped up the bag and carried it out into the corridor.

A plastic sign with the stylised diagram of a running man directed him towards the fire escape. The lift opened at that moment, disgorging two people. Pip waited until they had shuffled away down the passage before pushing open the double doors and stepping out into the night. Without hurrying he walked down the flights of iron steps, past the heat and clatter of the hotel kitchens that belched out from a first floor window, into the alleyway below.

It was one of those scruffy, unplanned places that are left when the rear end of two large buildings have been reversed into each other. No soft lights and muzak here, just garbage bins and a couple of stray cats who patrolled the area with their tails stiff and fluffy as pipe cleaners.

In Oxford Street he hailed a passing taxi.

'Where you going?'

'I'll tell you on the way.' Pip jumped into the back and turning around in the seat he watched out of the rear window until he was satisfied that he hadn't been followed before giving the driver instructions to take him up to Hammersmith Hospital.

'You going in for an operation then?'

'Just visiting.'

'Only I see you're carrying a bag with you. I thought you might be checking in.'

'I've been staying in a hotel.'

The driver sensed from the tone of Pip's voice that further questions might jeopardise his chances of a tip and turned his attention back to the road.

Hospitals carry more residents than a cruise liner but despite this they are lonely places, the uncarpeted floors, the complete absence of decoration conveying the impression that the final building work has been indefinitely suspended.

'Visiting hours are over, sir.' The nurse at the reception desk broke the bad news to him.

'I'm looking for Dr Jameson.'

She looked doubtful. 'I'll try for you, sir. He might have gone home by now.'

Pip waited in the hallway, looking around at the flower boutique that was closed until the morning, the automatic coffee dispenser, the rows of red plastic chairs that had been moulded to suit the requirements of the modular backside.

'He's not in his room, sir.' The nurse's voice betrayed little enthusiasm for her chosen vocation. 'I'll try paging him if you like.'

A wheel-chair trundled past, carrying a complaining woman to some new destination, and two nurses went out into the night chattering to themselves. Somewhere down the passage a vacuum cleaner was at work.

'Pip!'

The soft voice behind him carried no trace of either Scottish accent or surprise. Pip turned to see Angus standing by the reception desk, looking neat and fastidious as ever in a crisp white coat and bright paisley bow tie that puffed from an elegantly starched collar.

'Evening, Angus.'

'What on earth are you doing here?'

'I've come for a check-up.'

Angus's pale grey eyes didn't waver as they took in the overnight bag that Pip carried.

'Check-up?' he queried. 'What sort of check-up have you in mind?'

'One that lasts until Friday.'

Chapter Eighteen

'Have you found anything yet?' Krasin asked.

Katya shook her head. 'Nothing. We've been through every picture returned in the last six months now. There's nothing that looks wrong. But it's so hard to tell, Vassily. The catalogue doesn't give anything like enough information.'

They were walking across the cathedral square of the Kremlin. It was a bitter day, the sky flat as a slate and waiting for snow.

'Look at the back of the paintings.' His breath streamed out with the advice. 'Check whether the canvas has been cut down to size, or whether there are any marks on it to suggest that it has been in Europe recently.'

Katya had been working in the Kremlin vaults for over a week. It was a formidable task. She hadn't realised quite how many paintings came and went in the course of a year.

As Krasin had predicted, the inventory was practically useless. It was carefully indexed and cross-referenced but the descriptions of the paintings were so vague that they were of no help to her.

The worst of it was the cold. Georgy had put two paraffin stoves by the table where she worked and lit them before she arrived in the morning but they never seemed to make any difference. And she didn't like to put her feet too close in case they gave her chilblains, so instead she wore two jumpers and thick woollen stockings and tried to think of something else.

'Doesn't the cold damage the pictures?' she asked Georgy as she came in one day blowing on her fingers. He nodded unhappily. The old man took any criticism of the running of the vaults to heart as though it was his personal responsibility.

'There is heating,' he told her, 'but it only comes on when the temperature goes below freezing.'

'Christ, it should have come on weeks ago in that case. Don't you feel it?'

He shook his head and said that he had grown used to it, from which Katya guessed that he kept himself well insulated with the bottle of pepper vodka he had tucked away in his locker.

Krasin walked up the steps of the Cathedral of the Archangel.

'Just keep looking,' he said to her. 'Something will turn up.'

The woman in the entrance held out her hand for a ticket but he ignored her and went inside.

'Some of the pictures are in a terrible state, Vassily.'

'In what way?'

'They're covered in dirt. There was a portrait of Lenin we looked at yesterday which had little holes in it.' She couldn't help smiling at the memory. 'Georgy reckoned it was woodworm but I'm pretty certain that someone has been throwing darts at it.'

Krasin gave a grunt as they crossed the magnificent tiled floor. It was dark in the cathedral but the mosaiced walls cast a glimmer of phosphorescence.

'Where had it been?'

'In an officers' mess in the Voronezh barracks.'

'It doesn't surprise me. Put men together for any length of time and they behave like animals.'

He didn't press her for more information and she was slightly relieved. She'd thought for a moment that he was going to make an issue of it. Moving away from him she looked at the tombs set out in rows along the wall.

'What should I do about them, Vassily?'

'If they're badly damaged they should be sent to the restorers. Georgy has the address.'

Katya was going from one tomb to the next, reading the names of the Czars who had been buried in the cathedral. Her hair was tucked into the collar of her coat and she was running a leather-gloved finger over the carved inscriptions.

Krasin watched her thoughtfully. Now that it was permissible to talk of the past, her generation was becoming curious about life before the revolution. It brought a little glamour into their lives.

'My mother's family came from Moscow,' she said after a few minutes, coming over to join him. 'They weren't titled or anything like that but they were supposed to have been quite rich.'

'How do you know this?'

'My mother always boasts about it.'

'You shouldn't dwell on these things, Katya,' he said quietly. 'It was a long time ago.'

'I know, but there's no harm in thinking, is there?'

Krasin turned and called to the woman who sat at the entrance, telling her he wanted to go through to the other side of the screen. She lumbered to her feet, considered objecting and thought better of it. Reaching up above the door lintel she took down a key.

'Have you ever been in here before?' Krasin asked as they came into the little room beyond.

Katya shook her head, gazing up at the wall of icons on the back of the screen. The drowsy smell of incense hung in the air.

'They all look rather grim, don't they?' she whispered.

'Saints tend to meet unpleasant ends – it goes with the job.'

Katya was craning back her head to see, the long curve of her neck exposed above her scarf. Krasin put his hands on her shoulders and stroking back the shaft of hair he kissed her in the warm place behind her ear.

She turned, pleased by the unexpected sign of affection.

He was standing close, his hips pressed against hers. She put her arms around his neck and they tottered back a few paces until she was half sitting on the stone block of a tomb.

His hands were on her shoulders, pressing her down. She resisted, surprised and a little shocked, holding him away with her elbows. Surely he couldn't be contemplating making love in here? It was unthinkable.

The gold chandelier above her pricked the darkness with points of light, the air was dusty with disuse. Krasin was persistent.

'Lie down.'

'Not in here, Vassily,' she hissed back at him under her breath, laughing a little unsteadily. 'Someone might come in.'

'They won't – '

He slipped his hand beneath her jumper and cupped one breast, nuzzling the firm nipple in the palm of his hand.

'I've locked the door from the inside.'

Katya fell back on the tomb beneath them, her skirt rucking up around her hips. To her horror she found herself wanting him now, the profanity of what he was intending beginning to excite her.

'No, Vassily,' she wailed, her mind still swimming above emotion. 'It's not right.'

'Don't struggle, my love.'

'Please no . . . Not in a church.' There was desperation in her voice. She was losing control of herself, the desire overwhelming her. 'For God's sake, Vassily, not in a church!'

Krasin was smiling as he knelt over her.

'No one is watching,' he reassured her, 'apart from a few saints and they don't count.'

The stone was hard and cold against her back, the glassy eyes of the icons stared down at her.

It was a wicked, wicked thing they were doing, she cried at him but the words were lost in the exquisite pain of the moment.

When they were through she lay on her back, her head toppling over the edge of the stone tomb, hair cascading down to the floor. Her lower lip was bleeding from where she had bitten it to stop herself from crying out, her skin was hot and flushed. But through the pounding of the blood at her temples she felt a profound sense of shame that lingered with her for the rest of the day.

'You look worried,' Georgy said as he deposited some pictures against the work-table that afternoon. 'You've been sitting there staring into space for the last hour.'

She shook her head and put on a bright smile for him. 'Sorry, I was thinking about something.'

He dusted down a canvas and laid it in front of her. 'Have you had a fight?'

She was startled that he could read her so easily. 'No, not a fight,' she said hastily then hesitated, letting out her breath in a sigh. 'Well yes, I suppose it was really.'

'You mustn't worry about it. It's just a lovers' tiff.'

She looked at his round face crumpled into an expression of concern. He was really very sweet.

'Do you think so?'

'Of course. It shows he cares.'

'I hope so, Georgy,' she said sadly.

On the way home that evening she met Tatyana. She was struggling up the street with two heavy bundles of magazines tied with string.

'Katska,' she cried, 'I haven't seen you for ages. How are you?'

She dropped the magazines on the pavement and they kissed each other on both cheeks.

'Do you want me to take one of those?' Katya asked.

'Could you? They're heavier than I expected. I weighed them but Ludmilla says the scales aren't accurate.'

'She's not still dieting, is she?'

'Not still, she stopped that one. This is a new diet.'

They dived down into the subway, jostling their way amid the rush hour crowd. Steam hissed out from the central grating, the concrete floor was wet from the tramp of passing feet.

'Does this mean she's hitched herself to some new man?' Katya wanted to know.

'A director of the Pedagogical Institute. Grey and venerable with bad breath. But she hasn't dropped Mikhail, that's the interesting part of it. She's running them both on half time.' Tatyana grinned back as far as her gold teeth, 'We've all been sworn to secrecy.'

'She should get her picture put up in the park for exceeding her monthly quota.'

The string round the bundle of magazines was cutting Katya's fingers and she shifted it to the other hand. She wanted to talk to Tatyana, to unload the confused feelings of guilt and pleasure that she had discovered since meeting Vassily and which she was finding increasingly difficult to reconcile in her mind.

But so far Tatyana had avoided any such discussion. Since she rarely spoke of her own personal affairs she had blocked Katya's attempts to bring up the subject and the unspoken words stood between them.

'You're two kilos short,' the librarian informed them after she had weighed the magazines.

'What do you make them?'

'Nine kilos.'

Tatyana clucked with impatience and scrabbling through her bag she took out a slip of paper, signed and rubber-stamped.

'I only need nine, it says so here.'

The librarian shrugged and impaled the form on a metal spike. Going down the shelves she drew out a paperback and handed it across the counter.

'What have you got?' Katya was interested.

Tatyana showed her the cover of the book. 'It's his new one. Everyone says it's good. You must read it after me.'

Outside, the snow that had fallen that afternoon glowed orange in the streetlights.

Tatyana slipped her arm through Katya's as they trudged back home. After two appearances before the disciplinary committee she had been allowed to keep her job in the ministry but been transferred to a different department on reduced pay. On top of this she had been given the statutory six months' correctional labour.

'Have you started yet?' Katya asked.

'Last Monday.' She turned down the corners of her mouth. 'It's so boring, kovshka, you've no idea. They were all there, Solovynov, Podurets, Rokotov of course – loving every minute of it – and that Party weasel from Accounts, I can't remember his name.'

'Kritovski?'

'That's the one. They sat around in a circle like a coven of old women and told me that I was an anti-social and a disgrace to the ministry and so on.'

Katya had never witnessed one of these sessions. She couldn't imagine how Tatyana would react.

'What did you say to them?'

'Nothing really. I just scuffled about and tried to look as though I was sorry. The Komsomol office told me that if I didn't do that they'd just extend the sentence.' She paused and looked at Katya. 'Sometimes you have to toe the line.'

From the tone of her voice Katya sensed that Tatyana was trying to apologise.

'You think I don't understand,' she added earnestly. 'But I do. It's all very well for Yuri and Alexsei to get high and mighty and say we should never compromise but it doesn't always work. Sometimes you just have to toe the line. Christ – if it had been left to those two I would still be stuck in that stinking jail.'

To Katya's relief the barrier that had grown up between them in the last few weeks fell again.

Tatyana must have felt it too for she grinned beneath her woollen hat and said, 'Why don't we go and have a drink at Fedorenko's? It's ages since we got tight together.'

Chapter Nineteen

Adrian Trenchard was the last to arrive for lunch.

Dressed in a pale cinnamon suit and open-necked shirt, a silk handkerchief spilling playfully from his upper pocket, he offered Hargreaves his hand.

'Bill, sorry to be so late. I was held up at the Neo-Geo launch and then went back to the gallery to find two calls waiting from New York.' Apologies fluttered from him like confetti. 'So tiresome. One of those days when one can't catch up with oneself.'

The butler hovercrafted a glass of champagne across the room to him but Trenchard brushed it aside.

'Just Perrier for me – ice and a twist of lemon. I can't face alcohol at this time of the day.'

'I think you know everyone here.' Hargreaves extracted his hand to indicate the other guests.

'Indeed I do.' Trenchard's gaze travelled round the room. 'And a very select gathering by the look of it. Charles' – he singled out one for immediate attention – 'loved your piece in *The Times* yesterday.'

'Sweet of you to say so.'

'And Freddie, I thought you might be here.' Trenchard was in his element. When he came to Pip he hesitated only for an instant. 'Have we met before?'

'At Sotheby's, about a fortnight ago.'

'Ah yes, I'm not sure I caught the name at the time.'

'Phillip Spencer.' Hargreaves played his rôle with dogged determination. 'He's been handling some legal work for me.'

'Of course, I think it must be the suit.' He indicated Pip's blue pinstripe as he passed on. 'It does so change a man's appearance.'

At lunch Pip found himself with a junior director of Sotheby's on one side – young, earnest and eager to see everyone's point of view at once – and a stout gentleman with a triangle of unshaven hair sprouting from red cheeks on the other, who couldn't get closer to the table than his considerable stomach allowed.

'Are you part of the art world?' Pip inquired politely.

'Far from it.' He gulped in some wine and chewed it thoughtfully. 'I'm only here because my family's kept its wallpaper hidden for the last two centuries.'

'Hidden? Where's it hidden?'

'Under five Gainsboroughs, four Lawrences, a couple of good Constables and a rather indifferent Turner.'

'No doubt to stop the colour fading in the sunlight.'

Among the other guests there that day was the curator of a museum in Leeds with loud opinions, and next to him a minute but perfectly formed Indian with the melting eyes of a young roe deer who confessed to a weakness for collecting antique clocks.

'They represent one of those happy occasions when human ingenuity and creative vision have been combined to produce something that is not destructive.'

On Hargreaves's left was the author of the piece in *The Times*. He was dressed in expensive beachwear, presumably to register that he came from a convention-free zone of London, with greying hair brushed forward in the manner of a bit-part actor from *I Claudius*, and engaged in a running battle with a journalist from *Vogue* who argued that Old Master painting was returning to fashion.

'It's historically more important,' she was drawling across her watercress soup. 'The Pontormo sale the other day proves it.'

'The Pontormo sale will be eclipsed by the next major Impressionist piece to go under the hammer.' He held his cigarette vertically to register his authority. 'There is no doubt where the big money lies nowadays, my pet, although I can't say I approve.'

Adrian Trenchard had been positioned almost directly opposite Pip and during the crossfire of talk the solicitor was able to observe him closely.

Charged with the high-strung, nervous energy of a ballet dancer, Trenchard kept up a constant patter of conversation with his neighbours as though determined to appear at his ease. It was only on one or two occasions that Pip had noticed his attention waver and flicker across the table towards him, shooting him a look that was at once quizzical and demanding.

'What do you make of the government's plans for the legal profession, Mr Spencer?'

The question cut into his thoughts. Pip turned to see the Indian waiting with his eyebrows raised in polite expectation.

'I imagine that some firms will get more work,' he replied smoothly, 'others will go down the drain.'

'Doesn't that worry you?'

'I expect to do very well out of it myself.'

'It's still risky.' The Leeds museum curator didn't like anything left to chance. 'The best laid plans of mice and men and all that.'

Lunch was almost over now, chairs drawn back from the table. Pip estimated the time had come to take charge of the conversation.

'The law is a risky business,' he said lightly. 'Only this week I had a bomb put in my flat.'

The remark silenced the room as effectively as the entrance of royalty.

'Did you say a bomb?'

'No, that's not strictly accurate. The gas was turned on and a light bulb broken to expose the bare filament. But I dare say it would have had much the same effect as a bomb.'

'My God, that's extraordinary.' The young blade on Pip's left sounded shocked. 'But why should anyone do that?'

Hargreaves was watching him with interest, elbows on the table, fingers pressed together in their accustomed position.

'It was done to prevent me exposing a fraud.'

Across the table Adrian Trenchard was pouring cream into his coffee, letting it flow round in a perfect unbroken spiral.

'For several years now paintings from the Russian reserve collections have been smuggled out of the country and sold here in London.'

'And you know who's doing this?' asked the journalist from *Vogue*, breaking the silence that had greeted this disclosure.

'I know who is receiving them in London.'

The flow of cream didn't waver.

'Have you told the police?' The museum curator was trying to impose common sense.

'I've spoken to them, certainly. But as yet I haven't given them any names.' He looked directly at Trenchard as he spoke. 'You see, the evidence is purely circumstantial. That's the irony of it. It would be flung out of court quicker than a journalist with a Japanese instamatic.'

With painstaking deliberation Trenchard took a mouthful of coffee and replaced the tiny cup on its saucer.

'But surely, Mr Spencer' – his pale gaze beamed across the table – 'if there has been one attempt on your life, there's every chance of another. Especially since the first one clearly failed.'

'That's true.'

'Doesn't that worry you?'

'It would be extremely foolish for anyone to try again.'

'Really, and why is that?'

'I have put everything I know down in writing. The names, the connections, even the conclusions I've drawn have been left in a sealed envelope in the safe of one of my partners. In itself it doesn't amount to much more than speculation.' He looked around at the assembled faces. 'But if anything were to happen to me it wouldn't half make interesting reading. Who knows, it might spark off an investigation from the Fraud Squad.'

Trenchard received the news without any apparent sign of interest. 'Why are you telling us all this?'

Pip smiled. 'I'm just passing the message around – on the off-chance it should reach the right ears.'

His heart was hammering with the adrenaline, his palms sweating. But when he excused himself from the table and went down to the gents' cloakroom a few minutes later he was glad to see that there was no sign of nervousness in his expression. The face that stared back at him from the mirror was impassive.

He was washing his hands in the basin when the door opened behind him and Adrian Trenchard came in.

Passing Pip as though he didn't exist he went into the cubicle, leaving the door wide open, and relieved himself noisily. It was only as he emerged and was running bony white hands under the tap that he spoke.

'I found your insinuations back there rather childish.'

'I'm sorry. Would you rather I had been more specific?'

'I'd rather you dropped the subject altogether, Mr Spencer. I cannot imagine what has started you on this wild-goose chase but I would suggest you forget it. That charade just now was extremely amusing but quite pointless.'

'I'm sorry you see it that way.'

'No one is interested in your outlandish ideas.'

Pip dried his hands on the towel with exaggerated care. 'This wild-goose chase, as you describe it, began a month ago with a rather vulgar Victorian painting.'

'I think we've been over all this before.'

'We have, only last time you lied to me.'

'Really, Mr Spencer, this is becoming preposterous.' Trenchard seemed bored rather than angry but Pip pressed on regardless.

'That American collector who died so conveniently was an alibi. You know it as well as I do. What you probably don't know is that I was asked to check up on that picture by a Russian. He phoned directly from Moscow suggesting I look into its background.'

'Is that anything to do with me?'

'He claimed to be from the Ministry of Culture, even gave me a number to contact him at his office.'

Trenchard was attempting to leave.

'By the time I rang it, it had been disconnected.' Pip stepped in front of him blocking his way. 'It was only later that I discovered that it isn't anything to do with the Ministry of Culture. It is a security number, one of a sequence used by the KGB.'

The colour had drained from Trenchard's cheeks. Was it fear or indignation? Impossible to say.

'Whoever rang me knew I would go to your gallery. And he knew exactly what the consequence would be.'

'This is mere speculation, Mr Spencer, as you have admitted yourself. If you had one grain of evidence you'd have used it.' Reaching out his arm he attempted to brush his way past. 'And now if you'll get out of my way I'm expected back upstairs.'

Pip hit him in the stomach.

The speed of the attack took Trenchard by surprise. Pip felt his fist drive into the muscles of the man's belly, heard the breath burst from his lungs as he doubled over.

Catching him by the throat he threw him back up against the wall. Trenchard's legs gave and he slumped in his grasp.

'I want his name.' Pip kept his voice casual. 'No more lies, no more evasions. Just his name.'

Trenchard's face was pressed against the white tiles, his breath coming in slow spasms as he fought for air. With a sudden struggling movement he wrenched himself free and staggered back across the floor.

'How dare you assault me!' he screamed.

The impeccable façade had cracked. He was suddenly frightened, vulnerable, but Pip didn't relax the pressure.

'Give me his name.'

'I can't.' Trenchard was leaning against the basins, supporting himself with his hands. His shoulders were slumped, chest heaving. 'You think you're so clever, Mr Spencer. You think you've found all the answers. But you're wrong. There's nothing you can learn from me.'

'Why are you protecting him? He set you up as well as me.' Pip reckoned it was time for a few home truths. 'He gave you the dirty work to do and you failed him. That puts you in an uncomfortable position.'

'It was not my fault – '

'Maybe not but how long do you think it'll be before we read that you've met with some small accident?'

A tap was running. Pip twiddled the gold knob and the room was suddenly engulfed in silence.

'You know too much for your own good.'

'I tell you I know nothing.' There was a hint of desperation in Trenchard's voice now.

151

'You've become a liability.'

Trenchard was getting back his breath now, his thoughts calming, reason returning. He was on the verge of confession, Pip could sense it.

'Your only chance is to help me,' he said.

'I can't –'

'You have to.'

Trenchard looked down at the floor. 'Not here.' He addressed the remark to the tiles. 'I can't talk here – somewhere else.'

'It's just a voice on the telephone. That's all there ever is. A bloody voice on the end of a line.'

'No name?'

'Nothing.'

They crossed The Mall into St James's Park. It was an afternoon of light but persistent drizzle, better for the ducks than the tourists who clustered on the bridge over the lake, grimly posing for their photos against the distant rooftops of Whitehall.

'Have you any idea what it's like?' Trenchard asked sulkily. 'To have to sit and wait, never knowing what he wants from you, where it will end? Sometimes I don't hear from him for months and then I'll get two or three calls in a row. A voice comes on the line telling me what I must do, where I must go.'

'Why do you obey?'

They had paused beneath a plane tree. Trenchard sat down on a bench, huddling into the corner of the seat as though for warmth.

'I have no option,' he said.

'He's blackmailing you?'

Trenchard didn't appear to hear the question. A grey squirrel approached him with quick, nervous movements, hoping that the hands that hung between his knees carried some offering. Trenchard stared at it in incomprehension before saying:

'He told me he had photos. He threatened to show them to my wife.'

The oldest method in the book, Pip thought to himself, but still the best.

'Then why not go to the police?' he asked. 'Dirty photographs might raise a few titters at the next police conference but nothing more. You can't be arrested for adultery.'

'You think everything is so simple, don't you.' Indignation sparked life back into Trenchard again and he spoke quickly and spitefully. 'This was not something I could take to the police. Not something that could be discussed man to man: a nod and a wink and keep it under your hat, constable. It wasn't like that.'

152

'I'll take your word for it.'

Pip didn't particularly want to know how Trenchard got his jollies but the connection was vital.

'When did this happen?'

'Some time ago.' Trenchard glanced up and then gave an impatient shake of his head. 'Ten, eleven years back, I can't remember exactly when it was I met him.'

'You met him?' Pip was astonished.

'Oh yes, I don't know his name, or even who he was but I met the bastard all right.' Trenchard's voice sank with the memory. 'It was at a wine tasting at Claridge's. He asked me about the galleries, how they worked, where they were. I thought he was just being polite. He was very polished, you see, very professional. From his appearance you'd never have guessed he was a Russian. He was so smart, so suave. More like some English aristocrat. It was only later that I discovered what he wanted.'

'You're sure this is the same one?' Pip hardly dared break the flow of words but Trenchard seemed eager to talk now, to get it off his chest.

'It was him all right. I recognised the voice.'

'Then surely you could have found his name.'

'There were over a thousand people at Claridge's that night.'

'But someone must have invited him. His name must be on a guest list. You could have traced it.'

'I didn't want to.' There was a flash of anger through the fear. 'Christ – you of all people should understand that. Look what they did to you. He has people watching all the time.'

Pip glanced around, half expecting to see these anonymous figures peering at them through the damp willows. But there was nothing. Two secretaries skittered along the glistening path, clutching a copy of *Cosmopolitan* over their hair-dos. Somewhere in the distance a band was pumping out selections of Gilbert and Sullivan to empty deck-chairs.

'It's not been easy.' Trenchard was beginning to sink into self-pity. 'I was expected to invent a background for the paintings he sent me. Each one had to be something different, something plausible that wouldn't raise suspicion. At first it wasn't too difficult. Only two or three arrived a year. I was able to prepare for them. For a time I even thought it was rather exciting. But recently there's been many more. Sometimes five or six at a time. I told him it was too much, I couldn't keep up with the demand. It was bound to go wrong. And now this.' He flapped a hand in the direction of the lake where ducks were gobbling at pieces of wet bread.

'What did you do with the profits?'

153

'They were put into a Swiss bank account. No name, just a number.' Trenchard became agitated again. 'That's the whole point. I've never known who I'm dealing with. I'm just the front.'

The clouds thinned at that moment and a vapid sun washed over the park, grasping at the moisture, sharpening the details to an extreme clarity.

Trenchard was wrong about one thing, Pip thought to himself. It was simple. Simple and effective. He had been anticipated, manipulated and then mercilessly exploited by an opponent more cunning than himself.

'What are you going to do?' Trenchard was watching him keenly.

'You must have some way of contacting him.'

'It's just a number. No one replies, it's connected to an answering device.'

'In England?'

He nodded.

'You'll give it to me.' Pip stated his conditions without preamble. 'I shall also want the details of every painting you have handled, along with the dates they arrived in the country and the names of the people you passed them to.'

Trenchard didn't try to argue. 'Are you turning this over to the police?'

'Eventually.' He wasn't offering charity. 'But not until I have passed the information on to the Russians. For better or worse this is their affair. They can look after it themselves.'

'But what about me, Mr Spencer? What happens to me?'

'I really don't know.'

'But you must help me. I'm a victim as much as you.'

'Let's hope they see it that way.'

The rain had freckled the shoulders of Trenchard's cinnamon-coloured suit and plastered his hair to his face but he was past caring. If someone had crept up and stolen his wallet at that moment he wouldn't have noticed. It's hard to dislike a man once he's shown himself to be vulnerable.

'Go to the police,' Pip said with sudden weariness. 'God knows, in the circumstances you might even get off with a fine.'

After they had parted, Pip stood where he was, head slightly stooped in the wet, hands in pockets, watching Trenchard walk away towards Admiralty Arch. A sense of frustration, of helplessness, surged up inside him. He had discovered all that he could and he still knew nothing.

The scent had gone dead.

Chapter Twenty

'I find this hard to believe.'

'No more than myself, Colonel.'

'This place is meant to be impregnable.' Krasin clipped the words in his anger. 'The whole point of keeping works of art in these mausoleums is that they are supposed to be safe.'

'Under normal circumstances they are, Colonel. There is no way they can be touched.'

'You can say that?' There was a streak of sarcasm. 'A major painting goes missing from your museum and you tell me that it couldn't have happened? I hardly find it reassuring.'

'No, that's not what I meant – '

The strength had gone from Tokarev's legs. He perched himself on the base of a statue and stared at the ground while one hand moved restlessly across the crown of his head, smoothing and re-smoothing the strands of hair. The other members of the committee stood around, studiously avoiding Krasin's eye.

'I still can't see how it is possible.' Tokarev appeared to be shell-shocked by the theft.

'You're sure it happened during the night?'

'Quite sure. The guards noticed it was missing when they came in this morning.'

'But you didn't inform the department until this afternoon.'

Tokarev was tasting something sour. 'We weren't certain it had been stolen at first. It could have been in one of the offices. Members of the staff occasionally take a painting down for their own research.' It sounded like a lame excuse for inefficiency and his voice weakened. 'We wanted to be certain before we contacted you, Colonel.'

Scared witless would be closer to the truth, Krasin reckoned. Terrified that they might lose their cosy jobs in the museum.

His hands clasped behind his back, he walked a few paces down the passage where the stolen picture had been on exhibition. There were only a few working lights on and the galleries looked larger and starker than they did in the daytime. He turned to Tokarev.

'Where exactly did it hang?'

Jumping to his feet Tokarev showed him the position on the wall. It was low down in one corner of the passage, the sort of place where it would have passed almost unnoticed. The only indication of its prior existence was an irregular shaped patch of darkened wallpaper.

Krasin studied it thoughtfully.

'What was this painting?'

'The Raphael triptych.' Tokarev rattled off the name, adding hopefully, 'It's very small.'

That was obvious. 'What about the alarm? Why didn't that go off?'

'I don't know. It's one of these infra-red systems. The beam doesn't penetrate into every corner of the room. Maybe the burglar managed to slip past it.'

Krasin glanced up at the little sensor that winked down at them from the upper wall.

'I doubt it,' he said.

Zakov returned at that moment and took Krasin aside.

'I've checked the entrances,' he said. 'There's no sign of tampering on the locks and the alarm circuits are untouched. The burglar must have come from inside.'

Zakov spoke with the easy untroubled manner that comes to all efficient but unimaginative men.

'My guess is that he hid himself in here yesterday evening while the museum was still open and then took it in the night.'

Krasin had been thinking the same. 'A professional job.'

'There's no doubt of that.'

He turned back to Tokarev who was waiting anxiously for the outcome of this private conversation.

'Major Zakov will conduct an investigation,' he announced. 'Naturally you will give him all the co-operation he needs.'

'Yes, yes of course.' Tokarev was eager to be helpful.

'In the meantime you will put a notice up in place of the painting to say that it has been withdrawn for routine repair. That should quell any unnecessary speculation.'

Tokarev was only too happy to agree. 'I'll have it done straight away, Colonel.'

Krasin went down into the hallway, Zakov at his heels. As he was leaving he turned to Tokarev.

'This is an extremely grave situation.'

'I am aware of that, Colonel – '

'After this painting has been discovered and returned, you and I will have to put our heads together.'

Tokarev looked as though he'd rather be struck by lightning.

'Discuss how such a theft was allowed to occur.' Krasin was

pulling on his gloves, adjusting each finger in turn. 'Decide where the burden of responsibility lies – who is to take the blame.'

Krasin noticed how the blood had drained from Tokarev's face and smiled bleakly.

'But I'm certain that with your help that will not be difficult.'

It was after nine by the time they returned to Dzerzhinsky Square. Even at this hour of night there were signs of activity, lights burning in many of the office windows.

'I want this business cleared up as quickly as possible,' Krasin said as they stepped out of the lift on the second floor. 'Top priority. I'll give you the back-up you need but find it.'

The stammer of a typewriter came from an open door as they passed. Some wretched secretary kept up late finishing her quota.

'Get on to border control tonight, warn them to be on the alert for stolen works of art.' Krasin gave his instructions succinctly. 'Emphasise that the painting they are looking for is no bigger than a postage stamp.'

'A photo of it would be useful.'

'Unfortunately that's out of the question. The damned thing would be spread all over the foreign newspapers by tomorrow morning.'

He left Zakov to put the wheels in motion and continued on down to his office. The curtains were open and the glow of the city washed the darkened room.

Sitting down behind his desk he waited for five minutes to elapse before flicking on his intercom and punching in the number of the security desk in the front hall.

'Could you send someone outside and ask my chauffeur to come up to my office at once?' he ordered.

Chibatar arrived without knocking. Closing the door softly behind him he moved forward into the pool of light cast by the desk lamp.

'Do you have it?' Krasin inquired.

Chibatar reached into his overcoat pocket and drawing out an object no larger than his hand he passed it across to Krasin.

The triptych was black and slightly clammy with age and shaped like the pointed windows of a Gothic cathedral. Three wooden panels, hinged on their outer edges, that folded into one.

Lifting the catch, Krasin parted the doors and looked at the central painting.

'Did you have any trouble taking it?'

Chibatar shook his head and his short blond hair flickered in the light. He seemed neither curious nor interested by the theft but met Krasin's eyes with his flat, unwavering gaze.

157

'Where did you hide during the night?' Krasin was interested by the details.

Chibatar's hands moved, telegraphing the answer and Krasin smiled as he read it.

'In Tokarev's office?'

The hands moved once more, explaining that he had found the door unlocked.

'I think we'd better keep that to ourselves,' Krasin remarked. 'The poor fellow would be mortified if he ever discovered.'

Chibatar couldn't help noticing how Krasin's fingers glided across the surface of the little work of art as he spoke, instinctively caressing and exploring the mirror-smooth paintwork.

'The real quality of a picture is lost in a museum,' he observed. 'There are so many packed together in a small space that they interfere with each other. It's only when you see one in isolation, like this, that you can appreciate its true value.'

If Chibatar agreed with him he made no sign of it.

'Do you know what it is you've stolen?' Krasin asked, slightly irked by this indifference.

Chibatar shook his head.

'It's by Raphael – commissioned by Pope Julius II shortly before his death. He wanted something small enough to carry with him on his journeys around Italy. Raphael thought that if he made it a triptych the painting inside would be better protected.' Krasin knew the history of the picture intimately. 'A hundred years later it was acquired by the Gonzaga family and then bought from the Italian Government by Count Alexandrei Ivanovich Talinin.' He clipped the doors of the panel shut again and placed it on his desk. 'Nowadays the Pushkin Museum catalogues it as the Raphael triptych – references to the past are not officially encouraged – but it is still better known as the Talinin Madonna.'

Chapter Twenty-One

'When can we expect you back at work, Comrade Leskova?'

'I can't say. It's not for me to decide.'

Podurets nodded thoughtfully, as though it might be for him to decide. He was pleased by his unannounced arrival in the vaults. It had taken Katya Leskova by surprise, caught her off guard.

'I appreciate the importance of this work,' he added. 'Although I fail to see why it requires the services of an interpreter.'

Katya picked up a painting that was leaning against the table leg and showed it to him. Pasted on the back of the canvas was a paper label, dusty with age.

'What do you make of that?' she asked.

The lettering was foreign and quite incomprehensible to Podurets. With the unpleasant sensation that he had been outmanoeuvred he changed the subject.

'Your travel visas have arrived at the ministry. I'll need your signature on the receipt.'

'Do you have it with you?'

'Travel documents can't leave the ministry until they're signed for.' Podurets knew the rules. 'You'll have to pick them up from there.'

As he walked back across Red Square he thought about Katya. He couldn't understand why she had been allowed to work in the Kremlin with no other supervision than that doddering old janitor. It was strange. There was something Colonel Krasin hadn't told him, something he was keeping to himself. Through the respect, the awe he felt for Krasin emerged the first prickle of suspicion.

'What was all that about?' Georgy asked after Podurets had gone.

'Oh, nothing really.'

'I can't believe he came all this way just to tell you your visa had arrived.'

'He was keeping his eye on me. He likes to do that.' Katya was pulling on her coat and hat, checking her hair in a pocket mirror. 'It's lucky he didn't come half an hour later or he wouldn't have found me here.'

'Are you off then?'

'I've got to go to a reception this evening. I must get home and change first. I'll make up the time tomorrow.'

On the way back she stopped to pick up her dress from the cleaners and buy some new stockings. By the time she arrived back at the apartment she was already late.

'I had to queue for nearly an hour,' she said furiously, hanging the dress on the back of the door.

Tatyana was sitting cross-legged on a chair. She didn't reply.

'And then they only had black, nothing in blue.' She contemplated the effect this was going to have.

'They won't match my shoes,' she said crossly. 'I don't want to wear the black ones because they pinch and we're bound to be standing all evening.'

There was a coughing sound from the lavatory. Katya glanced at the clock and saw it was already six forty.

'Oh God – look at the time. I haven't even done my hair yet.' Krasin usually sent his car round to pick her up but this evening he'd told her she'd have to make her own way to the reception as he needed it himself. She tried to estimate the timing. 'What's the quickest way to the Gagarin Mansion, do you think?'

'You'll have to take the metro to Pushkinskaya and then walk up Strastnoy Boulevard.'

'How long do you reckon it'll take?' She was holding up her hair, wondering whether it looked better that way.

'About twenty minutes.'

Tatyana's voice was mechanical, strangely devoid of interest. Dropping her hair Katya glanced round at her.

She was sitting quite still, her hands clasping hold of her ankles, gazing back at Katya intently, as if trying to beam thoughts to her by telepathy.

From the lavatory came the sound of retching again. Tatyana didn't move. With a sudden thump of awareness, Katya realised something was wrong.

'What was that noise?' she asked quickly.

'Ludmilla – she's not feeling well.'

There was a silence between them. Hurrying across the room Katya rapped on the door.

'Are you all right?' she called out.

There was a groan from inside and a slow fumbling movement like someone turning in their sleep. At the sound Tatyana drew in her breath and bared her teeth in a fierce grin.

Katya spun round on her. 'How long has she been in there?'

'I haven't been timing it.'

The door was unlocked. Katya pulled it open. At once the sweet, corrupt stench of vomit struck her.

Ludmilla lay in a huddle on the floor where she had fallen, her face hidden from sight, one arm thrown out across the porcelain bowl.

'Oh my God,' Katya whispered.

Reaching down she grasped her by the shoulders and lifted her up into a sitting position.

There was a sheen of sweat on Ludmilla's face, her hair clung limply to her forehead and temples. Through the clothing Katya could feel her body shivering in long shuddering spasms.

Tatyana had leapt from her chair and now stood in the doorway above them. Katya looked round at her, her voice sharp with anxiety.

'What's happened to her?'

'She's sick – like I said.'

At that moment Ludmilla groaned and moved.

Staggering to her feet, the dead-weight of the body heavy in her arms, Katya dragged her out into the living room and laid her down. Ludmilla's eyelids fluttered at the disturbance. Vaguely Katya rememberd reading somewhere that a person could choke if they lay on their back. Pushing Ludmilla over on to her side she jumped to her feet and ran to the door.

Tatyana caught her by the arm.

'Where are you going?' she demanded angrily.

'To ring the doctor – '

'She doesn't need a doctor.'

'How can you say that, Tasha?' She could hardly believe her ears. 'Just look at her. She could be dying.'

Tatyana brushed the possibility away with a jerk of her head. 'It'll pass over. In an hour or so she'll be fine.'

They faced each other. Katya was breathing heavily from the exertion of lifting Ludmilla but she collected herself and spoke steadily.

'What have you done to her, Tasha?'

She shrugged.

'Tell me.'

'She ate something that didn't agree with her – '

Katya didn't recognise Tatyana at that moment. Her hatred had taken possession of her completely. It was an aura around her, a physical presence.

'What exactly did she eat?' Katya asked carefully.

'No more than she deserves – '

Tatyana stood above the prostrate figure on the ground, her legs straddled, eyes glittering.

It was like taming a dangerous creature. Katya lowered her voice and asked again.

'What have you done to her?'

Tatyana hesitated, her head thrown back, debating whether to let her into the secret. Then she relented.

'Polyanki.' It was the Russian for poisonous mushrooms and her lips curved into a smile as she pronounced the word.

'Oh Christ, Tasha.'

'I pickled them first to disguise the taste.' Tatyana was pleased by the ingenuity of the deception. 'She gobbled them up without a murmur. Asked for more. It's her own fault if she's so sick.'

'How could you?'

'Teach her a lesson – conniving little bitch.'

'Why for God's sake?' Katya was losing her patience. 'What's she done to you?'

'What's she done to me?' She sounded incredulous and her voice rose on the crest of the words.

'You could have killed her.'

Tatyana whisked away into the bedroom and returned a moment later. In her arms was the fur coat. She threw it down on the floor. Katya looked at it in amazement.

'But that's mine – '

'I found it in her locker at the ministry. She's been flaunting it all over Moscow.'

Sleek and black as a living creature the coat lay between them. Katya's mind was reeling in incomprehension.

'But how did she get it?'

'Where do you think she got it? From Vassily Krasin, that's where.' Tatyana spat out the accusation. 'It was his part of the bargain. The pay-off.'

'I don't believe you.'

Tatyana smiled again. 'Don't you? Then ask him.'

'Is it true, Vassily?'

'Of course it's not. I hardly know the girl. Why should I want to give her a fur coat?'

'In return for information.'

'Really, Katya, that's ridiculous – '

'Is it? Then where did it come from?'

The magnificent, chandeliered room was humming with polite conversation. Krasin dropped his voice below the level. 'Look,

162

do we have to talk about this now? This is a reception. You're supposed to be enjoying yourself and I have people I must talk to.'

A waiter came between them, gliding a tray of glasses within range. Katya wasn't to be distracted.

'Vassily! This is important, she's terribly ill. I thought she was going to die.'

He offered her a glass of champagne. 'Have a drink and don't make a scene.'

'I don't want a drink – '

With a shrug Krasin put it back on the tray. 'Very well,' he said calmly. He was not to be rushed into answering Katya's furious questions. 'But she's recovered now, has she?'

'Slightly. When I left she was at least conscious again.' Katya felt a rush of guilt. She should never have told him of the poisoning. It was a stupid, thoughtless mistake.

Krasin nodded in greeting to a couple who were passing. 'Well that's something. At least, I suppose it explains why you were so late arriving this evening.'

'I couldn't possibly leave earlier.'

'No, I agree.' He was at his most amiable. 'It's an excellent excuse. I can't think of a better.'

'How dare you suggest that!'

'Isn't it what you said?'

'You know perfectly well it's not!'

Across the crowded room General Chernov watched the argument from the comfort of a silk-upholstered sofa. He saw Katya stamp her foot in anger and turn away. Krasin didn't appear to be disturbed by the outburst, but then he never was.

The woman sitting on the sofa beside him didn't notice Chernov's momentary distraction and continued to gush with information.

'My husband's conference ends on Friday,' she was saying, inclining towards him. 'We'll have to return at the weekend.'

Chernov turned back to her, solicitous once more. 'So you're on your own all day.'

'It's a wife's lot – ' The heavily mascaraed eyelids fluttered messages and Chernov smiled as he read them.

'That seems rather unfair. Why should he have all the fun?'

'I hardly see him these days.'

Chernov looked down at her cleavage, noting the well-bolstered breasts that surged from the front of her dress. They were white and dusted over with powder.

'Then you must allow us to show you something of our city in the meantime.'

163

'In this weather?' she countered playfully. 'Surely it's too cold to be outside.'

'There's a great deal to see indoors,' Chernov informed her, deciding that she wasn't half as attractive as he thought when he'd asked to be introduced. Lumbering to his feet he turned and cranked his neck in a little bow.

'Ask at your hotel. I'm sure they'll arrange for a guide to take you round.'

As he moved away, leaving the wretched woman to wonder where she had gone wrong, his aide drifted into his wake.

'Who is that argumentative girl talking to Colonel Krasin?' Chernov asked him, nodding in the direction of Katya.

'She's the interpreter from the Ministry of Culture, General.'

'I thought she must be.'

Chernov's shrewd blue eyes took in the dark hair that fanned out across her bare back, the slim waist and graceful pose of the girl's body. He gave his high whinnying laugh.

'I can see now why she is proving to be such a distraction to the colonel.'

The aide was well trained in his unofficial duties. 'Do you wish to be introduced, General?'

'I don't think it's the right moment to intrude. It appears they are having some sort of domestic altercation.'

'Where did she get that coat from then?' Katya demanded hotly. She wanted a direct answer from Krasin. He gave a shrug as though the answer were obvious.

'From Yuri, I imagine.'

To his relief she hesitated. He could see that she hadn't considered that possibility.

'But why should he give it to her?'

'Maybe because he's in love with her.' He spoke in a flat, off-hand voice, willing her to believe him.

'Yuri? In love with Ludmilla?'

He saw her nose wrinkle as she tested the idea on herself. Krasin had the advantage now. Taking her by the arm he led her out of the crowded reception hall. At the head of the stairs he released her.

'Did you not know that?'

She shook her head.

'Yuri Stephanovich and Ludmilla have been lovers for some time.'

'But why has she never said anything about it to us?'

'Do you expect her to?' Krasin was reproachful. 'I can't believe your friend Tatyana would be too pleased to hear the news.'

Katya leaned back against the marble banisters as she put the pieces together in her mind. A few of the guests were leaving, carrying frayed scraps of conversation down the stairs as they went.

'Added to which,' Krasin said lightly, 'I've heard Ludmilla keeps a few ageing admirers in tow. I don't think she'd want to queer the pitch with them either.'

Krasin was pleased with his explanation. It was simple and plausible. From what he knew of Ludmilla he estimated she was the kind of girl who might be secretive about her affairs, particularly if they proved inconvenient. He added a final touch.

'She's hot as a bitch in season. When I brought those flowers round the other day she asked if she could be of service to me too.'

'She did?'

'Told me she was better in bed than you.'

Katya flushed as though she'd been slapped in the face. All other considerations fled from her mind.

'What did you say?'

Krasin was apologetic. 'I told her I'd take her word for it but I wouldn't be needing a demonstration.'

'That was nice of you, Vassily.' She was pleased by the indirect compliment.

'Now,' Krasin said, holding out his hand. 'Shall we go back in before the drink runs out on us?'

Chernov glanced up as they returned. Noticing that the girl was looking radiant once more, he turned to his aide.

'It looks as though normal service has been restored again.'

Krasin didn't feel sorry for Ludmilla. She had got what she wanted and paid the price for her greed afterwards. It was usually the way with informers.

He scarcely thought about her as he drove out through the suburbs of Moscow on the following morning. Snow crunched under the tyres, the air was cold and crisp, the sun a diffused glow in the sky.

Krasin opened the heating control on the dashboard to maximum but it had no effect. The damned thing was broken. He flexed his frozen fingers on the wheel and cursed the fact that he couldn't have taken the Rolls.

But it was too eye-catching, a car that was all too easily remembered, and Krasin didn't want to draw attention to himself that day. Rather than the tailored suits he usually wore he had put on a grey mackintosh and peaked cap, the anonymous clothes of a working man, and he made sure to hold the departmental car he had borrowed out of the reserved central lane.

As he reached Izmaylovskiy Park he turned up north. The streets were broader here, the five onion domes of the Church of the Intercession looming up above the trees, ghostly in the mist. This was one of the old residential districts of Moscow and had preserved something of its former elegance.

He parked the car in front of a large house. The façade was wooden with a high porch and ornamental veranda. For some minutes he sat in the car and looked at it, taking in the climbing wistaria that had run rampant, the central heating ducts and zinc gutters that had been added uncaringly in recent years. It was not thought suitable to lavish attention on the upkeep of old buildings. They were the property of a disgraced régime and must be treated with contempt.

He let himself in by a side door that opened with a shudder. Krasin had taken some care in arranging for the keys to be brought to him, applying for them in the name of a film company who had requested permission to work on location in Moscow and sending one of the secretaries to pick them up from the office.

Thoughtfully he walked through the deserted rooms of the ground floor. He had discovered from the housing committee who controlled the district that this had been one of the residences of a foreign embassy until lately. But since then it had been abandoned, too large to be used privately and too old to be worth converting.

The air was stale. There was dust on the few pieces of furniture and the woodwork was porous from neglect but he congratulated himself on the discovery.

It was perfect for his purposes.

Chapter Twenty-Two

'Izmaylovskiy Park?' Katya's voice on the phone was impressed. 'That's very grand, isn't it, Vassily?'

'Possibly, but it's not in very good condition.'

'I didn't know you were getting a new house.'

'Neither did I.' Krasin played down the acquisition. 'And I haven't decided yet. I want to take another look at it before I make up my mind. Perhaps you'd like to come next time?'

'I'd love to.' Katya leapt at the offer.

'I'm going round on Sunday morning. I'll be interested to see what you think of it.'

'How exciting, Vassily!'

He gave her directions to the house. Before ringing off he asked diffidently, 'How's it going down in the vaults?'

'We found a couple of pictures that might be interesting.'

'Really. I'd like to see them.' He thought for a moment. 'Maybe I could come in some time early next week.'

'That's too late, Vassily. I'll be in London.' She sounded hurt that he should have forgotten. 'I'm leaving on Monday.'

'Of course you are.'

She made a suggestion of her own. 'If you didn't mind them being taken away from the vaults for a few hours, I could bring them over on Sunday.'

'That's an idea.'

'They're not very big.'

'Ask Georgy to take them off their stretchers,' he said. 'Then you can roll them up.'

After he had rung off Krasin strolled down the passage.

It was nearly done now, he told himself. Two more days and the whole business would be finished.

He had no regrets. It was a woman's rôle to suffer. Nature gratified their pain with pleasure. Krasin had known this since he was a child.

The discovery had come one cold Sunday afternoon when he was ten or eleven years old. His family had been paying their monthly

167

visit to his uncle's house. When lunch was over, the adults settling back to talk and smoke, he had been given a book of Old Master paintings to look through. They were dull, grey pictures and he had turned the pages listlessly until he came across one in particular. It was a painting of a beautiful girl dressed in flowing robes who knelt before a spoked wheel holding a thin rapier in her hands. She was gazing out at him, her fingers caressing the long blade, lips smiling in anticipation.

As Krasin looked at the painting, at the soft flesh beside the sharpness of steel, he had experienced a sudden warm flood of excitement. It caught his breath, made his heart race and to his acute embarrassment he'd felt his undeveloped penis grow firm, pressing up uncomfortably against the thick material of his trousers. His mother must have guessed something of the sort for she'd snatched the book away from him, scolding him with a clip round the ear but the image had burned into his imagination. Even now as he walked down into Dzerzhinsky Square, he could visualise the brown eyes, the serene smile on the saint's lips, the look of sensual fulfilment with which she greeted her death.

That's how it would be for Katya. He was sure of it.

She walked from the metro station, occasionally breaking into a trot to warm her feet. He was waiting for her when she arrived and let her in through a side entrance toothed with icicles. He had opened some of the shutters at the back of the house and the reflections from the snow cast a clear, cold light on the ceilings.

'It's wonderful,' Katya breathed as she followed him through the empty rooms.

'I thought you might think so.'

'However did you find it?'

'Just chance,' Krasin replied. 'A camera crew had asked the department for permission to film here. I put in a housing application and it was accepted.'

'Just like that?' She was amused.

'I sweetened the offer slightly.'

She didn't dare ask him how. 'Isn't the rent going to be enormous?'

'I'll just have to do a lot of business entertainment. Let the State carry some of the burden.'

They came into the drawing room. A few sticks of furniture had been left behind and there were pages of ancient newspaper scattered about the floor.

Krasin was thinking of the future. 'Furnishing it is going to be a problem.'

'Don't you already have quite a bit?'

'I do. But that's going to stay where it is.'

Katya turned and looked at him. He was leaning against the boarded-up fireplace, one arm resting on the mantelpiece, his expression pensive. She wasn't sure she had heard him right.

'You mean you're going to have two houses?'

'Yekaterina likes it where she is. She has friends in the area, you see. People she knows.' He gave a shrug. 'She doesn't want to leave.'

Katya felt her heart give a leap but she held perfectly still. This was suddenly very important. Krasin had never mentioned his wife before, never even alluded to her. Had it not been for the fact that she wasn't allowed near his apartment Katya might have convinced herself she didn't exist.

'It seems unnecessary to force her against her will,' Krasin added, pushing himself upright and coming across to her. 'If that's where she wants to stay so much the better.'

Katya could feel the ache of suspense in her stomach. Was he saying he was going to separate from her?

'That's why I wanted you to take a look at it.'

Her voice was unsteady. 'Do you mean I can come here?'

'Would you like that?'

He stroked her temples, running his hands down over her hair and the small of her back until they rested on her hips. She responded lazily, drawing in close, curving her body into his.

'Yes,' she said simply. 'I'd like that.'

'I thought you might – '

Carefully he untied the bow at her throat, pulled the fine black ribbon free of the collar.

'I'm tired of all these borrowed apartments.'

'Are you, Vassily?' Her smile was secretive, inviting as she watched his hands through lowered lashes.

'It's so undignified.'

One by one he undid the buttons of her shirt, gliding his palms on to her shoulders so that it parted and fell down her arms. The flesh of her body was taut and firm beneath his fingers, the lacy material of her bra standing out very white against the butterscotch skin.

Giving a flick of her wrists, she freed herself of the shirt and slipped her arms around his neck.

'It's cold,' she whispered into the black hair.

'I've brought some rugs.'

They made love on the bare floorboards, sharing the warmth of their bodies. Krasin was gentle, almost timid, caressing her with the tips of his fingers, cupping the firm, pointed breasts in his hand before exploring downwards over the hollow of her belly to the wet softness between her thighs.

With small kisses across his chest and shoulders she responded to his touch, occasionally catching the flesh between her teeth as desire flooded through her, taking control of thought and action.

He could hear her breathing deepen in her throat, felt its warmth on his bare skin. As he came into her she lifted, arching her hips to his, the rhythm of her body joining his in sudden frantic passion. Then, falling back, arms and hair spread out in disarray, she lay quite still and for a while she seemed to drift, her lips parted, eyelids half closed.

Wrapping the heavy rugs he had brought in from the car around their shoulders, Krasin leaned on his elbow and looked down at the serene, lovely face. The memory of the kneeling saint rose before him, the two images meeting, becoming one.

Opening her eyes Katya stared up at the ceiling.

He saw the pupils contract as she focused and moving her head to look at him she asked, 'Are you going to miss me when I'm gone, Vassily?'

He ran his finger down the line of her cheek until it touched her lips and nodded.

'Yes, I'll miss you.'

St Catherine, that had been the title of the painting. It was strange, they even shared the same name and he added softly, 'But you mustn't be afraid. It's right this way.'

It had been the thought in his mind. The words slipped out unintentionally.

Katya didn't appear to notice however. Her mind was locked on the past. Getting to her feet she walked bare-footed across the varnished boards, looking around her.

'What do you think this room used to be?' she asked.

'I don't know.' Krasin rolled over on his back to consider. 'A drawing room maybe – or library.'

'I think so.' She nodded seriously. 'It must have been so beautiful in those days.'

'It could be again.'

From where he lay he could see her silhouetted against the cold light of the window, the rug twisted around her naked body. With one hand she was holding it against her breasts so that it fell down her back like a strapless evening gown. Krasin took his chance with the moment.

'Katya?'

She looked round at him.

'Will you do something for me?'

She came and knelt on the floor beside him, her expression suddenly intent.

170

'Of course, Vassily.'

He judged it the ideal moment – while she was content and satiate, the glow of love-making still on her. Sitting up he hugged his knees in his arms.

'I have something I want you to take to London.'

'What sort of thing?'

'It's a package, quite small.' He sounded non-committal. 'You can carry it in your pocket.'

For a moment she studied him gravely and then suddenly, with a quick flick of her head, she grinned at him. 'Have you been writing illegal poems, Vassily?'

He gave a little grunt of amusement as he stood up and going across to his overcoat he felt in the pocket.

'Nothing so romantic, I'm afraid,' he said, drawing out a small packet. 'It's just some documentation that needs delivering. I'd rather it was done personally.'

Katya examined the package on the train back home. It was no larger than a book, wrapped in brown paper and sealed with wax. Pasted to the surface was a security pass, dated and stamped.

'Where do I take it, Vassily?' she had asked him.

'You will be told all that when you arrive. Someone will contact you at your hotel.'

Katya had made light of the errand. 'It all sounds very mysterious. Is it a secret of some sort?'

'In a way,' he'd replied. 'At least, it must be kept secret from one or two of my colleagues in the Kremlin, which is why I don't want to send it through the normal channels.'

'How will I know this man when he calls?'

'His name is Tobias.' Krasin had pronounced the word carefully so that she should remember it. 'He will ring you as soon as you arrive in London and explain where you are to meet him.'

Tucking the package back in her bag Katya glanced down the aisle of the train. The compartment was almost empty, no one was paying her any attention. She felt alone and private.

They had parted in the doorway of the house. Katya would have liked to have lingered a while, to have whispered the soft, hurried assurances that lovers exchange before they separate, but Krasin was expecting a visit from a member of the housing committee and had thought it best she wasn't there when he arrived.

His manner had been detached, almost abrupt as he kissed her goodbye, but Katya was so brimmed full of happiness at that moment that she had scarcely noticed.

* * *

As soon as she'd left Krasin walked back into the empty room where they had made love, folded up the rugs and put them in the boot of the car.

The two paintings she had brought with her were lying on the floor nearby. He unrolled them in his hand. They were ugly and valueless. He couldn't remember whether they had come from London or not and he really didn't care.

Katya had taken them from the Kremlin repository, she had signed for them in her own name. That was the only thing that mattered.

Going upstairs he searched the upper rooms methodically for some minutes until he came across a loose floorboard. He touched it with the toe of his shoe, felt it move before kneeling down and prising it up with his fingers.

Beneath was a dark cavity. Taking the roll of canvas he slid it down between the floor and ceiling, pushing it well back out of sight before replacing the board. Gently he blew on the dust that had been disturbed, letting it resettle in the area. Then standing back he reviewed the effect.

Satisfied, he went down into the hallway and put on his coat and hat, pulling the peak down over his eyes and leaving by the side entrance.

The sun was bright on the snow but it brought no warmth and as he trudged up the street he could feel the cold biting at his cheeks and ears.

There was a public telephone on the corner but to his annoyance he found it was occupied by a red-faced woman engaged in a long conversation, the heat of her body misting the glass cubicle.

Krasin waited some distance away, stamping his feet on the pavement and flapping his arms across his chest.

When she had finally exhausted herself and shambled away he picked up the receiver, pushed five copecks into the machine and dialled the Ministry of Culture.

Podurets was expecting the call and answered immediately.

'Good afternoon, Colonel.'

Krasin was cautious. 'Can anyone overhear this conversation?'

'No. I am alone in the office.'

'I want you to come over here at once,' Krasin told him. 'I have made a discovery that you should see.'

Podurets hesitated. 'May I ask what?'

No you can't, Krasin thought with a flash of irritation. Just do as you're damned well told. But aloud he said, 'It's best not to talk of these things on the phone, Comrade Dmitri.'

There was a silence on the line.

Krasin waited. What had got into the little man? he asked himself. He rapped out a question.

'Are you still there?'

'Yes, Colonel.' Podurets's voice was formal. 'You must forgive me, Colonel, I don't understand what it is you expect of me.'

'I expect you to take the metro out to Izmaylovskiy Park and meet me there.'

'But this is most irregular – '

Krasin had no time to reason with him. Instead he pulled rank. 'I am giving you an order, comrade. Do I have to remind you of the consequences of disobedience?'

The question had the right effect. 'No, of course not, Colonel.'

'Then do as I say.' He gave directions to the house. Before ringing off he added, 'And you'd better leave a contact number for anyone trying to reach you.'

He read out a series of numbers, made Podurets repeat them and put down the receiver.

Podurets wasn't sure he had come to the right house. It looked deserted. The shutters were closed, snow piled thick against the doorway. He tried the bell but there was no response.

Moving back into the street he scanned the upper storeys but there was no sign of life. It was then that he noticed tracks in the snow leading round to a side door.

It was unlocked and swung open when he knocked. He stepped inside and found himself in some sort of scullery. Two large enamel basins stood against the wall. The floor was stone, the air heavy with disuse.

'Hello?' he said into the silence.

Podurets was sure he wasn't mistaken. The colonel had given him the number in the street, described the front of the house.

Shutting the door behind him, he ventured through into the next room, his feet leaving wet prints on the floor. It was dark and musty, the sunlight peering in through chinks in the shutters.

Double doors led through to the tiled hallway. The front entrance was bolted from inside, he noticed. Bare wires dangling from the wooden framework explained why the bell hadn't worked.

Krasin was leaning against the mantelpiece. One hand was thrust into his pocket, the other held a silver flask from which he was drinking.

'So you decided to come after all, Comrade Dmitri,' he said pleasantly.

Podurets turned. He had been anticipating this moment. On the journey over he had prepared his lines, rehearsed what he would say to Krasin. But seeing him standing there his nerve failed him and he said, 'I did as you told me, Colonel.'

'You took your time.'

'It's Sunday.' He heard himself apologising. 'The buses don't run so frequently.'

Krasin took a final pull at the flask and tucked it into his upper pocket.

'Did you come straight here after I rang?'

'Yes, Colonel.'

'Good.' Krasin studied him appraisingly, his head tilted back, eyes hooded.

Instead of the foreign tailored suits he usually wore he was dressed in a long grey coat and workman's cap. It had a brutalising effect. Podurets had heard the rumours that Krasin had started life working in a steelworks. For the first time he was able to believe it.

'When I rang you just now I thought you sounded concerned, Comrade Dmitri,' he said.

'I would like to know what you want of me.'

Krasin gave a curt nod of his head and strolled away towards the far room.

'Katya Leskova was here earlier,' he said looking around the empty floor. 'She was rather taken by the place. For some reason she thought she might be allowed to live here.'

Podurets gave a faint murmur of interest. They were quite alone, he realised. Krasin had brought no one with him. Not even that strange mute chauffeur of his.

'She brought a couple of paintings with her,' Krasin continued. 'I hid them under the floor upstairs. Not very original, I grant you, but convincing nevertheless.'

'I don't understand, Colonel . . .'

'No, you probably don't.' Krasin had turned and was smiling at him, his eyes bright as a ferret. 'But then you have never been required to understand, Comrade Dmitri, have you?'

He was standing close, watching, waiting. Podurets felt the first grip of fear in his stomach.

'I really don't know what you mean, Colonel . . .'

'Your rôle has always been to believe, hasn't it? Never to ask questions, simply to accept what you are told.'

Podurets's eyes were flittering around the room. 'I must ask you to explain yourself, Colonel.'

'Must you?'

Krasin seemed to be enjoying himself. Picking up a brass lampstand that lay on the floor he cradled it in his hands.

'They're bound to find her fingerprints,' he said, looking at the base, estimating the value. 'She wasn't wearing gloves, you see. She took them off when—'

The sentence broke off.

Podurets stepped back, his body turning but Krasin's reactions were quicker. With a fluid movement he spun around, pivoting on his toes, and swung the brass lamp up into Podurets's face.

There was a soft thump of contact.

Podurets gave a grunt and tottered backwards. For a moment there was no other reaction. Then his legs buckled and he sank to his knees, looking up at Krasin with an expression of stupefied wonder on his face.

Dropping his arms, Krasin turned from him in disgust.

Podurets's head lolled; his eyes were fixed on Krasin's back but they were no longer focused. He had lost the sequence of events. There was a whistling in his ears, a sound of infinite space.

Many years before, at a time and place Podurets could no longer remember, someone warm and large had held a shell over his ears, told him to listen to the sound of the sea.

He could hear it now, a distant roaring, growing louder.

The blood flowed warmly down his cheek. He could taste it on his lips. His head had fallen back, the collar was digging into the flesh of his neck. Vaguely he saw the ceiling above him but it was no longer fixed and moved before his eyes. His mouth opened and he heard himself give a long choking cry.

At the sound, Krasin spun round, the lamp held in both hands and with the full weight of his body he hit him again.

The force threw Podurets backwards on to the ground, the black astrakhan hat spinning away into the shadows.

His arms were spread out wide. The elbows pressed downwards. With a great effort he arched his back, lifting himself from the floor. And then, with a sigh, the strain went out of him. His body slumped, contracted slightly. A pool of urine appeared between his legs and spread out across the dry floor.

Krasin saw the muscles relax, waited until the body lay still and then reaching down he lifted one eyelid. Satisfied that the job was done he went outside and threw the brass instrument down the garden.

It landed silently in the snow, a soft dent marking its fall.

175

Chapter Twenty-Three

'He still hasn't come in to work, Colonel.'

'That's most unlike him.'

Krasin was reading as he spoke, his concentration fixed on the documents on his desk. With a quick, practised movement he scrawled his signature on a page and turned to the next, glancing up at Zakov who stood in the doorway awaiting further orders.

'Have you tried his home number?' he inquired. 'He could be off sick.'

Zakov shook his head. 'There's no answer from there either. His secretary told me he would have rung in if he was feeling ill.'

'Damn the man,' Krasin said mildly, putting down his pen and giving the subject his full attention. 'The one time I need to speak to him he decides to take the day off.'

'He was in the office yesterday.' Zakov ventured the information. 'He left a number on his desk where he could be contacted before going out.'

'Have you tried it?'

'Twice. But there's no reply. The line's disconnected.'

Krasin drummed three fingers on the leather-topped desk. 'Is it a local number?'

'Suburban. North-east section of the city by the look of it.'

'Find the address,' he said, returning to his work, dismissing the problem from his mind.

As soon as Zakov had closed the door he sat back with a sense of satisfaction. It was twelve forty. Katya's plane should be making its approach to Heathrow airport at that moment. The flight had been on time, he had checked that earlier in the morning. There was nothing to be done now except settle back and wait for events to take their own course.

It took Zakov less than ten minutes to track down the address and return to his office.

'It's a private house out by Izmaylovskiy Park,' he said. 'The number was ex-directory.'

'Let me see.'

Krasin took the slip of paper and studied the address for himself. Zakov saw a frown flicker across his brow.

'Do you recognise it, Colonel?'

'I've heard it,' he replied thoughtfully.

'Apparently it was used as a domestic residence of the West German Embassy for several years.'

Krasin linked the two in his mind, shook his head. 'It's more recent than that,' he said, staring across the office. 'I've seen this address somewhere recently. Just the other day.'

'Can you remember the context?'

Krasin pondered. It was on the tip of his tongue.

'No,' he said quietly, drawing on the memory. 'But I saw it recently . . . We both did – I'm sure of it.'

He looked up at Zakov for corroboration but the major's blunt features remained impassive.

'Doesn't mean anything to me, Colonel . . .'

'It was on the computer screen.' Krasin could visualise it now.

'In one of the files?'

'Probably – '

'The Leskova girl.' Zakov was beginning to pick up the scent. 'Could it be something to do with her? We examined her file only the day before yesterday.'

'Let's take a look,' Krasin said, jumping to his feet and going next door, intention translating into action.

Zakov sat himself before the computer console, hammered in commands. At once data streamed down the screen.

'Where's she been living since she arrived in Moscow?' Krasin was leaning over his shoulder, the green light of the computer illuminating his face.

'Smolenskaya,' Zakov read from the section. 'Nowhere else.'

'And before that?'

'Her father's Georgian. Spent some time in Moscow as a student.' The cursor flicked across the screen, new files appeared. 'Lived in communal accommodation belonging to the university. Nothing in the eastern district.'

'There must be some connection.'

'He was only here three years.'

'I'm certain I've seen that name somewhere.'

'Wait.' Zakov was ahead of him now. 'Her mother's family is Russian. They lived in Moscow.'

Krasin watched as new facts were dredged from the memory banks. 'Any good?'

Again Zakov shook his head.

'But we checked further back,' he added, thinking for himself

177

now. 'She told you her family had been wealthy before the revolution.'

'That's right – '

'We checked into it last week.'

His excitement was infectious. Krasin could feel his heart beginning to flutter.

Zakov was feeding in new instructions. A file spread across the screen. It was the assessment of Katya's family status in Czarist days, a prerequisite of her security rating.

'That's it,' Zakov said, his voice falling to a growl of satisfaction at the discovery. He stabbed the screen with his forefinger and turned to Krasin.

'The house belonged to Katya Leskova's great-grandfather.'

Krasin made no movement while his eyes scanned the screen, reading the illuminated letters. Then he straightened.

'Get out there,' he commanded with sudden intensity. 'As quick as you can.'

'Very good, Colonel.' Zakov had jumped to his feet.

'Take a couple of men with you,' Krasin called over his shoulder as he stormed through to his office. 'Turn that place over. I want it clean as a whistle by the time I arrive.'

He picked up his phone, cradled it in his neck, holding up his free hand to prevent Zakov from leaving.

'Wait a moment, Major – '

Zakov hovered in the doorway.

Krasin dialled the Ministry of Culture, barked an extension number at the switchboard. 'I want to speak to Comrade Podurets's secretary . . . Yes, I know he's not there . . . just do as I say.' He drummed his fingers with impatience as he waited. 'Hello . . . No, it's Katya Leskova I want. Has she left for London yet?'

He listened for a moment, giving the odd grunt of agreement and then put down the phone.

'I have a nasty feeling we're too late,' he said to Zakov. 'She left first thing this morning.'

The porter put down the two suitcases.

'Bathroom. Toilet,' he said airily, showing her the switches. 'Anything else you want just ring the reception desk.'

He handed Katya the keys and went out, looking her up and down with interest as he closed the door.

As soon as she was alone, Katya inspected the hotel room. It was small and incredibly neat. The single bed was turned down. There were framed prints on the wall. A folder of headed notepaper lay on the table, along with envelopes and brochures. Next to it was a kettle and a porcelain pot containing sachets of tea and coffee and milk in little plastic cartons. On previous trips she had discovered that, unlike the drinks in the fridge, these came free. If you hid them in your suitcase each day, more arrived in the morning. The same with the boxes of scented soap.

Going next door she stripped off her clothes and ran a bath, adding the bottle of oil. She lay for some minutes, revelling in the deep, fragrant water, letting the dirt of the journey soak away, feeling the stress of travel turning to drowsiness.

The flight from Moscow had taken a little over three hours. There were only five officials in the delegation along with the administrator and herself and so her duties were not going to be heavy. At Heathrow airport they had been met by a representative from the Arts Council, a fussy young man with a crumpled suit and damp handshake who had been visibly relieved when he found how easily he could communicate with his Russian protégés through Katya.

He had arranged for two cars to drive them to the hotel, insisting that she sit with him on the journey so that he could go over the agenda for the week. He talked quickly and nervously and from time to time she'd felt his eyes sliding off his notes to explore her legs and waist as he tried to reconcile what he was seeing with his image of Soviet Russia.

Ducking her head back into the water, Katya washed her hair and getting out of the bath she wrapped herself in the long white robe provided by the hotel.

There was a knock at the door.

'Who's that?' she called out, twisting a towel around her head.

'It's me – Vladimir Grigorvich.'

He was the delegation administrator, a thin, stringy man with the long hair, bad teeth and slightly unkempt appearance of a music teacher.

'I'm sorry to bother you, Comrade Leskova,' he said hastily as the door opened, his eyes flicking over her shoulder. 'I thought I should check that you've settled in satisfactorily. But if I'd known you were having a bath . . .'

His voice trailed away.

'It's all right,' Katya told him. 'Come in.'

Strolling back across the room she sat on the edge of her bed, crossing one leg over the other. The dressing gown parted, revealing a length of smooth brown thigh but she didn't appear to notice and made no attempt to cover herself.

She's very bold this one, Vladimir Grigorvich thought to himself as he ventured a couple of paces into the room. Two of the delegates had already made their interest known to him but he'd been quick to quash it. Katya Leskova was forbidden territory. He'd been warned of this in his brief. From what he could gather she was the property of some high-ranking member of the KGB. Girls like this usually were, he reflected sadly as he glanced around the room.

'When you have a few moments to spare,' he told her, 'the reception desk would like you to fill in the registration forms.'

She nodded. 'I'll be there in a moment.'

'And we'll be needing two taxis here at half past seven.'

Katya was towelling her hair. Getting to her feet she strolled into the bathroom.

'I'll be going out some time this afternoon,' she called back to him. 'There is something I have to deliver.'

The administrator's ears pricked up at this. He'd been told nothing of any deliveries taking place.

'When will this be?' he inquired politely.

'I'm not sure,' Katya told him, coming back and tossing her clothes down on the bed. 'But I'll be back well before dinner.'

'I understand,' he said quickly.

So, Katya Leskova was more than just an interpreter, he told himself as he walked back down the passage. Not that there was anything new in that. Girls were often employed by the KGB to act as couriers. In retrospect he should have guessed something of the sort from her suave turn-out, the smart clothes she wore, the confident, rather aloof way she carried herself.

But Vladimir Grigorvich was not at all pleased to have learned of her intentions so late. It was humiliating. Security was his responsibility. He should have been briefed before they left the country. As soon as he returned he'd file a complaint.

'When was this?'

'It must have been some time over the weekend,' Krasin replied. 'The coroner's report suggests the body had been dead for at least twenty-four hours when my men discovered it.'

Chernov's hard blue eyes met his for an instant and then picking up the photos he studied them in silence before throwing them back on the desk in disgust.

'But how did it happen?' he demanded.

'He must have followed her to the house, caught her red-handed.'

'And she killed him?' Chernov couldn't believe what he was hearing. 'A slip of a girl like that? I wouldn't have thought she had the strength to do such a thing.'

'Necessity often finds strength,' Krasin replied. 'We found the instrument she used. It was hidden in the snow some way down the garden.'

With a grunt of exertion Chernov tipped himself forward and peered at the photos spread across the desk.

'A man she's worked with for two years,' he complained. 'One of her own kind. It makes me sick to think of it.'

Krasin held himself quite still, one leg crossed over the other as he listened. It was strange, even Zakov had been shocked by the discovery of Podurets's body. For some reason the knowledge that the crime had been committed by a girl made it that much harder to accept. He made a small gesture with his hand.

'I blame myself, General. Comrade Podurets had made his suspicions known to me on several occasions. If I had investigated the girl's activities earlier this might never have happened.'

Chernov considered the apology momentarily.

'It is not your fault, Vassily,' he said with a jerk of his head. 'You were not to know he was going to attempt anything like this. The man was a fool. He should have kept you informed of his intentions.'

Opening the box at his elbow Chernov took out a cigarette, lit it from the gold desk lighter and took three quick, greedy pulls at the filter. A web of smoke lifted around him, suddenly flashing to silver as it caught the afternoon sunlight. He stared through it, eyes slitted in consideration.

When he spoke his voice was detached.

'I want this finished quickly, Vassily.' Discussion of the past was over, Chernov was thinking to the future. 'We can't afford a scandal. Right now the whole world is watching us, wondering what makes us tick. This is not the time to make mistakes. Do you follow what I am saying?'

'I think so, General.'

'Good.' Chernov brushed the photos aside, signalling the end of the meeting. 'Keep me informed of your progress, Vassily.'

Krasin went outside into the street. After the stuffy, over-heated office, the cold air felt good, invigorating and he drew it into his lungs with a physical sensation of pleasure.

The Rolls was parked further up the road. Krasin threw himself into the back seat.

'Take me up to the Lefertovo jail.'

'Have you got anything from him yet?'

The sergeant shook his head. 'Only that he is a patriot and a war veteran.'

'I bet you've heard that line before.'

'Just a few hundred times.' The sergeant completed the formula of words without lending it humour.

They turned right into a long passageway, their footsteps ringing out loud in the silence. The windows were set high in the walls and covered with wire mesh. In the distance Krasin heard a cell door slam, a raised voice barking orders.

The Lefertovo jail has had its share of celebrities. Solzhenitsyn, Daniloff, Sakharov had all spent time here. Men were locked up for their thoughts as much as their deeds. Krasin gave an involuntary shiver. He detested the place, as he detested these prisoners with their high principles, their ridiculous moral stances.

The sergeant nodded to the duty officer as he passed.

'Do you want me to come in with you, Colonel?' he asked, jingling his way through a bunch of keys.

'Not on this occasion.'

'I'll wait outside then.'

Krasin watched him thrust the key into the lock. His head was bowed, the line of his neck exposed between the collar and the rim of his hat. It made him look suddenly young and vulnerable. Some mother's boy rather than a jailer.

The cell door swung open.

Georgy was sitting on the bed, his hands in his lap, feet dangling. At the sight of Krasin his face cracked into a grin.

'I knew you would be coming, Colonel.'

Krasin stood in the entrance, sensing the cramped space, the stale air.

'Did you, Georgy?' His voice was remote.

'I told them that as soon as you heard of this you would be coming round here.'

The sergeant was leaning forward, his hand on the door handle. 'If you want me just give a knock, Colonel.'

Krasin heard the door close behind. Georgy was watching him expectantly. He didn't appear to be frightened but that was often the way with prisoners when they first arrived. It took time for the reality to dawn in their minds.

'Do you know why you are here, Georgy?' he asked.

'It's about the girl.'

Krasin nodded slowly. 'You must tell them what you know about her. Don't try to resist them.'

'But I don't know anything, Colonel. I keep telling them this but they don't listen to me.'

Krasin sat down on the edge of the bed. 'They can hurt you, Georgy. Do you understand what I'm saying? Unless you help them with their inquiries they will stop you from sleeping. They will keep you awake until your mind goes soft.'

Georgy was listening attentively. He was wearing his blue jacket with the ribbon of medals on his breast, the stitching crude and uneven. Dangling from his pocket was a rubber strap.

Krasin reached over and drew out a pink object, holding it up for both of them to see.

It was a bathing cap.

'I was going down to the Veterans' Club when they brought me here,' Georgy explained.

Carefully Krasin fitted the cap on the old man's head, pulling it down around his ears.

He said, 'I've seen men go mad from lack of sleep, Georgy.'

'But what can I say to them, Colonel?'

Krasin was leaning back, studying the effect of the cap. 'Tell them how she kept coming down to the vaults each month. Tell them how she brought pictures with her, how she left them there in place of others.'

'But it wasn't like that, Colonel – '

'You forget these things. I can understand, it's natural at your age.'

'She was only there a few days.'

Krasin stood, preparing to leave. 'She has been stealing pictures from the vaults.' He rapped on the door. The bolt clanked back. As the door opened he turned back into the cell. 'Tell them how she tricked you, Georgy, and then they'll let you go.'

Chapter Twenty-Four

It was raining as Katya came out of the hotel. The doorman standing back in the shelter of the awning gazed up at an overcast sky.

'Can I get you a taxi, miss?' he asked.

'No thank you. I'll walk.' There was no need to tell him that she hadn't the money for a taxi. She looked down the glistening pavement. 'How do I get to Marble Arch from here?'

He gave her directions. 'Take you about ten minutes, less if you hurry.'

Turning up the collar of her coat, she held it against her cheeks as she walked up into Piccadilly. Her hair was tucked into her fur hat to keep it dry. In her pocket was the package she had brought from Moscow.

It was just after three; she had plenty of time.

Two women barged past her as they came out of Fortnum & Masons, their heads down, umbrellas set against the wind. Cars were bundled up against the lights. On a newspaper stall by the railings of Green Park a poster blazed out the day's headlines: 'Berlin wall comes down – dramatic pictures'. Katya read the words without paying them any attention. Her thoughts were reaching forward to the coming meeting.

The telephone call had been paged through to her room. It had been a man's voice on the other end of the line. Quiet, well spoken. He had given the name Tobias.

'You have something for me, I believe?'

'That's right.'

Without further discussion he had given her instructions. 'Go to the car park at Marble Arch. It connects to the Underground station. You can't miss it. I'll meet you there.'

It was not what she expected. When Vassily had given her the package to deliver she had assumed she would be taking it to an office, a government building, possibly even a police station. Certainly somewhere official, somewhere public.

A car park didn't sound right.

'The caretaker has confessed.'

'I thought he might,' Chernov replied. He had been to a meeting of the Supreme Soviet and was still dressed in full uniform, a patch of medals the size of a chessboard on his breast. One by one he unpicked the buttons of his jacket and tugged it off.

'So what did you discover?'

'Much as I expected. He confirmed that Katya Leskova has been systematically pilfering paintings from the Kremlin vaults for the last two years.'

Beneath the immaculately pressed uniform jacket, Chernov's belly was restrained by a corset. Heaving in his stomach, he released the straps and sat down with a groan of contentment.

'I assume she is not going to get away with this, Vassily.'

'She will be apprehended, General. It has already been arranged.'

Chernov's blue eyes moved, quick and bright in fleshy sockets. 'Do you need assistance from the department?'

'I have a contact in London. He has been briefed.'

'But is he reliable?'

'It will be discreet, General. As you wished.'

Chernov nodded, laying fat palms on the arm-rest of his chair. 'And what of this caretaker from the vaults? What is to become of him?'

'He will be transferred to a work-camp in the east.'

Chernov breathed through his opened mouth, his stomach rising on the swell. So that was to be the way of it, he thought. Both the subject and the source silenced at the same time. It was neat. Oh yes, it was very neat. He studied Krasin through hooded lids.

He was leaning back against the mahogany sideboard, his ankles crossed, the hard winter light casting his face into sharp relief. God, he was a good-looking son-of-a-bitch, Chernov told himself, and poised like a ballet dancer. But then maybe that's what he was, a performer, an actor of parts.

Krasin glanced down at the floor and then up again. 'There is one other thing, General.'

'And what is that?'

'A few days ago a painting was taken from the Pushkin Museum for routine restoration work to be carried out. The restorers have no record of it arriving.'

Chernov pushed out his small, wet lower lip as he listened.

'Checking through the log-book I discovered that Katya Leskova was at the workshops on the day the painting should have arrived.'

'You think she has pinched it?'

'I would have thought the possibility was too strong to ignore. It is very small, you see. Small enough for her to have carried through customs control in her pocket.'

'And is it valuable?'

Krasin made a slight gesture of his head as though the subject were distasteful to him. 'Extremely. It is the Talinin Madonna. In the West it could command thousands, possibly millions of dollars.'

'Then you must retrieve it, Vassily.'

'I shall do so.' He straightened, preparing to go. 'With your permission I shall leave for London immediately.'

'I think you should, Vassily.'

After he had gone Chernov turned to his aide. 'What did you make of that?'

'It concerns me that his judgement may be clouded,' the aide replied carefully. 'He has been sleeping with this girl. He is evidently attracted to her. I wonder whether his actions may not be affected by sentiment.'

Chernov stared at him for a moment and then he laughed, his shoulders picking up the high-pitched note and shaking in sympathy.

'Sentiment?' he echoed. 'Vassily Krasin? He doesn't know the meaning of the word. Don't you know that when he was fifteen he denounced his father to the KGB? Stood by and watched him taken away in the night.'

'But why?' The aide was shocked.

'It was his entrance ticket to the security forces, a token of good faith. That's how he started out.'

The aide stared back at him. Again laughter registered on the Richter scale of Chernov's body.

'Oh yes, make no mistake about it. Whatever he intends for that girl, it won't have been inspired by sentiment.'

It was cold in the underground car park.

Katya walked down the long avenues of vehicles, looking at the numbers painted on the concrete beams above her head. She had been told which section she was to go to, where she was to meet Tobias. It was right at the back of the car park, a dank, oil-stained space against the far wall.

There was nobody there.

Pulling her glove back from her wrist she checked the time. Fifteen minutes to go. It seemed an eternity. She wanted to get this over with, hand over the package and get back to the hotel.

She positioned herself where she was visible beneath one of the overhead lights and waited, hands thrust down into her pockets, feet set close together.

186

Water dripped from the ceiling. The air was filled with the acidic stench of urine, petrol and exhaust fumes.

She could feel the weight of the package in her pocket. Pulling it out she examined the outer wrapping as she had a dozen times before. Vassily had told her it was documents. She could recall his exact words, the expression on his face as he'd explained what she had to do. His colleagues in the Kremlin mustn't know of its existence, he'd said. But surely now that she was in London it no longer had to be kept a secret? This man Tobias could have come to her hotel. Why did they have to meet in this stinking place?

The sound of footsteps broke into her thoughts. Katya pushed the package back in her pocket.

A man in a dark suit was coming towards her. She felt her heart patter awake. Was this him, she wondered. It was impossible to tell. Tobias had declined to describe himself. 'I'll know you,' he had assured her when she'd asked. But nothing more. No indication of his appearance or how she would recognise him. Just the number of the bay and the time.

The man had stopped. She saw him put his briefcase and raincoat on the roof of a car and reach down to unlock the door. She didn't know whether she felt relieved or disappointed. With a sudden deafening roar the engine fired. The car reversed out and drew away. She heard the tyres squeal as it turned at the far end of the car park and then it was gone.

Silence rolled in around her.

Katya glanced at her watch. Still ten minute to go. Where was he, for God's sake? Briefly she considered leaving the package, hiding it somewhere and going. If she wasn't there to meet him he would be bound to ring, wouldn't he?

Abruptly she turned and walked back through the sea of parked cars. It was better to keep moving, to think of something else, that way she didn't notice the twisting of the nerves in her belly. Yellow plastic signs pointed towards the Underground station. Katya pushed through swing doors into a white-washed subway. Strip lights above, graffiti shouting at her from the walls. The air was cleaner here, the lights becoming brighter as she approached the station. An old man sprawled on the ground was playing the mouth-organ. A few coins lay like tiddlywinks around his hat.

For ten minutes she wandered about the hallway of the Underground station, welcoming the presence of the strangers who thrust through the barriers, the bustle of other people, the sound of their voices. Again the image of Vassily rose in her mind. She pictured him as they had parted, as though seeing it for the first time; the

187

slight smile that had played on his lips, the coldness as they'd kissed goodbye.

It was three thirty. She looked back down the subway, coming to a decision in her mind.

Taking the package out of her pocket she reached under her coat and pushed it into her waistband as she had often done with her purse. She was wearing a broad patent-leather belt and the little package fitted neatly against the small of her back. Straightening her coat she returned to the car park.

There was still no sign of Tobias when she arrived.

Behind her she could hear the distant reedy sound of the mouth-organ, punctuated by the slow drip of water. She crossed her arms, hugging herself for comfort.

'Miss Leskova?'

The voice came from behind. She turned quickly.

He was standing in the shadow of a concrete pillar. A dark silhouette. Impossible to see him more clearly.

'You have brought it?' he asked.

Katya stood back, keeping in the light.

'Yes,' she said carefully, 'I have brought it.'

His hand came out from the darkness, the palm opened. 'You will give it to me, please.'

This was the moment she had been anticipating. Now that it had come she wasn't sure she could go through with it. But the words she had prepared came out automatically.

'I don't have it.'

A sharpness of tone. 'You've just said you've brought it.'

'I have done – but it's not here.'

'What are you talking about?'

Katya raised her arm, pointing back towards the entrance. 'I left it in the station.' Her voice was trembling as she spoke. 'I'll give it to you there.'

There was a moment's silence and then Tobias stepped forward. In the orange overhead light she saw that he was wearing a long overcoat, the lower part of his head covered by a scarf, the upper by a felt hat, so that only his eyes were visible. They blinked at her.

'Open it.' He nodded to the bag hanging from her shoulder.

Katya unclipped the flap, holding out the contents for him to see. He reached forward and again his eyes blinked.

Vaguely she registered that he was short-sighted.

'Undo your coat,' he ordered.

She did as she was told, holding out her arms. He ducked forward, running his left hand swiftly over her hips and waist, moving it up over her ribs.

She could feel the little package pressing against her back, only inches from his fingertips. He was going to find it, she was sure of it. She steeled herself for the moment of discovery.

Reaching up he checked the lining of her coat, the back of his hand brushing against her breast as he fumbled in the inner pocket. Drawing it out he tried the outer pockets and stepped back again.

'You stupid little cow,' he whispered. 'Where is it?'

He was as frightened as her. She could sense the fear on him like the scent on an animal. He was breathing hard, the whites of his eyes bright in the darkness.

Slowly Katya lowered her arms. 'I told you. It's in the station.'

'The station? Whereabouts in the station?'

She tried to picture the place but her mind had frozen. There was no answer, no image of the place.

'Where have you put it?' he asked fiercely, anger breaking through the control.

'I'll show you.'

'Tell me – '

'No!' she cried, backing away from him, fearful, close to tears. 'I'll show you when we get there.'

Again the eyes blinked at her. She could see him thinking, adjusting to this change of plan. He gave a jerk of his head.

'Let's go then.'

As Katya turned he fell into step beside her, coming up close. His right hand was in his coat pocket. He lifted it, touching it against her back.

'Walk beside me,' he said quietly.

Katya stared ahead of her. She could feel the bulk and weight of the gun as it nudged between her shoulder-blades. She'd guessed he was carrying one, sensed it in the way he'd kept the hand buried in his pocket, in the stiffness of the arm.

The subway floor dropped away before her, then rose again. She felt a sickness, a dull aching pain in her legs and in the palms of her hands. Her only thought was to get out of this place, to be back amongst people again. Nothing else mattered for the moment.

The passage seemed longer than it had before, an endless ribbon of concrete floor and white walls. Two men were approaching from the opposite direction. Only boys really, fair-haired, confident in tee-shirts and trainers. Then a woman with a loaded carrier bag in each hand, a small child beside her, complaining loudly.

None of them gave the tall girl in the fur hat or the man who held close to her a second look as they brushed past. From the way his hand rested on her hip, from the embrace of the coat around her back, they could have been lovers. Only the quick jerky movements of his head, the look of strain in the girl's dark eyes suggested otherwise.

'Where is it?' Tobias asked as they came out into the station.

Katya was looking around herself, searching for inspiration. She heard the clank of the ticket barriers, saw the escalators beyond. She needed an answer, something to give her more time.

'It's in there,' she said suddenly, pointing towards a tobacconist's kiosk.

Halfway across the marble-tiled floor she felt Tobias hesitate, followed the direction of his gaze. Standing by the ticket barrier was a policeman, a fresh young face beneath the peaked blue helmet. He was watching the steady flow of traffic through the station without interest, letting the time pass, his thoughts elsewhere. Tobias nudged the gun high against her back again.

'Keep going.'

The kiosk was brightly lit. A woman sat behind the counter. She looked up at them listlessly. Katya glanced around the shelves, uncertain of what happened next. She hadn't thought beyond this moment.

Tobias spoke for her. 'My friend left a parcel here a few minutes ago, I believe?'

'Not here.' The woman was defensive. She turned her attention to a man who butted in front of them, asking for the *Evening Standard*.

'Are you sure?'

The woman was taking money, handing back change. 'I haven't seen a package.'

Tobias turned on Katya.

There was no more time. The deception was over. She felt a sudden clarity, as though a bright light were shining down on her. She could sense people on either side, knew what she had to do. Tobias was grasping her by the arm, jerking her away from the kiosk.

It had to be now.

In a high, clear voice she said, 'This man is holding me against my will.'

For a moment she thought no one had heard. They looked at her stupidly. The woman in the kiosk, the man turning with the newspaper in his hand, an elderly couple carrying luggage. They just stood staring at her. Panic rose in her throat.

'Listen to me, please – you must listen!'

Tobias had let go of her arm.

She drew away from him, the adrenaline burning through her body giving her words a sudden urgency. 'This man forced me to go with him. I think he means to harm me.'

There was a murmur of interest from the crowd. Here was a spectacle, a curiosity, something worth watching.

Tobias had taken a step forward but Katya leapt back out of his reach.

'Don't touch me!' she screamed. In the emergency of the moment the words came out in Russian.

There was silence. She could feel the eyes of the whole station on her, startled faces taking in the strange language.

Katya felt suddenly isolated, a stranger in a foreign country. She was surrounded by people who didn't know what she was saying, who didn't understand what was happening.

Eyes stretched wide with fear, lips parted, she faced Tobias across the hallway. He met her gaze for an instant and then glanced quickly to his left.

The policeman had heard the commotion. He was taking an interest, coming over to investigate. Tobias's head snapped back to her, his expression darkening.

Katya saw him move. Turning around she broke through the crowd and bolted for the stairs. Raised voices followed her. Someone was shouting, telling her to stop.

Without looking back she tore up the dirty steps, taking them two at a time, her coat flying about her legs. Her high heels slowed her, turning her ankle so that twice she stumbled, grasping out at the handrail for support, pulling herself to her feet again.

Tobias was close behind. His footsteps were loud on the stairs, breath coming in short spurts. Katya kept on going, driven by the fear that coursed through her veins, by the image of the man who followed.

The street was above her. She could see the inky smudge of the sky, smell the fresh air. Sobbing for breath she reached the top and looked around her, confused and disorientated.

It was still raining. Shop windows glowed in the gathering darkness. Further down the street a man was selling chestnuts from a barrow, the coals in his brazier pricking the twilight with red eyes.

She ran down the pavement, pushing her way through the slow, ungiving current of pedestrians. Before she had gone more than a few yards Tobias caught up with her. The force of the collision threw her back against the barrow which rocked with the impact, chestnuts scattering across the pavement, a hiss of sparks rising into the night.

Katya felt her spine jar against the shaft and then a sudden pain which leapt upwards in her like a flame as one of the steel supports of the brazier dug into her waist, tearing through the fine material of her shirt. With a cry of pain she twisted around, throwing Tobias from her.

The sudden movement caught him off balance. He let go of her, pitching forward, his arms outstretched.

Katya had jumped back. Her hands were on her face, the fingers splayed out wide. She watched in horror as he fell across the barrow, heard the crack of splintering wood, saw the brazier begin to topple, the weight inside shifting.

Beside her the owner was shouting hoarsely; the acrid stench of smoke was in her nostrils. A great swarm of sparks rose into the air, hissing and crackling angrily as the red hot coals hit the tarmac and spewed out across the road like a flow of lava.

Tobias had fallen amongst them, his arms thrown around his face. She heard him scream in pain. The gun he had been carrying spilled from his pocket and skittered away into the kerb by Katya's feet.

Bending down she picked it up.

With a quick, convulsive movement Tobias struggled to his feet. His body was doubled over with pain, one hand thrown across his chest and clamped beneath his other arm. He glanced up at Katya, his eyes blinking at her in disbelief.

In the distance came the sound of sirens wailing. Tobias heard them, sensed them coming like the scent of danger. With his head down he pushed through the crowd and vanished into the darkness.

Katya stood and watched him go. A space had cleared in the street around her. The police officer had reached the top of the stairs and paused, assessing the situation. The radio on his lapel was crackling, a hush had fallen over the crowd.

Holding out his hand the policeman began to inch his way towards her.

'Give that to me,' he said.

Katya couldn't think what he was referring to.

'Come on, miss.' His voice was calm, reasonable. 'Do yourself a favour now.'

She looked down at the gun in her hand. That's what he wanted. But he couldn't be imagining that she was going to use it, could he? That was absurd. She'd just wanted to take it away from Tobias.

'That's it, miss. Hand it over.'

The sirens were closer now. She could see the blue lights spitting out in the darkness.

The police officer had his hands up in a gesture of surrender as he came towards her.

She backed away. It was not her they should be arresting. It was Tobias. The gun was his. She had just picked it up off the street. They must have seen that. Oh God, surely they must have seen that. Her mind told her to stop, to reason with them but her body was aching to get away from these strangers with their stupid gaping faces, aching to get away from this callow young man who approached her.

The spectators watched in silence. They saw the girl give a shake of her head and stumble back a couple of paces. Thrusting the gun into her pocket she turned and ran. In the release of tension a great sigh rose from their throats, immediately breaking into individual cries that lifted above the rest.

Katya heard them as she tore down the street and they urged her to keep on going. The pavements were crowded so she kept to the kerb of the road, feeling the gun banging against her thigh like a stone in her pocket. Above her head, Christmas decorations freckled the darkness with lights. In front of her was a bus stop, a knot of people blocking her way.

She swerved out into the street, heading for the other side. Brakes squealed in protest. A taxi skidded to a halt, tyres biting the road for purchase, its bonnet down, butting into her as it stopped. Katya stumbled and fell. The driver was out, shouting obscenities after her as she picked herself up and continued on her way. On the far side of the road she dived down into a side street. It was narrower, less well lit but almost deserted.

As she ran, bright images flashed across her mind. She saw Tobias's hand reaching out from the darkness of the car park, felt his hand searching across her body. She remembered the cold, stark moment when she had spoken out in the Underground station; the stupefied expressions on the people around her; the scream of pain as Tobias fell on the burning coals; the seething upward rush of sparks; heard the soft, soothing tone of the policeman's voice.

Every muscle in her body was hurting, her breath coming in great gasps that seemed to tear the lungs from her chest. She was scarcely moving faster than a walking pace now but she didn't allow herself to stop until she had crossed over Piccadilly and threaded her way down through the smaller streets.

In St James's Square she leaned against the railings, holding on to the black painted shafts for support while she fought to regain her breath. Her side was hurting, sharp spears of pain jabbing up beneath her rib-cage. She pushed back her coat and found that her shirt was wet with blood.

The gates of the gardens in the centre of the square were open. Katya sat on a bench and examined the wound. The metal edge of the barrow had torn a gash in her waist. It was the length of her finger, jagged and raw. Already the skin around had darkened into a livid bruise. The blood had soaked down over her skirt in a dark stain. She could feel it beginning to dry, the material sticking to her hip.

193

Taking a handkerchief from her pocket she pressed it over the cut. The bleeding had practically stopped. She pulled her belt up until it held the scrap of cloth in place and drew it tight. It felt better, the throbbing retreated slightly.

She slumped back on the bench, her face raised to the sky, arms spread out on either side. With the calming of her heart-beat her thoughts began to steady, events falling back into sequence. The evening air was cool on her skin. The rain had stopped and the earth smelled fresh and dank.

Something was pressing against her back. She reached under her coat, pulled out the little package and looked at it in surprise. Here was the cause of the trouble, the reason she'd gone to meet Tobias and she'd almost forgotten its existence.

She turned the package in her hand and then with a sudden gesture of impatience she put her finger beneath the seal and tore it open. The contents was tightly wrapped in polystyrene packing. Katya stripped it off layer by layer and drew out the tiny wooden triptych.

At first she couldn't see what it was. Then she found the catch, opened the two doors and looked down at the Talinin Madonna.

It was exquisitely beautiful. A sunlit landscape that sank away into brilliant ultramarine hills. The Virgin Mary sat cradling the child Christ between her knees, holding his hand as he stepped on to the ground. But it was the expression on her face that held Katya's attention. She was gazing out of the picture with a slight, sad smile of resignation on her lips.

For a few minutes Katya stared at it and then, shutting the twin doors, she refastened the catch and tucked the painting away in her pocket.

This was what Vassily had asked her to take across to London. Not documents, not something that his colleagues shouldn't see, but a minute painting. She had no doubt that it was valuable. He would never have gone to such lengths if it wasn't.

She gazed across the darkened gardens, the realisation of her own stupidity breaking over her like a black wave.

Vassily had lied. He had told her she was helping him in his work, acting as a legitimate courier. Instead he had given her a priceless work of art. Something that he didn't own. And she had smuggled it into the country for him.

Katya's head fell forward on her breast. She had always known he was lying to her. From the day she met him she'd sensed he was deceiving her, leading her on.

Only she had loved him and so she'd chosen to ignore it.

194

Chapter Twenty-Five

The commissionaire of Evans-Greatheart spooned sugar into his tea and sipped it comfortably. Another half an hour and he'd be handing over to the night security. Most of the staff had gone home, only a few lights were still burning in the offices above.

He looked up as the girl came in.

She seemed nervous, ill at ease. As she approached the desk he noticed the ladder in her stockings, the stain on the damp overcoat that she held wrapped around her waist.

'Can I help you, miss?' he asked politely. Not his place to judge the clients.

Her dark eyes flittered about the hall and returned to him.

'I want to speak to Mr Spencer.'

Foreign accent. He couldn't place it. 'He's not here, I'm afraid. Mr Spencer was in court this afternoon. I imagine he went straight back home afterwards.'

He could see the disappointment in her face.

'I must speak to him – '

'He'll be in tomorrow morning, miss. Can't it wait until then?'

She shook her head numbly. 'I must see him now. It's urgent.'

'Like I said, he's not here.'

'Can you tell me where he lives?'

'I'm not allowed to do that.' He looked at her more carefully. 'I've seen you before, haven't I?'

The girl stiffened at the suggestion – wary as a stray cat, this one – and then assented.

'Yes, I was here about a month ago.'

'A client of his, are you?' The commissionaire was beginning to mellow. She was in trouble of some sort, you didn't have to be a psychiatrist to see that. And Pip Spencer was not one to leave his work behind him when he left the office.

'Please,' she said quietly. 'It's very important.'

Reaching down to the desk drawer he hefted out a telephone directory and pushed it across to her.

'He's in the book, miss. Nothing to stop you looking it up for yourself.'

The flat was in a tall Victorian apartment block off the Bayswater Road. There was a bank of buzzers beside the entrance. Katya pressed the one beside Pip Spencer's name.

There was no reply.

She leaned against the brick porch and waited. The pain in her side had steadied into one single, nagging continuity. She put her hand into her pocket and tried to subdue it with the pressure of her palm but there was no response. The flesh felt hot and troubled beneath her fingers.

'Are you waiting for someone?' A woman had bustled up the steps and was fiddling a key into the lock. Katya straightened expectantly.

'I was looking for Phillip Spencer.'

'Ah yes.' The woman hesitated, assessing Katya with the shrewd eyes of a window-shopper and then held the door open. 'Well you'd better come in, dearie. You can't stand out there in the cold.'

Katya took the lift to the second floor. She knocked on his door but there was still no answer. In the warmth of the corridor she felt suddenly light-headed, unsure on her feet. There was a flight of stairs further along the passage. Katya went over to it and sat down with a bump, putting her head on her knees.

The decision to seek out Pip Spencer had not come immediately. Her first instinct as she'd sat in St James's Square had been to get back to her hotel. Clean herself up. Work out what to do next from the security of her room. But when she'd reached the street where her hotel was situated she found blue lights flashing. A police car was parked outside the entrance foyer. Further down the road was another, the door open, a uniformed officer talking rapidly into the shortwave radio.

Katya had shrunk back into the shadow of the building. They had traced her. Somehow they had discovered her name, identified the hotel where she was staying.

For over an hour she'd wandered about the city, the bleak reality of her predicament beginning to dawn on her. Briefly she considered going to the Russian Embassy, giving them the little painting and trying to explain how she came to have it, but she'd dismissed the thought as quickly as it came. They wouldn't believe her. It would be her word against Vassily Krasin's and she knew how that would end.

She remembered standing on the edge of a park pond looking at the darkened surface of the water, searching for the answer to a problem that appeared insoluble.

196

She needed help, someone to speak on her behalf. Pip Spencer's name had reached her and she'd clutched at it like a drowning man to a straw. He had met her before. He knew about the thefts from the Russian collections. It was just possible he might be able to help.

But now, as she sat on the stairs outside his flat, a new and more disturbing thought struck her. Pip Spencer was a lawyer. He was bound by a code of practice she knew nothing about. He might be obliged to report her, hand her over to the police.

The lift doors opened and a man stepped out into the passage.

It was him.

He was dressed in jeans and a grey herring-bone jacket which made him look younger than she remembered, but she recognised the sandy brown hair and blue eyes instantly.

He was searching in his pocket for the latchkey and hadn't noticed her crouched there on the stairs. Katya got to her feet, waited until he had the door open and ran down the passage.

'Mr Spencer—'

The door was half open. She pushed against it, slipping into the flat behind him.

'—I must speak to you.'

Pip Spencer closed the door.

The girl had wriggled past him so quickly that he'd scarcely noticed her. His surprise at seeing her was instantly blunted by recognition, the one coming a split second after the other.

Katya had pulled away from him as she came inside and now stood in the centre of the floor with her feet set slightly apart. She'd dug the gun from her overcoat pocket and was clasping it in both hands, her wrists bent down by the weight, the barrel waving erratically.

He put down his briefcase and straightened slowly, giving himself a few moments to collect himself.

'What in God's name are you doing here?' he asked.

'I need your help.'

The gun was aimed at his chest but with such a degree of approximation that he guessed if it were to go off the bullet could hit anything from the stereo set beside him to the chandelier above her head.

Taking his eyes off her, he moved over to the window and jerked the curtain aside, glancing down into the street. A couple were standing on the pavement immediately below him, further along a car was parking. Apart from that the place looked deserted.

'How did you get here?' he asked.

'I walked.'

'Were you followed?'

Katya shook her head. 'There was no one. I checked.'

'Well that's something.' He dropped the curtain and turned back into the room. 'You realise that half the metropolitan police force is out looking for you?'

The gun barrel wavered. She was very pale, he noticed; beneath her honey-toned skin the blood had drained from her face and lips leaving dark circles around her eyes.

'Your embassy is raising hell.'

'I've done nothing wrong – '

'That's not what they are saying. According to them you've stolen a painting from the Russian Government.'

'I haven't stolen anything,' she shouted furiously, giving a toss of her head as though trying to clear her mind. 'I didn't know what it was I was carrying. I thought it was documents, just pieces of paper – something that had to be brought to London.'

'You believed that?'

'It was wrapped up. I didn't see it.'

'But you must have—'

'Listen!' Katya cried at him. 'Just listen to me and don't talk. I was given a package, told to take it to a car park. I didn't know it was a painting. I didn't know anything at all. It was a trick, the whole thing was a trick.'

She paused, breathing hard. Pip could sense the violence of the struggle in her mind. Reason and caution were fighting for control. She needed his help but she was unsure whether she could trust him. It was common enough. He had known clients scream abuse at him as they confided their secrets, frustrated and humiliated by the experience of confessing to a solicitor.

The incident at Marble Arch tube station had been on the evening news. He had heard it on the car radio as he was driving home. It had even occurred to him that the Russian girl they were describing might be Katya Leskova. But her appearance in his flat had come so suddenly that he hadn't been given time to think, to put the pieces together. He was only aware of the wild eyes, the angry voice, the snout of the pistol pointing at him and he responded to them intuitively, speaking gently, trying to calm her.

'Put the gun down, Katya.'

'They'd set a trap for me,' she cried. 'You have to believe me – someone has to believe me.'

'It's all right – '

'I haven't stolen anything.'

'I know – don't be frightened. You have done the right thing coming here.'

198

He could see her registering his words, uncertain whether to accept them yet. The gun barrel dipped a few degrees. He took the opportunity to move towards her.

'Now put that cannon down and we can talk about it.'

'No!' She shied away from him, reversing into a table. 'Stay where you are.'

The gun was aiming at him again. She wasn't going to use it – he was fairly certain of that – it was just a symbol, a charm to ward off the evil eye, but there was every chance it might go off by mistake and so he kept his distance.

'Whoever is responsible for those paintings being smuggled out of Russia, it's not you.' Pip laid out the few facts he knew – a peace offering, a token of good faith. 'It's a man. I don't know his name but I do know that he has black hair. He's sophisticated in his manners – dresses more like an English businessman than a Russian.'

His words seemed to smack her in the face. She stared at him in amazement, the gun dropping to her side.

'How do you know this?'

'I asked some questions of my own.'

She stepped backwards, knocking against the table. A framed photo fell over with a clatter. Crossing the room Pip took the gun from her limp hand. She didn't resist, the fight had gone out of her. As he unpeeled the fingers from the butt of the gun she fell against him.

'Here,' he said, staggering slightly under her weight. 'I think you'd better sit down before you wreck the place completely.'

She allowed herself to be led to a chair, her coat falling open as she collapsed down into it. Pip saw the dark stain of blood.

'What in God's name have you done to yourself?'

'I hit something.'

'You can say that again – '

'Why should I?' She was puzzled.

Pushing back the skirts of her coat and loosening the lower buttons of her shirt he examined the wound. The bleeding had practically stopped but he could see that it needed attention. Further questions would have to wait. Going into the bathroom he collected a few things from the cupboard and went back to her.

'Take your coat off.'

She gave a murmur of complaint but did as he ordered, dropping it to the floor by her feet. Kneeling down on the ground he loosened her belt and drew it aside. The handkerchief beneath was blackened with blood and fastened hard to the flesh. Carefully he began to peel it away. At once he saw the muscles of Katya's stomach contract

199

and she drew in her breath with a hiss of pain. He dampened the handkerchief with warm water and it came off more easily.

'How did you get my address?' he asked, removing the scrap of cloth. The raw wound beneath was swollen and pink as the inside of a cat's mouth. As he washed it, pricks of fresh blood appeared along the torn edge, ruby red beside the old.

'I went to your office,' Katya replied through clenched teeth. She was holding her shirt away from her waist, apprehensively watching his hands as they worked.

'You didn't tell anyone who you were?'

She shook her head. Pip felt the movement in her body without looking up. Unscrewing the lid from a bottle of TCP, he moistened the end of a towel and held it ready.

'This is going to sting,' he warned.

She drew back her head, closing her eyes as the sharp antiseptic bit into the wound but she made no sound. Running a bandage twice round her body Pip drew it tight, holding the end in place with plaster.

'There,' he said, sitting back on his haunches and examining his handiwork. 'How do you feel?'

Tentatively Katya touched the bandaged area. 'Not too bad. A bit dizzy.'

'What you need is tea.'

'Tea?' She paused, checking that she'd understood the word correctly and then pulled down her shirt angrily. 'Are you making fun of me?'

'You've lost a lot of blood,' he told her, going into the kitchen. 'You need something hot and sweet.'

As he fiddled about in the kitchen, searching out tea, filling the kettle, he watched Katya through the opened hatch. She was sitting on the edge of her chair looking around herself, taking in the room as though seeing it for the first time. It was a pleasant, masculine place with low lights, rows of books and the slight disorder that comes with bachelor living. After a few minutes she seemed to relax and sat back, pulling her fur hat off. Her hair spilled down around her shoulders, dark and shining as polished mahogany.

Pip poured boiling water into a mug, prodding the tea-bag with a spoon. He had no idea what to do with Katya Leskova. She had come looking for help but he wasn't sure whether he could give it. He couldn't hide her in his flat. Eventually she would have to be turned over to the police. And yet, at the same time, he wanted to help her. He couldn't escape a vague feeling of responsibility for this girl.

He glanced up at Katya. She had found the auto-control of

the video on the table beside her and was examining it with some curiosity.

Take one step at a time, he decided. First he should find out what had brought her here. The decisions could wait until later.

'It's lucky you came when you did,' Pip said, carrying the steaming mug back into the living room. 'I'd been thinking of going out to a film.'

Katya sipped at the tea gingerly and gave a gasp as it hit her stomach, warmth spreading through her veins like a bush-fire.

'I put some whisky in it,' he admitted.

She nodded and drank again, this time more greedily, her body craving the sweetness. Pip watched her for a few moments, noting the flush of colour that touched her cheeks, then going over to the desk he examined the gun she'd brought.

It was a Zastava Model 70, manufactured in Yugoslavia. Not a make he'd come across before but the mechanism was conventional enough, a standard blowback semi-automatic. Pip unclipped the magazine and pulled it from the grip before cranking back the slide. The ejector slid the shellcase from the breech and lobbed it into the palm of his hand. It was short and solid, a .380 calibre hollow-point, also of Yugoslavian manufacture. He clipped it back into the head of the magazine and reinserted both into the butt of the gun.

Katya was watching him with interest.

'Now,' Pip said, lowering the hammer on to the empty chamber with his thumb and putting the gun into the drawer of his desk. 'If I am going to be of any help to you, I need to know exactly who it is you are running away from.'

The Aeroflot flight SU 241 from Moscow stood on the tarmac at Heathrow airport, the high-pitched whine of its turbines falling in disappointment as the jets were closed down.

Vassily Krasin remained in his seat. Outside it was raining lightly, the water crawling down the darkened oval of the window.

The air-hostess leaned across the empty seats, offering him the advantage of her opened cleavage.

'Colonel Krasin?' His diplomatic status put respect into her voice. 'If you would care to come this way, your car is waiting.'

A black Mercedes was parked on the runway. A junior attaché stood waiting by the open rear door, feet apart, hands folded protectively across his genitals. He introduced himself as Alexsei Sheverdayev.

'You have heard the news, Colonel?' he asked as the car drew out on to the M4.

Krasin nodded.

'The English police are co-operating. The girl has no money, nowhere to go to. In our opinion she cannot last in a strange city for long without being discovered.'

Krasin looked out at the fast-moving lanes of traffic. 'Let's hope that is the case.'

Sheverdayev was uncomfortable in his grey worsted suit. He plucked at the collar and changed the subject. 'Do you wish to be taken directly to the Embassy?'

'I shall not be requiring their services. Arrangements have already been made for a suite at the Connaught Hotel. I find it more convenient in the circumstances.'

'Very good, Colonel.'

'In the meantime I want a press release issued. If you do so immediately it will still make the evening news.' Krasin was collected, dispassionate. 'You will explain that Katya Leskova is required back in Moscow to answer charges of theft against the government. She is also to stand trial for the murder of her head of department whose body was discovered yesterday morning.'

'That's not true!'

Katya was standing before the television, her hands on her temples, fingers buried in her hair, watching the nine o'clock news with rising indignation.

'I didn't kill him,' she cried out. 'How can they suggest such a terrible thing? I didn't kill him – I didn't kill anyone!'

The bulletin had been short and factual. Her full name had been given, the screen flooded by an identikit picture that looked no more like Katya than any other girl in a fur hat. It had explained that she was armed and dangerous and warned the public not to approach her.

Pip went across to the television and prodded the switch, cancelling the rest of the news. Katya was still staring accusingly at the blank screen.

'Why do they say this about me?'

'I don't know. They must have evidence of some sort. They seem certain of their information.'

'They can't be. It's just lies – a pack of lies.'

She appeared to have been annoyed more than frightened by the news report, clenching her fists and stamping her bare feet on the floor as the accusations against her were listed.

'Who is this man who's died?' Pip asked.

'The head of my department at the ministry.'

'Did you have reason to kill him?'

202

'No!' She spun round on Pip, flaring up at the suggestion. 'He was just someone I worked for. Not even important – a little nobody.' The recollection of his death struck her and clapping her hands over her ears she reproved herself under her breath.

'No,' she said quietly, 'I didn't mean that. That's a terrible thing to say of anyone.'

It had taken time for Pip to get the facts from Katya. She had told him what she knew but the explanation had come in short snatches, incoherent and jumbled in sequence, a torrent of disconnected events. He could see that she was only just beginning to put the pieces together herself and as she spoke she'd leapt backwards and forwards in the narrative, occasionally letting out a cry of despair as she pounced on some new detail.

Pip had never known a girl so expressive. She carried her emotions in her face, her hands, in the movements of her body. Earlier, he had persuaded her to change out of her blood-stained clothes and put them in the wash. After an initial reticence she'd accepted, going through to the spare bedroom to put on the dressing gown he offered her. It was too large for her slim body and as she'd poured out her story the collar had spread across her shoulders, the cuffs falling over gesticulating hands, skirts whipping about her legs.

Most of the time she'd talked freely, determined to prove her innocence, but there was one subject on which she'd refused to be drawn. Vassily Krasin. Whenever his name had arisen she'd fallen silent. This was private, he realised, forbidden territory. Twice when Pip had pressed her for more she'd brushed the questions aside. But the sharp intake of breath at the mention of his name, the flash of lightning in her dark eyes had given him some sort of answer.

'Could he have killed this man?' he asked her now.

'I don't know. Yes . . . I suppose so.'

She walked across the room and with a sudden movement flung herself down in a chair, burying her head in her hands.

'It's hopeless – '

'No, it's not. You mustn't think that.'

She made no movement. He'd noticed the border between hope and despair was unprotected in her mind. She moved openly from one to the other.

'It may look hopeless but that's an illusion.' He dropped to his haunches before the chair. 'This man has built up a whole framework of circumstantial evidence around you. But circumstantial evidence is very fragile, Katya. It's like a card house, take one small piece away and the whole thing comes crashing down.'

Katya lowered her hands and looked at him suspiciously. His

tone was gentle, encouraging. He explained what he meant.

'In ten years I've never known a charge based on falsified evidence stand up in court.'

'Haven't you?' Katya wasn't impressed. 'In my country it happens all the time.'

'Yes, well fortunately we're not in your country.'

She brooded on the geographical advantage for a moment, her eyes dark and troubled and then turning back to him she asked: 'Why has he done this to me?'

Pip had asked himself the same question. 'I imagine he did it because you happened to be there, Katya. It was convenient. You were the right person at the right moment.'

'He intended it from the very start,' she said bitterly. 'That's what he wanted. When he first introduced himself to me at the ballet he must have had it all planned out.'

Pip watched her as she spoke and again he felt the resentment in her. It ran dark and deep.

Getting to his feet he went through into the kitchen. Katya heard him clattering through cupboards and a few minute later the rich, sweet smell of onions cooking in butter reached her. She followed him to the door.

'What are you doing?'

He poured a tin of tomatoes into the pan, adding herbs as the liquid fluttered to the boil.

'Making something to eat. You do eat, I suppose?'

Her eyebrows arched as though he had suggested something improper. 'I'm not hungry.'

'Well I am, so you'll just have to sit and watch.'

Katya went over to the window and stared out into the night. Above the rooftops she could see the dark void of Hyde Park, the distant lights of Knightsbridge twinkling beyond like buildings along a river bank. She fixed her mind on Podurets, summoning his face before her, trying to find some trace of sympathy. It didn't come. She told herself that she was a wicked heartless girl but the rebuke didn't find its mark either.

From the oven Pip watched her, saw her biting her upper lip. He asked a question to distract her.

'What are you doing here in London?'

She turned from the window. 'I was with a delegation from Gosconcert.'

'Where's that?'

Pip's ignorance of these things flicked a smile to her lips for an instant.

'It's a union, not a place. They're over here to arrange a tour for

204

the Moscow Radio Symphony Orchestra, set up recording rights, all the usual things.'

'And how are they going to get on without you?'

Katya was about to answer when she gave a gasp and clapping her hands to her face she looked at him in horror.

'There's a banquet this evening,' she said, her eyes dancing with sudden mischief. 'There are going to be speeches.'

'Can't they give them without you?'

'No.' She shook her head, half laughing. 'I have the translations ready for the press. They're in my suitcase.'

'They've probably found them by now.'

It was the wrong answer. Katya nodded, the irrelevance of the problem returning to her, the smile dying again. Coming across the kitchen she leaned on the worktop, and watched him listlessly as he cooked.

Pip was sorry to have broken the spell. For a moment there she had been transformed, the burden had been laid aside. Now it was back again. Taking the pan of spaghetti off the oven he took it to the sink and tipped it into a colander.

'What's going to happen to me?' she asked.

'Tonight you will stay here,' he replied concentrating on the steam that belched up around his hands. 'In the morning I'm going to take that little picture of yours and show it to the police.'

'No,' she said.

'It's the only way, Katya. They have to know about this eventually.'

'Not the police!'

'I won't tell them where you are, only that I have been in contact with you.'

'No!' Katya had drawn herself up to her full height, her eyes black with anger. 'I forbid it. If you go to the police they will pass the information on to my people.'

'That's not true, Katya.'

'They will report me. I'll be arrested – I know it.'

Pip faced her across the small kitchen. 'I can talk to them, Katya. You must trust me.'

She banged her clenched fists down on the worktop.

'Not the police!'

Chapter Twenty-Six

Detective Inspector Chatham held the Talinin Madonna in the palm of his hand as though it were an open hymnbook. He wanted information but he probed for it with the discretion of a nun.

'When you say you've been in contact with the girl,' he said, 'what exactly do you mean by that?'

'I mean I have talked to her.'

'By telephone, or face to face?'

'I don't think that's important at present.' Pip side-stepped the question but Chatham pursued it.

'How did you get your hands on this painting if you didn't see her in person?'

'Let's just say it was passed on to me.'

Pip kept his voice disinterested. It was a game so far, a delicate piece of manoeuvring. Chatham asked his questions and he released small, guarded pieces of information in return. In itself the exchange wasn't relevant. They were both simply using it to establish their separate territories, to define the borders, open lines of communication. The real bargaining would come later.

'How exactly did she make contact with you, Mr Spencer?'

'Through the office.' Pip stretched the truth to suit his requirements. 'And for that reason I'm treating her as a client of the firm.'

Chatham nodded. He appreciated the arrangement although it brought him no personal joy. His attention was still fixed on the tiny painting in his hand.

'This is the damnedest little thing I've ever seen,' he observed. 'I assume it's valuable?'

'I imagine so. It belongs to the Pushkin Museum.'

They both knew this much already.

'Are we talking in terms of thousands of pounds, hundreds of thousands, or millions?'

'I really couldn't tell you.'

Pip had wanted to take the painting down to Christie's and show it to Bill Hargreaves to have a more precise valuation but it was not practical. So far only Chatham knew that he had it and that's the way it would have to remain for a while.

Chatham was examining the picture critically.

'I can't see it myself,' he complained. 'If I had that sort of money I can think of better ways of spending it.'

'That's why they get sold.'

'Good point.' Chatham chewed over this scrap of wisdom. He had the appearance of a man who wanted little more from life than regular meals and a round of golf at weekends.

Pip had given him no warning of his arrival. He wanted to talk to Chatham but he also wanted to keep it informal. If he'd rung earlier the would have found himself in a sealed interview room with interested eavesdroppers, a tape recorder running.

'Looking at it from my side of the fence,' Chatham commented, 'it's the size of these things that makes them dangerous. The moment you get large sums of money tied up in small objects like this you have a crime waiting to be committed.'

'She didn't steal it.'

Chatham showed no sign of having heard him. With infinite care he set the painting back on his desk, the doors opened so that it stood upright like a dressing-table mirror.

'She had it with her when she came into the country,' he pointed out mildly.

'It was wrapped up. She thought she was carrying documents.'

'Through customs?'

'It had a diplomatic pass.'

'That's her line, is it?' There was a slight tension between the two men now, the steel beginning to show beneath the silk exterior. 'If you'll forgive me saying so, Mr Spencer, you know no more about this business than I do. You're simply repeating what you've been told.'

'I know that she went to see a solicitor as soon as she found what she was carrying.'

'That, I admit, is in her favour.'

'It was a crude attempt at an assassination that went wrong.'

'She was the one with the gun.' Chatham quoted the eye-witness reports at him.

'It fell on the ground. She picked it up.'

Chatham rested his chin on one black-haired fist and stared across the glass enclosure he called his office. Pip could see him weighing the situation in his mind, watching the tilt of the scales as each particle of new information was added.

'Are you going to be in contact with her again?' he asked, altering tack.

'That is up to her. But I would expect so.'

'Do you know where she is now?'

Chatham put the question lightly, innocently and Pip smiled to himself. He had been expecting to be asked this for some time now. He gave the reply his earnest consideration.

'I could find out if necessary,' he said eventually. 'If you wanted to meet her I dare say it could be arranged.'

'Meet her? God forbid.' He reacted to the offer with horror. 'That's the last thing I want just now. If I met her I would have no alternative but to take her into custody.'

'Would you?'

Chatham looked straight into his eyes and then nodded.

'I would. We are officially co-operating with the Russians on this one, Mr Spencer.'

So that was the way of it. Chatham had made his position clear. But the subject was not closed yet. Pip could tell from the tone of the policeman's voice that he was open to negotiation. Possibly even expecting it. He put his case bluntly.

'She didn't do it.'

'So you keep saying.'

'You know she's innocent as well as I do.'

'I know nothing of the sort.' Chatham showed the indignation of a man who has had words put into his mouth. 'All I know is that I have been given two conflicting stories. There's no reason why I have to believe one rather than the other.'

'But your instincts tell you that I am right.'

The tension was there again. Chatham didn't want to be press-ganged into taking sides.

'Contrary to popular belief,' he replied tartly, 'policemen don't rely on their instincts. They rely on evidence, Mr Spencer. Hard, uncompromising evidence. The type that stands up in court, the type that wins cases. In the last few weeks you've drawn our attention to the death of an old man, then an alleged bomb in your flat and an art dealer who has confessed to handling stolen pictures. Now you want us to believe that all these events are interrelated and linked to a high-ranking KGB officer in Moscow. What you haven't given us is any evidence.'

Chatham picked up the expanded polystyrene cup and took a mouthful of coffee. It was cold. Pulling a face he put it down again, coming to a decision.

'Speaking off the record, I won't deny that what you say is interesting. It's consistent and it fits in with a few observations of our own. But I need some sort of proof. Bring me one piece of hard evidence linking this Russian with the paintings that have been sold in London and I'll throw the book at him.'

A knock on the glass door punctuated the promise. A policewoman in a crisp white shirt poked her head into the room.

'The superintendent has just come in. Could you spare him a moment?'

Chatham rolled his weight forward on the chair and stood up with a grunt of exertion.

'Will you excuse me a moment?'

After he had gone Pip looked round the office. It wasn't decorated. The objects that scattered the place were simply the extension of Chatham's working life: empty coffee cups, files of papers, loaded filing cabinets, mugs filled with chewed pencils. There was no reference to his personal life that he could see. Not even a framed photo of his passing-out parade at Hendon.

He glanced down at his watch. It was nine forty. He wondered what Katya was doing back at his flat. Before leaving he had given her strict instructions not to answer the phone or open the door to anyone until he returned.

Katya's attitude had changed overnight. The previous evening she had been violently opposed to him going to the police. They had argued about it for hours. It had been well after midnight before she went to bed, too exhausted to keep her eyes open but still fighting sleep, unwilling to give in.

In the morning she had been more docile.

'You can see them if you must,' she had told him as she drank her coffee. 'There's nothing I can do to stop you.'

Pip couldn't tell whether she had decided to trust him or whether this was simply an inherent Russian fatalism surfacing in her mind. He'd noticed she had a capacity for theatre. Many of the things she said were emotional, over-dramatised.

'Why don't you throw me in jail yourself,' she'd said at one point in the evening. 'If that's what you want so badly, take me down to the police station and have me locked up.'

Chatham had come back into the room.

'Sorry to keep you waiting.' He dug his hands into his pockets, rattled small change. 'So you'll keep me in touch?' He was cultivating the air of a man who has lost the thread of the conversation.

Pip picked up the Talinin Madonna and closed the two doors. He offered it to him.

'Do you want to keep this here?'

'God, no.' Chatham's bushy eyebrows leapt at the suggestion. 'I haven't officially seen that thing.'

Pip put it into his briefcase, fastened the clasps and spun the combination wheels out of habit. Chatham watched him thoughtfully.

'A word of advice – '

Pip looked up.

'I should look after that thing carefully.'

'Why's that?'

'That Russian you mentioned.' He flicked his fingers in search of the name.

'Vassily Krasin – '

'That's him. He's here in London. Flew in last night.' Chatham jerked his chin towards the closed briefcase. 'He wants the painting.'

Breakfast at the Connaught Hotel is said to be the best in the country. It's a claim that is tested each morning by a select circle of politicians, senior civil servants and businessmen.

In the panelled dining room, the ritual silence that accompanies the English breakfast was being strictly observed. Conversation was contained. Thoughts were centred on headline news, leader articles and the fluctuation of share prices.

Vassily Krasin touched his coffee cup to his lips. The table before him was laid with crisp white damask, polished silver and porcelain. A single rose stood in a crystal vase. The only thing to mar the view was the sight of Vladimir Grigorvich, he delegation administrator, sitting opposite him.

Krasin put his cup back on the saucer.

'You knew about this?' There was a hint of disbelief in his voice.

'She said she was going out, Colonel. She didn't say where, only that she had something to deliver.'

'And you let her go?'

'I had no alternative. I assumed what she was doing was sanctioned by your department.'

Vladimir Grigorvich squirmed in his seat, his eyes flicking across the bare cloth before him. When he'd arrived a waiter had glided up to his elbow, waiting to take an order but Krasin had brushed him away. He wasn't sharing his breakfast with a delegation administrator. He was surprised, and a shade saddened, that the waiter couldn't see that. The English had practically invented the class system but of late they seemed to have lost the touch.

'You were in charge of security on the delegation. I find it extraordinary that you didn't exert your authority.'

'She said that she would be back within a few hours. I had no reason to doubt her.'

'Did you not see the package she was carrying?'

'Only briefly, Colonel.'

'And you didn't think to ask what it was?'

'No, Colonel.'

Of course you didn't. Krasin never thought for an instant that he would have. Russians were notoriously indolent and encouraged to be so. That was the beauty of the system. No one ever took the initiative. There was not a quota for initiative. It wasn't part of the five-year plan.

'You appreciate that I have no alternative but to hold you responsible for her defection?'

'I cannot accept it as my fault, Colonel.'

Krasin shrugged. He could feel the pale yellow eyes of the man on him, sense his loathing across the table. It didn't worry him. Quite the reverse, it gave him a small thrill of pleasure. He always found the impotence of weaker men slightly amusing.

Flicking his napkin from his lap he dropped it to the table and stood up to leave.

'In the meantime I shall require your assistance.'

'But my duties to the delegation – '

'I am relieving you of those for the time being.'

Reaching over, Krasin plucked the rose from the vase and snapped of the stem before fitting it into his button-hole. As he did so he held out one hand to Vladimir Grigorvich.

'Do you have a pin?'

'No, Colonel.' Again the administrator was made to feel inadequate. Krasin ignored his discomfort and stopping a waiter he asked him to bring him one.

There was a silence as they waited.

'What is it you want of me?' the administrator ventured after a few moments.

'I need to speak to Comrade Leskova this morning. Persuade her to give back the Talinin Madonna.'

'You know where she is, Colonel?'

The waiter returned bearing a pin. Krasin clipped the stem of the rose to the back of his lapel, viewing the result critically before turning to Vladimir Grigorvich.

'Naturally I know where she is.'

Katya sat at the antique desk and tried to make sense of her thoughts. In front of her was a pad of paper; several pages had already been torn off and lay around her, crumpled up into tight balls. She'd never been good at writing. She knew what she wanted to say but when she tried to put it down on paper the words became tangled.

It had been Pip's idea that she should make a written statement. He'd thought it might be helpful if she explained exactly what had happened to her since her arrival in London. 'Put down every little detail you can remember,' he had said before going out. 'Don't leave anything out. You can't tell at this stage what might be important.'

It was not as easy as it sounded. Explaining what she had done was simple enough; trying to explain why she had done it was another matter altogether.

'Just do your best, Katya. No one can expect more.' For some reason the teacher's platitude came out of the past. Throwing down the pencil in disgust she slumped back in the chair, arms spread along the rests and stared out of the window at the dank, cold morning. Above her grey skirt she was wearing a shirt with blue stripes which Pip had lent her that morning. Like all his clothes it was conventional but of extraordinarily good quality, the material smooth and silky to the touch.

Getting to her feet she strolled over to the mirror and examined the effect with satisfaction. It was several sizes too large and ballooned out above her belt, but with the sleeves rolled back and the top buttons opened she decided it suited her, the bagginess flattering her slim figure, the masculine cut lending her a look of executive severity. She wondered whether Pip found her attractive. The thought came from nowhere and she brushed it aside angrily. It had been instinct that led her to this flat. She had needed Pip's professional help as a solicitor, nothing more. She had absolutely no desire to be involved with him personally.

And yet she was curious. She wanted to know what went on behind that impeccable façade of his.

Thoughtfully she twisted away from the mirror, craning back over her shoulder to check her reflection from behind, noting that her skirt was creased. It had been washed but still not pressed. Going through to the kitchen she searched for an ironing-board. She knew she was inventing small, unnecessary occupations for herself but they were comforting. They filled the time, stopped her brooding on questions she didn't want to answer at present. She guessed Pip had set her the task of writing for the same reason.

When it was done she hung the skirt on the back of the door to air and wandered back into the living room on bare feet. The tails of her shirt reached down to her knees, the sides slashed to the waist to reveal the smooth curve of her thighs as she moved. Picking up the sheets of paper she glanced over them, checking what she'd written so far. The window beside her rattled in the wind.

Idly she looked up.

Vassily Krasin was standing in the street below.

The sight of him slammed into her like a body-blow. Giving a small, choking cry, she staggered backwards. The pages dropped from her fingers. She felt the strength go from her legs, lost her footing and collapsed in a heap on the floor.

It couldn't be true, she told herself frantically. Vassily was in Moscow. He shouldn't be here – he couldn't be here. No one knew where she was.

Shakily she drew herself up on to her knees. Pushing her hair from her eyes and lifting her head she peered down into the street.

There was no sign of him. She moved nearer to the window. A few people were passing, their hands dug into pockets, umbrellas up. But Krasin was not amongst them.

Katya forced herself to relax. It was a trick of the eye, she told herself sternly. She'd caught only the briefest glimpse of him. It must have been someone else completely, a man who happened to be of the same height and build as Vassily.

She stood up, burying her flushed cheeks in her hands. The adrenaline had trickled from her stomach now, leaving a warm glow of relief. She felt slightly foolish, a small child frightened by shadows.

At that moment the bell rang.

She jumped at the sound, backing away from the door. It was him. This time she knew it was him. She looked around the room and then down, suddenly conscious of her bare legs. Darting into the kitchen she snatched her skirt off the hanger and dragged it on, stumbling against the ironing-board in her haste.

The bell rang again. A longer, more insistent demand this time.

She ran back into the living room. Her mind was no longer concerned with how he had found her or what he was doing in London, only with how she could get away from him. Wildly she looked about herself. He mustn't find her, mustn't know she'd been here.

Picking up the scattered pages of notes, she crumpled them up in her hand and stuffed them in the pocket of her skirt. As she did so there came the soft ting of a bell in the passage outside.

Katya froze at the sound.

The lift had reached the second floor. She heard the doors open.

Krasin stepped out of the lift with Vladimir Grigorvich a pace behind him and walked down the thickly carpeted passageway.

Outside Pip's flat he paused, looked in both directions and knocked lightly on the door.

There was no reply.

Krasin ran his hand down the frame of the door. It had two locks, a large mortise beneath the handle and a smaller Yale above. Krasin pressed on each one in turn, testing the resistance of the woodwork.

As he'd hoped, only the Yale was locked.

213

'Do you want me to force it?' Vladimir Grigorvich sounded hopeful for the first time that morning but Krasin restrained him.

'That will not be necessary.'

Taking his wallet from his upper pocket he slipped out a credit card.

'Do you know what this is?' he asked.

Vladimir Grigorvich nodded. Credit cards, unheard of a few years back, were now a common enough sight in Moscow.

'They serve a dual purpose over here,' Krasin continued conversationally, pressing it into the crack of the door-frame. 'One of these will buy you practically anything you want.' He felt the catch draw back before the fine plastic blade. 'They will also open locks, so that you can be deprived of your possessions as quickly as you came by them.'

He turned the handle and pushed open the door, glancing quickly around the living room of Pip's flat.

It was silent, deserted.

'Which is why they call them access cards,' Krasin added softly to himself as he moved into the centre of the floor.

Behind him, Vladimir Grigorvich closed the door.

With a small gesture of the hand Krasin beckoned him to check through the rest of the flat while he stood quite still. He had never met Pip Spencer. He was just a name, a distant voice on the telephone. This was the only direct contact Krasin had had with the man.

His first impression was of affluence. The furniture, the Persian carpets, the hi-fi and video sets neatly tailored into the bookshelves were expensive. And a bachelor, every indication was of a single presence in the room. It was not new money either. The art nouveau figure serving as a paper-weight, the Chinese vase in the passage holding umbrellas and tennis racquets both suggested a certain lazy familiarity with wealth. There were drinks laid out on the sideboard but he wasn't a smoker; the only ashtray was positioned too far from any chair to be functional.

Rapidly the image of Pip Spencer grew in Krasin's mind, expanding and adapting as he absorbed new details. He believed in first impressions. For those with no experience they could be misleading, but with instinct and training they revealed more valuable information than a departmental dossier.

Moving over to the bookshelf he checked the titles. Novels mostly, a few heavier volumes beneath concerning the law. He ran his eye over the rows of CDs and tapes. Jazz here, and a few light classics: Rachmaninov, Sibelius, nothing too strenuous.

Vladimir Grigorvich came back into the room.

'The place is clean,' he said flatly. 'There's no sign of her ever having been here.'

214

Going through into the kitchen, Krasin put the palm of his hand close to the iron. It was warm.

'I think you can do a little better than that, comrade.'

Vladimir Grigorvich disappeared back into the bedrooms while Krasin strolled across to the window and stared down into the street. Despite his earlier confidence, he had been guessing when he said he knew where she was hiding. If she had turned herself in to the Russian Embassy or the English police he would have heard about it by now and so he'd assumed she had sought out some private contact of her own. But coming to Pip Spencer's flat had been a long shot.

'Look at this, Colonel.'

He turned from the window. Vladimir Grigorvich had returned holding a white shirt in his hand.

'Where did you find that?' Krasin asked sharply.

'In the washing machine.' He twisted the label out of the collar for him to see. 'It's hers.'

Krasin didn't need to read the cyrillic lettering to know that it was Katya's. He recognised the pleats, the small strawberries that were embroidered down the line of the buttons.

As he took it from Vladimir Grigorvich a sudden, vivid picture of Katya sprang to mind. She was lying on the tomb in the darkness of the Archangel Cathedral, her corduroy skirt rucked up around her waist, her long legs in their woollen stockings and black boots spilling on to the ground on either side. This was the shirt she had been wearing that day. He remembered how he had loosened the buttons one by one, slipping his hand on to the softness of her breasts beneath.

He remembered too the expression on her face when he'd lifted himself off her afterwards. She had been breathing hard, her lips parted, damp hair sticking to her forehead. A wild, wanton expression. But her eyes had been glittering in the candlelight, black with shock and anger.

Krasin smiled to himself. He'd always aroused Katya and offended her at the same time. That's the way it had been with them from the start. She'd desired him but never trusted him. It was just fortunate that one instinct had smothered the other.

He handed the shirt back to Vladimir Grigorvich.

'Search the place.'

The man began to work over the flat, starting with the bedrooms, ferreting his way through drawers and cupboards. He was good at his job, Krasin observed. His touch was light and feline. Nothing was disturbed, every object was replaced exactly where it had been.

As Krasin watched him his thoughts returned to Katya. She

215

had been here a few minutes before they arrived, ironing clothes, preparing to go out. It was unfortunate – no, it was annoying – that she had made contact with Pip Spencer. Together, they presented a threat, he had to admit it. They knew more than he wanted.

Reaching out one hand he touched the Hockney etching that hung on the wall, straightening the frame a fraction. It didn't matter, he told himself. If he could just recover the Talinin Madonna nothing else would matter. Katya could go to hell for all he cared.

Vladimir Grigorvich had moved through into the living room now and begun checking the bookshelves, systematically lifting them out to see what lay behind. Krasin leaned back against the desk, his arms folded.

There was a sound in the passage outside, a creak of the floorboards.

He looked up, suddenly alert. Out of the side of his eye he saw Vladimir Grigorvich halt, a handful of books clutched in his hand.

A key rasped in the lock. The handle beneath it turned.

Krasin straightened in readiness.

It was an elderly woman who bustled in. She was wearing a light brown mackintosh and carrying a loaded bag in one hand. Busily she removed the key from the lock and tucked it away in her pocket. As she turned she caught sight of the two men.

'Holy Mother of God—'

She gave a gasp, as though she had been under water for the last few minutes and stopped dead in her tracks, one hand jumping up to cup an enormous, terylene-covered bosom.

Krasin didn't wait for her to speak.

'Who are you?' he asked quietly.

Vladimir Grigorvich had slipped the books back in place and moved away from the shelves. He was standing beside him, uncertain how to respond, waiting for instructions. Krasin could feel the tension in the man's body, sense the anticipation.

The woman let out her breath with a rush. 'Lord, didn't you give me a fright standing there like that.'

'I apologise – '

She was the daily, the cleaning babushka, Krasin realised. Her bag was stuffed with clean laundry, a pair of carpet slippers balanced on top. He should have guessed it from the start. She wasn't dangerous but she'd seen them here in the flat. That was enough.

He moved towards her.

'We're waiting for Mr Spencer.' The door was still open, he noticed. It would have to be quick.

His hand came out of his pocket.

'Then you'll be waiting some time,' the woman told him grumpily. 'He's never here of a Monday morning.'

'So it seems – '

The lift stopped outside, the doors clanking open. Krasin paused. He glanced round at Vladimir Grigorvich. There was the sound of voices in the passageway.

He slipped his hand back in his pocket, relaxing, his smile suddenly charming.

'He asked us to meet him here,' he told her, 'but I think he must have forgotten.'

'He'll be in the office.'

'I'll give him a ring, fix another time.'

Now that she had recovered from her initial shock, the woman was becoming wary.

'Who are you?'

'Friends of his – '

'He never said anything about friends coming here in the daytime.'

Krasin brushed past her, Vladimir Grigorvich on his heels. The woman followed them out into the passage.

'I'll need your names,' she called after them.

Krasin ignored her. Going downstairs he pushed open the front doors. Vladimir Grigorvich followed him.

'Do you want me to go back, Colonel?' he asked.

'No.' Krasin felt angry, cheated. It had been an undignified episode. 'The painting isn't there.'

'But she spent the night in the place.'

'She'll have it with her. They wouldn't have left it.' Krasin paused on the corner of the street, giving his orders. 'You will stay here. I have business to attend to elsewhere but the moment she returns I want to hear of it.'

'Very good, Colonel.'

'If she leaves again stick with her.'

Chapter Twenty-Seven

'It's your fault.'

'I didn't tell them, Katya.'

'I knew this would happen,' she cried. 'I should never have let you go there. It was a stupid idea from the start.'

'The police weren't interested in where you were. They didn't even ask.'

'Then how did Vassily know the address?'

'I don't know – '

'He came straight to the flat.'

'He must have worked it out for himself. It wouldn't have been difficult.'

'You mean the police worked it out for him!'

'They wouldn't have done that.'

'They must have – '

The taxi slowed as it approached Hyde Park Corner. Katya slumped back in the soft leather seat and stared out at the tightly bundled traffic around them.

Krasin's unexpected appearance had shaken her badly. Her eyes were unnaturally bright in the dark of the cab, Pip noticed, and although she sat quite still her fingers were twisting at a button of her coat.

'None of this would have happened if you'd done as I asked,' she said resentfully.

'You can't just hide from him, Katya.'

'No?' She rounded on Pip again. 'It's better than sitting still and being arrested by your pig-police friends.'

Pip glanced at the back of the taxi driver's head. Fortunately the man had shut the glass partition that separated them and was busy listening to the radio.

'The police didn't tell Krasin anything.' He held his voice low. 'The officer I spoke to specifically said he didn't want to know where you had gone.'

Katya gave a snort. 'Really?' she said. 'Then he lied to you.'

When he'd returned from Scotland Yard Pip had been astonished

218

to find Katya in the street outside his flat. She had been waiting in the newsagent's shop further round the square, keeping in amongst the safety of strangers. As he passed she'd darted out and run down the pavement after him.

'He was here!' she'd screamed as she caught up with him.

'Krasin?'

'About an hour ago.' Her breath had come in great gulps as she spoke. 'He came straight here, just broke in.'

They'd gone upstairs. In the doorway of his flat Katya had stopped, hanging back. She'd seen Krasin leave earlier but she was still apprehensive, unwilling to go in.

'If I hadn't seen him in the street he would have walked right in on me,' Katya told him.

Pip was roaming around the flat, searching for any sign of the intrusion.

'How did you get away?'

'I climbed out of the window in the bedroom.'

He gave a grunt of understanding. There was a fire escape up the back of the building. She was lucky to have found it.

'I went down a ladder,' she said reproachfully, venturing forward a few paces. 'But it didn't reach to the ground.'

'That's to stop people climbing up the other way.'

'I had to drop the last bit and there were a whole lot of dustbins and rubbish underneath. I landed right in it.'

From the accusing tone of her voice he gathered that this was his fault. Everything was his fault at present.

'Just be glad it was there at all.'

'I could have broken my leg.'

Pip discounted the possibility. Walking past her he examined the edge of the door-frame. There were no scratches on the paintwork, nothing to suggest that the lock had been forced.

'He must have used a piece of plastic.'

Katya wasn't interested in how he had managed to get in, only in the reason.

'What did he want?' she demanded.

'The painting, I imagine – or you. Probably both.'

The answer hit her hard, as he'd intended it to. He was getting fed up with her constant accusations. He knew that she was frightened, disorientated, but there were times when she behaved like a spoiled child. But then from what he could gather that's exactly what she was, the favourite daughter of some senior official in Georgia, cherished and slightly pampered – if such a thing was possible in her god-forsaken country.

Katya had folded her arms and hugged herself for comfort.

'He'll be back then,' she said.

Closing the door Pip came into the centre of the room. There was a note from his daily on the desk. He hadn't noticed it before.

She watched him as he read it over.

'What are you going to do?' she inquired.

'I don't know – '

'He knows we're here. He'll be coming back. You must do something!'

Pip looked up from the note. 'It says that there were two people waiting to see me. Who was the other one?'

'Vladimir Grigorvich. He was the administrator on the delegation I was working for.'

'Administrator?'

'The security man – KGB.'

The taxi pulled out of the flow of traffic around Constitution Hill and swung down towards The Mall. Pip glanced out of the rear window. He had been checking it intermittently since they left his flat.

'This administrator friend of yours,' he said. 'What's he look like?'

Katya shrugged. 'Short, scraggy little man.'

'Long brown hair?'

'Yes – why?'

'I think we've got him on our tail.'

Katya jerked around in the seat to see but Pip stopped her. Reaching forward he tapped on the glass partition and gave the taxi driver new directions.

'Could he have been the man who met you in the car park last night?' Pip asked, settling back in the seat.

'Tobias?' Katya shook her head violently. 'No, he was quite different.'

'You said you didn't get a proper look at him.'

'Tobias was English. I could tell from the way he spoke.' She sounded positive.

The taxi drew to a halt. An attendant in a bright green uniform with gold braid had stepped forward to open the door.

Katya climbed out, looking up at the high, salmon pink building. 'Where are we?'

'Harrods.'

Pip peeled off notes, paid the taxi. The black Mercedes that he had spotted earlier was parked further up the road; the driver had got out and was browsing over the magazines on a newspaper stand. Taking Katya by the arm he propelled her in through the high, plate-glass doors that the attendant now held open.

220

She was inclined to be difficult. 'I can't think what we're doing in here.'

'That's because you're not English. If you were you'd know this is the best place in London for losing people.'

'You think you can shake him off in here?'

'I can't think of a better way.'

'Jesus Christ,' she muttered under her breath. 'You've had some crazy ideas in your time.'

They had come into the Men's section, carved woodwork and elderly assistants striving to recreate the atmosphere of tailors' shops that had been driven out of business years ago.

Katya strode down the rows of city suits and tweed jackets with designer patches, her head down. Pip caught her by the arm.

'Don't go so fast.'

'Someone's going to recognise me,' she hissed back at him.

'No one's even looking at you.'

It wasn't strictly true, Katya had already collected a couple of interested glances but not for the reason she was thinking.

'My face was splashed all over the television last night – or have you forgotten?'

'It wasn't. What they showed was an artist's impression of a terrorist with short hair and a fur hat. It looked no more like you than Raisa Gorbachev.'

'Thanks very much.'

They turned down into a passage inset with glowing showcases. Pip pictured the administrator following behind, keeping his distance, anticipating their movements. He fought the desire to look back over his shoulder.

'Just pretend you're a nice English girl,' he told Katya, 'brought up on a pony and a private income and no one will give you a second thought.'

Slowly they moved from room to room, pressing their way through the oozing, cosmopolitan crowd, occasionally stopping to look at the display cabinets, sensing the sudden changes of sound and smell of the huge store, the warm scent of leather and canvas in the luggage department, the cool freshness of flowers, the resonance of marble floors in the food halls, the saltiness of iced shellfish, the dull musk of meat and poultry.

'Is he with us?' Katya asked as they reached a room of pale cream and sleek logos.

'I can't tell – '

An assistant had glided out into their path, a perfume bottle in one hand.

'Would you care to test our new range?' she wondered.

Katya was going to walk on past but Pip stopped her.

'Try it – '

She looked at him quizzically, then held out her wrist while Pip let his eyes run listlessly around the room. It wasn't as crowded as the others. Only a few shoppers trickled between the counters, aimless, slightly bored. No one went to Harrods because they needed to. They went to pass the time, to amuse themselves with their money.

Katya was sniffing tentatively at the scent.

'It's a bit sweet.'

She offered her wrist to Pip. The perfume that reached him was heavy, sickly, better suited to a middle-aged cleavage than the throat of a young girl. He gave it his full attention, using the moment to look back towards the entrance.

Vladimir Grigorvich had come into the room. Catching sight of them he drifted aside to examine the colour chart of nail varnishes.

'What do you think?' Katya wanted his opinion.

'It's rather too Old-Vienna for my liking – drawn curtains, sex before lunch, that sort of thing.'

There was a smile in her eyes as they moved on.

'Did you see him?' she murmured.

'He's on the other side of the room. I can't tell if he's by himself or not.'

The wide doorway led through to the fashion jewellery. Pip went to a counter on the far side. At once an assistant in a black dress that clung to her credentials slid up to them.

'Can I help you?'

'I'd like to see those, if I could.' Pip pointed down into the glass cabinet.

With a silent, hydraulic smile the assistant drew out the tray and offered it to him. Pip picked out the nearest piece of jewellery, held it up to the light.

'I can put it on if that would be of any help,' she offered.

'No, that's all right – '

The wall behind the counter was a single sheet of mirrored glass that reflected the shelves of glittering objects. In it Pip could see the administrator clearly for the first time. He was standing some distance away, studying the floor plan of the store, hands thrust into his pockets. A small nondescript man, invisible in a crowd, dressed in a corduroy jacket and black polo-neck shirt. He was on his own, Pip was fairly sure of that.

He was suddenly aware of the assistant's face beside him, attentive, expectant.

'Is there anything wrong, sir?'

'No, not at all. It's very nice – don't you agree?' He turned to Katya for corroboration.

'I prefer this one,' she replied, picking up another. It was a tiny golden bumble-bee set with stones.

Pip's tone was dry.

'Do you – '

He hadn't realised that while he had been watching the administrator, she had been giving the jewellery her serious attention. He took it from her, putting it back on the tray. Keeping his voice down he said, 'Did you hear the ping of a bell just now?'

Katya looked up.

'Yes,' she said, 'I heard it.'

'That's the signal that the lift doors are opening. They're round the corner in the passage.' He glanced in the mirror again, checking Vladimir Grigorvich's position, estimating the distance between them. 'They stay open for about ten seconds – '

The assistant was looking at him vacantly, puzzled by this shift in the conversation.

Pip smiled at her, moved down to the next counter, Katya beside him. He picked up a thin gold necklace, draped it over his hand.

'Next time it rings,' he told her, 'count up to three and then go straight to them.'

'They gave me no warning, Colonel. By the time I got there the doors had closed.'

'Did you not see which floor they had gone to?'

'It's a large store – like a maze.' Vladimir Grigorvich wanted him to appreciate his dilemma. 'I'd not have found them again.'

Krasin cursed silently to himself. He'd been to Harrods often enough. It was the ideal place to drop a tail, he knew, large and crowded with more doors than a railway carriage. He shifted the receiver into the other hand. 'What were they doing there in the first place?'

There was a pause at the other end of the line. 'It looked as though they were shopping, Colonel.'

'Shopping? For what, for God's sake?'

'Jewellery . . . and perfume.' The administrator's voice withered as he heard the improbability of the reply for himself.

'They were on to you,' Krasin replied sharply.

'I cannot believe it – '

'There was no other reason for them to be there.'

Krasin paced the floor of his hotel room, the telephone in one hand. The trolley beside him carried the remains of lunch, an empty champagne bottle inverted in the ice bucket. He wanted it removed, the sight of the débris disturbed the elegance of the surroundings.

'Were they carrying anything with them?'

'She had a handbag.' Vladimir Grigorvich was eager to be helpful. 'He was carrying some sort of case.'

'A briefcase?'

'No, round, soft – more like a small sports bag.'

They'd moved out of Spencer's flat. That damnable old woman would have told them what she'd seen. They'd have realised that their cover was blown and cleared out. The Talinin Madonna would be with them, probably in the case Spencer was carrying. But where would they have taken it? There were a thousand hotels in central London alone. For the first time Krasin felt the ache of frustration. He was off his home territory and surrounded by imbeciles. If he were in Moscow now he could track down a couple of strangers within hours.

The silence hummed on the line.

'Do you want me to return to Spencer's flat?' Vladimir Grigorvich only floated the suggestion.

'No, come back here. Wait for me in the foyer until I return.'

Krasin drew on his overcoat and wrapped a grey cashmere scarf around his throat. Checking his appearance in the mirror he left the hotel and walked over to Kensington Gardens.

It was the sort of damp, overcast day that gives November a bad name. The air was fresh and quite still, recovering from the shock of the earlier shower.

Tobias was waiting for him on a park bench near Watts's equestrian statue. He stood up as Krasin approached, one hand in his overcoat pocket. His first question revealed the state of his nerves.

'Have you found her yet?'

'She is with Spencer.' Krasin offered no sort of greeting but walked on. Tobias fell into step beside him.

'The solicitor?'

'She went to him last night. It's not important.' Krasin didn't want Tobias to think he had lost control. 'There is nothing they can do.'

The path before him was metallic with rain, the avenue of trees above a blue-black bruise against the sky. When they reached the Round Pond Krasin paused, turning to Tobias.

'What went wrong?'

He asked the question simply, as though he wanted only an answer rather than an explanation. Tobias shrugged.

'She tricked me.'

'In what way?'

'When I asked for the Madonna she said she'd left it behind in the station. It turned out to be a lie.'

Clever little bitch, Krasin thought. Somehow she'd smelled the trap. Feminine intuition maybe, or an over-active imagination. Katya had always been quick on the uptake. But it was Tobias's fault. Like all amateurs he had laid a plan that was too elaborate. Keep it simple and cover your tracks afterwards, that was the way. The risk was greater but there was less to go wrong.

'You should have finished her,' he said flatly.

'What, with a hundred eye-witnesses to give a description?' Tobias felt he had the right to sound indignant. 'I'd never have got away with it.'

Krasin took his word for it. He jerked his head towards the hand that Tobias was holding in his overcoat pocket.

'What happened to that?'

'I told you, it was burned – '

'Have you had it looked at?'

'I couldn't, could I?' Tobias's reply came with a slight flush of anger. 'If I'd gone to the hospital with a burned hand it might have raised some nasty questions.'

That was his look-out. Krasin gave a shrug of his shoulders and moved on. A formation of geese was patrolling the edge of the pond. The water beyond looked bleak and uninviting.

'Where are the model yachts?' he asked. 'There used to be yachts all over the place.'

'You don't see them much these days.'

Not for the first time Krasin experienced a soft stab of disappointment. Nothing was quite the same. His memories of England had been brighter, somehow more serene than now. Maybe that was because six years ago it had all been unattainable – a dream. For a few moments he stood looking towards the outline of Kensington Palace before turning his attention back to Tobias.

'I'll not be seeing you again.'

'What about the Madonna?'

'I shall sell it myself – privately.'

'That was not what we agreed.'

'No.' Krasin couldn't deny it. 'But then your performance last night wasn't what we agreed; your pathetic attempts to silence Spencer were not what we agreed, were they?' He stared hard at Tobias while he spoke as though willing him to deny the allegation. 'When I recover the Madonna it will be mine. I shall sell it independently.'

'I have already arranged for a buyer.'

'Then I shall find another.'

Without another word, Krasin turned on his heel and walked back down the avenue of bare trees.

'You said Tobias was English?'

Katya nodded. 'He has to be. His accent was perfect. It's impossible for a Russian to get that good.'

'But you can't say what he looked like?'

'I hardly saw him.' Katya's fingers were splayed out wide as she fought for the memory. 'It was all so quick, so sudden, there was nothing about him that I can describe.'

The tube thundered through the tunnel, the wind ramming past the windows, wheels squealing on the tracks, drowning the sound of their voices as they sat with their heads close together. It had been Pip's idea to take the tube. It was an anonymous way of travelling.

'Why do you want to know about him?' Katya asked.

'I don't know – he's the one unknown. Maybe if we could find out more about him we'd be getting somewhere. We need a link, something positive to take to the police.'

He had turned away as he spoke and looked down the length of the crowded Circle Line carriage. Katya studied his profile thoughtfully, noticing the way his hair spilled forward over his eyes. She had underestimated Pip. When they stopped outside Harrods she'd thought he was playing games, but she was wrong.

The escape had been easy. As the lift doors opened Pip had crossed the passageway, jumped into another that had taken them down a floor and then moved quickly through the china departments until they found an emergency staircase. It led down to a side door at the rear end of the building. Katya had clapped her hands with satisfaction as they came out into the street.

She was feeling strangely exhilarated now. She wanted to help him, to remember something that might be useful.

'He kept blinking at me,' she said, snatching an image from her memory.

'What's that?'

'Tobias. All the time he spoke he kept blinking at me. I think he must be short-sighted.'

'Really?' It wasn't much but Pip was interested.

They came out of the tube at Tower Hill, the fresh air a relief after the tunnel.

'Where are we going?' Katya asked.

He nodded down towards the river. 'St Katharine's Dock.'

They crossed the street, diving down beside the cast-iron girders of Tower Bridge. A stiff breeze was blowing up the Thames, chopping the water, annoying the seagulls.

'This is the view on all the postcards,' Katya said, looking down to where HMS *Belfast* sulked on its quay. Each gust of wind brought new smells of salt and mud, mixed with the warm toffee aroma of the Courage brewery opposite.

Skirting the Tower Hotel they walked along the dockside. Moored to the quay between the racing yachts and expensive gin palaces was a Thames barge, a squat, tough-looking boat, the kind of thing that used to hump coal up the Medway. Since then it had died and been reincarnated as a corporate-entertainment vessel, the deck winches painted in red gloss, cargo hold tricked out with lace curtains and carpets. Vulgar as flying ducks but more profitable.

'Who owns this?' Katya asked as they walked down the gangplank. It ended in a mat saying, 'Welcome aboard'.

'A client of mine. He owes me a few favours.'

'Does he know we're here?' Katya had taken off her shoes in case the heels damaged the wooden deck and was holding them in both hands.

'That's who I rang before we left.'

The key was hidden beneath the forward rope locker which was presently moonlighting as a wine cooler. Pip opened the companionway hatch, went down into the reception area.

'They take this thing out to sea?' Katya asked, padding down behind him on stockinged feet.

'God no, it stays where it is. It's part of the window dressing around here.' Admittedly it looked more like the setting for a Victorian orgy but Pip kept the observation to himself. Katya was thinking along similar lines.

'What did you tell the owner you wanted it for?'

'I didn't. He'll assume it's something disreputable. I explained we didn't want to be disturbed and he gave me a wink.'

'On the telephone?'

'It's an audible wink.'

Dumping the bag he was carrying on a chintz-cushioned bench Pip pulled back the zip. He had thrown a few essentials together before leaving. Right in the centre, wrapped in a towel, was the Talinin Madonna. He drew it out and handed it to Katya.

'Put this somewhere safe.' He started back up the companionway. Katya's voice stopped him.

'You're not going, are you?'

'I must.'

'How long will you be?' She felt a sudden rise of panic at the thought of being alone.

'An hour, maybe a bit longer. You'll be quite safe here. Lock the door after I've gone.'

Chapter Twenty-Eight

To the north of Notting Hill Gate is an area that doesn't get its picture on the postcards. There are estate agents' signs in first floor windows, the corner shops keep the security grills up in the daytime and throw their empty cartons into the street. It's run-down, seedy – a part of London where owners don't get fined when their dogs crap on the pavement.

Vassily Krasin found the address he was looking for. It was a bed-and-breakfast near the Westway flyover, a narrow four-storey building with an anorexic hedge outside.

The reception counter was deserted, a television groaning in the room beyond. Krasin pressed on the plastic buzzer.

A man appeared in the doorway.

'Do you run this place?' Krasin asked him.

The man leaned on the counter and spread his hands as he considered his answer. Cheeks unshaven, shirt parted over a stained vest. He could have been a finalist for the beer-gut of Britain award.

'What of it?' he asked.

'I want a room.'

The proprietor's eyes frisked him over slowly and suspiciously. Krasin felt a flush of anger. He should have been warned. Dressed in his immaculate black overcoat and cashmere scarf he stood out like a sore thumb. He'd be noticed – remembered afterwards.

'Is there anything wrong?' he asked sharply.

The proprietor shook his head. 'How long do you want it for?'

'A few hours.'

He reached behind him, unhooked a key at random and tossed it on the desk. 'Just warning you, it's not the naffing Savoy.'

Krasin picked up the key, checked the number and put it down again. 'I want room one hundred and forty-one.'

'We don't have a hundred and forty-one.'

'That's not what I was told.'

'Oh yes, who by?'

'I heard it faces east – '

The proprietor chewed mechanically and then gave a nod as

though Krasin's words had brought up something that had been troubling his stomach. Going into the back room he returned with another key.

'I'll need three hundred quid for it.'

'I was told one-fifty.'

The proprietor shrugged. You didn't have to be a fucking genius to see that Krasin was worth more.

'Take it or leave it,' he said complacently. 'Three hundred's the going rate.'

Krasin wasn't going to make a scene. Thumbing six notes from his wallet, he folded them in his fingers and passed them across the counter. The proprietor stuffed them into his back pocket, the lethargy of idleness still on him.

'It's up here,' he said, flapping back the counter and waddling away to the staircase.

Krasin followed him to a first-floor landing. Somewhere in the distance a baby was bawling; the smell of frying fat hung in the air. By the time they reached the top floor the proprietor was wheezing like a punctured geyser. Unlocking an unmarked room he pushed open the door and handed Krasin the key.

'I'll be downstairs when you've done.'

Krasin went inside, closed the door behind him and locked it again. The room was furnished with an unmade bed and a wardrobe, the single window offering him a glimpse of rooftops, TV aerials and the concrete piles of the flyover. Putting his briefcase down on the bed he took off his scarf and overcoat and folded them alongside.

The wardrobe was heavy and it took him several minutes to manoeuvre it away from the wall. When he had it a couple of yards back he knelt down on the ground, ran his hands across the wooden boards, found the joint he was searching for and lifted out a rectangular section of the floor. It was well disguised; had he not known where to look he could have passed it over.

The small-arms were tightly packed into the cavity beneath, each one greased and still wrapped in the manufacturer's oiled paper. Wedged in beside them was a stout cardboard box. Krasin pulled it out and broke the seal of the lid.

Inside were three blocks of Czechoslovakian Semtex wrapped separately in polythene. He lifted out the top piece. It was soft, slightly pliant and to his satisfaction he observed that it was a dull yellow colour, like a slab of marzipan.

There are two brands of the infamous plastic explosive. Semtex 1A was developed in the early seventies for civil purposes and is used universally for mining and rock-blasting. It is easily recognisable by its rusty red colouring. What Krasin held in his hand was the rarer,

229

and infinitely more devastating, Semtex H. This was developed after the Vietnam war for military use and contains elements of the white crystalline solid Cyclonite, better known as T4 or Hexagon. Undetectable to X-rays or sniffer dogs, Semtex H is a vital weapon in the terrorist's arsenal. Its detonation velocity is 8000 metres per second, considerably higher than that of TNT, so that a piece the size of a 10p coin can puncture the pressure hull of an aircraft, while 300 grams will blast it to pieces.

Krasin laid the block down on the ground, took the knife from his pocket and flicking open the blade he ran it through the firm, buttery material. There was no danger; Semtex H is quite safe to handle, only a sharp electric current will detonate it. He weighed the smaller of the two pieces on the kitchen scales that had been left there for that reason. It was just over a pound. That was enough for his purpose.

Wrapping the explosive in newspaper he put it into his brief-case. The rest he returned to the cardboard box which he tucked back under the floor. Krasin wasn't sure where this consignment of Semtex had come from but the markings on the box suggested it was part of the Omnipol sales to Libya that had taken place in the late seventies. Only a fraction of this had been used in the last few years.

The detonators he found were clockwork and also made in Czechoslovakia. Krasin was glad of this. More sophisticated digital devices had been marketed recently but they were harder to set and in his opinion less reliable. He took one out and tested the mechanism. It was a simple ratchet system, not unlike a small egg-timer, that could be set for anything from thirty seconds to forty-five minutes. Satisfied it was working he put it in the briefcase and shut the clasps.

Returning to the cavity in the floor he examined the cache of small-arms with his gloved fingers, estimating the make of each weapon through the oiled paper without disturbing them. There was a Kalashnikov – or possibly it was the Yugoslavian equivalent, the M70AB2 – two Czech Scorpions and a number of handguns. Krasin took one of these out and stripped off the paper. It was a SIG-Sauer P230, designed in Switzerland and made in West Germany, an efficient, well-balanced pistol but not what he would have expected to find in an arms dump of this nature. He selected the appropriate eight-round magazine, snapped it into the butt and pulled back the slide, feeling the first round shunt up into the breech.

Crumpling the heavy oiled paper in his hand he threw it back into the floor cavity and replaced the boards. Then he worked the ward-robe back into its original position. When it was done he put on his overcoat, draped the scarf around his shoulders and went downstairs.

There was no one on the reception desk. Lifting the flap, Krasin went round behind the counter. There was a cushion lying on the chair. He picked it up and moved through into the room beyond.

The proprietor was watching television and didn't hear him come up from behind. Clamping the cushion to the back of the man's head, Krasin pressed the muzzle of the pistol into it and fired once. There was a Bugs Bunny cartoon on the television and the muffled shot was lost in the loud, exaggerated voices.

The proprietor had half turned as he felt the unexpected pressure of the cushion and so the bullet passed in through his ear. His body kicked at the impact and slumped forward in the chair.

Krasin didn't bother to check whether he was dead. He didn't need to. No one lives to see their brains join the colour scheme of the wallpaper. Dropping the cushion, he tossed the gun across the floor. Then reaching down he retrieved the six fifty-pound notes from the proprietor's rear pocket, slipped them into his wallet and went back to the reception desk.

Beneath the counter he found the guest book; it had a pencil attached to the spine by a string. He turned to the last entry and jotted the name 'Katya' into the top right-hand corner, just casually, as though he were taking it down on the phone. On reflection he added a question mark, then tearing out the page, he balled it in his fist and dropped it into the waste-paper basket.

The police would find it there. It would take them time but they'd find it eventually.

Krasin walked down as far as Holland Park and then took a taxi. As it swept him up the tree-lined avenue he stared out of the window, watching the girls who passed on the pavement. He didn't give the events of the last hour a second thought but the adrenaline was still burning in his veins and he found himself suddenly needing a woman, the comfort of her body, the easy gratification of desire. He knew the doorman on a hotel over in Mayfair who could provide him with a prostitute, one of the glitzy expense-account girls who handled the passing executive trade, but Krasin had never had to pay for sex in the past. He expected it to be offered to him.

He studied a leggy blonde who was looking in the window of a travel agent. Despite the weather her skirt was short, tight, revealing. Dressed like that you'd think she was a pushover but he knew this wasn't necessarily true. In many ways these little Western tarts were harder to pull than Russian girls. They were more worldly, less susceptible to status and wealth.

The taxi dropped him by the Brasserie in South Kensington. It was only six but most of the tables were already taken. As Krasin pushed through the glass doors a waiter bustled up to him.

'For one, monsieur?'

Krasin ran his eyes around the crowded room. 'No, I'm meeting someone here.'

'Ah yes – and the name is?'

'Krasin, Vassily Krasin.' At that moment he spotted a familiar figure sitting alone at a table in the far corner. 'It's all right,' he added smoothly, 'I can see him.'

As he made his way across the crowded room, Krasin felt an unexpected gleam of pleasure.

'So you made it then – '

The man at the table had stood as Krasin approached. He turned to greet him.

It was Chibatar.

Katya hid the Talinin Madonna in a ventilation duct.

She had spent much of the afternoon looking through the barge, searching through cupboards and lockers, more out of curiosity than for any particular reason.

The ventilation duct was a rectangular hole in the overhead deck about the size of her hand. She'd noticed that the brass grill that covered it was loose. Standing on the bed she reached up, pushed it to one side. She felt inside. There was a dry, dusty space between the two layers of the barge's deck.

She fetched the painting from the next room and opening the doors she looked down at the grave smile on the Madonna's face, the intense blue of the sky behind. It was a sad picture, she decided, beautiful but sad. Closing the doors she slipped it into the gap in the ceiling.

On second thoughts she put the gun up there too.

Pip hadn't seen her take it. He had been on the phone when she opened the drawer of his desk and slipped it into her pocket. Pulling the gun out she examined it in her hands. It was a large, ugly machine, black and functional. Nothing about it was decorative, every part served a purpose, even the scoring along the wood panels on the butt.

She pushed the gun into the ventilation duct alongside the painting and arranged the grill back in position again. Stepping down off the bed she inspected the result, her head cocked to one side.

She was feeling restless, cooped up in this floating isolation ward. Pip had come back around three that afternoon and left again almost immediately without saying where he was going. She'd tried venturing up on deck for some fresh air but a man on the quay had started talking to her and she'd hurried back down again.

232

Drawing the ridiculous lace curtains she took a shower and changed the bandage round her waist. The cut was no longer hurting as it had before, only the occasional stab of pain now reminding her of its existence, but there was a stiffness to the bruised flesh that made even small movements uncomfortable.

She went through to the forward cabin – the barge was equipped more like a penthouse suite than a boat – and lay down on the purple counterpaned bed, beneath which, she had been intrigued to discover, were black satin sheets.

'I don't think you'll catch anything off them,' Pip had assured her when she'd showed him the discovery. 'But I can't promise it.'

Close to her hand was a telephone. Everything on this boat was close to hand, she noticed. But there was no one she wanted to talk to. She stared up at the ventilation duct where the Talinin Madonna was hidden.

An idea struck her. She was wrong – there was someone she wanted to talk to.

For a moment she lay quite still, considering it, then kicking her legs over the side of the bed she picked up the phone and listened to the tone. It seemed to be working.

Holding the receiver in both hands she tried to concentrate her thoughts above the sudden hammering of her heart. Would it work, she wondered? Probably not. But worth a try.

Tapping in the overseas number for Russia, she followed it by the area code for Moscow. She heard the relays make the connection and added the number of the ministry.

She glanced down at her watch as she heard it ringing, mentally adding an hour to the time.

'Ministry of Culture,' came the girl's voice at the other end.

'Will you put me through to the Finance Department, please?'

'Just a moment – '

Katya could feel the butterflies waking up in her stomach as she waited. A woman answered the call.

'Finance Department.' She sounded bored.

'Is Tatyana Vasnikova there?'

'Who's speaking?'

'Natasha Kominski – Chamber of Deputies, Accounts Department.' She invented the first name that came into her head, pronouncing it with the irritating perkiness she thought the girl might suffer from.

'Just a moment.'

She could hear an exchange of voices on the other end and pictured the receiver being passed from one to the other, the puzzled expression at the meaningless name. Then Tatyana was speaking to her.

233

'Yes?'

'Tasha – it's me.'

There was a moment of complete silence.

'Katska?' She sounded wary as she said the name, as though this were some sort of trick.

'Are you free to speak?'

'Wait.' The phone clattered down. There was a pause as Tatyana moved to another extension and then her voice came in a rush, soft and urgent.

'Where are you, in God's name? We've all been sick worrying about you, Katska. Do you have any idea what's been going on back here?'

'Just listen, Tasha –'

'Are you all right?'

'Yes, I'm fine but I need you to—'

'They say you killed Podurets. They found him at that damned house you went to –'

'I didn't kill anyone, just listen for a moment, I can't speak for long.'

'What's going on? The police have been round to the apartment, turning the place upside down. We've all had to make statements—'

'Tasha!' She had to shout. 'Just shut up for a moment and listen. There's something you must do for me.'

'Does anyone know you're here in London?'

Chibatar shook his head, a quick factual gesture that needed no elaboration.

Krasin held out his hand. 'Let me see the passport.'

It had the dark green cover of the West German Republic and was made out in the name of Hans Fischer, a salesman of computer software from Essen. Krasin flicked through the pages. It was a work of art in many ways. The photo of Chibatar showed him in a sober grey suit and tie, both of which Krasin had no doubt could be proved to be of German manufacture, sitting in a booth of a railway station that could probably also be identified if necessary. Overall a beautiful job.

'What are you over here for?' he inquired as he handed it back.

The fluttering of Chibatar's hands explained that he was in London to attend an international conference for the dumb.

'Is there such a thing?' Krasin's tone was suddenly dry.

Chibatar nodded.

'It sounds like a contradiction in terms, if you don't mind me saying so.'

The ex-GRU man smiled gravely, the cornflower blue eyes gazing across the table without humour. There was an aura of calm, of spiritual fulfilment to the man, as Krasin had noticed so often before. It was in those eyes, the set of his head, the slow, unhurried movements of his body. Chibatar seemed always in control of his thoughts and actions. In that respect they were alike.

'How did you get over the border?' Krasin inquired.

Chibatar hadn't used any of the usual channels. He hadn't needed to. He had simply walked out of East Germany through one of the holes that had recently been breached in the Berlin Wall.

'That easy?' Krasin had seen pictures of the cheering crowds surging through into West Germany, searchlights reaching into the sky, the Brandenburg Gate looming up above. It was the end of an era, as the media were determined to point out, but not without its advantages.

'It may not be too good for the generals,' he said, 'but it's going to make our work a great deal easier if this goes on.'

The waiter was at his elbow, cradling a bottle for him to see. Krasin accepted a measure of wine in his glass, tasted it and nodded his appreciation.

'Pouilly Fuissé, 1976,' he informed Chibatar. 'It's really very good. You must try it.'

Chibatar shook his head. He didn't drink of course, Krasin was forgetting that. He turned to the hovering waiter.

'You'd better bring some mineral water for my friend.'

Chibatar waited until the waiter had removed himself before signalling a question.

Krasin read the sharp movements of the hands.

'Where is she? I imagine she's holed up somewhere with that solicitor friend of hers. In a hotel – or someone's flat.'

Chibatar inquired how he intended to find her.

'She'll come to us.' Krasin was quite confident of it. He sipped at the iced wine and settled the glass back on the table. 'She's gone into hiding but it can't last for long. She has to break surface eventually.' He glanced up at Chibatar and smiled. 'All we have to do is have a drink and wait.'

Chapter Twenty-Nine

'It was my own fault.'

'In what way?'

Katya's lashes dropped and she studied the glass in her hands. 'I let him make a fool of me,' she said quietly.

Maybe it was the wine or the warmth of the pub they were sitting in, she wasn't sure, but she could feel the conversation slipping into an intimacy she hadn't experienced before. Certainly not with Vassily. He had mistrusted confidences, avoided them whenever possible – always the lone planet around which everyone else must revolve.

'It was silly really,' she added. 'Tasha warned me, over and over again but I didn't listen to her.'

'Tasha?'

'Tatyana. She's a friend of mine – the one I rang this afternoon. She said that Vassily would be wanting something from me.'

'But you didn't believe her?'

'I don't think I wanted to – '

Pip said nothing but she could feel his eyes on her, studying her profile, the line of her throat and the shaft of hair that shone in the light.

She hadn't intended to confide in him when they sat down. But now that she'd started she found she couldn't hold it back, the sluice gates opened and the whole pitiful story poured out of her. She told him of their meetings, her hopes, expectations, even snatches of conversation they'd exchanged.

'The worst of it was he knew he could do it,' she explained, fingering the wax that trickled down the side of a candle. 'Right from the start he knew that he could make me do exactly as he wanted. He was so confident, so sure of his own power. That's what I can't forgive.'

'No?'

A bead of wax trickled down the candle and she caught it on her fingernail.

'No,' she said softly.

Like the sudden warm release of tears after pent-up emotion,

Katya felt calmer now she had talked of him. She'd never been able to do so before, not even with Tatyana. There had always been a barrier, an emotional tension between them that prevented it. The realisation made her self-conscious.

'But you don't want to hear all this.'

'Why not? It's interesting – '

'The first time I met you I thought you weren't interested in anything I was saying. It made me so cross.'

'You took me by surprise. I was expecting someone rather different.'

'Different?' Katya wasn't a particularly vain young woman but she liked to hear about herself. 'In what way different?'

'Tougher, grimmer – a sort of Communist boot.'

She laughed, throwing back her head. Her wine glass was held in both hands, elbows on the pub table, so that her body arched towards him, the small breasts pressing out firmly against her shirt.

'Did you know?' she asked, her expression growing serious again. 'About me and Vassily?'

'I guessed there must be something of the sort.'

'I didn't realise it was so obvious.'

Kicking his legs over the bench, Pip went to get them some supper from the bar.

'What do you want?' he asked.

'I don't know. Anything – whatever you're having.'

She sipped at her wine as she waited. The Dickens was much as she'd imagined an English pub, warm and wooden with boisterous male voices all around, although Pip had assured her that this was an illusion. Real pubs, he explained, had sticky carpets and tatty dart-boards.

'Haven't I seen you somewhere before?'

The voice cut into her thoughts and she glanced up over her shoulder. There were two of them, young men with jackets off and ties loosened in their collars.

'No,' she said hastily. 'I don't think so.'

'Could have sworn I've seen you somewhere before.' The boy's eyes had narrowed as he heard her accent. 'Never forget a face.'

Katya looked towards the bar but there was no sign of Pip. The two boys hung over her.

'You're foreign, aren't you?'

'Yes – '

'Where are you from then?'

She felt the sudden cold grip of fear in her stomach.

'I'm Greek,' she replied. People often mistook her accent for Greek. It was not implausible.

The boy sat down opposite her, his smile suddenly insolent.
'I don't believe you.'

The study was in darkness. General Alexandrei Chernov lumbered across to the desk and snapped on the lamp. He had been taken away from his dinner and was in no mood for prevarication.
'What does she want?'
'To speak to you, General.'
'That is out of the question. Does she realise what the time is?'
Throwing himself down in a chair which squealed under the impact, he wrenched the cork from the bottle he was carrying and poured the spirit into the glass.
'Take a statement from her, Major, and show it to me in the morning. I can't deal with her now.'
Zakov stood before the desk, feet set apart, hands folded behind his back. An immovable object.
'She refuses to speak to my men.'
'Then throw her out in the street.'
'She is most persistent, General. All evening she has been waiting at the office, refusing to go away until she's spoken with you. We threatened to put her in jail for the night but it had no effect.'
Chernov swirled the oily spirit around in the glass and throwing back his head he swallowed half in a single gulp before letting out his breath in satisfaction. Southern Comfort – the Americans might have the military instincts of a wet-nurse but they knew how to make good Bourbon. He studied Zakov's impassive features.
'You think I should see her, Major?'
'She has been in touch with the Leskova girl in the last few hours. It might be worth hearing what she has to say.'
Chernov drained the glass and belched loudly. Not a pretty sound but permissible, he felt, from a man of his rank.
'Very well' – impatiently he waved away his indecision – 'send the little slut up here.'

'God, they gave me a fright.'
'Who – those two little snotties?' Pip put the tray down on the table and sat down.
'They said they recognised me. For a moment I thought they were telling the truth.'
'They were just trying to chat you up.'
Katya laughed, a little shakily. 'I know, but it took me a few seconds to realise it.'
'Tell them to push off and play with their portable phones if they

238

do it again,' Pip replied. He had brought poached trout and salad with new-baked bread. With it was a bowl of whelks. 'I thought you should try these, speciality of the house.'

'One of them kept saying he'd seen me before.' Katya's mind was still on the two boys with the insolent smiles.

'Hardly an original line.'

'I nearly fainted.' Taking one of the whelks he offered her she put it in her mouth. It was hard and rubbery. She chewed it for a few minutes without success before swallowing it whole.

'That's horrible,' she said.

'You're not supposed to eat them. They're just for exercising your jaw muscles.'

'Is that true?'

'One should last you all evening. They're very economical.'

Katya laughed again, this time more freely. Thumbing the cork from the bottle Pip refilled their glasses. He liked it when she laughed. Her head went back, dark hair spilling from her shoulders while her eyes held his, soft and slightly mocking.

Reaching out she stopped his hand.

'What's wrong?' he asked.

'That label.' She was tilting her head to get a better look at the bottle.

'What of it – ?'

'Nothing.' She gave a toss of the head, dismissing the subject again. But Pip had seen the glint of recognition.

'You know it?'

'Yes,' she said lightly. 'It's the same as Vassily used to drink.'

It was a 1985 Chardonnay. Pip turned it in his hand, reading the label. It was bottled for a company called Ravenstoke & Co. of London.

'Are you sure about this?'

She nodded and said she was quite sure. Pip was cradling the bottle as though it were a precious antique.

'I didn't realise you could get French wine in Russia.'

'He had it imported specially. He was very proud of it.' She was surprised by his interest. It was infectious. 'Is that important?'

He put the bottle back on the table.

'A few weeks ago I needed the name of a wine importer – this is the one.'

'But why?'

'Because with it I just might be able to prove that Krasin has been smuggling pictures out of Russia.'

* * *

239

When he returned to the Connaught Hotel, Krasin found Vladimir Grigorvich waiting for him.

'Will you be requiring my services any longer, Colonel?'

The man had been sitting in the foyer for the entire evening, Krasin realised.

'Stay where you are. I shall need you later.'

Vladimir Grigorvich's face crumpled as he attempted to phrase a delicate matter. 'I have had nothing to eat all day, Colonel.'

'Ask the waiter to bring you a sandwich.'

'They refuse to serve me.'

Krasin was already walking away towards the stairs. 'Don't worry, I shan't be long. Wait there until I ring for you.'

In the privacy of his room he laid his briefcase on the small writing table, took out the block of Semtex and removed the newspaper it was wrapped in. Earlier that day he had bought a six-volt battery and a box of cigars. They were Romeo and Juliet No. 3. Slitting the seal of the box with his knife, he prised open the lid and emptied the contents into the waste-paper basket in the bathroom.

It took him less than ten minutes to assemble the bomb. He began by laying the battery in the side of the cigar box, its screw-cap terminals facing inwards. Havana cigars come with a wafer of wood lying on the surface. Krasin broke a piece off and laid it alongside the battery as added insulation. Then taking the Semtex he pressed it into the remaining space of the box, working it into the corners. The explosive is blended with latex and mineral oils to make it malleable so that it can easily be moulded into the back of a radio, an empty aerosol can or a toothpaste tube. He had even heard of it being carried through customs modelled into the shapes of children's sweets.

Driving his thumbs into the centre of the soft yellow material he scooped out a nest into which he pressed the timing device. It had two detonation leads, one red, the other black, ending in brass electrodes. These he dug into the Semtex about an inch apart.

When he had finished Krasin glanced at his watch. It was 10.38. He set the timer for forty minutes and then carefully he coupled the device to the battery terminals. Closing the lid of the cigar box he slipped it into a brown paper envelope on which was pasted a customs pass. Sealing the end he put it back into his briefcase.

Now that it was done Krasin relaxed. Going across to the sideboard he poured himself a glass of brandy and sat down to wait.

'What is it you want, girl?'

Chernov spoke slowly as though to a retarded child. Tatyana's eyes had darted about the room as she was brought in but now they held his.

'General Chernov?'

'That's me – '

'I spoke to Katya Leskova this afternoon. She rang me from London.'

Holy Saints, she was a fine-looking creature, Chernov observed, well built, with the fierce features of a raven.

'You come here,' he asked heavily, 'wasting the time of my officers, barging your way into my house, to tell me this?'

'She needs your help.'

'Help.' Chernov tossed back the word as though it were a currency that had lost its value in the modern world. 'The only help I can offer is to advise her to give herself up to the police.'

Tatyana held herself erect, the coins around her head wrinking back the lamplight.

'She has done nothing wrong.'

'She is wanted for the murder of Dmitri Podurets.' Chernov's voice was cold.

'Katya would never have killed him.'

'Her prints were on the murder weapon.'

'Then she was tricked into putting them there – '

'And the paintings that were taken from the vaults, the Madonna that was stolen from the museum. I suppose she was tricked into taking them too?'

Tatyana gave no reply.

With a spasm of disgust, Chernov brushed her away. 'Go home, girl, and stop wasting my time. Your friend will be caught and tried. There is nothing more to be said on the subject.'

Zakov moved to take hold of her but Tatyana was quicker. Slipping from his grasp she sprang forward, standing above the desk.

'It was not Katya who committed these crimes. It was one of your men, one of your own sort.'

'Is that so – '

'Please – don't send me away until you've heard what I have to say.'

Chernov's small eyes didn't waver in the moon of his face. 'And has this man a name?'

'Krasin – Colonel Vassily Krasin.'

She had strayed into dangerous territorial waters. Chernov hunched his shoulders. 'Take care of what you say, young lady.'

'It's the truth.'

'In your opinion.'

'No!' There was a fury to this girl, a violence. Tatyana's eyes

241

flashed as she spoke. 'He tricked her into doing what he wanted. Don't you see that? He played on her affections, deceived her. But what is worse – what is unforgivable – is that he has tricked you too, old man.'

'You are insolent –'

'All these years he has worked for you he has been making a fool of you. Using his position to feather his own nest.'

'That is enough.' Chernov growled his warning but Tatyana was no longer listening.

'If you were not so blind—'

'Silence!' He slammed his hand down on the desk. 'I will not be spoken to like this.'

Tatyana paused, breathing heavily. She had gone too far and she knew it. There was a sudden fear in her eyes but with it Chernov detected something else. Was it defiance – a gleam of triumph even?

'All I'm telling you is the truth,' she said quietly. 'Has the time come that I cannot tell the truth?'

Chernov levelled a finger at her.

'There is only one thing I detest more than insolence and that's computers.'

He settled back in his chair, letting his words sink in. The girl made no reply. He turned to Zakov but he too was puzzled by the remark. Without warning, Chernov's shoulders began to shake and his high-pitched laugh broke out.

'All the files, the print-outs, what do they know? They tell me this one's a dissident, an anti-social. But she has fire, eh Zakov? She's not afraid to speak her mind. That must count for something, mustn't it? It must register somewhere in the calculations.'

He turned back to Tatyana who was watching him warily, suspicious of this sudden change in manner.

'Sit down, girl.'

'I'd rather stand.'

'Sit down and shut up! You've already tested my patience far enough for one day.'

She did as she was told, scuttling across the room and perching on the edge of a chair. Chernov gave a grunt of approval and pouring himself another glass of the toffee-coloured spirit he downed it in one.

'None of what you tell me is news.' He pronounced the words slowly as though dictating. Tatyana made to speak but he swatted the unasked question with a swipe of his huge hand.

'Oh yes, you think we just sit here on our backsides, letting the cobwebs grow over our heads. But we are not as dull-witted as you would have us. We know about Vassily Krasin. He has been stealing paintings from the reserves for some time now. We know too that he killed that little apparatchik Podurets although for the life of me I don't know how he organised it.'

Silence had settled like dust in the study. Tatyana was the first to break it.

'Then why do you not arrest him?'

'When the time is right we will handle the matter, rest assured of that, Tatyana Vasnikova. But these things cannot be hurried. They take time and patience if they are to be done properly and there is still a great deal to be learned of Vassily Krasin. In the meantime – ' he turned his attention to the more immediate problem – 'I suggest you tell your friend to hand herself over to the English police as soon as possible. While she remains on the loose I cannot answer for her safety.'

'But I don't know how to get in touch with her.' Tatyana was astonished he thought she could.

'Did she not say where she was?'

'I asked but she wouldn't tell me. She was frightened the phone might be tapped.'

Again Chernov's shoulders shook and the high asthmatic laugh reached across the darkness towards her.

'In that case you had better say a prayer for her.'

Three minutes after ten there was a knock at the door.

Krasin ran his eyes quickly around the room, checking that nothing was out of place.

'Come in.'

The door opened to admit Chibatar. With the familiar flutter of his hand he greeted Krasin who remained seated, one leg crossed over the other, his glass in his hand, appraising his visitor through lowered lids.

'Did anyone see you?' he inquired.

Chibatar shook his head and indicated that he had come in through the side entrance as he was instructed. He seemed neither disturbed nor concerned by the order but stood in the middle of the floor with the same distant expression that Podurets had once noticed. He was dressed in a plain grey double-breasted suit and white shirt, the tie as close to pure black as a pattern can get.

Krasin gave a nod of approval and getting to his feet he went across to the briefcase.

'I have recovered the Madonna.'

Picking up the package he tapped it on his palm before tossing it casually back into the briefcase and shutting the clasps.

'I must go out now,' he said setting the combination locks. 'There are still a few details I need to attend to. I want you to stay here with it in the meantime.'

Chibatar had raised his eyebrows in interest when he saw the package but otherwise he made no attempt to inquire where or how the Madonna had been recovered.

'I shouldn't be more than an hour,' Krasin added, putting on his overcoat and shrugging it into place. 'Lock the door after I've gone and wait for me to return. On no account open it for anyone.'

As he went out he turned and looked back at Chibatar. The ex-GRU man was standing with his hands in his pockets, calm and unflustered, his blue eyes drained of colour in the lamplight. Maybe it was as well that they had never been able to communicate more freely, he reflected briefly. Conversation might have bonded them. As it was he knew the man only by his actions and not his thoughts. He smiled.

'I'll see you later.'

Krasin left the hotel by the side entrance and walked up into Grosvenor Square. The air was cold with a stillness that would bring frost in the small hours. Crossing Bond Street where the evening traffic still stammered at the lights, he turned down towards Piccadilly, moving quickly, partly to keep himself warm and partly to put distance between himself and the hotel. But with every step he felt an exhilaration growing in his chest, a glow of achievement. For the first time in his life he was free. He had left behind his job, his rank, even his name and the thought gave him a physical sensation of pleasure.

Earlier that day he had booked into Browns Hotel as Rudolf Hellsmesberger, a businessman from Vienna. In his pocket he carried a passport made out in the same name and at that moment the passport and the clothes which he was wearing on his back were all that he owned in his life.

Not that it mattered. Rudolf Hellsmesberger was an extremely rich man.

Chapter Thirty

Five people were killed in the explosion which tore a hole in the side of the Connaught Hotel, hurling débris into the street and shattering windows for a hundred yards in every direction. Fifteen more of the guests were admitted to hospital that night with serious injuries.

Although the outer wall had remained firm, the partitions and ceiling joists around the bomb had given way causing the floor above to collapse inwards, trapping the occupants of the rooms beneath the falling rubble.

The police were on the scene within three minutes of the detonation, ambulances, fire brigade and press within ten. By the time a section of the Anti-Terrorist Squad arrived, the street had been sealed off and the hotel evacuated.

The bomb had triggered at 11.22 p.m. Eyewitnesses who had escaped unscathed told police and press of the sharp report, the sudden, violent shock wave that had carried through the building and gave shrill descriptions of the flash of fire, the acrid smoke that had filled the corridors, while the cameras closed in on the nightclothes they were wearing, the superficial cuts and bruises they had been lucky enough to escape with.

By midnight the survivors had all been accounted for, the dead identified amongst the remains of the shattered hotel rooms, and the laborious process of forensic examination put into motion.

Vassily Krasin read of the bomb attack in the morning edition of *The Times* as he sat waiting in a car opposite Pip Spencer's flat.

He was glad to see that the report devoted much of its attention to his own death, describing him as 'a high-ranking Soviet official presently in London to conduct an investigation into the illegal importation of Russian art treasures'.

A spokesman from the Embassy had assured the newspaper that his death was a severe loss to the State in both professional and personal terms and hoped that the perpetrators of such a callous act would be brought swiftly to justice.

No one had claimed responsibility for the attack but the newspaper report confirmed that the police were looking into the possibility that his murder might be linked with the Russian interpreter who had evaded arrest on the previous day.

It was as much as could be hoped for in the time, Krasin decided, tossing the paper aside and stretching himself in the car seat. No doubt there would be more in the later editions.

He glanced down at the time. Nine fifteen. He had already been waiting for over an hour.

Climbing out of the hired Mercedes he walked stiffly over to the phone booth on the corner of the square and put a call through to the news desk of the *Evening Standard*. After a brief exchange he was transferred through to the editor. The conversation that followed was short and one-sided. Krasin made a statement he had prepared and put the phone down. The editor attempted to stall for time, to find his name but he was saying no more than he intended.

As he strolled back to the car Krasin breathed in the sharp morning air. A watery sun had appeared above the rooftops but it hadn't the guts to melt away the frost. He paused and stared through the bare trees of the square at Pip's flat but no one had come or gone in the last half hour. Settling himself back in the car seat, Krasin adjusted the back-rest to a more comfortable position and resigned himself to the tedium of waiting.

It was after eleven when a taxi drew up in the street. Pip jumped out on to the pavement, Katya close behind him, and turned to the driver.

'Will you wait here a moment?'

'Suit yourself – the meter will be running.'

'We won't be more than a few minutes.'

They took the lift, finding the second floor flat neat and tranquil in the cold November light. No indication of their hasty retreat the day before.

Pip went over to the bookshelves, drew out the Telecom business directory and flopped it open on the desk. He'd scrawled the name of the wine importer on the inside of a book of matches and, flipping it open, he checked the spelling before thumbing through the pages for the entry.

They had heard the news of Krasin's death on the radio that morning, the announcement butting its way into their lives, terse and brutal.

It had caught Katya quite unawares. As she'd listened to the detached BBC voice the colour had drained from her face, an involuntary shiver had run through her body and putting the cup she was holding on the table she'd sat down heavily.

Pip glanced up from the desk.

She was standing now with her hands in her overcoat pockets, feet close together as though she were chilled to the bone, staring out of the window. He couldn't judge what she was thinking. After the initial shock of realisation had passed, Katya had become remote, preoccupied. For one so expressive she had a remarkable ability to lock her emotions away in her mind.

At first he had imagined that she was grieving, silently and privately to herself but now he was not sure. It was too simple an explanation. There was a serenity to her, a sense of deep inner peace. It was as though she had resigned herself to a fate she could no longer escape and had drawn a new strength from the understanding.

'Are you all right?' he asked.

She turned from the window, breaking out of her reverie and flashed him a quick smile.

'Yes, I'm fine.'

He'd lost touch with her, he knew that.

The night before she had wanted to talk. When they'd returned from the pub she had said good night and had gone through to the forward cabin. He'd heard her moving about next door, undressing, preparing herself for sleep. But an hour later the door had opened and she'd slipped back into the room. Silently, on bare feet, she had come across to him and sat on the end of the bed.

'What's going to become of me?' she'd asked in a small voice.

Sitting up in bed Pip had hugged his knees with his arms. He knew the question had been on her mind for some time.

'You'll go back to Russia once we have all this straightened out.' He'd tried to give the words a confidence he didn't share.

In the light of the porthole he had been able to make out the grave, aristocratic features of her face.

'I'll lose my job,' she'd replied simply. 'The State won't allow me to work after this. I might even . . .'

Her voice had trailed away in the darkness as she contemplated possibilities she didn't want to hear.

'Do you have to go back?' he'd asked. 'Maybe it could be arranged for you to stay here.'

Her eyes had held his as she pondered the idea. Then she'd shaken her head.

'No, I must go back.'

'But why?'

'It's my home.'

'But if you can't work there any more – '

Her voice had been insistent. 'It's still my home. I couldn't live anywhere else.'

247

Krasin's death had only made the chance of her returning safely more remote. Closing the telephone directory, Pip straightened up.

'Okay, let's go,' he said. 'I've got the address.'

Krasin was given only a brief glimpse of them as they came out of the building and bundled themselves back into the waiting taxi. But in that time he was able to see that Pip Spencer was no longer carrying the sports bag he'd arrived with. Katya had her handbag but from the careless way it was swinging from her shoulder he took a guess that it didn't hold the Talinin Madonna.

They'd left it behind.

Krasin cut the engine which had been turning over in readiness and waited until the taxi had vanished out of sight before climbing out of the car and strolling over to the block of flats.

Ravenstoke & Co. occupied a low brick building in Elizabeth Street. It was grubby with age and set back from the road so as not to embarrass the other façades. An archway led through to a cobbled yard where a van was parked. What had once been a stable was now a lavatory, the hiss of running water issuing from the half-opened door.

The office was on the first floor, a handwritten sign pointing the way up a flight of metal steps. A girl was sitting behind a desk mounded with paper work.

'Can I help you?' she asked getting up and coming to the door.

'Maybe you can.' Pip was solicitous. 'We're trying to trace the date of a wine tasting that you put on.'

'A wine tasting?'

The girl was short and elfin with a wave of dark hair that seemed too heavy for her head. She found the request a strange one and looked quickly and keenly between them.

Pip explained. 'It was held at Claridge's about ten years ago.'

'Oh Christ – years before my time.' From the way she rolled her eyes he gathered she wasn't offering odds.

'Do you keep any sort of record of these things?'

'I'll give it a try.'

Moving back into the office, the girl slid open the drawer of a filing cabinet and began rattling through the contents. There were bright maps of the wine regions of France on the wall above her head, a busty calendar from a haulage company below.

'Have you asked Claridge's?' she called over her shoulder. 'They might know of it.'

'I tried them. They said you'd have the details.'

'We don't do many tastings off the premises.'

Pip could feel the first ache of anxiety as he waited. It wasn't going to work. He glanced at Katya who was standing in the doorway of the office distractedly gazing round at the cases of wine stacked up on the warehouse floor.

'I think this one was put on for the art trade,' he added.

The girl said, 'Ahh,' as though he had been holding back the one relevant piece of information and pushed the drawer closed with a practised thrust of her hips. 'That'll be one of the Connoisseur Evenings.'

Opening the drawer beneath she pulled out a file.

'Those are charity dos,' she explained, sitting down behind the desk. 'We do quite a few of them around the country.'

Katya had come back into the office now and watched in silence as the girl shuffled her way through the loose paper in the file.

She found the wine tasting. It had been held at Claridge's on March 23rd 1981. The file had a facsimile of the invitation card and a list of the wines put up for approval. Pip needed more than this.

'Do you by any chance have a list of the guests who were invited that evening?'

The girl pushed the hair from her eyes and stood up.

'Possibly.'

Krasin unzipped the bag and pulled the contents out on the bed. A towel, sponge bag, roll of bandage and two white bathrobes. No sign of the Talinin Madonna.

Methodically he began to search the flat. Katya and Spencer had been up here for only a few minutes. It hadn't been long enough for them to have put it anywhere obscure.

After ten minutes without success, Krasin paused. There could be a safe in the flat. Solicitors often held valuable documents for their clients. It was not unlikely that Spencer would have some private place to lock them away at home. He checked behind the pictures, beneath the carpets but there was no indication of one.

He ran his eyes around the room, reassessing the problem. He was sure they hadn't taken the Madonna with them. They'd left it – somewhere they'd left the damned thing.

A single telephone directory was lying on the desk. Beside it was a book of matches.

Krasin crossed the room and picked it up.

On the cover was the logo of the Dickens pub in St Katharine's Dock. Krasin knew the place vaguely. It was up in the City, near Tower Bridge. He flicked the book open. Inside was written the name Ravenstoke & Co. So that's where they'd been going in such a hurry. Quite how they'd come up with the name he had no idea. Not that it was of any importance, he told himself, tossing the matches back where he'd found them.

There was nothing useful they could learn from Ravenstoke & Co.

'No,' she said.

'You've no way of finding out?'

The girl shook her head. 'I don't think we keep the guest lists.'

'Who gets invited to these wine tastings?'

Pip could feel an impatience, a frustration burning in the pit of his stomach. For a moment he'd thought they were in with a chance. Now it was gone. The girl pushed the heavy swag of hair from her eyes.

'It varies,' she replied. 'Clients, friends of the directors, anyone who might be useful really. It rather depends on where it's held.'

'I see.'

Katya had been silent since they came into the warehouse, watching and listening without speaking but now she asked a question.

'Does the name Krasin mean anything to you?'

'Colonel Krasin – ?'

'That's right. Do you know him?'

'Yes, of course.' The girl's voice had quickened again. 'I mean, I've never met him but I've often written to him.'

'You supply him with wine, don't you?'

'He's one of our oldest customers.' She was slightly bemused by the conversation now.

'Would he have been invited to that wine tasting, if he'd been in London at the time?' Pip asked her.

'If he was in London . . .' She didn't want to commit herself. 'Yes, I suppose so.'

'But you can't be sure?'

The girl shook her swag of dark hair. 'It's possible. But there's no way of being certain.'

'Can I help you, sir?'

The Dickens had just opened its doors for lunch. The barman was polishing a wine glass with quick twists of a cloth. His voice had the sing-song quality of one who's repeated the words so often he's forgotten their meaning.

Krasin glanced down the length of the bar. Only a few customers had come in so far, seizing on tables in the furthest corners.

'Do you have rooms for the night?'

'No rooms, sir.'

'I thought pubs took in guests?'

'That's just the name we use. This is more in the way of a

wine bar.' The barman wasn't going to be involved in a battle of semantics. Krasin turned and looked through the bottle glass windows.

'Where would I find somewhere to stay around here?'

'There's the Tower Hotel. That's the nearest.'

Krasin walked across the docks to the large anonymous block of concrete which blotted out the view. The doors opened, sucking him into an air-conditioned interior of soft lights and obedient service.

'I'm meeting a couple of business colleagues,' he told the receptionist. 'They booked in last night.'

'What name, sir?'

'Spencer.'

Not that he'd have been stupid enough to use it, Krasin reflected. The receptionist confirmed this for him with a bright, synthetic smile that he'd have willingly slapped off her face.

He walked back to the Dickens, past the avenues of moored boats, his breath streaming out around him in the cold air. He glanced across the docks at the smart waterfront apartment blocks. Jesus, this could take all week.

'I'm trying to trace a couple of friends,' he told the barman. 'They were here last night.'

'Them and a thousand others, sir.'

The barman wasn't in the business of remembering faces and made it clear with an expectant raise of the eyebrows. Krasin allowed him to prod a double whisky from the optic.

'These two you might have remembered,' Krasin said, handing over a five-pound note. 'Particularly the girl. She's tall, very elegant with long brown hair that reaches halfway down her back.'

'Sorry, sir. Can't say it rings a bell. We're kept pretty busy of an evening.'

The place was filling up, customers beginning to jostle for attention. The barman moved away.

'Is she Greek?'

Krasin turned around.

The question had been asked by a boy in his early twenties. He was sitting on a stool further down the bar with another of the same age. Both had bright, crafty expressions and pints of lager on the counter.

'This girl with the long brown hair,' the first one said, 'is she Greek?'

Krasin was on the point of turning away when he caught himself. A smile came into his eyes. It was light and engaging.

'Now that you mention it,' he said, moving down the bar towards them, 'I think she might be Greek.'

'Where do we go from here?'

'Back home, I suppose.'

They walked up Elizabeth Street until they reached the broad, tree-lined avenue of the Upper King's Road. They hadn't managed to prove anything but it had been worth a try, Pip reflected gloomily as he looked around for a passing taxi. What else could they do?

'Oh my God – '

Katya had stopped abruptly in the street and was staring at the headlines of the *Evening Standard* that blazed from a newspaper stall:

RUSSIAN GIRL WANTED
FOR MURDER OF ARMS DEALER

Pip bought a copy and returned to where she was waiting.

'What does it say?' she asked anxiously.

'The police think they've found proof that you're responsible for the bomb last night.'

'But how?'

'An arms dump has been discovered in a hotel up in Notting Hill Gate.' He was skimming quickly through the columns of print. 'The proprietor was found dead, your name was found in the register.'

'It can't have been!'

'An anonymous caller tipped off the paper this morning.'

Pip went back to the start of the story and began reading it through more carefully. When he looked up Katya was gone.

'Where are you off to?' he asked, catching her up further down the road.

'I must go to the police.'

'Not yet.'

'It's the only way,' she replied quietly. There was no anger, the serenity he had noticed earlier had returned. She smiled at him and added, 'Isn't that what you said I should do from the start?'

'Yes – but not now. Not after this.'

'I have to.' She saw that he was about to argue and stopped him with a shake of her head. 'You've been very kind, Pip. I know that. You've done everything you could for me. But it's not going to work. My only chance is to turn myself in, go to the police and then to my own people and try to explain what happened.'

Gently she removed her arm from his grasp.

Pip watched her walk on down the street. She had never believed he could prove her innocence. She had come with him, watched him try but in her own mind she'd known she could never break Krasin's grasp.

'Wait!' he called after her.

She turned, half in surprise.

'I've got an idea,' he said as he reached her. 'It's an outside chance but it's worth a try.'

Chapter Thirty-One

There were three of them round the table, all giving him the hard stare treatment. Two were from the Yard, the other a private under-secretary from the Home Office. Detective Inspector Chatham sat to one side, an impartial and slightly nervous observer.

The room was small and stuffy. A tray of coffee had been put on the table to lend the hastily assembled meeting an air of conviviality but so far nobody had touched it.

'I heard you had fresh evidence, Mr Spencer. What you have given us so far is nothing more than speculation.'

It was the private under-secretary who spoke. He had the spruce, clipped manner of a Guards officer and had already made it clear that he was pressed for time.

Pip was not to be hurried. 'For almost ten years now a Cork Street dealer called Adrian Trenchard has been selling stolen pictures from the reserve collections of the Kremlin. This much is already on record.'

He glanced round at Chatham who acknowledged the claim with a quick nod of the head. Turning back to the table he added, 'The man who supplied Trenchard with these paintings was Colonel Vassily Krasin.'

Silence in the room. The Police Commander with the gold braid piped on to his uniform was the first to speak.

'Can you substantiate that?'

'Trenchard told me that he had been blackmailed into handling the pictures by a Russian. He didn't know the man's name or who he was, but he did remember that they'd once met at a wine tasting. This I've recently discovered took place at Claridge's on March 23rd 1981. Krasin was also there that night.'

'Colonel Krasin is now dead, the motives for which are still unclear, and so can't speak for himself. But I think you should know that he denied ever attending any such occasion. One of my officers raised the question with him yesterday.'

'Then he is lying.'

'We're talking about something that took place ten years ago.

Trenchard's memory is bound to be clouded. It certainly can't be considered as the basis for evidence.'

'Krasin was there that evening.' Pip was certain of what he was saying. 'The event was put on by a firm called Ravenstoke & Co. Krasin was a client of theirs. He would have been invited.'

He had their full attention now.

'And these wine merchants are prepared to confirm this, are they?' It was the detective superintendent who asked.

'Not directly. They can confirm that Krasin was a client.'

'I see . . .' Pip saw a flicker of disappointment on the policeman's face. 'But nothing more? They can't say definitely that he was there that evening?'

'They don't keep records of the guests they invite.' It sounded lame in his own ears. He was losing their interest. Behind him Chatham shuffled his feet as he recrossed his legs.

'Then it is an interesting coincidence. Nothing more.' The private under-secretary was glancing up at the clock, preparing to leave. 'I have to say, Mr Spencer, that when you claimed to have fresh evidence we were hoping for something rather more tangible.'

'Then you might be interested in this.' Pip put his briefcase on the table and opened the lid.

'It occurred to me that an important charity event such as this – staged at one of the most famous hotels in the world – might have featured in one of the social magazines.'

The private under-secretary had paused in the act of standing up. He held Pip in his bland stare for a moment and then sat down again.

'And was it?'

'Earlier this afternoon I went down to the offices of the *Tatler* and had a look through some of their back numbers.'

Pip took out a photocopied page and pushed it across the table. The middle picture on the left-hand side showed a group of guests in black tie, glasses in hand. Around the figure of Vassily Krasin he had drawn a circle in red ink.

'It's small,' he said, 'but a good likeness. I'm sure if you were to show it to Trenchard he could confirm that this was the man who spoke to him that evening.'

'What did they say?'

Katya was waiting in the shelter of the cafeteria. Seeing Pip approach across the deserted park she jumped to her feet and hurried towards him.

'They want you to come in straight away,' he replied.

'Did they like the picture?'

Pip smiled at the question and told her that they'd liked it. The rain was sparkling in Katya's hair.

'What took you so long?' she asked breathlessly. 'I've been waiting hours.'

'They made me kick around while they contacted the Russian Embassy.' Pip held the collar of his jacket to his throat as he spoke. 'Moscow has dropped charges against you.'

Katya gazed at him in astonishment.

'Dropped them – but why?'

'I don't know. Your people told the police that they want you to turn yourself in as quickly as possible. They were going to put an announcement out on the radio.' Pip could think of no good reason for their sudden change of attitude. But who was arguing?

'Where's the Madonna?' he asked.

'On the boat.'

'I thought you brought it with you – '

Katya shook her head. 'I left it there. I thought it would be safer.'

'Go and get it. Bring it along to Scotland Yard. I must go back and sort out a few things before you arrive.' He turned and began walking towards the entrance gate. 'Ask for Detective Inspector Chatham when you get there,' he added, swinging back to her, 'have you got that?'

She nodded eagerly.

'I'll see you then.'

Krasin stood beneath the dripping awning of a yacht club and watched the rain drilling holes in the smooth water of St Katharine's Dock.

The two boys in the pub had identified the barge where Katya had spent the night. You can't miss it, they'd said, pointing through the forest of masts.

'What's her trouble then?' one of them had asked. 'She been messing about with someone she shouldn't have?' They'd had it all worked out in their minds, put two and two together.

Krasin had smiled thinly and said it was something like that and they both nodded knowledgeably.

'Had to be – jumpy as a grasshopper she was.'

Krasin looked out through the opened doors of the pub. 'It's the Thames barge, you say?'

'The *Magpie*. We saw her going back on board.' The boy turned to his friend for support.

Krasin thanked them curtly and left. As he passed, one of them caught him by the arm.

'Here.' He wanted the low-down. 'What you going to do to her when you catch her then?'

Krasin didn't bother to answer.

Poor Katya, he reflected as he walked down the quayside towards the squat bulk of the barge. She must have thought she was safe enough tucked away in this place. She hadn't bargained on a couple of punks with egos inflated to bursting point picking her out in the crowd. But that was all it took to tip the scales.

A man in black tie and a frilly white shirt was standing at the head of the gangplank. He held out his hand as Krasin approached.

'Can I see your invitation, sir?'

'For what?'

'You're part of the Frazer-Hancock lunch?' The politeness in his voice was thin as paint.

'Not exactly.' There was some sort of party going on in the hold of the boat, Krasin realised. He could hear the muffled rumble of conversation coming up through the companionway. At that moment a couple with a newspaper held over their heads splashed up beside him, flashed their invitation and hurried on down the gangplank.

'Don't want to hang around there,' the man called back to him, 'catch your death.' The girl giggled. They were looking forward to a good afternoon.

Krasin turned to the individual in the black tie who was regarding him coolly.

'I was here yesterday,' he said. 'I think I must have left something on board.'

'Stay there, sir. I'll ask one of the waiters.'

A boy dressed in a white shirt and black waistcoat that didn't reach down to his trousers appeared on deck. His eyes darted furtively between the two of them.

'Gentleman's lost something,' the black tie said.

'It's a brown envelope,' Krasin clarified. 'About the size of a book.'

Realising he wasn't being reprimanded, the waiter applied his mind to the problem. He shook his head slowly. 'Can't say I've seen any packages. You can take a look for yourself if you like.'

A burst of laughter reached Krasin up the stairs. The place must be stuffed like a blood sausage. He smiled and turned away.

'Don't worry,' he said drily, 'I'll come back later.'

From where he stood now he could see that barge clearly across the water. Taking the flask from his pocket he unscrewed the cap and took a pull of whisky.

As he did so he caught a movement on the far shore. A girl in a long blue overcoat had appeared from the direction of the Tower Hotel.

It was Katya. He knew it. Even from that distance he recognised her figure, the stride of her legs.

He watched as she reached the gangplank, saw her talking earnestly to the bouncer and then disappear down inside.

'How much longer's she going to be?' Chatham was slumped down in his chair.

'I guess she'll be there by now.'

'You're sure she's coming in?' The waiting was getting to him. 'She's not going to play silly buggers with us again, is she?'

'No,' Pip replied. 'She's not.' He was standing at the window, staring down into Victoria Street.

'How's she travelling?' Chatham asked.

'Tube, I imagine.'

He gave a grunt. 'Best way at present. There's a protest march along the embankment – CND, Greenpeace, one of that crowd. I can't remember which exactly.'

From the tone of his voice Pip gathered they were all much the same to him. Through the misted window pane he could see the brake lights of the cars beneath winking up at him.

'Have you ever met this Krasin?' Chatham asked from behind him.

'I spoke to him on the phone.'

'Sounds a right bastard.' Charity was running low that afternoon. Two representatives from the Russian Embassy had arrived and were getting the red carpet treatment on the floor below. The private under-secretary from the Home Office was out in the passage, fretting about the time. Pip had taken sanctuary here in Chatham's office while they waited.

He turned from the window.

'I can't see how he expected to get away with it.'

'Who, Krasin?' Chatham couldn't see the problem. 'He was just going to take the money and run, wasn't he?'

'They'd have come after him.' It had been bothering Pip for the last hour. 'The moment he didn't come back with the Madonna the Russians would have guessed what he was doing. He'd never have got away with it.'

'Change of identity, new passport?'

'He'd have been looking over his shoulder for the rest of his life.'

'Maybe he could have fixed it so that his disappearance looked more permanent.' The remark was tossed off the cuff but as the words came out Chatham caught himself. 'You're not thinking . . . ?'

'The body in the hotel,' Pip asked. 'It was him?'

'Who else could it have been?'

'You identified it positively?'

'How could we? There are no records to compare it to.'

For a moment they stared at each other and then Chatham was on his feet, moving towards the door.

'Where is she now?'

'St Katharine's Dock.'

'Jesus Christ – I'll get a car.'

'You're not drinking, darling.'

The large florid man in the blue blazer splashed champagne into a glass and pushed it at her.

'No, sorry. I'm not one of the guests.' Katya tried to squeeze past him but he wasn't giving way.

'Now that you're here – '

Katya gave a quick shake of her head. The barge was packed tight with loud jostling people. Cigarette smoke clung to the ceiling, sudden bouts of laughter hit her.

The florid man was insistent. 'Come on, darling. Don't be a pooper.'

'No, please – '

'Can't have you not drinking. It's a crime.' Someone jogged the glass spilling champagne down her front. Katya tried to extricate herself.

'I'm just here to pick up something I left last night.'

'Last night, eh?' Sounded useful. 'Something black and flimsy, I hope.' He was enormously pleased by the reply and repeated it to the others. There was laughter and more suggestions.

'Show it to us when you find it,' another called after her as she pressed through the crush.

There were three more of them in the forward cabin.

'We've got to go in at the grass roots,' the executive in the clerical grey was saying. The woman with her hips pressed towards him replied, 'Oh quite.'

'Get in there and start pitching.'

Katya looked up at the ventilation duct. Beneath it another of the guests was lying sprawled on the bed, his glass perched on his chest.

'Are you two wankers going to talk about anything else or are we going to have a party?'

Katya closed the door behind her.

'Excuse me,' she said. 'Could you wait outside for a moment? I have to change my clothes.'

The sharpness of her voice punctured the conversation. The clerical grey turned round.

'What was that?'

'Don't know.' The man on the bed looked baffled. 'Lady wants to get undressed by the sound of it.'

'Don't let us stop you then,' replied the woman in a voice that had been dried on blotting paper.

Katya smiled tightly and held the door open for them to leave. 'I won't be more than a few minutes.'

Krasin drew back into the shadow of the tunnel that runs beneath Tower Bridge.

He had seen Katya come back up on deck. There were two men with her. They seemed intent on making her stay and he watched with slight amusement as she detached herself from them and hurried away.

It was still raining and she had her head down as she trotted along the quayside, her face buried in the upturned lapels of her coat. Beneath her arm was the brown paper envelope.

Krasin reached into his pocket, touched the familiar shape of the switchblade. He could hear the tapping of Katya's heels as she approached, see the slender ankles, the curve of her legs beneath her coat.

She didn't notice him standing in the dark of the tunnel. He waited until she had passed before calling after her.

'Katya – '

She stopped in her tracks and swung round.

The police car hit sixty as it plunged through the red lights in Birdcage Walk, the wail of the sirens scattering the pedestrians as it approached.

Ahead of them Pip could see the traffic locked solid in Parliament Square, a huge unmoving substance that nothing was going to shift.

The driver was listening to the short-wave radio.

'I'll cut up north,' he called back over his shoulder. 'See if I can find a way through into the Strand.'

'You'll do better to cross the river,' Chatham grunted from the back seat.

The car mounted the pavement, skimmed along the line of static cars and swung up into Whitehall. Pip felt the machine accelerate sickeningly. Trees flashing past the window, the high buildings of the Foreign Office, the sudden open space of Horse Guards Parade and then with another squeal of tyres they were out into The Mall.

Chatham was leaning forward, staring morosely over the driver's shoulder. 'Damned marches. A whole lot of noise and fuss and what do they achieve? Fuck all.'

The car skidded to a halt under Admiralty Arch.

'It's no good, sir,' the driver said calmly, slipping into reverse, weaving his way backwards into the oncoming traffic before swinging around into the other lane. 'I'll have to double back and try to get up into Piccadilly.'

'Katya – it's me.'

Krasin stepped out of the shadow of the tunnel to give her a better view of himself.

She didn't move. Across the ten yards that separated them she looked at him steadily but said nothing.

'You don't seem surprised, kovshka.'

She shook her head slowly.

'How's that?'

'I knew you weren't dead, Vassily.'

In the sallow light he could make out the firm sculpture of her cheeks, the softness of her lips. God, she was a beautiful creature. He hadn't forgotten, just forbidden the memory.

'Why do you say that?'

'The bomb in your room,' she said simply. 'You would never have allowed it to happen to you.'

'How very perceptive you are.'

He moved towards her but Katya stepped back quickly. Her voice had been quiet, almost weary but her body was tense as a racehorse's.

'Please don't come near me, Vassily.'

'I need the painting.'

She shook her head. 'I'm taking it to the police.'

'I must have it, Katya.' There was a note of reproach, as though she should understand his point of view. 'Surely it's not too much to ask?'

'No.' She shook her head and hugged it to her breast.

'But it's of no value to you – ' He held out both hands to her as though greeting some old friend but she skittered back on stiff legs.

'Don't come near me, Vassily!'

'Really, Katya, this isn't necessary.'

Dropping his hands he smiled, breaking the tension between them and took another step towards her.

Katya saw the distance closing between them and turning on her heel she ran out of the tunnel into the rain and sudden brightness of daylight. Krasin caught up with her before she'd gone more than a few yards down the embankment.

As he took her by the arm she spun around.

'Keep away from me,' she hissed.

In her hand was the gun. She'd tugged it from her pocket as she ran and now held it out at arm's length. Krasin held perfectly still.

'Put that down, Katya.'

'I'll use it if I have to, Vassily.'

'Don't be stupid.' He was watching the barrel as it pointed at him, estimating the firmness of the grip, the distance that separated them. He gave a shake of his head.

'Why are you doing this to me?' He sounded puzzled. 'You don't want to hurt me, do you?'

There was a flicker of uncertainty. He saw it.

'Not after all we've meant to each other.'

She drew in her breath. 'You tricked me, Vassily.'

'No, Katya – no.' The accusation was unfair, misguided. He shook his head sadly. 'You don't believe that. You can't. It was just a misunderstanding. I've been looking for you ever since I heard what happened.'

'Don't lie to me.'

Krasin smiled. The words were defiant but there was no conviction in them. She wanted to believe him. He was sure of it.

'You've had a terrible time, Katya. I know that.' His tone was gentle, caressing. 'But it's over now.'

He saw the gun barrel waver.

'We can start again, forget the past and make a new start. You'd like that, wouldn't you?'

'It's too late, Vassily.' She lifted her head and looked him straight in the eye. 'I'm taking the painting to the police. If you try to stop me I'll kill you.'

'Don't be silly, Katya.'

'I mean it – '

Not in cold blood she wouldn't. Not with the intimacy they had known, the experiences they shared.

Krasin's confidence was in his smile, in the slow, casual movement of his body as he drew close to her.

Katya was still pointing the gun at him. Her eyes were round, lips slightly parted.

'I'll do it, Vassily – I swear it!'

'No, Katya.' He reached out his hand for the envelope.

As he did he froze.

With a little sob in her throat Katya had stepped back a pace and pulled the trigger.

Chapter Thirty-Two

The hammer fell with a click on the empty chamber.

Katya stared at the gun with incomprehension. Then there flickered through her mind the image of Pip as he'd handled it that first night, drawing out the magazine, ejecting the shell into his hand before putting it away in the desk.

She remembered the sequence of actions. With her other hand she yanked back on the slide, feeling the weight of the spring as it reloaded the breech and released it again. But Krasin was quicker.

Stepping forward he caught her by the wrist and wrenched the weapon from her grasp. His face was white with anger. He had misjudged her. For once he had overestimated his influence.

'You stupid little bitch!' he whispered.

Swinging back his arm he hit her across the face. The weight of the gun knocked Katya off her feet so that she fell outstretched on the ground.

She had dropped the Madonna as she was running. It lay back by the entrance to the tunnel. Krasin retrieved it, quickly pulling away the envelope to check the painting inside.

Katya picked herself up from the wet paving stones on which she had fallen into a kneeling position. The barrel of the gun had struck her on the cheek just in front of the right ear and the blood, loosened in the rain, was streaming down the side of her face, warm and salty in her mouth.

She touched it, looked down at crimson fingers.

'I loved you, Vassily,' she said quietly. 'Did you know that?'

Krasin was examining the surface of the painting, checking that it hadn't been damaged. Katya repeated the question.

'Did you know that?'

He glanced up, a quick impatient gesture. 'It was your concern,' he said shortly. 'I am not responsible for your feelings.'

Katya knelt in the rain and regarded him steadily. 'You didn't need to trick me, Vassily. Don't you understand that?' She wanted him to see the waste of it all. 'You didn't need to deceive me into doing what you wanted. I would have done anything for you if you'd asked me.'

'I didn't want your love, Katya Leskova.'

'It would have been so simple – '

'You brought it with you. It was your invention. It meant nothing to me.' Krasin had closed the doors of the Madonna and tucked it into a lower pocket inside his overcoat.

He came back and stood above her.

Katya knew his intention. She could read it in his eyes, in the set of his mouth, but she was too tired, too drained emotionally to fight him any longer.

There was no escape, she knew that.

Glancing quickly in both directions Krasin had drawn the switch-blade from his pocket. She heard the snap of the spring, saw the glint of the steel.

He stepped forward, reaching out to her and it was at that moment that the bullet struck him.

She didn't hear the shot, only its impact on his body as it threw him back against the embankment wall.

For a moment he stared at Katya in confusion, trying to understand what she had done, how she had pulled this trick on him. And then very slowly he turned, each movement cautious, hesitant as though he were performing a balancing trick that required every ounce of concentration and looked back in the direction of the shot.

Katya huddled on the ground. In the silence of the grey afternoon she could hear a voice screaming, a high, plaintive sound, and it was only as it died away that she realised it was hers.

A look of amazement had come over Krasin's face. He was trying to speak but the words were no longer there. Blood wriggled from the corner of his mouth. A tiredness had crept over him. He looked back at Katya but he was no longer interested, no longer in control and slumping back against the wall he fell to the ground.

Katya crouched against the cold stone, her hands wrapped over her head, trying to make herself as small, as invisible as possible. The stench of mud was in her nostrils, rain plastered her hair to her cheeks. Far away she could hear sirens wailing. Then footsteps approaching along the embankment.

'Are you all right?'

It seemed hours later that she heard the question, although it could only have been a matter of seconds.

Slowly she unfolded her arms and looking up she saw Chibatar standing above her.

'Push through them,' Chatham ordered.

With the siren going, the police car nudged into the thick column of protest marchers. Placards waved drunkenly, figures knocked and butted against the body. Someone slammed his hand down on the roof.

'Jesus Christ,' Chatham said, staring fixedly ahead. 'Don't run one down whatever you do. I can't face the headlines in the tabloids.'

The car rocked on its suspension as the figures thrust up against it. A face pressed against the window and mouthed silently at them, the voice lost through the glass. Chatham was muttering under his breath. 'Make a bit of noise, clutter up the street and think they've changed the bloody world.'

Pip sat quite still and watched as the car nosed through the slow unyielding mass, felt it suddenly leap forward, the engine roaring into life as it broke free and headed out on to London Bridge.

She stared up at Chibatar in astonishment.

'Are you all right?' he repeated.

Katya said, 'Yes,' too stupefied by the sight of him, the sound of his voice to say more. Bending down Chibatar caught her by the arm and unceremoniously pulled her to her feet.

She gave a yelp of protest, suddenly galvanised into action by the physical contact and tottered backwards on unsteady legs.

The wail of police sirens was closer now.

Chibatar unscrewed the silencer from the muzzle of his pistol, tucked both parts away in the upper pocket of his raincoat and went across to where Krasin lay.

Katya looked away quickly. She was shivering with cold and fright but too stunned even to notice. Weakly she leaned against the wall and gazed out across the river.

Chibatar returned a moment later carrying the Madonna. He checked it was in one piece and tucked it away out of sight.

'Why in God's name didn't you just give it to them as you were told?' he asked.

Chapter Thirty-Three

Victoria Station at 10.22 in the morning. Pip stood beneath the departure board feeling cold and slightly depressed. Stations usually had that effect on him. It was the scale, the noise of the places, the sense of impending departure.

Across the crowded floor he saw Bill Hargreaves coming towards him, wearing a black overcoat that had seen better days.

'You left a message at the office.' He sounded interested by the distraction.

'I thought you'd like to see the Madonna before they take it back to Moscow.' Pip opened his briefcase and lifted out the triptych.

'I read about the girl in the papers this morning,' Hargreaves commented as he cradled the painting in the palm of his hand. 'It sounded terrible.'

'She'll be here in a moment.'

Pip glanced over towards the entrance. He'd seen Katya the night before but he hadn't had a chance to speak to her alone since they parted by the cafeteria in St James's Park.

It seemed a century ago.

Hargreaves was fumbling at the catch of the triptych with his thumb. When he had it open he turned the painting face down so that the twin doors fell apart, then inverted it again. Hardly the most respectful way of handling a masterpiece but effective.

'Remarkable.' His square glasses twinkled as he studied the Madonna. 'Really quite remarkable.'

'It is valuable I assume?'

'Oh yes.' There was little doubt of that. 'Raphael never painted anything else like it, apart from a few small pieces in his very early years and they don't have the quality of this.'

'What sort of figure are we looking at?'

'It's almost impossible to tell with a work like this. It would attract some important bidding.'

'Millions?'

'Several.'

The others had arrived. Pip took back the Madonna and shut it away in his briefcase.

'They're here,' he said.

Hargreaves was looking distracted. He glanced down at his watch then around the station.

'I must put a call through to my office,' he said moving away in search of a phone booth. 'I'll join you in a minute.'

Pip went across to the Russians who stood by the ticket barrier of the Gatwick Express. There were five of them in all. The Embassy had sent three delegates to see them off.

Katya stood to one side of the group. She was dressed in a grey trench-coat tightly belted at the waist, her hair tucked up into the fur hat she had been wearing when she first broke into his flat. She flashed a smile at him as he approached but didn't speak.

Chibatar detached himself from the others and came over to meet him. His face carried its distant, dreaming expression as though he were considering the solution to some complicated chess move.

'So,' he said in slow English. 'We are all set then?'

'I think so.'

They had dined together the night before at the hotel where Katya was staying. Chibatar had listened to his proposals thoughtfully.

'Yes,' he said when Pip had finished. 'I think this is right. It's better that we co-operate.'

'It will require authority from the State bank.'

'That can be arranged.'

Katya sat listening intently as they spoke without making comment. It was only as dinner was drawing to a close that she said, 'Who put the bomb in Vassily's room?'

'He put it there himself,' Chibatar replied. 'He wanted me to be killed in his name.'

When he offered no further explanation Pip asked, 'How did you know it was there?'

Chibatar swept his pale gaze round at him and for a moment he considered the question before saying, 'It was not difficult. When I was given instructions to come into the country unannounced I had some idea of the rôle I was expected to play. So I searched the room.'

'You didn't think to just defuse it?'

'It would not have worked that way,' Chibatar replied quietly. 'He would have known I was on to him.'

There was something awe-inspiring about the man. There were no doubts in his mind, no areas of indecision. He spoke and acted with complete certainty.

Operating under the direct command of General Chernov, he

had been transferred from the GRU, where he had distinguished himself as an intelligence officer in the Afghanistan war, to work as Krasin's private chauffeur, carrying out his orders, overseeing his plans, all the time silently watching and waiting, assessing the extent of the man's guilt. For three years he had served under Krasin, rarely letting him out of his sight, always on hand, always ready, like some angel of death, to intervene when the moment came.

'And in all that time you never once spoke to him.' Pip was uncertain whether he was impressed or revolted by the man's cold-blooded dedication to his ultimate master. But Chibatar had regarded him with his unwavering gaze and said, 'It was easier that way. If you don't speak you can't give anything away – not even loyalty . . .'

'So who was in Krasin's room when the bomb went off?' Pip asked him.

The question had been hovering since Katya brought up the subject. Chibatar was not inclined to give a name.

'Someone else,' he replied. 'It's not important. He was down in the foyer of the hotel, waiting to serve Vassily Krasin. I gave him his chance.'

It was after midnight when Pip left the hotel and went out into the night. Chibatar accompanied him to the door.

'What will become of Katya?' Pip asked him.

'She will be looked after. In the eyes of the State she has committed no crime.'

It had been a statement rather than an opinion but Pip had walked back to his flat still not knowing whether he felt good about it or not.

The train had arrived, the gates clanking open, passengers pouring out.

'I will be in touch with you when I reach Moscow,' Chibatar told him as they came on to the platform. Then he nodded back towards the station and wished him luck.

It was the only time Pip had seen him smile.

His parting with Katya was brief and unsatisfactory, as these things usually are.

She paused in front of him, held out her hand.

'You have my address?'

'Yes – I have it.'

'I'll see you next time I am in England maybe?'

As she spoke she gave him a hard, searching look but it was neither the time nor the place to say more. Reaching up she kissed him quickly on the cheek.

Doors were slamming along the length of the train. A whistle sounded. As she was getting on the train he stopped her.

'Katya – '

She turned quickly. Expectantly. But he merely handed her a small parcel wrapped in brown paper and said, 'You left these in my flat.'

'Oh, yes, thank you.'

The train had drawn out of the station when Hargreaves came hurrying down the platform full of apologies.

'Sorry about that. Bit of a crisis back at the office,' he explained. 'Have I missed them?'

'Yes, they've gone.' Pip was heading back towards the gate.

'I'd better be getting along too.'

'I'll walk with you.'

The train pulled out over Chelsea Bridge, the wheels suddenly hollow as they crossed the river.

From his seat, Chibatar watched Katya through lowered lids.

She was sitting very straight, knees together. On her lap was an opened magazine but she was staring out through the dirty glass of the window, her thoughts far away.

After a few minutes he saw her give a start as she remembered the little parcel that Pip had given her. Taking it out she removed the paper and opened the lid of the box.

Inside Chibatar caught a glimpse of something small and glittering. From where he sat it looked like a tiny golden bumble-bee. Katya gazed at it for a few moments and then carefully wrapped it up and put it back in her pocket.

It evidently had some meaning for her, he didn't know what. But he could tell by the radiance of her eyes as she sat back in her seat that it brought her some happiness and he was glad for her.

'It's over then.'

They walked out through the ticket barrier. Pip said, 'There is still the problem of Tobias.'

'Tobias?'

'He acted as the go-between.'

'Really?' Hargreaves didn't sound too interested. 'Have you got any sort of lead on him?'

'None. Except he must be connected to the art world.'

'I suppose he would be.'

'Tobias.' Pip paused for a moment. 'It's an odd name. I looked it up in the encyclopaedia the other night. The only reference I can find is to some Old Testament character who travelled to Medea with an archangel. A pretty obscure story to anyone but an art historian. They'd know it. Apparently it appears in endless Renaissance paintings.'

'That's right,' Hargreaves agreed. 'Tobias and the Angel.'

'I think I'm right in saying that he's always represented as a traveller.' Pip pursued the image. 'I expect that's why our man gave himself the name. He was the one who travelled backwards and forwards to Russia, ferrying the paintings across the border.'

They came out through the main entrance of Victoria Station. Hargreaves was in a hurry to move on.

'Well I wish you luck,' he said. 'It doesn't sound as though you have much to go on.'

'No.' Pip nodded back towards the empty platform. 'Katya was the only person I know who might have identified him – that is, apart from you.'

Hargreaves looked at him in astonishment.

'Me?'

'While I was looking through those pictures in the *Tatler* I couldn't help noticing that you were also at Claridge's on that night.'

'Oh, I see.' Hargreaves gave a little shrug. 'Yes, I probably was. It's hard to escape these trade events.'

'I expect you saw Tobias without realising it. He would have been there. I imagine he was the one who introduced Krasin to Trenchard that evening. It must have happened right in front of you.'

Hargreaves had stopped on the pavement and was looking at him quizzically.

'Why are you telling me all this?'

'I thought you should know,' Pip replied. 'The only thing Katya could tell me about Tobias was that he was short-sighted. She said he kept blinking at her – as I imagine you would if you weren't wearing your glasses.'

'My God,' he said slowly. 'You're not suggesting—'

'I discovered from the Aeroflot office that you've made regular flights to Russia in the last ten years.'

'So what? It's part of my work.'

'Yes, I realise that.' Pip sounded apologetic as though he knew he was jumping to conclusions and felt it was not in the best of taste. 'That's why I couldn't be sure until just now.'

'Just now?' he said sharply. 'What happened just now?'

'I gave you the Madonna.'

'And?' Hargreaves still couldn't see the relevance.

'It's surprisingly difficult to open the doors, isn't it? The catch is so small. Most people use both hands but I noticed you only used one. You kept the other in your pocket all the time. I couldn't think why.'

270

There was a stillness in the other man now.

'That is,' Pip added, 'unless it had been hurt in some way.'

When there was no reply he nodded towards Hargreaves's pocket. 'That is why you're keeping it out of sight, isn't it?'

Hargreaves glanced round the entrance hall, saw the uniforms of the police who stood waiting. Slowly he nodded his understanding.

'Is this why you asked me here this morning?'

'I needed to be sure.'

'Are you arresting me?' He didn't want to play cat and mouse any longer.

'They will want to question you.'

Hargreaves looked at him steadily, assessing his situation. 'I'm not saying anything more until I've seen my solicitor.'

'As you like. It's going to be a long and slow business.' Pip warned him of what lay ahead. There was a slight weariness in his voice. He wanted to get this over with now.

'In the meantime you and I have a job to do.'

Hargreaves was looking across to where a police car was parked up by the Buckingham Palace end of the station. He swung back.

'Job? What sort of job?'

'The Russian Government is going to recover the money from Krasin's Swiss bank account,' Pip told him. 'With it you and I are going to track down the paintings that were taken from their vaults and buy them back.'

'Why in God's name do you want to do that?'

Pip thought of the conversations he'd had the night before, the train that was presently drawing out of London and said, 'I don't know, to be honest. Let's just put it down to Glasnost.'